# The King Edward Plot

*Robert Lee Hall*

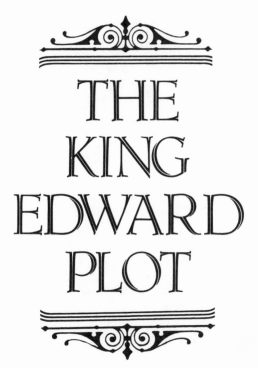

# THE KING EDWARD PLOT

McGRAW-HILL BOOK COMPANY

*New York   St. Louis   San Francisco
Mexico   Toronto   Düsseldorf*

The author gratefully thanks the Ramona Street Regulars, past and present. Thanks also to Thursday's Children, present and future; to Pat, my British connection; and to Dean and Shirley Dickensheet.

Book design by Anita Walker Scott.

Copyright © 1980 by Robert Lee Hall.

Library of Congress Cataloging in Publication Data

Hall, Robert Lee.
The King Edward plot.
I.  Title.
PZ4.H17885Ki [PS3558.A3739]     813'.5'4     79-20435
ISBN 0-07-025609-8

1 2 3 4 5 6 7 8 9 DODO 8 7 6 5 4 3 2 1 0

Published in association with
SAN FRANCISCO BOOK COMPANY.

*For the beautiful Cornelia Clay*

# ❧*Editor's Note*❧

1906. *La Belle Epoque.* Edwardian England. King Edward VII, beloved of his subjects, called "Good Old Teddy" by the man in the street, is firmly on the throne. The Great War is eight years in the future.

And yet . . . Europe is gearing for battle. A militaristic fanatic rules Germany—King Edward's nephew, Kaiser Wilhelm II. Intensely jealous of his uncle, he is convinced Great Britain plans to encircle his country with alliances, thus stifling his plans for expansion.

The following recently discovered manuscript tells a heretofore untold tale of those days: on the surface, sunlight-dappled and carefree, ending a century of progress; underneath, dark with international rivalries, plots, and counterplots.

A true tale? This much is known: its protagonists existed; Somerset House records their births. The Diogenes Club still stands in Pall Mall. Number 221B Baker Street is legend. And Sandringham looms on the Norfolk plain. John Singer Sargent's portrait of Madame Sophie Bernard hangs in a private collection in Paris.

The spirit of the tale is accurate too: the spirit of brave Englishmen.

*Robert Lee Hall*

*Note found among the effects of the heirs of Simon Bliss:*

The world is not yet ready for the truth about the events in which my three friends and I were so intimately and perilously absorbed. Nevertheless, believing that the story ought not to be lost, I have asked them to pen their parts in it. They have agreed. I have assembled the narrative as seemed best to me. Tomorrow I shall place the manuscript in my bank for safekeeping. I hope the age that reads it at last is a safer one than ours. Though I shall not live to see that time, I am pleased to leave this record. An old man has his vanity, and it is good to know that the deeds, by which we proved our loyalty to king and country, shall not be forgotten.

Simon Bliss
Diogenes Club, London
December 23, 1906

I

Murder at the
Diogenes Club

# Herbert Munns's Narrative

### I

My name is Herbert Munns. In 1875 at the age of sixteen, quiet and shy but determined to work hard, I was taken on as messenger boy at Cox's Bank, Charing Cross. Quick with figures, I rose to apprentice bookkeeper and at the age of twenty-two was given a place behind the counter. There in that cold marble room, surrounded by clerks perpetually scratching sums with their pens and coughing and sniffling discreetly as if any loud sound might prevent the money in the steel vaults from accumulating interest, I spent the next quarter of a century. Early on I married, but my young wife, Emily, died of enteric fever. After that I lived alone in two rooms in Porchester Road and crowded onto the Circle Line each morning and evening in a dull routine. I developed sprinklings of gray in my moustache, grew spectacles on my nose, and husbanded the hopes of my youth. Emerging from the fug of the bank each evening, I smelled on the air of the city something indefinable which quickened my pulse and made me dream. Perhaps it was this dreaming which prevented my advancing at Cox's. Pensively I strolled the Victoria Embankment; reflected in the rolling Thames were glittering lights, invisible from my barred cashier's window, which called me to a life I yearned for but which, seemingly, I never would achieve.

It is quite certain that no one who saw me then—drab,

3

unprepossessing, meek—would have imagined I could be part of a great adventure.

The world was changing. The new century arrived. Queen Victoria departed this earth. It had seemed she would go on forever, but there was a new sovereign, King Edward VII, and in August 1902 I strained with the throng in Trafalgar Square to catch sight of him in his grand coronation procession. He had waited fifty years to be king; I wished him well.

My mother had died when I was young. In 1905 my father passed on, leaving me an inheritance on whose interest I could live. I made a hard decision: I quit my place at Cox's Bank and began to look about for new lodgings. I was determined at the age of forty-six to make something of my life, though I had no idea what that should be.

My only friend from the bank was old Stamford, under whom I had been apprenticed. "I know a flat in Baker Street," he told me over a pint of bitter some weeks after I had left my job. He gave me the address, and I went round the very next morning to see it. The owner of the building was Mrs. Martha Hudson, a plump, pleasant woman in a print dress and starched white apron. She explained that she planned to retire to the South Downs and wanted to let her ground-floor rooms, which she had occupied for thirty years. The rooms were satisfactory, the rental reasonable, and Mrs. Hudson was well pleased with me. Furthermore, her house, number 221B, was the three-storied red brick building where the great detective Sherlock Holmes had lived for many years. It seemed a fitting place from which to launch my new life, and so I engaged the rooms on the spot.

I remember that morning quite clearly. The sky was fine and blue. We chatted on the stoop. As we did so, a cab drew up at the curb, and down stepped a slender young man with finely cut features, dramatically flaring nostrils, and longish blond hair which must have been carefully cut to achieve its insouciant, unbarbered look. He appeared to be getting home after a night of revels, for he wore at 10:00 A.M. an evening tailcoat of dark blue with black satin lapels and gold buttons, a white tie, and a gleaming silk hat pushed forward at a raffish angle. In one hand he swung an elegant Malacca

4

stick; in the other he carried a pink rose, which he sniffed thoughtfully as he strolled toward us.

He answered Mrs. Hudson's reproving look with a bright "Good morning." Glancing up at the sky he continued, "Beautiful morning, in fact—and an excellent night's sleep at my club. I say, I'm sorry I didn't inform you that I should be away last night, Mrs. Hudson." He leaned jauntily on his stick and frankly looked me up and down. "Who's this?"

Rather awed by the young man's aplomb and dashing appearance, I did not show how taken aback I was by his rudeness.

"Mr. Herbert Munns," Mrs. Hudson told him. "He's to share the house with you. Mr. Munns, this is Mr. Frederick Wigmore."

The fellow pumped my hand. It was hardly an auspicious greeting; I did not like him at all.

He beamed at me, rather vacuously I thought. "Splendid to meet you! My friends call me Wiggins." A doubt crossed his face. "You do like music, I hope."

"Much as any man," I replied uncertainly.

His smile returned. "Then it really will be splendid! For now I must dash. We will talk later. You will discover many things about me, as I shall about you." Glancing with obvious disapproval at my brown tweed suit and ordinary bowler hat, he added, "We shall both have to make allowances. Good day!" And he strode into the house.

"He is an actor," Mrs. Hudson said. She looked at me anxiously. "I hope it will make no difference."

From an upper window of 221B Baker Street the young fellow's strong tenor voice warbled "A Wandering Minstrel."

"I am looking for a difference, Mrs. Hudson," I assured her. But, glancing at the window, I could not repress misgivings.

2

Early in January 1906 I moved into 221B Baker Street. Mrs. Hudson had left a divan and a few tables and chairs but had taken the rest—potted palms, embroidered pillows, antimacassars. My rooms therefore awaited the impress of my

5

personality. On that first day I placed 'round the sitting room my meagre odds and ends—photos of my dead wife and parents and a few bright, sad souvenirs of holidays at Margate and Brighton. On the bookshelf I fit novels by Hall Caine, Charles Garvice, and Marie Corelli, from which I could recall not one character or scene. I stood back to view the effect but was singularly disappointed. A steady rain beat against the Baker Street windows. The light was cold and gray. Determined to be optimistic, I lit a fire in the grate and sat before it in my shirtsleeves. I rubbed my hands to work up enthusiasm. But it was no good.

I had just managed to sink to the very lowest ebb, and was cursing myself for a fool for thinking I could change my life, when a gay Offenbach aria floated down the stairs, followed by the sharp rap of knuckles on my door. Puzzled, I opened. Carrying two glasses and a bottle of Wachters Royal Charter champagne in a bucket of ice, Frederick Wigmore stood before me. I could not speak for staring at his attire, a voluminous white-and-blue-striped caftan which made him look like an Oriental prince. Blinking innocently, without a by-your-leave, he brushed past me to place the glasses and champagne on the low table by the fire. Then turning, hands on hips, he frowned. "My dear fellow, what a dreadful expression!" An engaging smile lit his features. "Greeting committee, don't you know." He held out a hand. "Welcome to Baker Street!"

We sat before my fire. I had not drunk champagne since my wedding day, and the tingling taste, the bubbles popping in my moustache, gave me the same sense of an unexplored world as had those bright, Thames-reflected lights. Young Wigmore chattered away about inconsequential matters until he had drawn me out of my funk. I was grateful and, much as I still did not know what to make of him, thought I might grow to like him after all. Shortly he fell silent and I began to talk. I was used to saying very little about myself, but the young man drew me out by just the right questions, with the result that at the end of two hours, though I still knew nothing about him other than that he was an actor, liked music, and dressed in a highly original style, he had my entire uneventful life story, including my awkward little idea, which seemed foolish and futile when I described it, of starting life anew at Baker Street.

"And how do you plan to go about it?" he asked, his blue eyes popping with interest.

"I don't know," I replied lamely, chagrined at the knowledge that he, twenty years younger than I, must know far more about life.

"You will manage it, Herbert," he said confidently. "I may call you Herbert, mayn't I? You'll want my help, of course," he added, as if there could be no question of that, "and I shall be delighted to give it, but . . ." he glanced at a fob watch which he pulled from the huge pocket of his caftan, "it is five o'clock, and I must dash." Jumping up, his cloak swirling like a Bedouin's, he hurried to the door, but when his hand was on the knob he turned with a sly expression. "Still, we might begin tonight, after a fashion—if you will accompany me to Paris . . ."

I rose. "To Paris?"

"Well, to its reconstruction in the Strand. At the Gaiety Theatre. There I stroll the sized, painted boulevards of the City of Light each evening. I'm quite popular, you know; I have three songs. What do you say, Herbert? Will you come to see me perform?"

I was touched by his offer but felt rather shy. I removed my spectacles and polished them with the soft, gray moleskin I kept always in my trousers pocket. "I am not a theatregoer, Mr. Wigmore. Perhaps I wouldn't appreciate . . ."

"Nonsense! No apologies or excuses! You have begun a new life. Why not take its first steps down the gangway of the Gaiety Theatre?" He winked. "I promise you, her bright lights and charming chorines are sure to make you forget Cox's Bank."

I still did not know what to do. There were a few drops left in my glass and I drank them down, but the champagne had gone flat. Flat, the taste of my life—I wanted no more of that!

Fitting my spectacles on my nose, I looked firmly at my new friend. "What time shall I be ready, Mr. Wigmore?"

"Hurrah!" He flung open my door. "Six o'clock. We shall dine at Romano's." He disappeared, only to poke his head back in a moment later. "You must call me Wiggins, you know!"

## 3

At Romano's we had *tortue, moules marinières, framboises,* and other things I had never tasted before and could hardly pronounce. "This is a meeting place of the well-to-do and the demimonde," Wiggins explained as he leaned back, flashed his smile about the elegant restaurant, and waved to several pretty young women of his acquaintance. "A gentleman does not bring his wife to Romano's," he confided waggishly.

After eating, we hurried down the Strand to the brightly lit Gaiety Theatre, arriving early so Wiggins could get ready for his performance. "You will be surprised, Herbert," he told me as we parted. The show was Ivan Caryll and Lionel Monckton's popular musical comedy, *The Spring Chicken,* its keynote the Entente Cordiale with France, which King Edward had made possible. I was indeed surprised. Disguised by make-up and padded out to middle-aged stoutness, Wiggins played Monsieur Boniface, an aging boulevardier always after the ladies. He delighted the audience with comic turns and sang his solos and a duet with Miss Gertie Millar very affectingly.

After the show he lured me into the florid depths of the nearby Adelphi Bar. When we had found a table among the crowd I stared with undisguised curiosity and dismay at the flamboyant theatrical gentlemen lining the bar. "The Adelphi is their second home," Wiggins told me. Many knew him and bounded over, all stage smiles, and my young companion unabashedly introduced me: "My new friend, Mr. Herbert Munns." I shook their hands, dazzled by the enormous stickpins they all seemed to wear. I remembered not a name.

My new life was breathlessly begun.

During a lull I complimented Wiggins on his performance. He was pleased but frowned. "Monsieur Boniface may be amusing to the public, but he bores me. I'm glad to be ending my part soon." He pushed his glass in circles on the tabletop. "I shall have some time for my hobby."

Pleased to have this entree into his life, I asked, "What is that?"

8

The glass continued in circles. "Oh . . . helping people."

"And how do you help them?"

He looked at me strangely. "Have you ever been in trouble, Herbert?"

The question surprised me. "With the police?"

He went back to the circling glass, and I felt a small chill. "No, but in need of them and unable to go to them. Or not convinced they could help even if you did seek them out."

"Neither of those. As I told you this afternoon, I've walked a straight and narrow path."

He brightened. "Still, you're taking new turnings—that's admirable! I like your courage!" He stopped pushing his glass. "But be careful. Some paths lead to dark ways. If ever you find yourself on one of these, come to me. It's my hobby to save straying wayfarers."

"How?"

He hesitated. "Oh, there are many methods. I am versatile!"

At this moment the barman called, "Time, gentlemen!" and we joined the flood of the Adelphi's colorful patrons out onto the bustling Strand. We went to the corner of Bedford Street to look for a cab. I was about to ask Wiggins more about his mysterious hobby when he gave me a thoroughly exasperated look. "Your tie, Herbert!" he exclaimed. "It really is disgraceful. And your trousers! May I recommend Sewall of Savile Row? He does splendid work and is quite reasonable. You really need a good tailor!"

I cannot pretend I was not stung. I bunched my fists and glared at this young man who could be so unfeeling. A retort hung on my lips; I would put him in his place! But at that moment I caught sight of our reflections in a draper's shop window: Wiggins tall and fine, standing at ease in the splendor of his evening clothes; whereas I, half a head shorter and slump-shouldered from my years at Cox's Bank, wore a rumpled brown suit and an out-of-fashion topper. My moustache was a bristling thing that gave me the look of a walrus. My spectacles were absurdly positioned halfway down my nose. At once my anger fled. Wiggins was right; I looked quite disgraceful. His words were not unkind. He had merely been frank, and I found to my surprise that I

9

liked him for it. If I wished to remain his friend I should simply have to get used to blunt honesty.

There was more I needed to do. I pulled my shoulders back, straightened, and discovered that my slumped posture was no irreparable defect. I smiled; the fellow in the draper's window already looked more like a man. I pushed my spectacles on my nose and felt almost rakish. What would proper clothes do?

"Can you also recommend a bootmaker, Wiggins?" I asked.

He beamed and clapped me on the back. "Indeed I can, old chap!"

### 4

If I thought that first evening had made us fast friends, I was mistaken. The very next morning Frederick Wigmore accompanied me to Savile Row, and in an elegant shop where I felt thoroughly out of place among hovering clerks, all tape measures and pursed lips, who obviously knew the young actor well—"Custom, Herbert; custom makes good friends . . ."—he urged me to purchase some rather flamboyant attire. Demurring, I settled for a plain brown suit and, for evening wear, a black frock coat and trousers. "Well, well, it will do to begin," Wiggins conceded.

As he led me to his bootmaker he spied someone he knew. His eyes lit. "I say! A friend of mine. Been chasing him simply for ages. Must run. Here, Herbert." He thrust the bootmaker's card in my hand. "Just up the street; you can't miss it. Frightfully sorry." And he disappeared into the throng.

The pavements were crowded. I did not know who he was pursuing. I wondered why he did not call his friend's name.

Feeling somewhat deserted, I bought two pairs of boots. When I returned to Baker Street I climbed the stairs to Wiggins' rooms to thank him, but got no answer to my knock, nor, though I stayed up late, did I ever hear him return. Wondering about my new life, wondering about Frederick Wigmore, I slept fitfully, so I was certain he did not come in that night. Perhaps he had spent it at his club.

It was my first lesson in Wiggins' elusiveness; I was to have others over the next few months. He had said he would help me, and he did, taking me to supper, to the theatre, and once to his club, the Siddons, an actors' lair, where I was inundated by stage talk. Frederick Wigmore led a colorful life, yet I sensed I was seeing only a fraction of the rainbow. When I overcame my shyness and went up to the rooms that once had been occupied by Sherlock Holmes, Wiggins greeted me in a friendly enough fashion. And, wearing his white-and-blue-striped caftan, the discarded booty of some officer of the Soudan campaign, he would stop by my rooms, too, though he never stayed very long and never at any time talked about anything that revealed a clue to the mystery which seemed to hang about him. He was always quite charming. He bewildered me. Was it only that I knew so little of the world? Or was I correct in thinking he was interested in me for some special reason? There were moments when he would look at me speculatively, as if measuring me for some task or favor, and once or twice I thought he was on the verge of putting his thoughts into words. But the time for that never came, and always, shortly after, he would smile, gaze placidly into space, and hum some light musical comedy air.

Several times I tried to ask about the "hobby" he had mentioned, but I soon learned that that was a sure way to drive him off, usually to some urgent engagement which he suddenly recalled. I stopped asking; I did not wish to pry. I had interests other than Frederick Wigmore.

One of them was my uncle, my mother's brother, Simon Bliss. I had not seen him since I had come to London as a boy in 1875. It was he who had found me my place at Cox's Bank—even then he was connected with money—but he had since been engaged in the overseas ventures which made him his fortune, and I had lost touch with him. Also, he and my father had not got on. "Damned queer bloke!" was my father's phrase for him. But Father had been a suspicious man, and I wanted to get to know Uncle for myself, he being my only living relation. His adventuring days over, Uncle kept a room at the Diogenes Club; so, shortly after moving to Baker Street, feeling nervous and unsure of his receiving me, I took myself 'round to Pall Mall and had myself announced. He was in. A small boy with large brown eyes showed me up to his room. I remembered a spry, vigorous man in his forties; I never had understood why Father thought him peculiar.

"Mr. Munns, sir," the boy said, backing out the door of the spacious third-floor room overlooking Pall Mall.

"Thank you, Jack." With the aid of a blackthorn stick, and looking like a breath of air would blow him away, a bent, baldheaded old man rose from a chair by the fire and held out a clawlike hand. "Herbert, I'll be damned!" he exclaimed in a cracking parchment voice, as he came at me with a scuttling walk like the hop of a beetle. His smile was a nest of wrinkles. His eyes were yellow as an owl's. And I knew from the surprisingly sharp vigor of his handshake that, though he looked frail, there was strength in my old uncle yet.

### 5

Uncle was in his seventies, a self-made man. Through with the bustle of amassing money—"Waste of my youth, Herbert!"—he had settled into London life "like a hand into a glove," as he put it. "Splendid fit!" he added, smiling. He was a student of human nature, he told me as we sat by his fire that first day, damp outside, a bleak fog pressing against the panes of the French doors that gave onto a little balcony from which he could survey the city. He knew society from top to bottom, it turned out; had even been a friend of King Edward when he was Prince of Wales.

"Bertie," he said, disconcerting me by referring to His Majesty by so intimate a name, "has his faults, but snobbery is not one of them. I hadn't a title, but I had money." Uncle chuckled. "That was enough for him."

He told me of great balls in Marlborough House and told tales, too, of the darker byways of the great city. He was a character in a surprising number of these stories, and I felt I had come upon a man equally fascinating as Wiggins. I listened, asked polite questions, fidgeted, and for the most part felt a drab, dull fellow for having nothing interesting to tell Uncle in return.

When I rose to go I was sure I had seen the last of Simon Bliss.

All along, the shrewd, yellowish eyes had been examining

me. "And you, Herbert, what of you?" he asked kindly, a hand on my arm.

Feeling ungrateful, turning my bowler wretchedly in my hands, I nevertheless blurted out how I had hated the years watching life pass me by at Cox's Bank, and how I had quit my place, wanting something more. "Though," I had to confess in some confusion, "I don't know what."

Uncle seemed pleased. "So you are my sister's son after all!" He patted me hard on the back. "Visit me, Herbert. Sit with me by my fire. Let us be friends."

I was pleased and grateful to do so and came to spend at least one afternoon a week with Uncle, occasionally at his Curzon Street house, but mostly at the Diogenes Club, for he preferred the club nearer the pulse of the city. I like to think he respected me—and I respected myself more for that. "You are intelligent, Herbert, genuinely common-sensical; that is rare. And you have a spark!" He seemed to trust my judgement and came to discuss many matters with me. He was more than a mere observer of life, I learned—far more than an old gossip, which was what my father had thought him. He was a sage of sorts, of a very practical cast, and people came to him for help—even, on occasion, the redoubtable Inspector Nelson Faraday of Scotland Yard. Mysteries fascinated Uncle; he was expert at solving them. Detective, I should have called him, and did, just once, to his face.

"Pah!" he said, scowling and thumping his blackthorn stick on the carpet. "I am nothing of the sort!"

But he was, he was.

My conversations with Simon Bliss in no way lessened my curiosity about Frederick Wigmore. There was romance in his living in Sherlock Holmes's former rooms. But I did not like to intrude on any man's privacy and so had to be content with observations and speculations. I had much time to myself and noted the number of visitors who climbed Wiggins' stairs at all hours. Some, dressed in the height of fashion, drove up in elegant broughams. Others, attired in the morning coats and black top hats of the professional world, came in hansoms. Some shabby souls arrived on foot. And there were children, too, scruffy little urchins who scrambled by my door. What was their business? And on what errands did Wiggins go with them to all parts of the city? My guess was that they were the "straying wayfarers" whom he had said he helped. But how?

Some of these clients must have paid Wiggins well, for he had a free hand with money. He maintained a wardrobe of the latest fashions. He dined at expensive places like the Savoy, the Carlton Grill, Romano's. He kept a manservant, a Cockney named Mr. Salt, a wiry, upstart little fellow whom Wiggins seemed to find highly amusing and to whom he gave great liberties. And Wiggins had a motorcar, his pride, which he kept along with his Admiral Nelson bicycle 'round the corner in a rented shed in Dean's Mews. The car was a sixty-horsepower F.I.A.T., "with four speeds and reverse, magneto ignition, and Bleriot Elliptique lamps," he pointed out proudly when he showed it to me one day. Politely I viewed its two-seated, white racing body and red uphol-stery. It was a pretty thing. "Two thousand pounds and cheap at the price," Wiggins told me. Thinking of the in-come on which I must live, I took out my moleskin and pol-ished my glasses in consternation at the young actor's extravagance.

My life could not depend upon Simon Bliss's and Wig-gins' patronage. Stimulated by Uncle's tales, I spent many hours exploring the city and found I enjoyed observing the affairs of the world. Too, I began to develop my interest in motors and mechanical things, a gadgeteering bent which I had always had without the time to indulge it. I set up a lit-tle workshop in one of my rooms. A mere tinkerer, one might have called me, but I was happy working there among odds and ends with the smell of machine oil about me. Pho-tography interested me, too, so I devised a darkroom in a cupboard, where I improved my technique with bromide paper. And firearms. Was it that they gave my life the touch of danger it lacked, for which I had left Cox's Bank? In any case, I came to own a number of pistols, blunt-barrelled, long-barrelled, heavy and light. I cared for them well; they would never fail me—foolish thought, as if I should ever de-pend upon one for my life. Occasionally Wiggins would ac-company me to a firing range, where we would practice our aims. He was a far better shot than I—expert—and I asked him where he had learned the skill.

"Oh, one picks up things," he replied in his offhand way, and I knew by his manner not to ask more.

Increasingly he cast his speculative look upon me, and I sensed that his as yet unasked question was imminent.

6

One Sunday in early June Wiggins suggested an outing to the Kentish woods. I agreed. We set out early—he in checkered dustcoat, yellow choker, and cap with great staring goggles; I wrapped in greatcoat and scarf, my bowler hat jammed upon my head. I clenched my teeth. In his little F.I.A.T. we rattled over the Thames and within an hour passed Greenwich. I tried to relax and enjoy the scenery, but Wiggins' erratic driving, with dramatic gestures to punctuate his shouted conversation, did not make me easy. I was glad when, about one, we stopped among some trees off Shooters Hill Road to eat the picnic lunch which Mrs. Cannon, our cook and housekeeper, had prepared.

We spread a blanket. I opened the wicker hamper while Wiggins popped the cork from a bottle of hock. We ate sandwiches and shared a cold bird. Stretched out a few feet away from me, Wiggins leaned on an elbow and thoughtfully surveyed the landscape. A breeze ruffled his blond hair. Mrs. Cannon had included half a dozen small fruit tarts, and he indulged his insatiable sweet tooth by popping them one by one into his mouth.

When they were gone, looking rather disappointed as he rustled among the picnic things to see if any of the pastries might have escaped his notice, he scowled at me. "You are very exasperating, Herbert," he said.

"I?"

"Yes—though I like your damnable discretion."

"Is that meant to be a compliment?"

"Yes. Blast! Are the tarts gone then?"

"It seems so."

"They were excellent!"

I did not comment that he had left none for me.

"See here, Herbert, don't you at all wonder about me?"

"Yes."

"About my hobby I mean. And my . . . visitors?"

"Naturally."

15

"Why haven't you asked about them, then?"

"I thought . . ."

"Never mind. You know, of course, that Sherlock Holmes once lived in Baker Street?"

"Indeed."

"But did you know that I knew him? Aha, I thought not!" He seemed pleased at my ignorance. "You see what asking questions may yield!"

"I thought you preferred me discreet."

"There are limits, Herbert!" His blue eyes were earnest. "I mean to tell you a story. It's not one I've told to anyone else. Not even Salt knows the whole truth of it." He took a deep breath. "I was once one of Sherlock Holmes's lads!"

"His lads?"

"The Baker Street Irregulars, the street boys he used to help him in his cases. Does that surprise you? I see that it does. I was not always Frederick Wigmore, the rising young actor, you know," he said proudly. "I have come a long way from my days of nosing about the city in Mr. Holmes's employ. I had neither parents nor home then. My reward was an education and a roof over my head. The detective took care of us right enough. When he saw I had a theatrical bent, he encouraged me. He was something of an actor himself, you know. When he retired just three years ago I took his rooms. Thinking he still lived there, all sorts of people came looking for him, and a good many told me their problems. I had some time between engagements and decided to try my hand at helping them. Why shouldn't I? I was trained by the great detective himself. Well, I've had some success; I've a small reputation. Naturally I keep my detective work quite separate from my stage career. People mistrust no one so much as an actor; that's why I never appear on stage in my own face. Disguise is a great advantage, Herbert. Now listen, I need help. And ever since I heard you were looking for something more out of life I've been watching you. I trust you." He sat up very straight. "I wish to make you an offer."

I gazed at the handsome young fellow. His tale did not entirely surprise me, for I already had guessed something of the sort—though not that he had known Sherlock Holmes, and I confess the fact gave me a little thrill. I thought how odd and fortuitous it was that both Uncle and Wiggins were in the same line of work. Yet my conservative habits were not to be overcome in an instant, and it was with some misgivings and a little shiver of uncertainty that I spoke: "What sort of offer?"

He gazed at me straightforwardly. "Simply this: I want you to be my partner."

"Your . . . partner?"

"In detective work, don't you know! Damn!" Impatiently he overturned the picnic hamper. "Is there nothing left? Listen, dear fellow, you are perfect for the job—honest, hard-working, intelligent, brave—and you have a special quality of—forgive me, I mean this as a compliment—of . . . forgettableness."

I pulled off my glasses and rubbed very hard at the lenses.

Wiggins gestured. "I mean, Herbert, you sink into a background. You are unobtrusive. To someone who knows you as I do, you're a splendid fellow, infinitely to be preferred to the flashy sort. But . . . you look like . . . well . . . like an Englishman, damn it all—*any* Englishman is what I mean to say. It's a sort of talent—blasted if I know how you do it! At any rate it's perfect for trailing suspects; they never would notice you. Too, you know the city. And you are a keen observer. Those pistols of yours, your knowledge of firearms—it could prove quite useful." He sat back. "Yes, all in all you're exactly what's wanted! You have my reasons, then—all except that, well, Herbert, damn it all, I like you! I don't want to lead you in under false pretenses; there's a very particular case I'm anxious for you to start on, and, to be frank, you would not just be wetting your feet but plunging right in—nothing dangerous, I trust, though one never knows. What do you say? Aha!" Pouncing upon a pastry crumb, he popped it into his mouth and made a great deal of it while he watched me wrestle with my decision.

I continued to rub at my glasses, the sun glinting off the rims. Wind soughed in the chestnut trees and swished through the tall grass in a nearby field. Horse-drawn waggons clattered on Shooters Hill Road, the occasional impatient motorcar bleating at them as it put-putted 'round. When I slipped my glasses back on, I saw very clearly that

17

an opportunity for a new life was here. It was not what I had imagined, but what had that been after all, other than a vague notion of finer things? It would be fine, wouldn't it, to quicken my blood?

"Of course I shall join you, Wiggins," I replied.

The actor's gleaming smile and a vigorous handshake were my reward, though neither warmed me. I sat in a chill, wondering what I had done, knowing that to please Wiggins and satisfy my own pride, which was rising far above what it had been, I intended to keep my word.

## 7

That evening, before a blazing fire in his rooms, Wiggins told me about his work. "Of course, the people who come here are those who cannot, or choose not to, take their problems to the police." He went on to describe the latest case. "I have in my time frequented houses which ... cater to a man's tastes, if you know what I mean." Understanding full well, I nodded. "And one of them—among the best—is run by Mistress Nance Castle, an old friend. I've helped her with one or two sticky matters, and the upshot is she's come to me again. Seems some smarmy bloke has badly disfigured one of her girls, a beautiful young thing whose looks are now quite ruined, and Nance wants me to find the man and make him pay. Don't make such a face! It's money I mean, that's all, to take care of the girl now that her career is spoiled. Ordinarily it wouldn't be much of a task, but the blighter is proving elusive—I can't get a line on him—and what with my time at the Gaiety I haven't the energy that I'd like to put in on the case. That's why I need you. Will you try your hand, Herbert? The girl, poor Rose Mappin, would be very grateful."

"I shall help in any way I can, Wiggins," I replied.

"Splendid!"

And so I became a detective. I liked the work, feeling that my quite ordinary appearance was an advantage, a "talent" as Wiggins had called it. Danger? There was none, or didn't seem to be, though what I discovered was odd indeed.

There were three detectives then—Uncle, Wiggins, and I. It only wanted a fourth to complete our quartet. Though I did not know it, I had met him: a small boy with large brown eyes. It was he who discovered the murder at the Diogenes Club.

## ❧Jack Merridew's Narrative❧

### I

My name is Jack Merridew. I am twelve years old, nearly thirteen. And I am proud to write this as Mr. Bliss has asked.

The morning it began seemed no different from any other in the year since I came from Hanwell School to the Diogenes Club as page to Mr. Simon Bliss. At 4:00 A.M. the distant scrape of Alfred the boilerman's shovel feeding the club furnaces made me toss in my iron bedstead. There was another hour of quiet; then the undercook, Mrs. Beddoes, shuffled past my door to go down to the still room to light the water heaters. Shortly after, the staff cook was up to prepare the servants' breakfasts. Then the housekeeper, Mrs. Broek, was shaking my shoulder—"Time to stir, Jack!"—and I knew it was 6:00 A.M., and I must see to the club members' tea.

I awoke in my tiny room on the top floor of the Diogenes Club on that October morning in 1906, as I had grown used to doing each day of my year of service. It was cold and dark, and I could barely see by the dim light seeping through the small, high window above my bed, but I was not unhappy. My cubbyhole in the servants' quarters was small and sparsely furnished, there being only an iron bedstead, a rickety deal table holding my lamp and books, and an old wardrobe where my page's livery was hung each night by the laundry maid. But it was all my own, and when I closed its door at day's end I could scurry under a warm eiderdown, light my lamp, and lose myself in the books Mr. Bliss brought me—Thackeray and Dickens, and French and Russian writers too. And I would scribble my thoughts into the journal he had me keep. It was not a bad life for an orphan boy of twelve who had had no prospects.

I lit my lamp and splashed water on my face from the enameled basin on the washstand. Blotting myself dry, I peered into the cracked mirror on the wall and brushed at my unruly hair. I quickly slipped on stockings, then the green breeches, jacket, and white Eton collar of my page's uniform, and opened the door to begin another day at the Diogenes Club.

First, below, to the servants' dining room. Breakfast was a slapdash affair. We snatched it when we could. Already several were at their places, washing down bread, drippings, and jam with cups of hot tea before hurrying off to chores. I took my place at the long oaken table. Dishes rattled and knives and spoons clinked as we greeted one another, ate, and gossiped about club members. As usual I only listened, taking in every word, which I would repeat to Mr. Bliss if I thought it would interest him.

Finished with breakfast by six-thirty, I went to the still room to help Mrs. Beddoes load trays of tea on the service lift before pulling the heavy cord to send them to the upper floors. Then, winding my way past the wine cellar, game larder, cold rooms, carpenter's shop, knife room, and boot and plate rooms, I hurried up the staff stairs at the back of the club to the third floor, where I began to help footboy Jimmy Thompson to unload trays. Hawk-nosed Mr. Stalker, the head steward, watched us sharply. Silently he took the trays, placed a folded newspaper on each, and delivered them to the bedrooms with a murmured, "Tea and *Times* on the table, sir," as he backed out and shut each door. There were thirty-two bedrooms to do, almost all occupied each morning, so it took nearly an hour to complete the task.

From my first day at the Diogenes Club I had had the privilege of bringing in Mr. Simon Bliss's tray when he stayed there. I am sure Mr. Stalker resented me for that, for he treated me very ill, though he was never kind to any lad. This morning he snapped at Jimmy Thompson to "look sharp in the dining room" before he strode off. Jimmy and I exchanged a wink. He scampered off. I took up Mr. Bliss's tray and went to his door.

Mr. Simon Bliss is thought one of the oddest men in London, but I love him. He has been both father and grandfather to me, and I shall always be grateful. I learned his story only after he came like a miracle to save me from Hanwell School. He was born in Grimsthorpe, Lincolnshire, in 1834, the son of a poor crofter, a good-natured man who drank too much and took wretched care of his frail wife and family. Mr. Bliss's mother could read and write and taught her five children to do the same, though it did them little good in poverty. At fifteen, young Simon Bliss left home to seek his fortune and found it in trade, becoming a wealthy man. But he was not in love with profit, so in the eighties, when his ventures were at their most thriving, he sold them—all his holdings in far-off lands—to live in London.

"I wanted a more settled life, Jack," he told me, "but I wanted to study humanity too. Where better than in London, that great, gray, smoky, seething city of cities, where every nation meets? So in old age I returned to her bosom, and I have never for an instant regretted it!" People thought him eccentric because he kept company with all sorts of people, high and low, royals and thieves, but that never bothered him. "The duchesses and earls may call me a queer old duck, but they let me in their parlours nonetheless. I amuse them! Ah, if only they knew how they amuse me . . ."

As for me, my history is short. When I was small my father and mother were employed as valet and head parlour maid by Lady Blassingame. At her fine Mayfair house I learned to read and write, even to speak French. "Learn all you can, Jack. You may one day be a gentleman too," my mother would say. But this pleasant life did not last. My father was killed at the relief of Mafeking in the South African War. Old Lady Blassingame died, and my mother was forced to take work in the paint trade. After three years she died of lead poisoning, so at the age of ten I was sent to the Hanwell School for Orphans and Destitute Children.

Hanwell was a dreadful place, cold and bleak. The masters were very hard. One day about a year after I came there, an old gentleman arrived looking for a boy to serve him. That gentleman was Mr. Simon Bliss. He interviewed many lads and at last called me into the drafty Hanwell corridor. I was frightened of him, though he was hardly taller than I. Bent, wrinkled, bald except for wisps of white hair about his ears, he tottered up with the help of a blackthorn stick and peered hard into my face. I spoke up brave as I could, hoping he would choose me. I told him the truth: how I used to play truant to wander London's byways and how I read books— *The Prisoner of Zenda, The Moonstone, King Solomon's Mines*—to take my mind off my misery.

I was smaller than the other boys, thin, and pale, and I thought Mr. Bliss would not want me. But after a silence he announced in his high, cracked voice, "You will do, Jack Merridew."

My heart leapt! "D-do for what, sir?" I dared ask.

He cocked his head like a parrot. "Oh, a great many things. You see these old legs?" Making a face, he struck his shanks with his stick. "They are not as limber as they once were. But . . ." he tapped his skull, "here is a mind with the vigor of youth, wise—though without so much wisdom as at twenty I thought it had. It's simple as this: my legs can't keep up with my brain, so I need an eager young fellow to hop about for me. A bright lad, not one of your dullards, a fellow who can understand what he's seeing." He looked at me sharply. "Are you such a lad, Jack Merridew?"

"I . . . I should like to be, sir," I stammered.

"I believe you would," he said, nodding, putting his hand on my shoulder. It was the gentlest touch I had felt since my dear mother's death, and my lips began to tremble. I was very ashamed of the tears that started to my eyes, but Mr. Bliss only scowled, first at the right wall, then the left, before snorting and thumping away down the corridor. "Let us leave this wretched place at once!" his voice echoed back to me.

And so I came to the Diogenes Club.

I packed up and said good-bye to the lads. Within an hour we were across the Thames, my mind in a whirl. The Diogenes is near St. James's Square, "among the forest of London clubs," said Mr. Bliss. Clutching a little knapsack of all my worldly goods, I stepped down from the hansom and gazed in awe at the wide, three-storied stone building. It looked like a picture of a Roman temple.

"What do you think, lad?" Mr. Bliss asked.

"Very fine, sir," I replied.

"Fine? Mmm." He rubbed his jaw, and I thought he did not think it so fine as I. "It was built in the 1850s by men of Manchester, railway barons—robbers I should call them. It was a rich snob's palace, but the founders drifted to other clubs or lost their money, and her character changed. Odd sorts who couldn't—or didn't want to—join other clubs attached themselves like barnacles until by the 1880s the place was encrusted with the most peculiar men in London— backward peers, furtive barristers who wouldn't meet your eyes, stuffy magnates who sucked on fat cigars. That was when I joined, Jack; it seemed just the club for me! At one time silence was the cardinal rule, and members were fined just for speaking in her hallowed halls—quite a challenge to a student of human nature! But that prohibition is long gone, and we are now much like any other club. No, there are not so many fascinating characters as before. Yet . . ." he smiled, "do you know what I have discovered to my very great pleasure?"

"What is that, sir?" I asked, looking up at him, his face reminding me of the face of a mummy which I had seen in the British Museum.

He winked. "That every man has his secrets! Come, lad!" Briskly he led me into the Diogenes Club.

### 3

As usual, I found Mr. Bliss still in bed when I entered his room with the tray on that bright, chill October morning. He was propped up by two huge pillows, reading a book, squinting as he ran his bony finger along the lines of print. He wore a striped nightcap and, as he frowned at me over the tops of his wire-rimmed spectacles, reminded me of Ebenezer Scrooge.

"Morning, Jack," he murmured.

"Good morning, sir," I said, going about my task.

Mr. Bliss's was a large corner room. French doors led to a balcony. Below was Pall Mall, bounded by St. James's Palace at one end and Trafalgar Square at the other. The room was crowded with booty from Mr. Bliss's adventuring days.

On the floor were carpets from Turkey and Persia. Near his high oak bed stood the simple, low, carved wooden throne of an African king, where the old man sat to pull on his boots each morning. Above the entrance door hung the head of a leopard which he had shot in Punjapore. There were bits of scrimshaw he had carved on a whaling voyage, lacquered Chinese boxes, a Japanese screen behind which he kept his basin, ewer, and washing things on a little stand. Beside the fireplace, on the tall bookcase spilling with books, sat a fat stuffed owl with eyes yellow and shrewd as Mr. Bliss's. Apollo he called it—"My oracle!"—and when some problem baffled him he would sit by the fire, smoke his long-stemmed pipe, and stare up at the bird as if it could give him counsel. A framed quotation from Alexander Pope hung above the mantlepiece: "The proper study of mankind is man."

An oval Benares brass tray with hammered designs of elephants hauling teak logs served as Mr. Bliss's tea table. I arranged the things upon it, then struck a match to the tinder which I had set in the grate the night before.

Mr. Bliss slipped from bed, his long, old-fashioned nightshirt dragging the ground. "I shall be ready in a moment, Jack. While I wash, have a look at this." I went over. "The *Almanach de Gotha*," he said, placing the heavy book on the edge of the bed where I could see. "A genealogy—collection of family trees—with the apes left out." He chuckled. "It never hurts to know who is related to whom, lad." He tapped a bony finger on the open page, where a maze of lines spread like the roots of a tree, with the names of nobles and royalty sprouting from the ends. "Here is Bertie—King Edward. See how he's related to nearly every royal house in Europe?" He traced the connections. "King Leopold of the Belgians, Tsar Nicholas of Russia, King Ferdinand of Rumania, Frederick of Denmark, Haakon of Norway, Constantine of the Hellenes—and, unfortunately," he scowled, "the blasted German emperor, Wilhelm II, a bloody fanatical fool, the most dangerous man in Europe!" He sighed. "Study it, Jack, study it. The knowledge may stand you in good stead some day."

"Yes, sir."

Mr. Bliss stepped behind the Japanese screen to splash

water on his face. While he washed I tried to make sense of all the lines in the *Almanach*, but the maze was too much for me; I would examine it later.

When Mr. Bliss had washed, I helped him into his old maroon dressing gown. He settled into his padded leather wing chair on one side of the fire. I—though it would have shocked Mr. Stalker if he could have seen us together, like chums—sat in the chair opposite. I poured tea. Apollo watched us from his perch. Above the hiss of the coal fire, sounds of early morning traffic drifted up from Pall Mall.

*"Hast du deine Deutsche Grammatik gestern studiert?"* Mr. Bliss asked. He was teaching me German.

*"Ja, mein Herr."*

*"Gut, gut."* He rubbed his hands and leaned forward. "Now, lad, what news?"

These were the words I heard every morning when Mr. Bliss and I took our places. It was understood that I was at his beck and call if he needed me, but I had regular duties in the Diogenes Club, just like Jimmy Thompson. "I want you to see what life is about, not be locked up with an old man, lad," Mr. Bliss had explained. I was happy to do anything he liked. My work in the club put me in the way of hearing the latest stories from servants and club members alike. I gave my report—nothing special. Retired Army Colonel Cooke was pressing his attentions on a pretty Irish maid; I had heard her sobbing over what to do about it to Mrs. Beddoes.

Mr. Bliss hated injustice. The maid was in love with a young footman; they planned to wed. "I shall have a talk with Colonel Cooke!" he exclaimed. "It would not do at all to have the girl seduced! If she got in the family way Cooke would drop her; so might her young man and then she would end in the streets. Yes, I shall see to the matter today. Is that it then, Jack? Mmm." He sipped tea, then cocked his head in the way he had when something was on his mind, his eye like the eye of a sparrow on a worm. "What do you know about Baron Sigmund Czinner?"

I felt a little chill when he asked me. I pictured the baron: short, stout, with thick, black hair and sharp, darting eyes. I never liked it when he looked at me. "He's been a member about two months, hasn't he, sir? Very rich. Foreign—German? He goes out a good deal, all over the city. He's always leaving messages with Mr. Wetheridge as to where he may be found."

"Is that all, lad?"

"I . . . think so, sir."

He leaned back and made a tent of his hands. "And what do you make of him?"

I knew what he meant and that I could be honest. "I don't like him, sir."

"Aha!" He slapped a knee. "Precisely! Nor do I, Jack, nor do I. Your instincts are correct. There is something very wrong about this Baron Sigmund Czinner. Foreign? Yes, Austrian. And he is indeed rich; he flashes his money about in very crude fashion—though I'm damned if I can discover how he came by it. It's surely not inherited; the fellow has no breeding. Busy, busy, he is, gadding about like an insect ever since he arrived on our shores six months ago. He's wormed his way deep into society."

"He talks to the servants, sir, takes them aside."

"Bribing them, no doubt, for information about club members. Is he merely a gossip? I think not. But what? His money's opened a great many doors; he proposes vague financial schemes—so some wealthy gentlemen of my acquaintance tell me—but more to test the wind than to do anything about them. Like an old badger he hoards secrets but gives none away. He's slippery, all right, avoids me; I can't pin him down. He bears watching."

"Yes, sir."

"Keep your eyes skinned and your ears open, lad."

"I shall, sir."

He smiled. "I know I can trust you. Now let us see the *Times.*"

I handed him the newspaper. He rattled it open. Every morning Mr. Bliss read aloud to me what he thought the most important stories, often political news, but sometimes bits of scandal or descriptions of grisly murders. Everything interested him. This morning he read an article about the building of the dreadnoughts. "We need those battleships, Jack, to keep our lead over Germany's expanding naval might!"

Then there came a particularly noisy rattle of the paper.

26

"Admiral Fisher is still pressing to combine the Channel and Atlantic fleets into one, I see. He's right to do it! It's a bad situation, Germany keeping her whole fleet within a few hours of our shores. Damn the German emperor!" He set the paper aside. "At least Bertie supports Fisher against Lord Beresford. And he stands by Haldane's wish to form a territorial army, too, in spite of Lloyd George's and Winston Churchill's economizing zeal. The king is by no means useless. Oh, he's far too concerned with making sure his decorations are stuck on in the right places, but without him the Entente Cordiale would not be. We need the friendship of the French—indeed, all the friends we can muster—not to mention ships and guns. Bertie sees that. He does some good." He sighed and shook his head. "But what a popinjay and a gadabout he is! Where has he hopped to now, do you suppose?"

"He's at Abingdon, isn't he, sir?"

"*Was* at Abingdon, at the Colebrooks' for grouse shooting. But is he there now?" He turned to the Court Circular, the list of the king's activities which was printed daily in the *Times*. "Ah, as I suspected, he has trundled on, this time to Londesborough with his gay party of friends—the Keppels, Count Mensdorff, Lionel Rothschild, Harry Chaplin." His eyebrows rose. "And two fresh names I see: the young Frenchwoman, Madame Sophie Bernard, and the German embassy's newest attaché, Herr Wilhelm Luscher." He dropped the *Times* and searched through the back copies of the *London Illustrated News* which he kept for ready reference in the stand by his chair. Taking one up, he folded back a page and handed it to me. "Have a look at Madame Bernard, Jack. What do you make of that face?"

He tapped a photograph with his pipe stem—two people on shipboard, the French wine merchant, Monsieur Armand Bernard, and his twenty-year-old bride. They had just arrived from France, the caption said. Monsieur Bernard had business to attend to in England and would be in London for the season. I glanced at the date of the paper—April 12, 1906, six months ago. Monsieur Bernard was a tall, sober-looking gentleman in a high silk topper. His bride, holding his arm, wore a frilly white dress, her hair up in curls in the latest fashion, with a little feathered hat on top. I could not help staring at her. She had an oval face; her smile seemed meant just for me. "She ... she's beautiful, sir," I stammered, looking up at the old man.

Mr. Bliss grunted, snatched the paper, and narrowed his eyes at it over his spectacles. "Beautiful? Indeed. Her eyes are green; her skin's like milk. I've met her two or three times, you know." He glanced at me sharply. "Beauty can be dangerous to men—and boys. Forget her, Jack." Quickly he turned pages. "Ah, here is Herr Luscher, Willy to his friends."

He showed me the paper again, this time a picture of a hunting scene at the royal lodge, Abergeldie. The king himself stood proudly beside forty braces of birds. Behind him, to the right, was a lean, blond young man with a curling moustache and a flashing smile.

"Handsome, what?" Mr. Bliss commented as he lit his long-stemmed pipe. "Another fascinating case which I must investigate. Herr Luscher hasn't been in England long, but nevertheless has won Bertie's friendship. What's his secret? Money? Wit? Those who know him say he's charming. I haven't met him, but intend to at the earliest opportunity." He put the newspaper away. "And where does Bertie encamp next, my lad?"

"That hasn't been published yet, has it, sir?"

He clucked his tongue. "You should know it just the same! This time of year he always returns to Sandringham, for his birthday on November the ninth. Sixty-five years old. Hmm. It will be a grand occasion, with too much food, silliness, and boredom for the ladies while the gentlemen are out killing birds. I wonder if Madame Bernard and young Luscher will be there. No matter." He glanced at the clock on the mantlepiece. "You must be off now." He gave a sly grin. "We don't want to make Mr. Stalker angry."

I collected the tea things. "Baron Czinner, Jack, watch him!" Mr. Bliss reminded with a deep look just before I went out.

"Yes, sir."

I left the old man in a cloud of pipe smoke, staring up at Apollo. On my way downstairs I kept seeing Madame Sophie Bernard's almond-shaped eyes. Green, Mr. Bliss had said they were. Could it really be so dangerous to think of them?

<h2 style="text-align:center">4</h2>

After my hour with Mr. Bliss, my place each morning was in the large, panelled dining room where breakfast was served until ten. Three valets carried trays of food to the tables laid with white cloths. I stood between the sideboard and the plate closet, alert for the nods and beckoning motions of club members who might miss a teaspoon or want a linen napkin, pot of jam, or newspaper. By eight-thirty I was in position, watching the clubmen come in.

About nine Mr. Bliss made his appearance in a brown tweed morning suit, the trousers fitting his thin legs like the casing of a sausage. Leaning on his stick, he stopped just inside the entrance doors and cocked his head, glancing 'round the room to see who was present and where each sat. Shortly he made his crablike way among the tables, stopping here and there for a word, smiling and patting shoulders before he ended at the table of his victim, retired Army Colonel Cooke. I had no doubt that he would soon convince the colonel, by one means or another, that he must refrain from badgering the poor Irish maid.

Baron Czinner came in soon after. I glanced at Mr. Bliss and saw that he saw the man and was watching him over Colonel Cooke's shoulder. By now Colonel Cooke looked very pale.

I watched Baron Czinner, too, and practiced the techniques of observation which Mr. Bliss had taught me. "You must be able to read a man at a glance, Jack!" he had said. I read "no good." Hands behind him, the baron rocked on his heels just inside the room. He was middle-aged, short, solid, and rounded from head to toe. Dressed in a white waistcoat and snug, dark morning coat, he reminded me of a penguin. His jowls were loose, his color pale as wax. His shining black hair was combed back, and he had a pencil-line moustache. His little, dark eyes were like raisins. His smile showed long teeth, and I shivered when it touched me.

Just as Mr. Bliss had done, the baron looked 'round before making his move. He had a sort of sliding walk, by which he came to a table near my station, where the Gray's Inn solicitor Sir Charles Ormsby sat alone with his long nose buried in a morning paper.

"*Bitte*, may I sit?" I heard Baron Czinner ask Sir Charles.

"My dear fellow, yes." It was a mumble. Sir Charles hardly looked up from his paper.

Baron Czinner's smile widened as if he had been granted a great favor. He dropped into the empty chair and fussily arranged his napkin on his lap. He folded his white, stubby-fingered hands, glanced about, cleared his throat, tapped on the cloth. At last he leaned toward Sir Charles and appeared to be asking questions of which I could hear none. He was secretive, all right. Sir Charles seemed annoyed. What did the baron want? Watching his smile and how his fingers rubbed the tablecloth, back and forth, back and forth, I could not believe he meant any good and was glad to see him confounded. Sir Charles was one of the club's most distinguished members and had little time for gossip. With a brusque "Excuse me, sir!" he abruptly rose and left.

Baron Czinner appeared not to mind. Keeping his bright, false smile, he buttered a scone and munched it while he sipped coffee. At last, dabbing the corners of his mouth, he rose to go. His look touched my face, and it was as if cobwebs had brushed it in an old house. The baron seemed to study me; then he breezed past with his sliding walk, trailing the scent of gardenia water. He left the dining room.

Mr. Bliss rose too. "Oily, he is," he muttered so no one else could hear as he passed near me. "What's his bloody game?"

5

At ten the maids bustled in to clear the breakfast dishes. I went to willowy, white-haired Mr. Wetheridge, the head hall porter. He was the sentinel of the club, his tall figure in green livery swaying to and fro all day by the great entrance doors as if the breeze they made in opening and closing moved him like a reed. My job until half-past eleven was to stand by to carry messages or to show visitors into the club. Bright flames danced in the fireplace opposite Mr. Wetheridge's box. Above the mantelpiece hung a portrait of Queen Victoria, looking very stern. She was King Edward's mother. I was proud to know my master, Mr. Bliss, was a friend of the king. His Majesty had a reputation for liking fun, and, gazing up at the late queen, so very unlike my own dear mother, I thought it would take a good deal of fun indeed to make up for even five minutes of that disapproving look.

Members came and went. Mr. Wetheridge carefully recorded their movements in the book of the day. I sorted the morning post and carried occasional messages on my tray to the smoking, reading, and card rooms. Always, if there were anything interesting in these notes, I remembered it for Mr. Bliss.

At ten-thirty Mr. Bliss passed through the vestibule to begin his daily outing. His wrinkled face peered from above the otter collar of his long, black, broadcloth overcoat. His silk topper was pulled well onto his ears. "I'm off, Jack! Morning, Wetheridge." He waved and went out. Through the glass panels in the entrance doors I watched him clamber into a waiting carriage on Pall Mall, his bent body looking as if a breeze would send it flying like a dried leaf. He had amazing energy. Every day he was away in a different direction—toward Belgravia, Bloomsbury, the slums off Mile End Road—collecting information about the city.

Shortly after Mr. Bliss departed, Baron Czinner appeared in the vestibule, stopping before the porter's box with his hands behind him, rocking on his heels. He did not look at me. The scent of gardenia water was very strong. I noted how fat his white fingers were and that he wore several rings set with large stones—red, blue, white. His smile showed his long, yellowish teeth. "I am here until this afternoon, Vetheridge," he said, pronouncing Wetheridge with a *V*.

The porter dutifully took up his book. "I shall note it down, sir."

Once more rising on his toes, the baron was gazing at me. Realizing he had been aware of me all along and knowing I had been staring, I felt hot to my ears.

"Ah!" he said softly, his raisin eyes wrinkling as they examined me. "You are Jack!"

I shivered. His tone reminded me of the Hanwell headmaster's when he hoped to catch some boy out at a lie. "Y-yes, sir," I stammered.

He nodded. "And Mr. Simon Bliss is your . . . protector, yes?"

"My protector, sir? He . . . he found me my place at the Diogenes Club, if that is what you mean."

"So-o-o." He bobbed his head thoughtfully. "You are helpful to him, I am sure. *Du bist ein braver Junge!*" He patted my shoulder.

I forced myself to meet his look, fearing he could read on my face every word of what Mr. Bliss and I had said about him. "Mr. Bliss was very good to bring me here," I gulped.

"And surely he is good to you still?" Glancing along the empty corridor, then at Mr. Wetheridge, who was occupied with his book, Baron Czinner lowered his voice. "You have his confidence; I am told that you do. Hmm. Mr. Simon Bliss is very . . . how do you say . . . spry for an old man. Off every morning—*wunderbar!* And where does he go, I wonder?" He rocked on his heels.

"I don't know, sir," I said.

"Oh, perhaps . . ." I heard a jingling in his pocket; suddenly his fat palm was full of shillings, among them a gleaming sovereign. I stared at the coins, then into Baron Czinner's eyes, which were hard and mean for all their jolly crinkles, and I felt great fear.

At that moment Mr. Wetheridge came from his box to hand me a note for the upstairs card room. I snatched it. "I'll go up at once, sir," I said, glad for the excuse to escape.

The baron's coins already were tucked out of sight. "I shall be in the smoking room, Vetheridge," he said in a bored sort of way and left us with his sliding walk, trailing gardenia scent. I saw Mr. Wetheridge wrinkle his nose.

I now had something to tell Mr. Bliss: that Baron Sigmund Czinner was interested in him as he was in the baron.

Visitors were not unusual at the Diogenes Club. However, I paid special attention to one who arrived at eleven; he was a short, portly man, sixtyish, balding, red-faced, weak-chinned, with ill-shaven cheeks and grease spots dotting his waistcoat.

"Samuel Jarrett to see Sigmund Czinner!" he snarled at Mr. Wetheridge.

I examined the man—Mr. Bliss would want to know

about him. Smelling of liquor, in his dishevelled state, he was far from a typical club visitor.

"*Baron* Czinner?" Mr. Wetheridge inquired doubtfully.

The man curled his lips and barked a laugh. "If that's what 'e calls 'imself."

Frowning, Mr. Wetheridge consulted his book. "The baron does not appear to expect you."

"Announce me, then, damn it all!" The man bunched his fists.

Mr. Wetheridge was very cool. "Have you a card?"

"Don't need no card!"

Mr. Wetheridge appeared to think while Samuel Jarrett fumed. "Very well. Jack, show this gentleman to the stranger's room. Then go tell the baron in the smoking room that Mr. Samuel Jarrett—that was the name, wasn't it?—is here to see him."

"Bloody right!" said the man, pulling himself up. Clumping on my heels and breathing heavily, he suffered me to lead him to the stranger's room, where visitors must wait while their club member friends are called for them. Just down the corridor from the vestibule, it was empty, and I left the man muttering alone while I went to the smoking room. There, a dozen or so members lounged in studded, red leather armchairs, reading or chatting. A few stood by the blazing fire. Baron Czinner appeared to have cornered a grizzled naval officer. "A Mr. Jarrett to see you, sir," I announced as I came up to them.

The baron's smile vanished. "*Samuel* Jarrett?"

"Yes, sir." I swallowed hard as the dangerous look surged in his eyes. "Shall I . . . shall I have Mr. Wetheridge send him away?"

"No," he said quickly. "Did you see this man? Fat? Red-faced?"

"Yes, sir. He's waiting in the stranger's room."

"Mmm. *Danke schön*, Jack." Seeming to want to make light of the matter, he rose with a little shrug of apology to the naval officer, whom he appeared to have been plying with brandy. "I shall see what this fellow wants." He hurried away.

I stayed for a moment to take some messages. On my way

back to the vestibule I noticed that the doors of the stranger's room had been closed. Through their glass I glimpsed Baron Czinner and Mr. Jarrett. The baron's face was pink with fury, and his mouth was moving angrily. His visitor didn't look like backing down. Wishing I could hear what they quarrelled about, I promised myself that Mr. Bliss would know everything I had observed.

A few moments later Baron Czinner hurried into the vestibule, his expression grim. "I have some business, Vetheridge! Whiskey and soda in the library! At once!" He stalked off down the hall.

Sighing and shaking his head, Mr. Wetheridge ordered a bottle of Dewars Special, a siphon, and glasses, and I carried them on a tray up the wide, carpeted stairs to the library on the first floor. Baron Czinner and his visitor were seated across from one another at a table in one of the bays. They were hidden from the entrance doors by the tall bookcases, their angry words, trailing off as I came in, muffled by thick carpeting. This was the least used of the club rooms; they could not have been more private.

The baron was enough himself to flash me his toothy smile. "Thank you, Jack." But his stubby fingers continued to drum on the tabletop as I set down the tray. Mr. Jarrett glared at him out of eyes blurred with drink. I withdrew.

At the club entrance Mr. Bliss was just coming in, earlier than I expected. With him was Inspector Nelson Faraday of Scotland Yard. I wanted to tell Mr. Bliss about the men in the library but saw I must wait, as it was clear he and the inspector meant to have a talk.

"We'll have more privacy in my room, Faraday," said Mr. Bliss, gesturing toward the stairs.

"Um," the policeman responded gruffly. He was a large, looming man with a squarish head and close-cropped hair. He wore gray trousers, a plain broadcloth overcoat, and, jammed well forward on his head, a billycock hat, under whose brim his slit-eyes glittered. "Hello, Jack," he muttered, as he handed me his broadcloth.

"Good morning, sir."

The inspector unbuttoned his black sack coat, which fell back like a curtain to show his belly in a red-checkered waistcoat. Hooking one thumb into his watch pocket and toying with his Albert chain, he scanned every corner of the vestibule as if it were no more than a lurk for thieves. His eyes were alive with suspicion. I never saw him without this expression; there was something terrifying about it, even to me, who had nothing to hide, and I knew it must melt any cracksman, footpad, or fence taken to answer questions in a Bow Street back room.

"Well?" the policeman rumbled.

"Let's go up at once." Mr. Bliss gave me a secret wink. "Lunch in my room, Jack. One o'clock. See to it."

"Yes, sir."

Dressed alike in black, Mr. Bliss a scuttling spider to Inspector Nelson Faraday's great black beetle, they mounted the stairs.

From eleven-thirty to twelve I helped the upstairs grooms remove dust cloths from the billiard tables, lay out London dailies on the round stands near the fireplaces, change pen nibs, and stack the writing tables with quires of pale-green club notepaper. Going below to get the paper and pen nibs, I came up by the servants' stairs at the rear of the building. These stairs lead by narrow passageways all over the club and exit directly into each club room. On my way past the library service door I paused. Were Baron Czinner and his mysterious friend still in the library? I could not miss this chance of learning something which Mr. Bliss might want to know, so, setting down my box of writing supplies, I turned the latch and cautiously cracked the door. The men were indeed there; I heard muffled sounds of argument. They could not see me because of the bookcases. Shivering with excitement, fearing to be discovered but taking the chance nonetheless, I listened.

Their words were hard to make out. Baron Czinner spoke softly. Mr. Jarrett was louder, but his words were slurred by drink. "Not for any amount of money . . ." I caught from him. Also something that sounded like "sand" and "ham" and something about "playing."

". . . tell all!" Mr. Jarrett roared.

I had to hear more. I opened the door wider and leaned into the room.

"It is not decent of you, Mr. Jarrett—nor grateful," came the baron's accented voice.

"Bah! A servant!" Mr. Jarrett spit. "Naught but a bloody servant is all I been to you and your fine friends! But I'm an Englishman, and now I see the thing clear I won't go through with it. Won't do it, no—not to poor bleedin' Teddy! But you!" His voice frightened me. "I'll do it to you, right enough. I'll tell all, I will!"

I heard the clink of a glass, and when Baron Czinner's voice came, soft, it frightened me even more than Mr. Jarrett's yelling: "Have another drink, Mr. Jarrett . . ."

Suddenly I heard footsteps on the stairs. My heart jumped. Swiftly I closed the door and picked up my writing supplies just as Mr. Stalker came into view 'round the narrow bend above. He glared but said nothing; he had not caught me listening.

Sorry I had not been able to hear more of the argument in the library, I edged past Mr. Stalker and hurried to my job.

## 6

From twelve-thirty until nearly two I was at my place by the sideboard in the dining room, at the call of the retired officers, solicitors, government officials, and businessmen of the city who bustled in for the midday meal. About one I carried a tray to Mr. Bliss's room, where he and Inspector Faraday were talking before his fire. I longed to stay with them, to hear what they discussed, but had to return to my place. I was gone no more than ten minutes. Baron Czinner did not appear for lunch.

From two until four I waited on the billiard rooms, helping Mr. Dorland, the marker. On my way up I stopped again at the library, but when I opened the service door I heard no voices.

There was little to do in the billiard rooms but stand about, occasionally handing a player a rest or long cue, or stoking the fire, and this afternoon there was no interesting conversation. I spent the time thinking about the bits of talk I had heard in the library. Samuel Jarrett had threatened Baron Czinner with telling something. What? Were "sand" and "ham" and "playing" clues? Who was "Teddy"? Mr. Bliss might know, and I was anxious to speak to him soon as I could. I would do so when my afternoon chores were done.

I left the billiard rooms at four and went to the library. It was my job every day before tea to see that the tables in each bay were stocked with paper and pens and that the pots of paste, sticks of green sealing wax, candles, and green-handled letter openers were in order. The library was so little used that often there was nothing to do, but I had to check. I entered through the service door and looked into the first bay. The clear afternoon light fell from the window at the end of the alcove across the writing tools on the long mahogany table and made the morocco bindings of the books in rows on the tall bookcases shine. Everything was in place. The second bay was like the first. But in the third, in which Baron Czinner and his guest had argued, I was surprised to find Mr. Jarrett still present, in deep sleep, with his arms crossed under his head, which was turned away from me. It was a drunken sleep, I guessed, for an overturned glass lay near him and the whiskey bottle on the serving tray was nearly empty.

Quietly I collected the glasses and the siphon and picked up the tray. I thought of waking Mr. Jarrett but decided that if he were roused to a headache he would abuse me, so I let him be. I was about to go out the service door when I remembered that I had not seen to the last set of writing tools. Placing the tray on the nearest table, I crept back and looked into Mr. Jarrett's bay. Everything was in place on the mahogany table except for the letter opener. Thinking it must have fallen on the floor, I made my way quietly as possible between the bookcase and table, peering under chairs as I went. I found nothing. Reaching the window, I turned to make my way along Mr. Jarrett's side of the table, when I saw his face for the first time. His eyes were open and staring.

"Mr. Jarrett?" I gasped.

He did not answer, and I touched his shoulder. He slid away along the table. One arm dropped from its edge. Then his chair tipped and he fell face up on the thick carpet, his body in a twisted pose.

Baron Czinner had won their argument. The green-handled letter opener was buried in Mr. Jarrett's chest, and his greasy waistcoat was dark with blood.

# ❧Simon Bliss's Narrative❧

My name is Simon Bliss, and my old eyes are clear enough in the long view—God help me, I hope the dread events which I see looming over Europe may prove an illusion!—but, damn them, they are not so good at seeing up close as they once were, and Baron Sigmund Czinner was too close, too bloody close, for me to get a sharp bead on him. What was the man about?

I hoped Jack Merridew—clever lad!—could find something to help me focus my aim. So I set Jack to watch on that October morning in 1906. I could trust the lad; he was quiet but spirited, fiercely loyal, and I never regretted taking him from Hanwell School. Afterward I sat and brooded for a time, hoping Apollo might inspire me, but the bird was singularly unhelpful. At breakfast I kept an eye on Czinner, but he only made my old bones ache. Shortly I went out on my morning rounds—the city always cheered me!—running into Inspector Nelson Faraday in Fleet Street. I had gone there to drop in on Alfie Whitehead, hoping for the latest gossip of the newspaper world, and I debated with myself before temporarily giving up my goal to ask Faraday about Baron Czinner.

I framed my question in my best offhand fashion, not wanting to put the wind up Scotland Yard. (I never liked the police nosing in matters that interested me until I had made all I could of them!) Faraday knew me well, knew I rarely asked anything without purpose, but it was with only the faintest of suspicious gleams in his narrow, dark eyes that he told me he had never heard of Sigmund Czinner.

"Ought I to have, Simon?"

"No . . ."

He didn't press me. Curious. Fidgeting with the Albert chain stretched across his great red-waistcoated belly, he obviously had something on his mind, and, wondering what, I changed my plans: "Luncheon at my club, Faraday?" I asked.

"Um. I'd like that, Simon."

It was like leading an old bull elephant to peanuts.

We went up to my room. Through the windows, beyond the Oxford and Cambridge Club, could be seen the roofline of Marlborough House, where I had sometimes attended parties at which Bertie and Alix, now king and queen of England, played pranks on their guests.

Jack brought up a tray—watercress salad, roast beef with horseradish, boiled potatoes and carrots, a gooseberry tart. Faraday and I sat at the small, round table near the French doors: he with a grunt plopping his great bulk down, I pulling a rug over my legs to keep them warm—damn the silly things one must do when one grows old! Faraday's belly snugly fit the table edge. Tucking his napkin in his waistcoat, he heaped his plate with food. I liked to watch him eat, in his honest trencherman's fashion. He was a man of fixed imagination—he always imagined the worst—but he was firm and incorruptible, a symbol of implacable law to the criminal world.

He began to speak of the king.

"Causing you fellows trouble again, is he?" I asked, eating little, watching him. I didn't think he had come yet to what was agitating him.

Faraday dispatched a potato with his fork. "Um. Yes." He chewed sombrely. "He's damned hard to keep track of, Melville tells me. Especially overseas, even with the foreign police to help. And we've often lost him in London. Would you believe, he's still at it?"

I could only nod. "It" was Bertie's habit of chasing women—and catching them. Few ladies refused him. In fact, many society Europas longed for the old bull's favor; perhaps they might earn their husbands an Order of Victoria. A corps of detectives under Mr. Melville was assigned to protect Bertie overseas and in London, but the king hated being watched and, incorrigibly, often snuck off to keep his rendezvous. He was nearly sixty-five, his amorous chases somewhat curtailed from younger days, but even his current *maîtresse en titre*, Mrs. Alice Keppel, could not completely keep him in rein.

I found this all quite amusing. "Indeed I believe he *is* still at it," I said, unable to keep from smiling. "Would that I were myself." Faraday only scowled. "But how the devil does Melville manage to lose the 'Uncle of Europe'? After all, his face is known everywhere."

"The king is damned clever, that's how," Faraday snorted.

"Why should it worry you? Melville's in charge."

He stared at me. "It's the times, Simon, the bloody times! I just want His Majesty safe."

I nodded again. I knew what he meant, and it did not cheer me. Bertie's behavior wasn't wise. There had been two serious assassination attempts against him in the nineties. President McKinley of the United States had been assassinated in 1901, and just months ago King Alfonso XIII of Spain had narrowly escaped the same fate. Decidedly Bertie should not go about without protection.

"It's the women!" Faraday complained. "You'd think at his age . . . well, at least we know the latest."

"And she is?"

He looked at me as he sawed his roast beef. "You may as well know. It's Madame Sophie Bernard, the Frenchman's wife."

"Ah!" This was a tidbit I should never have got from Alfie Whitehead. "Of number 24 Norfolk Street, right?"

"You seem to know everything," Faraday grumbled.

"Not this latest bit of news. Well, well. Monsieur Bernard's money comes from the vine—estates in Burgundy and the Rhone. While he sells his excellent product to merchants and wealthy English gentlemen with great cellars, Bertie has taken his young bride as mistress. I wonder if Bernard regrets bringing her over."

"I should think so."

"She's beautiful, all right, and clever—though I thought Bertie had grown to prefer maturer women."

"He prefers women, period," Faraday said gloomily.

"Mmm." While the inspector reached for the gooseberry tart, I mused, a parade of names floating through my thoughts: Lillie Langtry, Lady Brooke, Sarah Bernhardt, La Goulue, the Princess de Sagan. These were Sophie Bernard's predecessors, and I could have summoned up many another less illustrious name to fill out the list of Bertie's past loves.

He lived according to the great unspoken maxim of society: all is permitted—provided that you are not caught. The rich and well-born turned a blind eye to every liaison, so long as the participants were discreet. But if any disagreeable affair reached the law or the press, there were only two alternatives for the guilty parties: suicide or exile. I had observed many strange ceremonies enacted in the worship of the adamantine fact. Now another was begun in Bertie's affair with Madame Bernard. It would be fascinating to observe the latest royal dance.

"His Majesty has bedded her rather quickly, considering she's been a wife barely six months," I commented. "She must have a keen eye on success. Melville will have to watch out; she may lead him—and Bertie—a merry chase."

I had been right in thinking the problem of keeping track of the king was not uppermost in Nelson Faraday's mind. Through eating, I lit my pipe; the detective a fat cigar. Faraday drummed his fingers on the tabletop. "Damned Foreign Office!" he muttered, blowing smoke.

"Yes?" I said quietly.

"I've had to give up some of my best men to them lately," he went on as if talking to himself.

"And why is that?" I asked.

He started, and his little eyes grew even narrower. "I don't know that I can tell you."

I merely sucked on my pipe.

"As spies, then, damn it all, Simon! You mustn't repeat it," he added truculently.

"Of course not. Spies . . .?" Thinking of the German emperor's mad conviction that England plotted to encircle his country, of its rapid build-up of arms, of our dreadnoughts soon to be launched, and of the unsettled state of affairs everywhere in Europe, I guessed what the detective was about to tell me.

"Recruits for Germany," he said. "Counterspies. For the War Office and the Admiralty too. They have our brightest, best-trained fellows at their beck and call. The thing is sanctioned by Whitehall, the commissioner sends down the word, and I must give up my men."

"You'll replace them. Meanwhile, the ones you lose go to

a good cause. It's time Whitehall took action. Germany has spied on us for years, collecting information about cities, roads, shipyards. We must start doing the same."

"I suppose so." I knew he must be thinking about what we had just said about Bertie's safety. He tossed down his napkin. "But I don't have to like it!"

"None of us will like it if we are unprepared," I said.

"For what?" he asked, but neither of us had the answer.

2

Shortly Faraday departed, and I was left in a morass of glum speculation, about Madame Bernard, Czinner, spies, King Edward. It was a thick stew; I did not know what to bite on first; so I was very glad when, at three, my nephew Herbert Munns was announced. I had him sent up at once. Always liking to see him, I was happy we had renewed our acquaintance after so many years. His calm, attentive way of listening and his shrewd common sense pleased me. Too, he reminded me of my favorite sister, Celia, whose son he was. I never hesitated to tell him anything. Perhaps he could help bring some order to the muddle of my thoughts.

"Herbert!" I said when Jimmy Thompson showed him in.

"Hello, Uncle." He came forward and gripped my hand in his cool, reticent way. He wore a tweed suit. His eyes, with their pouches of middle age that always made him look a little sad, reminded me of those of a favorite loyal old hunter with which I had once stalked game.

If anything, overpolite, Herbert turned his bowler hat in his hands until I gestured to his usual chair opposite me. "Sit, nephew, sit. Well . . ."

We began to converse in the easy way we had.

I asked how his new life was progressing. I knew very little of it, only that he had formed a friendship with a young actor who lived as he did where Sherlock Holmes once had, in Baker Street. (Coincidentally, Holmes's brother Mycroft had been a member of the Diogenes Club in its odder days.) Frederick Wigmore was his friend's name. Herbert was rather secretive about him, and of late a sly sparkle had enlivened his usually dour face when he mentioned the actor.

"Oh, my new life is something more than I expected," he told me, chewing his words before he spoke them. He was judicious, but I caught a secretive glint in his eye and wondered what he was up to. First I would get his opinion of Sigmund Czinner.

The moment I mentioned the name I saw him start. He pulled off his glasses, and I wondered if he did so to hide his agitation.

"Czinner?" he repeated.

"Baron Czinner. Do you know him, Herbert?" I asked, watching him closely.

"No-o," he got out, rubbing his lenses with a moleskin. "No, I don't." He fit the glasses back on and gazed at me placidly. "What of him?" At that moment Herbert Munns interested me exceedingly.

Swallowing my curiosity, I told him what I had observed of the baron.

"And what do you make of it all?" he asked.

I thumped my stick on the carpet. "That's just it, I don't know!"

"Have you tried the direct approach?"

"Asked him straight out, do you mean?"

"Yes."

"No, damn it all! He's amazingly slippery; he avoids me. I've been reduced to laying silly traps, but he always wriggles free."

Herbert pursed his lips. "It does sound as if he has something to hide. He knows your reputation for ferreting out things?"

"He knows my reputation and everyone else's; that's what makes me suspicious! What's the man's motive? In England less than a year and already he's bought his way into society? There's something disreputable about him. I'm having a devil of a time uncovering his past."

My nephew appeared to be thinking. He sat in his still, calm way, spine stiff, legs neatly crossed, hands folded in his lap. He chewed on his moustache ends, the only outward sign of mental activity. He shifted his position. "Uncle, perhaps I . . ." he began.

I leaned forward.

Just then, without knocking, Jack Merridew burst in, his large eyes popping. In his green club livery his chest heaved; his face was pale. "Sir . . . sir . . ." he gasped.

"Yes, Jack?" Alarmed, I pulled myself up with the aid of my stick.

The lad stared back and forth between Herbert and me.

"We may trust Mr. Munns," I said. "Out with it!"

He needed no more prodding. "A dead man, sir! In the library! Baron Czinner has murdered him!"

## 3

"You are sure the man is dead?"

"Yes."

"A club member?"

"No, sir. A stranger. A visitor to Baron Czinner. Mr. Samuel Jarrett. I served them whiskey in the library. I heard them argue."

"Have you told anyone else?"

"I came right away to you."

"Good lad!" I clapped him on the shoulder, then turned to my nephew. "Herbert?"

He had risen. "I am with you, Uncle."

"Let's be off, then."

We left my room, I with feelings of both foreboding and excitement; evidently my suspicions about Baron Sigmund Czinner had been horribly justified.

Jack turned to the right, toward the stairs leading to the library one floor below. I stopped him. "No. The dead man will not vanish, but the baron might, if he hasn't done so already. This way first." Cursing the three-legged state that made me go so slow, I led them down the corridor, counting off door numbers as I went: "Fifteen . . . sixteen . . . seventeen. Here it is, number eighteen. Quiet!" I knocked. There was no answer, no sound. I knocked again and we hung fire. At last I sighed. "Skipped, has he? I wouldn't stay either. Still, he may be hiding, hoping we will go away. His room doesn't have a balcony; there's no other exit. Jack, I want to open this door. Fetch me the twirls."

The lad ran off. Rubbing his bushy moustache, Herbert stared speculatively at the lock. "If we had time I would do it without twirls," he said, surprising me once more.

Before I could ask the source of his boast, Jack was back, in his hand the ring of keys of various types which I kept secreted in one of my lacquered Chinese boxes for just such an occasion. I had rarely used them, but they stood me in good stead now. Within a moment of the lad's handing them over I found one that turned the lock.

"Wait, Uncle," Herbert said, placing a hand on my arm. "The baron has murdered a man." And he surprised me a third time by pulling a pistol, a gleaming, short-barrelled Webley's .38, from an inside coat pocket. "This should do the trick, don't you think?"

I stared at the pistol, then into my nephew's mild gray eyes. The secretive glint was there again; I thought he was half amused—and proud. "A far better weapon than my blackthorn stick. Amazing, Herbert! Surely you didn't get that at Cox's Bank."

"No." He gestured at the door. "Baron Czinner?"

Reserving my questions, I nodded. "Indeed. Stay back, Jack." I turned the knob and pushed.

It was dark beyond. No one rushed to escape. Entering cautiously, I located the wall switch and flooded the room with light. It was windowless, small, and high-ceilinged, with a bed, wardrobe, chest of drawers, armchair, and writing desk. There were some hunting prints in slightly foxed condition on the cream-colored walls. The effect was anonymous as an hotel room and looked unlived in.

I turned to Jack. "Quick, lad, go down to Mr. Wetheridge. Find out if the baron left by the front entrance. Make some excuse—say he and I were to play cards and that I'm looking for him. Off you go! Herbert and I will be in the library when you return."

Jack hurried out. I closed the door so no curious groom, maid, or footboy would discover us.

Herbert put away his pistol. He glanced coolly 'round the room, seemingly unperturbed. "What now, Uncle?"

I cocked my head at him. "What would you do, nephew?"

"Oh, search," he said at once.

"Don't stand there, then!"

I went to the chest of drawers, he to the mahogany wardrobe. I found a few starched shirts, collars, and ties. The baron hadn't packed; neither had he left anything that revealed anything about himself. Disappointed, I turned to watch my nephew expertly digging his fingers deep into the

45

pockets of the dozen or so coats and jackets and the trousers that hung in the wardrobe. Turning, he spread his hands. "Nothing."

"Not even a scrap of paper?"

"Not the stub of a theatre ticket."

"Press on, then."

I went to the writing desk. Herbert walked into the cupboard, his voice floating out hollowly as he rummaged: "Why don't we leave this to the police?" He emerged, again with empty hands.

"Because," I replied, rising from my equally fruitless search of the desk, "it was I who suspected Baron Sigmund Czinner, and I won't have Nelson Faraday and his men trampling over my territory before I've thoroughly examined it."

"Barren territory, it seems," he commented, sucking on his moustache.

"That in itself tells us something," I snapped. "Help me with the bed!"

We pulled apart the bedclothes and looked through them. While he replaced them I searched in odd corners—behind the hunting prints, under the washbasin. I forgot all my arthritic twinges in my eagerness but received no reward. There was simply no hint of the man—no photographs, no books, not even a dropped collar stud or tie pin.

"Thorough, hasn't he been, Uncle?" Herbert said when we had looked everywhere and come up with nothing.

"Thorough indeed!" I sniffed the air. "There is something, however . . ."

"What's that?"

"His blasted gardenia scent!" I thumped my blackthorn on the carpet. "Damn! Close the wardrobe, Herbert. Let us see this dead man in the library."

4

There was no commotion outside the library doors; no club member had used the room between the time of Jack's awful discovery and Herbert's and my headlong arrival. Herbert and I went in. A man lay in the third bay between the right bookcase and the long reading table, in plain view of the centre aisle that traversed the room from entrance

46

doors to the small service door at the back. He was quite dead: protruding from his chest, just under the ribs, was the green handle of a club letter opener. The man's waistcoat was streaked with blood. Spreading under the grotesquely twisted left arm was a stain which the Diogenes Club would not soon wash out. Standing, the fellow could not have been more than five-and-a-half feet tall. He was perhaps sixty, fat, balding, high-complected, ill-shaven. His white lips were parted in a sort of snarl, his slightly protuberant eyes open in a glazed death stare. He looked oddly familiar.

Herbert stared palely, and I saw his lips twitch as he swallowed. He might carry a pistol, but he was apparently unused to dead bodies. I had rarely seen one so unpleasantly dead as this, but that could not stop me. "Watch the doors," I said.

"Yes." Herbert seemed happy to remain in the centre aisle.

Kneeling with a grunt, I concentrated on Samuel Jarrett. He reeked of liquor. First I examined his clothing, putting my hand into every pocket but finding nothing. The man had been stripped clean as the bedroom we had just left. Czinner had not wanted his victim soon identified. Only the waistcoat contained something: a hunting watch on a brass chain. Removing it, I probed the watch pocket. Empty, I thought at first. Yet there was something: two objects, very small—tiny pebbles?—almost lost in dust and lint. Carefully I edged the objects out, placed them in my palm, and gently blew away the dust. Little chips of blue glass, they appeared at first. And yet they were more than that I knew! Frowning, I looked from them to Samuel Jarrett's staring gray eyes and back. A premonition which I could not quite explain caused me to shudder, and I at once wrapped the bits of glass in a linen handkerchief and slipped them in my coat.

What was it about the dead man's face...?

The watch was cheap and ordinary, a make which could be bought anywhere. No clue there. My legs ached from kneeling, and, thinking there was no more to discover, I was about to return the watch to its pocket when I thought to open the back. I received my reward. In the portrait space was a piece of thin paper. Eagerly I took it out and unfolded it, read it, then read it again. Once more I looked at Samuel

Jarrett's countenance—the wide, bald brow; red cheeks; haughty mouth; aquiline nose; the odd, slightly protuberant eyes—and I knew why I had shuddered. I closed the watch and replaced it in Jarrett's waistcoat, but kept the paper, slipping it in a pocket. I rose with a grunt.

"Well, Uncle?" Herbert said, turning from the doors.

I took out my pipe, lit it, and, deep in thought, gazed out the window, where autumn light was deepening over the city. "Odd. Damned queer," I said. "Serious perhaps, Herbert. I may be mistaken, but this thing may go far beyond the Diogenes Club, to the very seat of power. Let us wait, however. I must have Jack's story before I rush into theories." I looked at my nephew's moustachioed face, composed again after the momentary paleness. "In the meantime, would you care to explain how you happen to carry a pistol? It's loaded, I presume."

"Oh, indeed." He hesitated. "My new life . . ."

"Go on."

He seemed embarrassed. "Spot of detective work, don't you know."

"Detective work?"

"Only a little. Quite unofficial. Amateur, you might say. Only . . ."

Just then, Jack came through the servants' entrance.

"We shall speak more of this later, Herbert," I said. "What news, Jack?"

The lad's brown hair was tousled, and there was a film of perspiration on his brow from running up the stairs. Nevertheless, he said gamely, "I didn't have to speak to Mr. Wetheridge at all, sir. I stole a peek at his day book. Baron Czinner left by the front entrance just before one."

"Good work, lad. Damn! Four hours' start—plenty of time for him to go to ground. We'll have a devil of a job flushing him, then!" I sat in a chair with Jack before me. "Now, I want you to tell me and Mr. Munns everything you saw and heard today."

Jack had been trained well and in five minutes had it all out: about Czinner's apparent attempt to bribe him for information about me, about Samuel Jarrett's arrival, the argument, the snatches of conversation, the name "Teddy" he had overheard—hearing it myself, I felt an inward sinking—

48

and the words "sand" and "ham," which I understood all too well. I glanced at Jarrett. Was that really the dead man's name? Whether or no, I thought I knew who he had been meant to be.

I shook my head. "So you didn't actually see the baron stab the man? Well, it's clear all the same that he did it. Mmm. Jarrett helped by being drunk when he got here. Czinner encouraged him to drink more, to prepare him for slaughter. Yet there's evidence of haste in the choice of weapon, first thing at hand. Why was it necessary to do it like this? Why couldn't he wait? Jack, you and Wetheridge both saw them come up; Czinner knew you had. He must've known he would be suspected—convicted most likely, too, on circumstantial evidence alone."

"*If* he got caught," Herbert put in.

"Yes. Which it isn't likely he intends to be. Jarrett threatened to 'tell all.' Whatever it was, it was worth taking a life and becoming a fugitive to prevent its being known. Blast Czinner, I knew he was up to no good!"

"Sir, Mr. Jarrett complained of being a servant of the baron and his friends."

"Yes?"

"He said he wouldn't work for them any more. Maybe he meant to tell what they'd hired him for—something shady?"

"Indeed. Just my thought. And Czinner murdered him to prevent that being known. Friends, eh? Who the devil could they be?"

"We have one name," Herbert said quietly, pushing his glasses up on his nose and coming near. "Teddy. Not a friend, though; more likely a victim. The dead man told Czinner he wouldn't do it to 'poor bleedin' Teddy'—those were his exact words?"

"Yes, sir," Jack confirmed.

"Oughtn't we to find Teddy, then, and warn him?" Herbert asked.

I nodded, somewhat savagely. "We ought indeed!" I bit hard on my pipe stem. "Though I believe we already have found him," I said.

I ignored their looks of surprise and put down my pipe. It was past five, the pink light of a fine October sunset showing through the bay. From the street below came the clip-clop of

49

horse-drawn carriages and hansoms and the rude chuf-chuf of motorcars. All along Pall Mall clubmen were arriving for the glass of whiskey or sherry in the smoking room before the evening meal. Later would come cards, billiards, or conversation by a roaring fire. Civilized England. And in the Diogenes Club library lay a dead man, a stranger, murdered with a club letter opener.

"You know who Teddy is, Uncle?" Herbert asked breathlessly. "Is it time for the police?"

"Nearly. But first I want to show you something." I took out the paper which I had removed from the back of the dead man's watch. "I found this on Jarrett's body, something Czinner missed. It was what he was looking for, I'd guess—what he killed for, partly. Here, have a look." I handed the paper to Herbert. "You, too, Jack; you're part of this."

The lad joined my nephew, who held the paper so they might read it together. It was small, about six by eight inches, a piece of private stationery. Diagonally across the upper left-hand corner was printed "Buckingham Palace." Under the date, 17 March 1906, was the directive: "Private, for Lord Hardinge," then:

My Dear Hardinge,

I am happy to welcome you back from your sojourn among the Russians to the circle of my most trusted advisors—Cassel, Lord Esher, Soveral, etc. And I congratulate you again on your appointment as Head of the Foreign Office. As you know, foreign matters have always been extremely interesting to me; it is there, I believe, that I have had my greatest successes, particularly with the French in '03. I hope we shall continue to see eye to eye regarding Haldane's army reform plans, which are absolutely essential with my jackanapes nephew as emperor of the Germans. When I return from my Mediterranean cruise, I shall look for your counsel.

Until then, all my regards.

It was signed by King Edward VII.

Herbert stared owlishly. "But this is a highly confidential communication!" He glanced at the dead man's shabby clothes and ill-shaven cheeks. "How did a fellow like this come to have it?"

"I expect he stole it from Czinner or one of his friends, whoever they may be. The snatches of conversation Jack

50

overheard suggest that that's the case. Jarrett meant it as blackmail. Czinner couldn't take the chance that he and his friends—fellow conspirators I should call them—had the letter." I frowned mightily. "Some great issue was at stake, something about which not a word must be breathed. Jarrett was in a drunken state, unstable, liable to do anything. So Czinner murdered him. He didn't find the letter on him and fled—probably scurried to Jarrett's digs to search for the thing. He won't have found it there either. Likely he's with the others now, informing them, changing plans."

"What plans?" Herbert asked.

Jack was staring out of his large brown eyes. "Sir . . . Teddy must be . . . His Majesty!"

I nodded, squeezing his shoulder. "Right, lad. 'Good Old Teddy.' "

"King Edward," Herbert breathed, beginning to rub very hard at his spectacles. "There's some plot against His Majesty?"

Sighing, I sank into a chair, feeling old, helpless, bewildered. The urgency of the matter must give me energy! I spoke, all the while holding the pocket where the two small circles of blue glass seemed to be burning a hole. "We must guess. From Jarrett's statement about 'poor bleedin' Teddy' we may assume he had been hired to do something to—or about—the king. He grew cowardly, saw his chance for fast money. Perhaps in addition a tug of conscience caught him up; we shall never know. At any rate he backed out. He had come by this letter—must've stolen it from the conspirators, as they somehow stole it from Hardinge. I wonder, do they have any other damaging private correspondence? The upshot of Jarrett's little scheme was murder, with Czinner now a fugitive . . ."

"Perhaps their game is up, then," Herbert suggested, replacing his spectacles.

"I should like to think so—and dare not." I took out my handkerchief and opened it upon the table. "What do you make of these?"

They approached and looked at the tiny blue chips. Herbert blinked; Jack's face lit.

"I know what they are, sir!"

51

I was very much surprised. "What, lad?"

"Well, sir, they're meant to be put in the eyes, to help a person see better. Remember when you had me carry a note to Lady Cromer in Wilton Crescent? She was having tea, made me come in and wait while she wrote out her reply. I stood apart, very quiet. All of a sudden she was blinking and crying out. Then she was crawling on the floor, patting the carpet. 'Help me to find it!' she cried. 'What ma'am?' I asked, wanting to help. 'A little circle of glass, you saucy boy!' she said. 'For my eye!' Well, sir, I searched and did find one—just like this, only made of clear glass—right in her teacup. She took it, dried it on her bodice, and popped it into her left eye. That surprised me. She blinked and looked very pleased. 'It helps me to see so I don't have to wear spectacles,' she told me. 'You mustn't tell anyone!' "

"Lady Cromer *is* vain," I commented, "—and you're quite right about these."

Herbert was nodding, poking gingerly at the lenses as if they were live insects. As a gadgeteer he kept up with the latest scientific developments. "I've heard of such lenses," he said, "though I've never seen one till now. Mmm." He peered at them closely. "The latest invention of optical science—float right on the cornea." He gazed at me. "They can be harmful unless they're ground by an expert, but they really do aid in correcting faulty vision, I believe."

"These were not meant to correct anyone's vision," I told him grimly.

He straightened. "No? What for, then?" I saw a little shudder cross his shoulders.

Not liking to do it, but wanting to give my theory the final test, as well as to show Herbert and Jack what I meant, I knelt and fitted a lens in each of the dead man's staring eyes. I stood. "You see?"

Making a face, Herbert came close and peered down. "The man's eyes are blue now rather than gray. But . . ."

"Samuel Jarrett is in disguise," I told him.

"Disguise?"

"Of course, imagination must supply a great deal. Do you by any chance know the color of King Edward's eyes?"

"No."

There was a pause, during which the sound of convivial laughter drifted up from the smoking room.

Jack said, very quietly, in a tone of dawning understanding, "Blue, sir, aren't they?"

Nodding, I stepped back from the dead man and pointed at him with my stick. "Imagine Mr. Jarrett alive, standing before us. About five-and-a-half feet, wouldn't you say? Not a tall man. And portly, almost obscenely fat from years of consuming ortolans, truffle-stuffed woodcock, and peach melbas? Imagine him with a handsome, finely trimmed moustache and a beard to cover his receding chin. Fix a haughty, regal look in those dead eyes. Make him resplendent in Garter robes . . ."

Herbert gasped. "His Majesty—the very image of King Edward!" And he tore off his spectacles and rubbed at the lenses exceedingly hard.


# ❧*Frederick Wigmore's Narrative*❧

### I

Frederick Wigmore's the name. Wiggins, don't you know. Of musical comedy reknown? Old Bliss—remarkable chap!—has asked me to pen my part of the tale about . . . well, we shall come to that in good time, shan't we? We shall come to a great many things. Where was I? Ah, yes—*The New Aladdin*; that's where it began for me, the one hundred seventy-third performance, when I spied my friend and accomplice, Herbert Munns, waggling his bush of a moustache at me from a front-row stall. He tapped his nose, our prearranged signal that he must see me. I tapped my nose in return—it added a nice comic touch to my scene. The audience roared with laughter at my antics as the Genie of the Lamp; no one could have played it better, I fancy. I finished my jujitsu number with Gaby Deslys, and shortly *The New Aladdin* was over for another night. Three curtain calls—I could not relinquish those—then I hurried to my dressing room, doffed my jewel-encrusted turban, scrubbed the cocoa brown from my face, and emerged moments later in evening clothes, a splendid new outfit, complete with cape, which my Savile Row man had worked up for me.

Herbert met me in the wings. Ordinarily placid, he seemed in a dreadful state of excitement.

"Heigh-ho, old chap. What's ruffled your feathers?" I squeezed his arm, but there was no answering smile in return. First glancing about the bustling backstage, his spaniel eyes sent me an appeal. We could not talk here, so I steered him toward the exit, past the Gaiety girls who were hurrying to meet their beaus. Several smiled at me stunningly, but this was no time for flirtation, and shortly Herbert and I ended in front of the Gaiety, surmounted by its green cupola and sylphlike golden trumpeter. The Strand was rent with loud traffic and ablaze with lemon-colored light from pavement to rooftop.

I turned to my friend. "Now, what's up?"

His moustache fairly bristled with excitement. "I've stumbled upon an extraordinary case. That is, Simon Bliss and I have stumbled upon it. I've convinced him that you can help."

I stood back and gazed at him in reproof. "Bliss? Your odd duck of an uncle? Really, Herbert, I don't need an old man's permission to take a case! Besides," I led him along the pavement, "our agreement is that *I* shall find the cases. Generals and foot soldiers, there must be both, and it must be clear which is which. I am the general, and—"

Herbert stopped abruptly. "This is no time for ego, Wiggins!" he muttered.

It amounted to insubordination, and I stared at him.

He met my gaze in his stolid way. "This happens to involve His Majesty!"

"How?"

He chewed his moustache ends. "That's just it. If we could say how, there mightn't be a case . . ."

I was intrigued, and, leaning on my stick, I mused, picturing the stout, womanizing old monarch. "King Edward? Mmm." I had met him once. He was a great theatregoer, and I had been introduced to him at the opening of the New Gaiety when I played Meakin in *The Orchid.* Impeccably dressed, he had waved a huge cigar as he joked with the gentlemen of the cast and charmed the ladies with his roguish smile, all the while rolling his guttural Coberg *r*'s. "A fine per-r-rfor-r-rmance, Mr. Wigmor-r-re!" he had complimented me. Then, coughing bronchially, he had trundled off with his retinue to some London night spot to drink and gorge himself. His appetites were enormous—a beautiful woman may very well have been dessert. I quite liked Teddy!

"I'll help if I can, Herbert, of course. But it's ten-thirty and I've had nothing to eat since midday."

"Uncle arrives in my rooms at midnight, just to meet you."

"There *is* time for supper, then!" I said. "Simpson's, I think." I insisted Herbert accompany me.

Simpson's Divan Tavern was just up the Strand. The headwaiter led us past the placard announcing "Dinner from the Joint: 2s 9d" into the great hall, with its groaning dumbwaiter in the center, black-cushioned lounges, and huge mirrors along one wall. On the opposite wall the painted murals of fish, flesh, and fowl were mellowed by age and London smoke.

We sat at a table with a white damask cloth. I narrowed my eyes at Herbert over my menu. "Now I think of it, wasn't it Simon Bliss gave you the hint that helped me to settle the Kempton Park matter just a fortnight ago?"

"It was. Just something he mentioned in passing, but I realized it would be useful to you. See here, Wiggins, you must respect my uncle. You have the habit of underestimating men, but Simon Bliss is not one to be treated like that. He's . . . he's a detective of sorts himself."

"Oh?"

Matter-of-factly, Herbert told me how his uncle had helped Inspector Nelson Faraday, with whom I had had dealings—I'm afraid the policeman did not care for me—to solve several cases, the Crichton murders and the Allington kidnapping among them.

I was miffed. "Why haven't you told me about this before?"

He was maddeningly cool. "I have secrets too, Wiggins.

And I have Uncle's confidence. I wouldn't betray it any more than I would yours. But now . . ."

"Now?"

"Now you must meet."

I had to laugh at his ominous tone. "Magnesium and water? There shan't be an explosion!"

He fidgeted with his menu. "I hope not. I know your temper."

"Quite under control."

"Good."

"And why am I not invited to Bliss's club? The Diogenes, isn't it?"

"It's rather in an uproar, I'm afraid. The police—"

I threw down my napkin. "Really! If your Simon Bliss is the type of fellow who invites in the police whenever . . . !"

He fixed his pouchy eyes on me. "You have more in common than you know. He's not told the police everything. But there was a murder, and—"

"Murder?" Things were brightening.

"Yes. And don't look so cheerful. It was a dreadful thing—bloody! The murderer was . . ." he allowed a little pause; he, too, had his dramatic effects, " . . . Baron Sigmund Czinner."

I gave Herbert full satisfaction, then, by bobbing my Adam's apple numerous times as I attempted to swallow. "You don't tell me?" I managed, thrilled. I knew the name too well.

He nodded. "I do." The wine steward appeared. "Beaune with the beef, don't you think?" Herbert asked with remarkable aplomb.

"I should think so. Now," I continued, leaning forward when the wine steward was gone, "the murdered man?"

"—looked like the king."

I whistled, sat back, felt a smile creep across my face and the warmth of excitement inside. A case indeed! "Tell me everything!"

He did. And by the time we were in a hansom rattling toward Baker Street to meet his uncle, Simon Bliss, I could not have been prised from the affair by even an expert cracksman's jemmy.

In Herbert's sitting room I lounged on the settee opposite the fireplace while he set a blaze going. Mrs. Cannon, whose bible was Beeton's *Shilling Cookery*, bustled in to leave a tray of bath buns and ginger biscuits. At the stroke of midnight the purr of a motor sounded outside, and just as the chimes of the clock died away, there came a knocking at the door. Seconds later Herbert let two persons into the room. One was a boy, perhaps twelve, small, quiet, with a thatch of brown hair and large brown eyes—Jack, who had discovered the murder, I assumed. The other was a thin, bent old man wearing a long coat with an otter collar and a bowler hat— Simon Bliss. I rose, keeping a sharp eye on the old man. A bit of a rival, I imagined him, and I wanted to get his measure. He used a stick, a blackthorn, but seemed agile enough. In fact, there was an air of energy about him. Over seventy, Herbert had informed me; I could hardly believe it from the spark in his gaze. He glanced 'round the room, seeming to be taking in every detail, cataloguing it. Herbert took his hat. He was bald, with a wispy, white fringe about ears that stuck out like a gnome's. If what Herbert had said were true, those ears heard a great deal.

"Here, sir." The boy helped him out of his coat.

"Thank you, Jack." The old man's voice was like the scraping of a limb against glass. He went directly to the fire, warmed himself, then abruptly turned to me. "Bliss," he said, thrusting out a gnarled hand. "Simon Bliss. And you are Frederick Wigmore?"

"Yes."

He squeezed my hand, his grip dry and firm. He cocked his head, the shrewd eyes never leaving my face for a moment. "My nephew's told me about you. One of Sherlock Holmes's lads—remarkable!" Suddenly he blinked. "Dear fellow, where is your caftan?"

I shot Herbert a glance. "Upstairs."

Simon Bliss clucked. "Pity. I should like to see you in it. Well, no matter; not every pleasure at once—saves something for later, what? Has Herbert described this afternoon's events?"

"He has."

"Oh, let us sit, let us sit!" He lowered himself into an armchair. "Jack, you here on the stool beside me. This is Jack Merridew, Mr. Wigmore, my page—and something more, a great deal more." He patted the boy's shoulder. "He discovered the murder, you see." Jack flushed.

"So I've been told." I resumed my place on the settee. Herbert sat in the chair opposite his uncle. We formed a circle before the fire.

"Well?" Simon Bliss asked.

"A fascinating bewildering matter," I replied, not sure what he expected.

"Yes, yes!" Impatiently he thumped his blackthorn on the carpet. "That's obvious. I must tell you, Mr. Wigmore, I didn't want to bring another person into the affair. It goes beyond Samuel Jarrett's poor bloody corpse, and the fewer people who know the details the better. But if what Herbert says about you is true, you may be put to some use. You're an actor, I understand?"

"I am. See here, I'm not accustomed to being, as you phrase it, 'put to use,' by anyone except myself. I do as I please. I shall be treated as an equal. We must get that straight before we go any further!"

I had come to the edge of my chair. Jack Merridew was staring. Herbert looked worried. Simon Bliss merely smiled with amusement, his face wrinkled as old parchment.

"Certainly. Presumptuous of me. Sorry. I should know by now to trust my nephew's judgement. He says you're a splendid chap, that's quite enough, and let's hear no more of it."

"Yes. No generals, please, Wiggins," Herbert put in quickly, softly. "It's His Majesty we must be concerned about, remember?"

I sat back. "Of course, but . . ."

"Quite right," Bliss said. "We shall all have our say. You first, Mr. Wigmore." Leaning forward, piling his hands on top of his stick, he gazed at me with high interest.

"One question first," I said. "How much do the police know?"

He seemed to approve. "Quite to the point. They know very little—that a man who announced himself at the Diogenes Club as Mr. Samuel Jarrett was found at four o'clock by Jack Merridew in our library, a letter opener stuck in his chest; that he came to see Baron Sigmund Czinner; that Czinner was the last person known to be with him; and that he and Czinner argued. Naturally the baron is high on the list of suspects. The police do not know the words Jack heard pass between the two men, nor do they know about the private royal correspondence I found hidden in Jarrett's watch or the blue-glass eye lenses which seem all too clearly meant to have turned Jarrett, who already bore a remarkable resemblance to His Majesty, into a facsimile of the king of England. That's what the police don't know. Knowing it, you know as much as we. Now, what do you make of it?"

"Oh, I know a good bit more than that," I said, pleased to announce it.

Simon Bliss watched me.

"And so does Herbert. Thank you, my friend, for leaving me the opportunity of revealing it."

"What's this, Herbert?" The old man glanced sharply at his nephew.

Herbert was rubbing at his spectacles. "It was up to Wiggins to tell you, Uncle," he murmured.

Bliss settled back, an arm on each rest, looking like Solomon before a judgement. "Do go on," he said to me, thrumming his fingers.

The coal fire hissed. I smiled. "I have a varied clientele," I began. "Some months ago Nance Castle knocked on my door."

Bliss fidgeted. "What of it? I know Nance well; she runs the finest house in London—Chelsea Gardens. Even Bertie chose from among its beauties when he was Prince of Wales."

"But it wasn't to reminisce about the Prince of Wales that Nance came to see me. She wanted a job done. A man who called himself Brown had been seeing one of her girls, a pretty little dollymop named Rose Mappin. This Brown bloke was well dressed, but there was something about him Nance didn't like, and he had tastes new even to her experience. He was pushing; Nance takes nothing from any man and would have thrown him out, but he was willing to pay

59

through the nose for what he wanted, and the foolish Mappin girl took a fancy to his money. So the thing was arranged. The man wouldn't meet her at the Gardens, though; he insisted on setting up rooms near Pelham Crescent—not unusual. But he got rough with the girl, beat her up, ruined her face—and expected to do the same with other young women. Nance was furious—she takes care of her girls—and had a great row with the man. She made threats; he disappeared. She came to see me, saying, 'Poor Rose is scarred for life. The bleedin' cove must pay!' I saw Rose's face; it was a nasty bit of work—only right that money should be forthcoming. Brown had been free with cash; he could afford it. The only problem was to find him.

"So I set out to track him down. Shouldn't be hard, I thought. But it was, and I began to believe Nance's instincts about him had been right. He had left no clue in the Pelham Crescent rooms; 'Brown' was surely not his real name. What was it, then? The only sure thing was, he was slick as a snake in slipping free. That's where Herbert came in; helping me to find the man was his first job. It wasn't easy, was it, old chap? But we did it. Brown had a network; we were bound to trip over one of its threads sooner or later. What do you suppose we found? That the man wasn't 'Brown' at all, but 'Seecombe,' an import–exporter with offices in Jamaica Road. He also was 'Dr. Scheele,' a sympathizer with the cause of Irish independence. And to certain dockside labor organizers he was 'Gundersen,' a socialist avid for labor reforms, willing to stir up trouble wherever he could." Taking up one of Mrs. Cannon's ginger biscuits, I popped it in my mouth. "And he was Baron Sigmund Czinner. Excellent biscuits, Mr. Bliss. Have one." I held out the tray.

Bliss shook his head. "No, thank you. Go on, Mr. Wigmore."

A second biscuit in hand, I sat back and crossed my legs. "There's very little else." I nibbled. "Herbert and I have had to walk on eggs. When the multiple identities began to crop up, I knew something extraordinary was in the wind and that I mustn't tip my hand or I would lose the game. It's only a week that Herbert and I have known 'Brown,' 'Dr. Scheele,' 'Seecombe,' and 'Gundersen' were all Baron Czinner. The fellow has a remarkable way with accents! Genuinely Austrian it seems, and genuinely a baron, recently titled. The Continentals are ... ah ... less fastidious than we in granting titles and orders."

The old man stuck a long-stemmed pipe in his mouth. "You amaze me, Mr. Wigmore. Thorough work! I congratulate you. So Czinner impersonated an importer, a home ruler, and a socialist?"

"Quite. He's as adept at disguises as he is at accents."

"An actor?"

"Of sorts."

He lit his pipe in smoking fury. "So was Samuel Jarrett. It's the purpose of all this play-acting that we must discover!"

"Sir," the boy spoke up for the first time, his tone familiar yet respectful. "The baron and Mr. Jarrett mentioned 'playing.' Were they talking about Mr. Jarrett's role, do you think?"

The old man nodded. "That's surely what they were doing, Jack. We know from the eye lenses and Jarrett's resemblance to Bertie that he was meant to play the king. But why?"

Bliss handed me the lenses and the stolen letter. I examined them. The hollow clip-clop of a cab sounded on Baker Street as the clock struck the half hour.

"So you shouldn't show these to the police." I passed them back.

"Would you have?" Bliss snapped.

"Perhaps not. I gather you mean for us to pursue the matter without official help, then?"

He looked very grim. "For the time being. If officialdom is drawn into it, we shan't be allowed any part at all. And," he chewed his pipe stem, "I'm convinced that will do the case no good. Inspector Faraday is a dogged fellow, but he has no finesse—blunders through locked doors without first peeping over their transoms." He shook his head. "That won't answer! You didn't see Samuel Jarrett. I did. In stature, weight, and features he was very nearly His Majesty. With these," he tapped the pocket containing the lenses, "and a beard that would have taken a mere fortnight to grow, he

61

might have fooled a great many people, and would have for ill purposes, I think, very ill indeed. We must unravel this plot without the police."

Herbert looked like objecting.

I thought it a splendid course. "I wouldn't miss it for the world!" I exclaimed.

"It's no lark," Bliss warned.

"Naturally not. But how urgent, I wonder. Samuel Jarrett is dead, Baron Czinner forced to flee the Diogenes Club. Won't those two facts hamper any scheme that may have been brewing?"

Herbert pulled out one of his dreadful Rajah cigars, his moustache twitching over the thing as, with little popping sounds, he puffed it alight. "If I may . . ."

We stared at him.

Smoke escaped his mouth like steam from one of Mrs. Cannon's kettles. "I've been thinking along those same lines, Wiggins," he said in his ponderous way. "It does seem, Mr. Jarrett being dead and Baron Czinner in flight, that the plot against His Majesty must be hopelessly crippled." His big basset eyes swam through the cloud of smoke. "But what if Jarrett already has played his part? His death won't matter then. Czinner has at least four aliases; he'll simply slip into one of them, won't he? Then he and his friends can go on with their scheme. Even if it's badly damaged, they won't give up." Another puff. "They've gone to a great deal of trouble already . . ."

Raising an answering cloud, Bliss thudded a hand on his knee. "Indeed, nephew, I'm inclined to think you're right. What Jack overheard confirms it. 'Think you can brush me aside?' Jarrett said—not the words of a man who had more to do. He had finished what he was meant to. Ruthless blighters! Perhaps they meant to kill him anyway and were just forced to it sooner than they had planned. At any rate, their plot will proceed without Jarrett; we must assume that it will."

"There are other reasons they'll go ahead, sir," Jack spoke up.

"What, lad?"

Eagerly he stirred on his stool, the coal fire framing his tousled head. "Well, sir, they don't know we have the letter and the eye lenses. They don't know I heard the argument in the library. They won't know we're after them, will they?"

Bliss patted his shoulder. "Indeed!" The boy beamed.

I began to be very glad we had Jack Merridew as an ally.

"The question," Bliss said, again putting on his scowl, "is how the devil can an impersonation of Bertie at some past time harm him in the future?"

We were silent for some moments, chewing on this hard nut. Beyond Herbert's cosy sitting room, London, in sleep, seemed to be menaced by dark clouds—a far cry from the bright stage lights and laughter of the Gaiety Theatre. Bertie, Teddy, His Majesty—jolly fellow, king of England!— the past two hours had changed my view of him. Now I was imagining him in peril. Was I justified? Yes, some plot was afoot. But what? And why? I thought of my mentor, Sherlock Holmes, and of how his keen eyes would have brightened, his nostrils flared, to have been on the scent! And I felt the old thrill of fear which I had experienced when, as a lad, I had lurked dark corners of the city in Holmes's behalf.

"S-sir?" Bliss's boy said in a tremolo, gazing up at the old man, who sat like a crone from *Macbeth*, stirring a brew of private thoughts. "W-will they murder Baron Czinner now?"

Bliss gave him a sharp look, crying, "Ah!" with a sort of pained acknowledgement.

"I mean, sir, the baron killed Mr. Jarrett to prevent his giving the scheme away. The police are after the baron; if they nab him they may force him to talk. So if Mr. Jarrett was worth killing to keep quiet, then . . ."

"Yes, lad, yes." Bliss looked fierce. "All the more reason for us to act on our own! We want Czinner alive! We want the truth out of him!"

"We know enough to suspect. We know so little else," Herbert murmured from his pall of smoke.

"We know what 'sand' and 'ham' mean," Bliss said.

"We do, don't we, sir?" Jack said, nodding.

It dawned on me. "Sandringham!" I exclaimed.

Herbert sat up straighter, blinking.

"Indeed," Bliss said. "Sandringham it must be, Bertie's country estate in Norfolk, to which in a mere three weeks he repairs with numerous friends and hangers-on for his sixty-fifth birthday party. I have been brooding on the mentioning of the name in Czinner's and Jarrett's conversation. Though Jack didn't at the time realize what he was hearing, he knows it was repeated often. Why? Because it figures in their plot—I'm convinced that it does! But how?" He scratched his jaw with his pipe stem.

"Some surprise for His Majesty's birthday?" I suggested.

"Not a cake!" the old man muttered.

"By no means," Herbert agreed.

The sound of Baker Street traffic had died entirely, leaving a muffled but throbbing stillness, London's steady pulse. The coals crumbled on the grate. The clock ticked softly as the hands crept toward one.

Bliss sighed and rose with the aid of his blackthorn. "Well? Well?" he said impatiently. Herbert fetched his uncle's overgarments. Jack pulled on a cap and wrapped a red scarf about his throat. Bliss tucked his head into his otter collar and went to the door, where he again shook my hand.

"You please me, Mr. Wigmore, have I told you that?" he said in his dry parchment voice. He smiled, and I saw that he was weary.

"I believe you please me, too, sir," I said.

He bobbed his head. "Good, good. If we are to work together let us take pleasure in one another's company. Our task itself may not be so pleasant. Come, Jack, the Diogenes Club awaits. Gentlemen, let us sleep on this very disturbing matter. Tomorrow morning in my flat in Curzon Street we shall hold a second council of war. Eleven o'clock, agreed? Until then, good night."

When they were gone, Herbert puffed his cigar at me, his hands behind his back. "What do you think, Wiggins?"

"Oh, I think we're in very deep. I think you're a sly fellow. I think your uncle is one of the most fascinating men I've met. Hmm. Perhaps I shall wear my caftan to Curzon Street, to give the old fellow some pleasure."

# ❧Jack Merridew's Narrative❧

Next morning 'round the big oak table at breakfast the servants could talk of nothing but the murder. I sat quiet and listened. Several admitted that Baron Czinner had tried to bribe them, as Mr. Bliss guessed, asking about politicians and financiers. " 'E was interested in anything, anything. *I* didn't crib!" There was a great buzz about this. "What was 'e always snoopin' for?" a steward piped up nervously. I recalled the coins the baron had clinked in his fat hand when he had asked about Mr. Bliss, and the mean look in his eye, which had frightened me. Was he a blackmailer, collecting scandals to use against well-known men, wondered the head cook, Mrs. Franks. "Don't know," ... "Can't say," ... "Very likely," came the answers.

"And what does Jack think?" boomed Mr. Stalker suddenly, peering at me out of his cool black eyes. "After all, it was he discovered the body. Did Czinner try to bribe *you,* boy?"

"Yes, yes," they all chimed in, eagerly looking my way.

I felt myself flush red. "I don't think anything. Don't know anything," I said, wanting to sink under the table.

"And nosy old Simon Bliss!" a snippy maid put in, sticking out her long neck. "What does 'e know?"

"Nothing," I told her. I was very glad, shortly, to get away.

I went up to help with the tea. Climbing the servants' stairs, I passed the library and couldn't help thinking about finding Mr. Jarrett dead and about how, later, the club in an uproar full of police, Inspector Faraday himself had questioned me in the very bay where the body had lain, its bloody stain inches from my toes. I did not know where to look—at the stain or at Inspector Faraday's suspicious eyes; there seemed no other places.

"You showed Jarrett to the stranger's room?" the policeman asked. "You announced him to the baron. You brought them whiskey here? That's all?"

"I . . . I heard them argue, sir."

"What about?"

This was hardest to manage: "D-don't know, sir."

"Um!" Very gruff. He creaked back and toyed with his Albert chain, and, feeling a criminal, knowing I was keeping things from him, I itched to dash from the room.

Upstairs, Mr. Stalker was sourer than ever. Thinking that Mr. Munns and Mr. Frederick Wigmore would be helping us cheered me some. I had always liked Mr. Bliss's nephew; he was a kind, soft-spoken gentleman. I was shy of Mr. Wigmore, though I liked him also—a handsome young actor and a detective, too, who had known Sherlock Holmes! I had read all the Holmes adventures that appeared in the *Strand Magazine,* and my heart had pounded to be in the very house where he lived before he retired to the South Downs in 1903. Would Mr. Wigmore tell me about Sherlock Holmes if I asked?

For now there were other questions. I saw them on Mr. Bliss's lined face when I carried in his tea and *Times.* I didn't like to see him so worried. Usually he was on top of things, but this morning he looked very glum. He sat by the fire in his maroon dressing gown scowling up at Apollo. He didn't return my greeting when I entered.

I arranged the tea things and sat opposite him.

"Damn and blast, Jack!" he said at last. Then he sighed. "Well, well, what news?"

I told him all the servants had said.

"Mmm. They protest their innocence, do they? But I'll wager they said a great deal once bloody Czinner's silver had crossed their palms. Nothing to harm anyone, I hope."

"Is the baron some sort of blackmailer, sir?" I asked.

"Could be, Jack. The question is, once he had something on a man, what would he have demanded to keep silent? Information perhaps. . . ? Do you know," he said, stirring, "Nelson Faraday sat in this very room yesterday and told me how all his best men were being recruited for spies . . ." He cocked a bleak eye toward the French doors. "A peaceful blue sky today." He jerked his gaze back, sharply. "But can we trust appearances, Jack?"

I didn't know what to say.

"Sandringham . . ." he went on, chewing his lip, "the final act. . . ?"

At this moment there came a knock on the door. I jumped up; it would not do my position with the servants any good if one of them saw me familiar with Mr. Bliss. "Come," Mr. Bliss called, and Mr. Stalker himself announced Inspector Nelson Faraday.

"Send him up. Stay, Jack," said Mr. Bliss.

Moments later the policeman trundled in, looking huge as a mountain. He wore his red-checkered waistcoat, and his narrow eyes as usual swept the room like lighthouse beams.

"Simon," he said gloomily and sank without further word into the chair I had vacated.

I busied myself with straightening Mr. Bliss's bedclothes.

"Have you collared Czinner yet?" Mr. Bliss asked.

"No," Inspector Faraday scowled. "A queer duck, he is! I went 'round to his other clubs last night. Belongs to five, did you know? Of course he wasn't at any of them. Hadn't been seen that day. What about him? I asked. A friendly chap. Rich. What else? Oh, they didn't know. Austrian? Yes, he was Austrian. Been in London six months. He talked financial schemes. What schemes? Well, manufacturing. Actually, he didn't so much talk as listen. A good listener. And smiled all the while. He was getting to know a lot of people. I questioned the servants. They were close-mouthed at first, and guilty-acting, but they came 'round. Czinner had paid some of them to talk about other club members. 'Gratuities' the servants called his money." He sniffed. "Bribery I call it. Of course, the usual descriptions will go out. Difficult beyond that, however. His room was stripped bare. And no one seems to know his banker. See here, Simon, you don't know anything, do you?"

"I'd like to know where Czinner's gone to ground and talk to him as much as you would," Mr. Bliss answered.

Shortly, after much huffing and puffing, Inspector Faraday rose, saying he would go down to have a second try at certain clubmen who had been seen with the baron at one time or another. "They were shaken yesterday. I'll see what I can get out of them today."

"The whole club is shaken," Mr. Bliss said, gesturing toward the *Times* which had featured the story. "It's rather a scandal."

"It will be even more of a scandal if I don't find Baron Sigmund Czinner. And this Jarrett bloke, who the devil was he?"

"Ah!" said Mr. Bliss. "I want to know that too."

When the policeman was gone I collected the tea things. Mr. Bliss went to the French doors to stare down Pall Mall toward Trafalgar Square, where pigeons swirled about the Nelson Column. "Tsk tsk, how much more discontent Faraday would be if he knew that the real crime is not yet committed. Samuel Jarrett's death was only a prologue. But to what?" He turned and thumped his stick. "We must prevent the thing, Jack!"

I was at the door with the tea tray. "They are dedicated criminals, sir."

He smiled grimly. "Just my thought, Jack: dedicated—to a cause."

"What cause, sir?"

"Ah, if we knew that. . . !"

"Mr. Jarrett might have told us. It's too bad his voice was stopped."

"Mmm." He scratched his jaw. "He spoke eloquently enough with that overlooked scrap of letter and the blue-glass eye lenses. He gave us our lead; it's up to us to follow it." For the first time he looked almost cheerful. "A challenge, lad! We must rise to it. Now be off; you're wanted in the dining room. I'll have Mr. Wetheridge replace you at the doors so you may be at Curzon Street at eleven."

# ❦Herbert Munns's Narrative❧

## I

I hardly slept for thinking about the body sprawled on the Diogenes Club library floor. In fitful dreams Samuel Jarrett's staring eyes, now gray, now blue, seemèd to watch me. Giving up on sleep, I rose early, lit a fire, and, as dawn spread above the roofs across Baker Street, I reflected on how changed my life was from the safety of a clerk's cage at Cox's Bank. Murder? I did not quite like that.

Yet it was, as Wiggins said, fascinating.

There was little movement in the street—a few drays, ice wagons—when someone knocked rapidly, almost imperiously, on the outer door. I had heard no approaching footsteps. Wondering who could be calling at 6:00 A.M., I went into the entranceway intending to let the visitor in, but Wiggins' wiry little Cockney, Mr. Salt, beat me to it. He clattered down the stairs on his bandy legs, almost knocking me down as he brushed by with a curt, "Guv'nor!" He flung the door wide.

On the threshold stood a dwarf—no, not a dwarf, a child, though his face, all odd bulges in which features seemed to have been scattered according to no known plan, looked that of a thirty-year-old. His eyes were black and snapping, his nose a pushed-in button, his mouth wide, mobile, and red in a complexion otherwise dun as a bog. His ears stuck out so far that one might have hooked umbrella handles on them, and his close-cropped hair darted up like a brush. His ill-fitting jacket and trousers were dingy as his smudged cheeks, and his shoes were little more than tattered scraps of leather. He was not four feet tall.

"Billy!" Salt exclaimed.

The creature swaggered into the house as if he owned it. "Mornin', Salt," he said brusquely. "Wiggins upstairs?"

"You know 'e is."

"Well, then . . ." With a glance at me, as if to say, "Who's this?" the little apparition marched up the stairs.

"Blimey!" Salt nudged me as he followed. "Royalty, don't yer know," he whispered, nodding at the boy's back. Then he winked, guffawed, and was gone.

Shaking my head, I returned to my rooms. I had seen Billy before. He often strutted up to Wiggins' rooms; when his business was done, he would dissolve like a wraith into the Baker Street crowd. Other equally disreputable-looking boys appeared at all hours before scampering off. "My irregulars," Wiggins had told me proudly, "my private police force." I did not know quite how they helped him.

Some time later I heard footsteps in the passage. Hurrying to my window, I saw Billy dart off along the pavement.

At eight I went up to Wiggins' rooms and knocked.

Salt opened the door. He wore tight-fitting brown-checkered trousers and a loud checkered coat. His black hair—dyed, I knew—was combed back and curled up wetly at his collar. Wiggins was not in evidence. With his usual grinning jerk of the head to usher me in, Salt left me to close the door and returned to laying linen, china, and silverware on the round oak table in the bow window overlooking Baker Street. This he did deftly with knobby hands which had known many trades in his forty-odd years. He whistled music hall tunes as he worked. I cringed to hear what he did to "Dolly Gray."

"Yer on a new case, I 'ear," he commented.

"Yes."

"Oho, 'ang onto yer 'at, I says!" He gave his leathery leer. "An' God save the king!" He arranged the knives and forks, stood back to squint at the effect, and seemed pleased. "Righto." Then he hurried to the door to grab his coat and bowler hat from the tree. "Cheerio, Munns. Tell Wiggins I'm off!" And breezily he departed.

I was used to his brisk ways and gave it hardly a thought, except to be reminded that Wiggins was unconventional in his relations with his manservant as in almost everything else. I took my place at the table. My young friend and I had got in the habit of eating together most mornings. I glanced 'round his sitting room, from which Dr. Watson had been dragged on many cases with Sherlock Holmes. It was much changed from those days of books piled in corners, press cuttings spilling from bookshelves, dottles of pipe tobacco on the mantlepiece. Wiggins would tolerate no clutter, and Salt was fastidious as a spinster in this matter. There was a russet-and-gold Bokhara rug. Two comfortable armchairs sat before the fireplace; between them was a low table with, neatly stacked, the latest, already dog-eared editions of the *Illustrated Police News* and *Lloyd's Weekly*, lurid publications which seemed to fascinate Wiggins. A large rolltop desk was against the far wall. There were also a tall bookcase with many bound copies of plays, a red leather settee, and a liquor cabinet containing glasses, a siphon, and bottles of whiskey. Theatrical posters bearing the illustrious names of Beerbohm Tree, Henry Irving, Duse, and Bernhardt were hung on the walls. Indoor plants, aspidistras and the like, completed the decor. Everything was in its place. In her cage by the bedroom door chirped Wiggins' pet canary, Columbine, blissfully unaware that murder had been done in the Diogenes Club.

"Good morning, Herbert!" Wiggins swept from the bedroom with his usual theatrical flourish. He wore a tan worsted walking suit, a four-in-hand scarf, and polished black shoes with tan spats. A tiny rose was in his lapel. He raised the sash of the bow window and sucked in air. "Splendid morning!"

"Indeed," I said rather glumly.

Wiggins sat opposite me, dropping his napkin into his lap. Small, white-haired Mrs. Cannon arrived with a tray of stewed fruit, porridge and cream, kippers, fried eggs, rashers of bacon, grilled tomatoes, toast, and a pot of steaming coffee. We commenced, I taking merely a bit of toast and kipper while Wiggins ate enormously and with relish. (My friend was maddeningly able to consume anything and keep his slender figure, whereas I must always watch my paunch.)

"You had a visitor this morning," I observed.

Finishing the last of three eggs, Wiggins replied in an offhand way, "Billy Gully? Did you meet him?"

"I can't call it a meeting."

Wiggins smiled placidly. "He *is* a rude little fellow. Bacon?"

"No, thank you. Who is he?"

He gazed out the window. "An urchin. You know our arrangement." He poured coffee. "Your uncle, Herbert, I quite like him. And this matter of the King Edward plot . . ."

"Salt called Billy royalty," I observed.

Heaping marmalade on toast, Wiggins laughed. "You aren't to be diverted, are you? Mmm, yes, Salt does have a way with words. Royalty, ha, ha! Not quite accurate, however. Billy is more of a general, in charge of my troops." He frowned, as if reminded of some sobering thought. "Don't fret, Herbert; this new case may very well cause you to see him in action. You've never met my irregulars have you? Well, you shall, you shall." He looked dismayed. "You aren't going to light one of those dreadful cigars!"

I had pulled forth a Rajah. "It's one of my pleasures, Wiggins," I said.

He wrinkled his nose. Wiggins rarely smoked, and then only imported Egyptian cigarettes in pink-tinted paper. "Think of my plants; I'm sure your exhalations are killing them! Do have the decency to go outside!" Suddenly, pensively licking marmalade from the corners of his mouth, he threw down his napkin and jumped up. "In fact, we shall both go out!" His blue eyes brightened. "A detour or two before we meet your uncle in Curzon Street, eh?" And he rushed into his bedroom, emerging a moment later wearing mocha gloves matching his trousers, a brown homburg, and carrying his Malacca stick.

My cigar sat, cold, in my hand. I allowed myself to be dragged to my feet.

"Come, Herbert! This King Edward matter must be seen to! Your latest invention, the small folding camera that fits in your pocket—it's in working order, I hope?"

I was used to Wiggins' whims, but was bewildered by this question. "It is."

"Splendid! Just what's needed. We'll pick it up in your rooms on the way." And he propelled me toward the door.

"Photographs, Wiggins?"

"Indeed." He was grim. "*Nature morta*—still life, very still. But first to Bond Street, Carlyle's, where Madame Sophie Bernard is on display."

2

In the season, from May to July, the great houses of Mayfair and Belgravia are freshly painted and window boxes bloom on the lower floors; gentlemen and ladies stroll Bond Street. But it was autumn, and society was gone to country homes; too, it was just 9:00 A.M., so Wiggins and I shared the pavement only with shop girls and clerks rushing to work as Carlyle's opened its doors.

We went into the art gallery and stood before *Madame Sophie Bernard*, by John Singer Sargent, England's most sought-after portraitist. He had done Madame Bernard in the dashing style I had come to know from numerous gallery visits with Wiggins, as much a connoisseur of painting as of crime. The room deserted except for us, we looked at the painting for long, silent moments, Wiggins standing, hands behind his back, wearing an expression I could not fathom. He loved mysteries; he would not tell me why we were here. "A suspicion, Herbert, a suspicion," was all he had said. Madame Bernard's husband had commissioned the painting; it was the habit to show such works publicly before they were taken possession of. The young woman was depicted sitting in a window, its leaded casements open to reveal the suggestion of a park—some great country house? In three-quarter view, she wore a simple pale-green gown cut low across her white bosom. Her red-brown hair was upswept and bound by a fillet of tiny blue and yellow flowers. Her bare arms held three malmaison lilies in the position one might have held a child. Her eyes were remarkable—sea-green, almond-shaped, slightly uptilted at the corners, giving a faintly exotic look to her face. Her mouth did not smile; she looked grave for one so young (the newspapers said she was twenty). Somehow Sargent had made her skin seem translucent as marble, and I wondered if in reality it could be so perfect.

After a moment I took off my glasses and polished them. She was the most beautiful woman I had ever seen.

I glanced at Wiggins, leaning on his stick in his usual fashion, one knee bent, hands dangling his gloves behind him. His expression . . . Was he smitten with Madame Bernard?

"A beautiful woman," I said. "What has she to do with the King Edward case?"

He stirred, his voice sombre as I had ever heard it. "She's beyond my fathoming for the present, Herbert—beyond even her husband, who commissioned this portrait as an homage. She's Teddy's mistress, his latest, that much I know; *he* has reached her. But have other men got there

73

first?" He shook his head. "I don't like to say it, but her beautiful face may be the face of the enemy."

"Whatever do you mean?"

He slapped his gloves on his palm. "Billy brought unsettling news, Herbert. I promise to explain in Curzon Street. For now . . ." He started for the door.

I followed, with one glance back into Sophie Bernard's green eyes. Magnetic, they seemed; capable of drawing a man's soul into them.

Outside, Wiggins hailed a hansom. "Scotland Yard," he called to the driver as I got in beside him.

"The police?"

"Not exactly. We have an appointment with a dead man."

## ❧Jack Merridew's Narrative❧

At breakfast the club was very gloomy, the members muttering about the scandal which the murder had brought down upon their heads. They chewed their whiskers and brooded. I heard nothing that could help Mr. Bliss.

Just before eleven I walked the short distance to Curzon Street. Mr. Bliss's house was a Georgian building of mellowed yellowish stone. It had white window shutters and a white door with a brass knocker and fanlight. Mr. Bliss had bought it a dozen years before, when he returned to London to live. "But I didn't like to be shut up in a house all alone," he told me. He much preferred his room in the club, where there was always someone to gossip with. Nevertheless, he kept the Curzon Street house open, a maid and cook ready there any time he needed them.

Nancy was the maid's name. "Hello, Jack," she said, opening the door at my knock. She showed me into the drawing room, where Mr. Bliss, Mr. Wigmore, and Mr. Munns already were seated 'round a low marquetry table by the fire. Mr. Wigmore was very finely dressed and had his long legs stretched out. Mr. Munns wore brown tweed. Mr. Bliss was in his black morning suit.

"Ah, Jack. Sit, sit." Mr. Bliss gestured to a nearby chair. "Herbert and Mr. Wigmore have just arrived."

"Yes, sir." They greeted me, Mr. Wigmore shaking my hand as if we were the best of friends. I took my place and listened, feeling very proud—unsure of myself too—because they let me into their confidence.

"Well," Mr. Bliss began, looking 'round at us all. "I have been at work prodding the bruised flesh of the Diogenes Club. I spoke to as many members as I could, discreetly you may be sure. Unfortunately, no one had any idea who Samuel Jarrett might have been, though they all were quite ready to believe Baron Czinner had stabbed him. Why? They never trusted Czinner, they said. I wonder what their opinion would have been before the murder. No matter. What had he talked to them about? Nothing we haven't heard already—politics, particularly behind-the-scenes matters, the drift of Whitehall's latest thinking. He seemed especially interested in military information, things that ought to have been kept secret—the deployment of ships, numbers of troops, and weapons, and the like. And, of course, any breath of scandal; he always had his nasty nose open for that. Blackmail may have been his aim in sniffing it out, to get something on important men as leverage in his search for political and military information."

"A spy, Uncle? Is that what you think he is?" Mr. Munns asked.

"Very possibly."

"But this impersonation matter...?"

"Mmm, yes, the heart of it—the false King Edward."

"Someone was meant to be deceived," Mr. Munns added.

Mr. Bliss cocked an interested eye at Mr. Wigmore. "You are the expert on play-acting, on disguise and impersonation. Herbert tells me you're a wonder on stage, that I wouldn't recognize you. I must see you sometime."

The young actor brightened. "Tonight?"

Mr. Bliss waggled a finger. "Only if the King Edward business doesn't occupy me. Do give us your opinion."

Mr. Wigmore looked pleased to have center stage. "I agree

75

with Herbert that some person or persons were meant to be deceived, but we may take it as certain that they could not have been His Majesty's intimates. Wonders can be done with make-up and disguise—I wish you had seen me in *The Prisoner of the Tower!*—and Jarrett had a natural resemblance to the king. But we must remember it was a resemblance only. Even if he wore those eye lenses, grew a beard like Teddy's, and did the royal growl to perfection, he couldn't have fooled anyone who knew His Royal Highness well."

"From a distance?" Mr. Bliss suggested.

Mr. Wigmore thought. "I believe so."

Mr. Bliss thumped his stick. "And why?"

"To discredit the king?" Mr. Wigmore suggested. "To make him appear to have done something rash, perhaps compromising—scandalous?"

Mr. Bliss smiled for the first time. "You're very clever, Mr. Wigmore; everything Herbert's told me about you is true. Yes, just my thought. Consider..." He leaned forward, peering at us. "Bertie—King Edward—is two men: one, Albert Edward, bon vivant, woman chaser, husband, father; the other, Edward VII, king of Great Britain and Ireland and of the British dominions beyond the seas, the Uncle of Europe, the foremost royal personage of our time, a man commanding great respect and affection worldwide. He *is* England." Mr. Bliss lowered his voice. "I put it to you that it is this second man, this symbol, who is the target of the scheme which we have stumbled upon." He sat back, his knobs of hands folded on his stick. "Thus it is England herself which is under attack."

There was a small silence. "England's reputation is to be compromised by compromising her king, you mean?" Mr. Munns breathed.

"That is exactly what he means," Mr. Wigmore said, no longer lounging but sitting upright, eyes bright.

Mr. Bliss looked grave. "The South African War made us see how unpopular we were, how isolated, and that we must make friends among nations to survive. We've accomplished that—indeed, in 1903 Bertie was instrumental in bringing about the Entente Cordiale—but the balance of power is precarious. Bertie is the symbol of our new-found respect.

The most popular monarch on earth, he represents England in the minds of people everywhere. If he were thought to have performed some damning act—"

"Then the monarchy itself would be compromised!" Mr. Munns said.

Mr. Wigmore nodded. "There might even be another republican crisis as there was in the seventies. Good God, England can't afford that turmoil now, or the loss of face she would suffer!"

Mr. Munns's eyes were very large behind his glasses. He removed them and rubbed hard at the lenses. I watched Mr. Bliss, whose lined face was grim. The shutters were closed, making the room dim except for our circle by the fire. From outside came the chattering of children's voices, the singsong cry of a muffin man, an organ grinder's tune. A van rumbled over the stone setts of Curzon Street.

Mr. Bliss stirred. "It's a devilishly clever scheme, but there is time for us to act, I think. As Jack pointed out, Czinner and his accomplices can't know we're onto them; they almost surely will go ahead. Jarrett's death will have been at the most a minor inconvenience, causing Czinner to go to ground. The planned scandal has not erupted; therefore it's yet to come, this trap to be sprung upon Bertie—and all of us. We must see it does not catch us; in fact, we may be able to turn it to England's advantage."

"If only we could, Uncle," Mr. Munns said.

"We shall see. Czinner and Jarrett spoke of Sandringham. Today is October twenty-fourth. In approximately three weeks Bertie goes there for his birthday party. Play-acting is our theme." He glanced at Mr. Wigmore from under his white brows. "What a grand setting for the climax—Sandringham, what?"

Mr. Wigmore's eyes sparkled. "Quite!"

"I think we should inform the police!" said Mr. Munns. He had put on his glasses and was blinking like an owl.

Mr. Bliss nodded. "You may be right, Herbert. We take a grave responsibility if we don't. Remember, however, that the king is closely watched—when he doesn't escape for his rendezvous. Nevertheless, I've taken it upon myself to contact Lord Esher. Oh, I gave him no details; after all, we've the slimmest of circumstantial evidence so far. But Esher is an old friend; he trusts my instincts. I said he must make sure His Majesty does not get free of his police guard, and His Lordship said he would see to it. That is, I think, the most we may do for the moment."

"We may do more than that," Mr. Wigmore put in, looking sly.

Mr. Bliss stuck his pipe in his mouth. "Oh?"

"Indeed. Herbert and I have already been at work, visiting Madame Sophie Bernard, at Carlyle's."

Mr. Bliss raised his head slowly from puffing his pipe alight. He glimpsed my puzzled look. "Her portrait, Jack—that's what the young rascal means. And whatever has Monsieur Bernard's young bride to do with the case?" he asked Mr. Wigmore.

"Perhaps a great deal. What did you think of her, Herbert?"

Mr. Munns looked close to blushing. "As I told you, beautiful," he said. "Striking. Quite. Her eyes . . ."

"Beguiling, yes, I agree. A siren? A witch?" Mr. Wigmore stretched out his legs. "I wouldn't like to be under her spell."

"She would use a man ill, do you think?" Mr. Bliss asked. He was watching the actor sharply.

"Oh, she would use a man as she liked," Mr. Wigmore said. "Not that I've ever met her, but I trust Mr. Sargent's artistic insights. Something . . . callous comes through in his painting of her. And," he paused, making a tent of his hands, over which he beamed at us, "I have just discovered that she is a friend of Baron Czinner."

Mr. Bliss pulled the pipe from his mouth.

Mr. Wigmore nodded. "It's so. As I've told you, Czinner had at least three aliases. About 'Dr. Scheele' and 'Gundersen,' the socialist, I haven't discovered anything more than what I've already described. But 'Seecombe' kept a dockside office. A lad in my employ—Billy Gully by name—has been keeping an eye on it for some time. 'All sorts o' blokes come an' go,' he's told me. This morning he made his weekly report. As you will have noted in the society pages, Madame Bernard spent a few days in the city before going to Londesborough. What the newspapers didn't report was that just four nights ago, dressed as her own maid, she slipped out of number 24 Norfolk Street, crossed Tower Bridge by hansom, and, in a dripping yellow fog which had most of London indoors, climbed the creaking steps of 187 Jamaica Road to the shabby offices of Seecombe Exporting."

"And—?" Mr. Bliss breathed.

Mr. Wigmore smiled. "You want more? You shall have it. Billy's eyes make no mistake. He crept upstairs after her and peeped through a crack in a shade. He couldn't hear anything, but it was she and Seecombe—Czinner—he saw, all right, in close conversation. 'Very serious, they was,' he told me. When this 'maid' left, Billy followed her—to Mayfair; that's how he discovered she was really Madame Sophie Bernard. The lad kept faithfully to his post for the rest of the week. 'Seecombe' hasn't been to his offices since. Billy reported everything to me just this morning. Naturally I sent him back double-time to keep watch."

Mr. Bliss jammed his pipe in his mouth. "More play-acting!"

"His Majesty's mistress consorting with a . . . a murderer?" Mr. Munns said. "What does it mean?"

"That Madame Bernard is mixed up in this, I'm afraid," Mr. Bliss replied. "Good work, Mr. Wigmore. You quite amaze me! How, I wonder, have our paths never crossed before?"

Mr. Wigmore looked smug. "We're both too clever."

"Hmph. Well." Mr. Bliss drummed his fingers, and his eyebrows dropped nearly to his nose. "I hope we're clever enough to bring Czinner to ground and to stop this bloody plot!"

"I hope so too," said Mr. Wigmore.

Mr. Bliss groaned up and went to the windows that faced Curzon Street. He peered through a shutter, then turned, leaning on his stick. He did not quite look at us. "Twenty years old . . ." he mused, and I knew he was thinking about Madame Bernard. I remembered her picture from the newspaper and knew why Mr. Munns had blushed; she seemed fresh as a flower. I could not imagine her with oily Baron Czinner. "So lovely a young woman caught up in a plot against the king of England? One doesn't want to believe it," Mr. Bliss said, shaking his head. He thumped his stick, and his eyes flashed. "But youth and beauty don't necessarily

79

add up to innocence! Who knows what influences Madame Bernard has fallen under—how she may have been misled—and what bad influence she in turn may bring to bear? Whatever her aims, she's Bertie's latest flame; she's turned his head. From what I've heard he's powerfully smitten, more so than with any recent woman. Therefore Madame Bernard is in a position to do great harm."

"We must keep an eye on her," Mr. Wigmore put in. "A not unpleasant prospect."

"Um." Mr. Bliss returned and stood, hands behind his back, beside my chair. "Keep an eye on her indeed—when she's in town. Presently she's at Londesborough however. I'll call Esher and have him put a discreet watch on the Frenchwoman whenever she's near the king; it will strain my credibility with Reggie, but it must be done. No word to His Majesty, of course; he would be furious if he knew anyone was acting on flimsy circumstantial evidence. A watch on his mistress? Imagine his fury! As for us, we have an additional job—to look into Madame Bernard's background, her connections. She may be innocent of the plot against Bertie, though I doubt it. We cannot take the chance that she is. Let us be thorough as we can, but cautious. Remember, our advantage is that our quarries don't know we're after them. Mr. Wigmore, did your lad Billy Gully report anything more?"

"No."

"Well, you know best how to employ him—perhaps in finding Baron Czinner. It also will help to know who Samuel Jarrett was. The police may learn that, but we can't count on it or on Nelson Faraday's sharing the information. Our work is cut out for us, gentlemen!"

Mr. Wigmore crossed his legs. "Herbert and I were already on the job. I think you'll be pleased." He winked at Mr. Munns, who looked a bit green. "We visited Scotland Yard this morning, didn't we, old chap? The morgue, to be exact. The orderly, Mr. Pickering, owes me some favours and was happy to slip us in. I had to get a look at Jarrett, don't you see. Awful, I don't like dead men! However, his resemblance to His Majesty was fascinating—not that one would see it if one didn't know to look. Herbert's mechanical genius came in handy. He's invented a small portable cam-

80

era, did you know? It folds up and slips right in his coat pocket. With Pickering on the lookout, he took some photographs of the dead man. When he develops and prints them, I'll give them to some . . . ah . . . bright little chaps in my employ. If anyone can trace Jarrett, they can; any one of them is worth ten of the police! Well," he put his hands on his knees, "what do you think?"

"You're certainly fast-moving, Mr. Wigmore," Mr. Bliss said. "We shan't have to worry about you not doing your job." There was a knock at the door. "Come," he called.

Nancy slipped in and curtseyed. "Luncheon is ready, sir."

We went to the dining room and took places 'round the table. There were platters of cold meat and a game pie. Mr. Wigmore heaped his plate, while Mr. Munns took little. Mr. Bliss ate nothing at all but sat fidgeting with his napkin; I could see he had something on his mind, so I was not surprised when after only a moment he scraped back his chair and rose.

"Damn, I must be off on the hunt myself; I'm impatient to begin! What is their bloody plot? Excuse me, excuse me." He went to the door. "Nancy, my hat and coat and scarf! And call a hansom! Gentlemen," he turned, "we shall meet again tomorrow to compare notes." Then he was gone.

I was shy with Mr. Munns and Mr. Wigmore, though the actor put me at my ease by asking me questions about how I had come to be Mr. Bliss's page. Still, I felt foolish and helpless. These fine gentlemen were doing everything to save the king, but I—I could do nothing it seemed.

# ❧Simon Bliss's Narrative❧

### I

I pulled my topper on tight, muffled myself to the mouth in a thick woolen scarf, and kept my knees tight together under the travelling rug as my hansom picked its way through the city. Baron Sigmund Czinner's money, the vague financial schemes he had broached to many wealthy men—these were what I hoped to find out about; my interlocutor to be the most celebrated banker in Europe, Lord Nathaniel Rothschild, head of the Rothschild clan. He knew money and the men who controlled it. If anyone could tell me about Baron Czinner's fortune it was Natty.

I peered out of my hansom. The sky was clean-swept, a pale china blue; the air cold and autumn-bright. And the teeming city was about me. A day to be alive! But I scowled at London this morning. An old man—damn, was I losing my patience with the world's foolishness? Past Berkeley Square we turned right, then left at the Devonshire Hotel into the stream of Piccadilly traffic. Old-fashioned, superannuated—that's what I felt. Beneath the mechanical noise of motorvans, motoromnibuses, landaulettes, and other motorcars, I could hardly hear the regular clip-clop of hooves and hum of metal-rimmed wheels that had been symbols of bustling London since my youth. I thought of Jack—earnest lad—and children everywhere; they would grow up into a far different world than the one I knew—a faster world, where electricity and petrol, not kings and statesmen, ruled.

Get hold of yourself, Simon! I bristled like a porcupine under my heavy coat. Whatever the world may be, it must be preserved. Decency must be preserved—that's the goal, old man! I concentrated on my task.

The Nelson column soared to the right, pigeons in Trafalgar Square. Then I was in the Strand, moments later at St. Clement Danes, then past Temple Bar, along Fleet Street where the great presses spewed forth London's dailies—MURDER AT THE DIOGENES CLUB! sidewalk placards proclaimed—and last up Ludgate Hill toward the noble dome and twin towers of St. Paul's. The cab turned off Cannon Street into St. Swithin's Lane, and I was in New Court, the financial center of Europe, of the world. This was the Bank of the Rothschilds.

I gave my name to the man at the gate. Recognizing me, he smiled, "Righto, sir!" and waved my hansom under the archway. I alighted and paid my driver. In the courtyard half a dozen couriers waited to take private messages to any part of London, and beyond. In the solemn entrance hall of the bank the usual flock of art dealers hovered to swoop on one or another of the brothers who might walk by. The Rothschilds had eyes as shrewd for Limoges enamels, silver-gilt nautilus cups, and Flemish miniatures as for investments, and many a dealer lived for a year on the profit he made from a morning's encounter with Nathaniel or Alfred or Leopold.

I was announced and shown directly through the executive offices to the inner sanctum known as the Partners' Room. Swarthy, sombre-eyed Lord Nathaniel Rothschild rose ponderously and came 'round his desk to greet me.

Seeing Natty, I recalled my first meeting with one of the famous family. A patron of the arts and trustee of the British Museum, Ferdinand Rothschild had heard of my reputation and had invited me for a weekend at Waddesdon to help him with a delicate problem: a priceless jewelled scarab had been taken from the Egyptian Collection by an art-mad lord of the land who believed his peerage entitled him to any national treasure of his choosing. "How may we recover the precious thing without a scandal?" was Ferdinand's question. I managed it; I helped to hush up the affair, too, in the process making a friend of the remarkable Ferdinand, who could tell an Ostade from a Teniers at a glance. Through him I had met the other English Rothschilds and over the years had served most of them in one capacity or another—as confidant, courier, friend. For their parts, they had not been remiss in advising me about investments.

I shook Lord Rothschild's hand, his grip firm and solid, one quick, efficient squeeze. Then, "Shut the door, boy!" he growled at the page who did not withdraw fast enough to please him. "And bring us some wine. Now. Sit down, Simon." He glanced at the magnificent ormolu clock on his huge desk—time was money. "For you, my friend, I can spare ... half an hour." Striding 'round the desk, he sat, folded his surprisingly delicate and perfectly manicured hands before him, and fixed me with his famous smouldering eyes. "What is your business?"

Natty Rothschild was amazingly direct. Briefly I regarded him: Bertie's age, sixty-four, and emperor of his realm as the king was of his. Bertie's beard was trim and white, Natty's thick and black. Bertie pursued women with amazing vigor. Nathaniel Rothschild pursued wealth with a restless energy which was unleashed on any man who wasted his time or, worse, contradicted him. Bertie could be petulant and cutting, but it was Natty who had the reputation of rudest man in London. His nickname was "king of the Jews."

Sitting in a black leather armchair, I glanced about the thickly carpeted, richly ornamented Partners' Room. Few besides the brothers ever were admitted here. The panelled walls were hung with ancestral portraits and framed mementoes of the Rothschilds' rise, including a receipt for £2,000,000 once paid to Wellington's army. Besides Natty's own, there were two other desks, presently unoccupied, belonging to the younger brothers. Blond, sybaritic Alfred's I recognized by the mink footwarmer peeping out from under it. Alfred never let banking interfere with his eccentric pleasures and rarely arrived at New Court before two. Gentle, sports-loving Leopold must be at Newmarket, where he bred racing horses, second in his affections only to fast motorcars. Leo cared nothing for high finance. The upper half of the room's entrance door was glass. No employee ever dared knock but must stand until noticed; then, if he were fortunate, he might be summoned in. Woe betide him who interrupted for no good reason!

Natty's dark eyes showed displeasure at my leisurely examination of the room, so I came to the point. "I want to know about Baron Sigmund Czinner."

His black eyebrows lifted. "Aha, the murderer!"

"Presumed murderer," I said.

"You deny he did it? But the papers are full of evidence!"

"I believe he did it," I conceded.

Natty looked smug as a judge.

We were interrupted by the arrival of the wine, a fine, wood-dry sherry served in gold-rimmed tulip glasses that sang at the faintest touch.

Lord Rothschild drummed his fingers and made displeased sounds in his throat until the page was gone. Then, nipping off the end of a cigar and reflecting only briefly, he said as if reciting from a ledger, "Baron Sigmund Czinner. Forty-five years of age. His rise has been remarkable. He began in the eighties in the offices of Steen and Goldschmidt in Vienna. In close touch with the stock exchange, he had a yearly income of £5,000 by the age of twenty. He invested in businesses in Egypt, Morocco, and Uruguay, seizing them by unscrupulous manoeuvres." He passed me the tooled box of cigars. "But his real money was made in the Balkans and Turkey, where he financed the Oriental railways for the sultan. Though he is Austrian—he negotiated his baronage in Austria by a clever application of funds—his main interests are now in Germany, in the steel mills of the Ruhr and the shipyards at Kiel and Hamburg." He handed me his gold nipper. "That is what I know of the fellow. Also—" he leaned forward to offer me flame from a lighter inlaid with mother of pearl, "that he is a dangerous foe."

"In the marketplace, you mean?" I puffed at my cigar.

"Yes. The Rothschild family has always obeyed certain rules. But Czinner—he is unscrupulous."

"In what ways?"

"In every way. I did not like the man, Simon! He had the audacity to visit me a month ago. He thought to have me, can you imagine?" Scowling, he clamped down hard on his cigar. "I heard his dangerous rattling the moment he slithered in the door. The *chutzpah ponem* might have choked or charmed a man less experienced than I!"

I was extremely interested in this encounter. "You sent him packing?"

"I did!"

"Not before you found out what he wanted, I hope."

Natty looked sly. "You *are* interested in him, aren't you?"

There could be no games with the shrewd old Jew. "Very much," I said.

He nodded. "I wish I could tell you more. Oh, I gave him his head, allowed him to think he was leading me a chase. First he wanted to know all about my financial affairs without revealing any of his own. That got him nowhere, I can tell you! Then he proposed schemes for building armament works in England. 'Do you think Whitehall might be interested in such plans?' he asked. He stretched back in the very chair you sit in, gazed 'round my office like he owned it, and waved one of my cigars—to give the impression my answer meant very little, I suppose. I gave him no answer; shortly I told him to go."

I understood Natty's agitation. Peace on earth had always been a Rothschild goal, conducive to high profits. Czinner made profits from warlike enterprises, which, if unleashed, would end peace and cripple the Rothschilds' empire.

"So Czinner's money is in steel and shipyards," was all I commented.

"Yes. And he has considerable influence in Berlin, along with the other mad anglophobes who prey on the emperor's fanatical hatred of England."

"Excellent sherry." I rolled it on my tongue. "It's odd, isn't it, that, supporting Germany's build-up for war, he should suggest manufacturing arms for England too?"

Natty glared at me as if I were a fool. "Not odd. He merely seeks profit regardless of principle. There are too many like him these days!"

"Mmm. One of his calibre is quite enough to be dangerous to us all. You may be wrong about his motive in coming to you, you know."

Not used to being contradicted about money matters, Natty flashed his eyes under the thick, black brows.

"I mean," I added quickly, "that Czinner must have known he could never finance the war industry on these shores. He broached his scheme only to find out if you knew Whitehall's plans."

Natty's severity gave way to glumness. "I can quite believe that," he said. "Why did he murder this Samuel Jarrett?"

"I don't know. I don't even know who Jarrett was. I hoped you might have some clue. I would very much like to . . . clear my club of scandal."

"Um." He nodded.

It seemed Natty had told me all he could about Baron Czinner, very little—enough, however, to confirm that the man had been a German spy, if not officially, at least in the capacity of furthering his business of manufacturing war machines. I was impatient; I had one more person to visit this day. But it would be rude to leave so soon, especially as some minutes of my allotted half-hour remained.

I leaned back and crossed my legs. "An excellent cigar, Natty," I said.

Pleased, he gazed at his, rolling it in his fingers. "They are, aren't they? The last of a consignment of 1888 Uppmanns, a gift from young Herr Wilhelm Luscher as a matter of fact."

"Oh?" Luscher was the man whose photograph—blond, handsome—I had shown to Jack only yesterday. He was a friend of the king; it would be a relief to spend some moments speaking of lighter matters. "I haven't met Herr Luscher," I said. "What's he like?"

"Haven't met him?" Natty chuckled through his black beard. "I would have thought he would be in your collection by now."

"He will be," I said, smiling back. "Our paths just haven't crossed. I'm interested in him of course. Attached to the German embassy under Count Hatzfeldt, isn't he? His name has been in the Court Circular damned often lately. And there are all those photographs in the illustrated papers— King Edward and Willy shooting, the king and Willy golfing . . . " I blew smoke toward the gilt bas-relief pattern of the ceiling. "For a man who's been in England only six months, Herr Luscher has got close to Bertie awfully quickly."

Natty shrugged. "No mystery in that. The king is easily bored; he has to have people to amuse him, and Willy Luscher is expert at that sort of thing—you know, not too deep and full of little jokes. Just what's wanted. In fact, Luscher seems to have been born to be amiable. And he appears genuinely to admire the king. Very likely it flatters Edward to have the dashing young fellow following him about. Of course, that isn't all of it; Luscher has other qualifications—passions for shooting, for horses, and for women. He's good-looking, quite the lady-killer. Mmm, I wonder how many noblemen's bored wives he's seduced. At any rate, to top it all off, he has the supreme advantage—" Natty gave a bearish wink, "money. His father is a wealthy manufacturer and spares the son nothing. So Willy rents a large house near Tunbridge Wells and royally entertains the royal circle."

"A money diplomat, eh?"

"Bluntly put, Simon, but there's truth in it."

"What does the father manufacture?"

"Woolens."

"A peaceful pursuit. And Luscher brings you gifts of cigars?"

"An offering to the House of Rothschild. A few months ago the young fellow was my guest at Tring Park. I wanted to meet this latest addition to the king's circle, whose wealthy father owns woolen mills in Germany. I'm cursed with always seeing the profit in friendships! Along with cigars to smooth the way, young Willy brought a suggestion that N.M. Rothschild and Sons invest in expanding the Luscher manufactory."

"To which you replied?"

Natty merely pursed his lips. "We are looking into it."

I smiled. "So Willy has charmed you too."

Thoughtfully, he stared at his cigar. "I like him well enough. Charmed? No one charms me, Simon! We discussed business. In company he seems lightweight, but over the bargaining table he is a shrewd fellow. He knows the language of money."

"Yes? And when he's with the king he speaks the king's language, and in a boudoir the language of love. Fluent in many tongues. I can't forget, Natty, that his native tongue is German."

Natty tut-tutted. "That doesn't become you, Simon! You're suspicious of Germany—I understand that. But of one German? You wouldn't say that all Jews are usurers."

"No, but . . . " I let the sentence die and glanced 'round the magnificent Partners' Room, which was like the audience chamber of a monarch. Through the glass-panelled door, in the huge business office clerks scratched sums and scurried from desk to desk in the most powerful Jewish citadel in the world.

Again Natty regarded his cigar, this time thoughtfully, pursing the red lips in his thick, black beard. "Come to think of it, Simon, young Willy once recommended Baron Czinner to me."

"Recommended?" Feeling my old heart thump in my chest as my thoughts began to race, I forced my voice to sound only mildly interested. I sipped the remarkable sherry and tasted not a drop. Luscher: German, close to the king. Czinner and Luscher had arrived in England separately but at about the same time, half a year ago. Both had driven wedges deep into English society in a short time.

"Yes," Natty was saying. "At tea in the drawing room at Tring as a matter of fact. Not that Willy brought Czinner's name up himself. No, it arose by chance. Ah yes, I remember; it was Madame Bernard mentioned it first." His dark, liquid eyes met mine.

I didn't blink.

"Madame Sophie Bernard?" I gripped my glass tightly, but I felt great excitement. Madame Bernard, too, had arrived on our shores six months ago!

Natty seemed to notice nothing. "I had several guests that weekend," he explained. "Monsieur Bernard was just arrived from Paris after his marriage. It was the first time I met his wife." He took a sip of sherry, not swallowing immediately but swirling it from cheek to cheek, savoring. "She's a beauty, Simon. Enchanting! Every man thought so—except Luscher, who paid her very little attention. Odd now I think of it, considering his amorous reputation. He appeared to avoid the husband too. In fact, there seemed something unspoken between the men, some bitterness, though perhaps it was my imagination. At any rate, Madame Bernard flirted outrageously, if charmingly. I thought even then that her poor doting husband ought to watch out. And I was right; he's been cuckolded—by the king himself. Ah well, noblesse oblige. The young Bernard woman has talents; she may be another Lillie Langtry! Too bad her husband so obviously worships her. He suffers for it, I'm afraid—a pity; he's upright, scrupulous, utterly trustworthy in business." Natty shook his head. "A hard heart, that's what it takes to survive in this world."

I puffed smoke, time to collect my wits. "And his flirtatious wife brought up Czinner's name? Why?"

"It was only in passing. He had some financial dealings with her husband, I think; that's how she knew him. At any rate, Luscher took the opportunity to say how his father had traded with Czinner to both their benefits. 'He's a fine man,' Willy pronounced. I remember being surprised at this nonsense. Even then—this was several months ago, as I've told you—I knew more than I cared to about Baron Sigmund Czinner, none of it good. I objected; I questioned Czinner's patriotism—an Austrian building warships for Germany and poisoning the emperor's mind against England! 'Oh, you must be mistaken,' Willy said, smiling and insisting he had never heard any such thing." Natty frowned. "I'm not used to being contradicted by young pups, and I assured him he could not deny that Czinner was helping to manufacture armaments which might cause the destruction of both our countries. He backed down at once and introduced some other topic—prospects for the Derby, I think. And that was that."

Lord Rothschild's swarthy face suddenly turned toward the ormolu clock, and he began to fidget with his sherry glass.

Crushing out my cigar—a gift from Willy Luscher; suddenly it left a bad taste in my mouth—I retrieved my blackthorn from beside my chair and stood.

"Thank you, Natty."

He rose, came 'round the desk, and brusquely shook my hand. "Profitable for you, has it been?"

I looked at him steadily. "I may not know until the ninth of November."

Regarding me with a set expression, he took this in but did not comment.

We walked to the door. Carrying a sheaf of papers, a young clerk waited beyond the glass, but Natty's frown made him scamper off. As we left the Partners' Room there was a change in the outer office, its bustle stilling to the rustling silence of an impending storm, in which pens scratched furiously and eyes darted watchfully from the mountainous piles of paper work on every desk. The master was among them.

Natty seemed not to notice the change. We walked down the centre aisle, I leaning on my stick, the powerful old Jew with his hands behind his back and an abstracted look on his face. "At Kiel and Hamburg," he muttered, "the shipyards financed by Czinner work night and day to launch faster cruisers and destroyers and to build deadly submarines. His mills in the Ruhr churn out cannon of every calibre. Meanwhile, he dances gavottes at English balls and lounges in the armchairs of your English clubs, while we Jews, who are your friends and prop up your economy whenever it is about to topple, must battle for a single seat in Parliament." He shook his head. "It is a mad world."

"Czinner will dance no more gavottes," I reminded him as we left the great office.

"Very likely." He continued to shake his head. "It's puzzling. In committing murder, in becoming a hunted man, Czinner gave up a fortune. What was his motive?"

"There was some great issue at stake."

"And still is?" The dark eyes watched me.

I returned the look. "I believe so."

"Um." He took my elbow. "You are onto it, are you? Have I helped?"

"Yes. Greatly, perhaps. Not a word of this, Natty—to anyone!"

"You can trust me."

I knew that I could.

In the entrance hall the waiting art dealers crept forward with their gem-encrusted cups and jewel-like little paintings, but Natty's scowl scattered them. "Ah, Simon," he sighed as we emerged into the courtyard, "the world is mad. We old men must save what of it we can, eh? But nothing is easy as it once was, nothing simple. In the old days, my father's days, the Rothschilds could prevent any calamity simply by withholding funds. Now . . . " His words seemed to shatter in the chill air.

"Indeed," I commented. We understood one another; no more need be said.

"And where next, in pursuit of your quarry?" Natty asked.

"Paddington Station. From there—"

"You must take my private landaulette!"

I thanked him. He squeezed my hand once more before I climbed into the motorcar. Pulling the lap robe over me, I gave the driver instructions. The vehicle started off. I glanced back. Framed in the archway, Lord Rothschild's bulk receded, one hand raised. "Luck, Simon!" I heard, his words a puff of cloud in the shadows of New Court.

## 2

The London crush: cabs, trams, and lorries in the roadway at midafternoon; the Oxford Street pavement awash with shoppers; the muffled mercantile roar, getting and spending bustle. Then Paddington Station and the 2:10 northwest, my destination Devonshire House, Chatsworth, to see Louise Cavendish. I settled myself into my carriage just as the train pulled out. The Duchess of Devonshire was a doyenne of English society; she also was German by birth and sniffed the air of both nations with a very sharp nose. I was presently not in Lottie's good graces, but my call to her that morning had piqued her curiosity enough to earn a grudging invitation. "Czinner?" she had asked. "The murderer? Of course I know something about him. A nasty little man! I am annoyed with you, Simon, but you may come to tea if you will promise to be amusing. I shall leave your name with Boothby." When I telephoned, I had intended to inquire only about Czinner, but now I had two other names to add to my list: Willy Luscher and Madame Sophie Bernard, the two people presently dearest in Bertie's affections—and both had known Baron Czinner. A trio of plotters?

Or a quartet? What about the cuckolded husband, Monsieur Bernard? I knew him and had believed he was upright as Natty Rothschild described him. Were we wrong? Could he be part of the scheme?

Damn! What scheme? We did not know even that! Drumming my fingers on the sill, cursing the arthritic twinges that throbbed like premonitions in my joints, I was glad I had telephoned Lord Esher; the police were alerted. Must they watch Luscher too? Yes, unless my talk with Lottie Cavendish absolved him. What had we—I, Jack, Herbert, Mr. Wigmore—stumbled onto?

No answers came. The Derbyshire landscape tumbled past the window, the train hooting 'round a curve. Reflected in the glass I seemed to see Madame Bernard's remarkable green eyes, her soft face. Her lips moved. "Bertie, Bertie

. . ." they seemed to say. To what fate did they lure the king of England?

3

I reached Chesterfield at three. In a hired carriage I arrived at the pretty village of Bakewell on the Wye by half-past the hour. Set against the craggy hills and steep, wooded dales of the Peak District, the classic stone façade of Chatsworth shortly came into view, and soon the dignified Boothby, head manservant of the manor, was leading me past the great painted hall, state rooms, and theatre gallery to the library, where the Duchess of Devonshire waited.

I found the duchess seated stiffly in an upholstered, cabriole-legged armchair near a book-lined bay, whose tall window admitted bars of clear afternoon light. Tea service was beside her: exquisitely wrought utensils and a profusion of cakes and cremes. Lottie surprised me by leaning forward— a concession; I heard the creak of her stays—to offer a single finger, which I kissed. "Your Grace," I murmured.

"Simon," she breathed in a voice that reverberated huskily with privilege; then, sitting back, she regarded me over the rim of her teacup with the cool, fixed expression of a monk.

As I sat I had to smile, and I fancied I saw an amused, if reluctant, answering sparkle in her hooded eyes. In her seventies, Lottie Cavendish was a remarkable woman. She had come to England as the bride of the Duke of Manchester and in her youth had been known as the most beautiful wife in England—though not the most faithful. For thirty years she had carried on an affair with the eccentric Lord Hartington, known in society as "Harty-tarty," and at the death of her first husband had married him, her second duke, giving her the nickname, the "Double Duchess." Now, bewigged and bejewelled, like the ruined shell of some castellated keep, with flower boxes blooming on the crumbling sills, she gazed at me suspiciously. In her sphere she was powerful as Lord Rothschild; she quoted prices on the stock exchange of reputation. By offering one, two, or three fingers when shaking hands, she indicated one's current social standing, and I felt privileged to have had a single finger. I had known Lottie

93

for many years, but of late, occupied in London, had been remiss in our friendship.

Unbending further, she poured me tea. "So. You have popped up after months of silence," she hissed. "It is not nice, Simon! There have been too many years of such rudeness. How often I've needed you to enliven some weekend or other! Even the king asks about eccentric old Simon Bliss—though, liking neither cards nor horse racing, you are not the best company for His Majesty. Still he likes you, I think, even if you do have the queerest friends. Why must you call on me only when you want something?"

This was a bad beginning. "You're quite right, dear Lottie. I need chastising; I can always count on you for that."

She blinked, then laughed her throaty laugh. I was greatly relieved.

"Quite right, Simon," she said. "I am good for something, then. Well, well. Have one of these little cremes. They're excellent! I shall watch you eat. My physician utterly forbids them! Baron Czinner? Baron indeed!" She sniffed. "That's right, pop it right down. Delicious? Czinner, yes—you shall hear all about him, just as you like."

I was content to listen, Lottie to speak. I was somewhat disappointed that she could add no new information, but she confirmed what I knew. Czinner had made deep inroads into society. "His money, Simon—how vulgarly he displays it! And how many eyes gleam at the sight of it, how many fingers twitch!" Yes, he was inquisitive. "A little ferret, scrabbling with his paws everywhere!" His loyalties? Lottie snorted. "In England he lauds all things English, cannot say enough good for our way of life, our 'picturesque landscape,' our 'sturdy populace,' our food. Really! I keep an extensive correspondence with my friends and relations in Germany. They know something of him, and there it is a different matter. He has the reputation in the highest circle, among von Bülow, Admiral von Tirpitz, and the Kaiser himself, of being the most vicious anglophobe, taking every opportunity to turn opinion against England." Her bosom, in its black décolleté dress, quivered with outrage, and the banks of pearls shook against her wrinkled throat.

Cautiously I introduced Madame Sophie Bernard's name.

"Now there is an interesting subject!" She smiled slyly. "Monsieur Bernard's pretty wife will go far!"

"She's already Bertie's mistress; everyone seems to know that. How much farther can she go?"

Lottie's mouth grew pinched. "Tsk tsk, how little imagination you show, Simon! A woman with *la Bernard's* . . . talent and . . . ambition can always find new challenges. Now—" a shrewd cocking of the head, "a question for you: why did you bring up her name?"

"I'm fascinated as you are by the latest gossip."

She looked skeptical. "More tea?" She poured two cups. "Do you know Sophie's husband?"

"I've met him once or twice."

She nodded. "A pleasing man, refined. I don't much care for the French, but I make an exception in his case. I'm very sorry for him, Simon; he's much changed. Last week my carriage passed him in Regent Street; I stopped to say hello. He looked a ghost, absolutely dreadful, and all due to this affair of his wife's with His Majesty. Well, what can he expect, what can he do? Nothing. He's really a fool to love that young beauty—genuinely love her, Simon! It's a mistake to love one's wife these days. And Madame Bernard gives his feelings short shrift. Imagine, in that state to have to tolerate her affair with Bertie! Well, it must be very hard on him—it is; it shows in his face. Then, too . . . " she sipped tea, "there are the rumours from Paris."

"Rumours?"

"You see, Simon, you really do need me. Rumours about Sophie's behavior during the time of the engagement, of course."

"Go on."

"You see, the young thing is supposed to have had an affair with Willy Luscher."

It took all my control to keep from sputtering in my cup. "One more affair in Madame Bernard's career, what can that matter?" I managed, crossing my legs and holding my saucer tightly in my lap. I could trust Natty Rothschild to silence; Lottie would scatter her suspicions like grapeshot.

She raised a brow. "So callous, Simon? It's not like you. Do you or don't you want to hear more?"

"Gossip? I'd love to have it all."

"You shall. But it's a delicate matter, Willy being to His Majesty what he is, the latest amusing gentleman. I'm sure the king doesn't know about the affair—and shouldn't. It would cause a stir, of more than embarrassment. You know," she glanced thoughtfully out the window, where the light was fading, "I think Bertie loves Madame Bernard? At any rate," her eyes came back to mine, "I have the story on good authority from Lady Jean Teresa, who was in Paris at the time. Willy was there too; it's a fact that his path and Madame Bernard's crossed many times socially. They crossed in Willy's boudoir, too, Lady Jean swears to it, and she's never been wrong that I could prove. Quite passionate on Madame Bernard's part, I understand; I wonder if she's over it. Of course, all this explains why the two behave so oddly when they're trapped at the same weekend together, which they often are. They avoid one another; what else can they do now that Madame Bernard is 'occupied' by the king?" She gave a low laugh. "It must be quite amusing now at Londesborough, with both of them and Alice Keppel, the former mistress, present. All of them, including Sophie's poor husband, will be at Sandringham on the ninth for the birthday party—Queen Alix, too, whom everyone loves, averting her violet eyes from the roundelay. You know, in this situation the players should envy the queen." She smiled wickedly. "Don't you wish you could watch, Simon? Don't you wish you were invited?"

I gestured dismissingly. "What do you make of Willy Luscher?"

"Oh, he's quite handsome; there's no denying that." Her tongue flicked over her lips. "A dear boy! Too bad his conversation is all horses, cards, and money. And to an old woman like me he doesn't vary the monotony with amorous whispers—though he's reputed to be practised at them. Still, he has his charm. He seems to see himself as a peacemaker. Perhaps he may do some good along that line. He's always promoting friendship between his country and ours. He does a bit too much of that sort of thing for my taste— though one must expect some of it, he being with the German embassy. I sometimes wonder if Willy isn't a trifle simple—but with looks, money, and position like his, intelligence would be an extravagance, don't you agree? What do you think of him, Simon?"

"I've never met him."

"But you would like to."

"If he's amusing, as you say."

"He's definitely not your sort! Nothing to reveal, no secrets. He was a friend of Sigmund Czinner's. What do you suppose Willy makes of Czinner's stabbing a man?"

I was careful. "If Willy is simple as you make him out, he probably makes nothing of it."

She looked sly. "And if he's not so simple . . . ?"

I shrugged.

"Why are you so interested in the murder, Simon?" The pearls rattled at her throat.

I told her what I had told Natty Rothschild: "I want to help my club out of a spot."

"You're always helping someone!"

I bowed my head. "May I help you in some way, Lottie?"

She held out her whole hand this time, as she rose. "Come to see me more often, that's all I ask. We have much in common, Simon—the past . . . "

Lottie and I had had a flirtation; we had known one another thirty years. "I promise to see you more often, dear Lottie." I kissed her hand. "And now—"

She sniffed impatiently. "Yes, yes, you must run off, and I must prepare for my bridge game tonight."

I went to the door.

"Simon?"

I turned. She stood in the dusk of the room.

"This Czinner affair would have been more of a scandal than it is if the list of the king's birthday guests had been published earlier. Bertie was interested in the baron's money as anyone; he intended to invite him to Sandringham on the ninth. Willy Luscher arranged the thing, I believe." There was a silence; I could not make out her expression in the gloom. "Fortunate, isn't it, that the official list has not come out yet, so that no connection can be made between His Majesty and the murder?"

"Yes. Very fortunate," I replied. "Thank you, Lottie."

In the entrance hall downstairs I ran into the duke. One of the richest men in England, old "Harty-tarty" wore the shabby, ill-fitting suit of clothes that was his trademark.

"Bliss!" He peered at me in vague startlement. "I thought you were dead!"

"Merely a rumour, milord," I replied.

"No doubt started by my wife!" he grumbled. Ponderously shaking his head, he took my elbow and walked me to the door. "A dreadful thing happened to me last February, you know."

"Dreadful?"

"Simply! I had a nightmare that I was making a wretched, dull speech in the House of Lords and woke up to discover it was true!" Guffawing, he slapped my back as he showed me out. "Splendid to see you, old chap. Do visit Chatsworth again—before both of us are dead."

4

My train roared back to London. I sat alone in the dimly lit carriage, puffing on my pipe and watching clouds scud across the sunset to pile up darkly in the west.

Connections, patterns—they crackled through my thoughts like lightning, bright lines above the dark landscape of the mystery. As the flashes touched one another they set off sparks which briefly illuminated the unknown terrain. Madame Sophie Bernard was the king's mistress. Samuel Jarrett had been meant to play the king. Baron Czinner had murdered Samuel Jarrett. In disguise Madame Bernard had visited Baron Czinner. Madame Bernard had spoken of Baron Czinner to Natty Rothschild. Herr Wilhelm Luscher had recommended Baron Czinner. Luscher was Bertie's bright new companion. Luscher had seduced Madame Bernard in Paris. Luscher had arranged for Bertie to invite Baron Czinner to Sandringham.

It could not all be coincidence! In it I glimpsed the threads of a plan, like a net, closing about the king of England. So Madame Bernard, Willy Luscher, and Baron Czinner were all to have been at Sandringham on the ninth! Czinner's name had been quietly struck from the list, but so far as I knew the young Frenchwoman and Herr Luscher still would be there. More than ever I was convinced that the king's Norfolk estate was where the climax of the plot was to take place.

Did I wish I had been invited to His Majesty's birthday? Lottie had asked. Yes! And at that moment, as the first drops of rain began to streak my carriage window, I determined that I would be.

# Herbert Munns's Narrative

## I

Hurry, Herbert! You are slow as a snail," came Wiggins' voice, along with a rapid pounding on my darkroom door.

"I can't work faster than my chemicals," I called out. "I shall be through presently."

When I emerged some moments later carrying a still-damp photographic print, I found my young friend impatiently striding back and forth before the Baker Street windows. On returning from luncheon at Uncle's flat, I had taken my plates directly into my darkroom, while Wiggins had gone upstairs to speak to Salt, who had returned from the mission he had undertaken earlier. I was startled to see that Wiggins changed from his dapper morning outfit into a pair of stout but well-worn trousers held up by a cracked leather belt, a rough stoker's shirt, a frayed jacket with but one button, and a pair of brogans which looked to have seen service where coal was shovelled. A faded red scarf was at his throat, and he clutched a dirty cloth cap.

Before I could comment on his peculiar costume, Wiggins held out his hand. "Well?"

"Success," I replied simply, passing him the photograph. "Careful not to tear it. It's wet."

Together we examined the features of Samuel Jarrett, fixed in the russet tones of bromide paper. Mercifully, the police doctor had closed the dead man's eyes.

Wiggins beamed. "Herbert, you are a genius!"

Used to my young friend's hyperbole, I merely sniffed. It was nonetheless a good job—sharp and clear.

Gazing in the mirror above my fireplace, Wiggins arranged the old cloth cap on his blond head. "Do you know, Herbert, lacking a Watson I've been thinking of writing my memoirs. 'The King Edward Plot'—that's what I'll call this little affair when I've solved it."

"*If* you solve it. Others must have some credit!"

"Oh, naturally. But," turning, he regarded me with his hands on his hips, "we shall accomplish nothing here. Have you more prints?"

"A dozen, as you asked. Why are you wearing those dreadful clothes?"

He smiled mysteriously. "A man's wardrobe should contain outfits for every occasion. I even have a spare, for you."

He handed me a paper-wrapped parcel. I opened it to discover worn trousers, a frayed tweed coat, and a battered old topper.

I stared up from the wretched garments. "Surely you don't expect . . ."

His expression became fixed. "You must wear them, Herbert. We are about to descend into the dreaded east, where city savages lurk in dark courts, pass like shadows along the walls, and kill for a half-sovereign without fear or favor." He went to my door. "Stack the prints in paper and bring them along; we can't wait for them to dry. Change your clothes too. I'll have Salt call a hansom." And he whisked himself away.

### 2

The East End of London—that was Wiggins' "dreaded east." He was right, of course; it was no place for a gentleman—or anyone who looked like one—and in my walks about the city I had always omitted its darker lurks. Ill at ease in my greasy trousers and coat embedded with the musty smell of poverty, I sat beside my friend as our cab moved across the city, Oxford Street becoming Holborn, Newgate becoming Cheapside, each change signalling a new and lower social stratum, as if we were really, as he had said, descending.

In disguise we were; it seemed appropriate for the case. It was 2:00 P.M. "Oughtn't you to be in rehearsal at the Gaiety?" I asked.

Staring out the window at the gray blocks of flats passing by, the young actor sighed. "No. Just this morning I telephoned my regrets to Mr. Edwardes that I would not be able to continue in his latest production. I didn't like to disappoint him, but I've not had a case like this one. I want to give it all my energies. Do you know, Herbert," he gestured out the cab window, "that this was once my home?"

We had passed the Old Lady of Threadneedle Street and by way of Cornhill and Aldgate High Street had reached the Commercial Road. We were in the heart of Whitechapel.

"I know that you were once a street boy, living by your wits, and that Sherlock Holmes took care of you and the other boys who acted as his private police force."

A reminiscing look came into Wiggins' blue eyes. "That was a score of years ago. Then I lived in Dorset Street, Spitalfields, called 'the evilest street in London,' and for a few coppers did many things of which I can't say I'm proud. That was before Mr. Holmes saved me, of course. Many's the day I was lucky to get even a two-penny meat-and-eel pie under my belt. Things have changed since then. The new thoroughfares have all but destroyed the old rookeries, where vice was the path of survival. But there still are boys to be saved."

"Like Billy Gully?" I asked.

Wiggins nodded thoughtfully. "Some day the way of life which has deformed Billy will be dead, I hope. Ah, well, the streets have done him some good, honed his cunning, given him a macabre sense of humor. He's a survivor, you will see!"

Knowing that Wiggins would reveal in his own time where we were going and why, I fell silent. He called to the driver to turn south on Cannon Street. The ways grew narrower and the houses more dilapidated, springing up grotesquely from the dirty cobblestones to lean precariously overhead on both sides in two jagged rows, like teeth about to close on the sky. Few figures moved in the streets, and these furtively. We passed squalid doss houses, where men bought a night's fitful rest for fourpence, and yellow-lit pothouses, from which muffled shouts of sad, ginny revelry drifted to our ears. There were no other carriages in these narrow lanes. Eyes stared suspiciously at our hansom as at an apparition. The eyes were hungry, and, shivering, I was glad to be in disguise.

At four we reached Wapping High Street. We left our cab behind and, seemingly aimlessly, strolled south. To our right was the Thames, to our left the London docks, where ships unloaded dried fruit, pulse and beans, tea, sugar, spices, grain, wool, ivory and hides, tobacco, and every other sort of commodity. I was growing impatient, when Wiggins turned and pushed through the doors of the Ramsgate, a noisy pub near Wapping Old Stairs. I followed. Inside, a boisterous clientele of seamen and of carpenters, turners, and wheelwrights who worked in the shops that kept the machinery of import running smoothly bellied up to the bar and quaffed great glasses of porter. Pausing just inside the doors, Wiggins caught the eye of the barman, a burly, mut-tonchopped fellow, who merely gave a significant little jerk of his head upward before he went back to wiping glasses with a dingy cloth.

At once Wiggins walked to a side door. With a brief glance back he led me through it, up a narrow flight of stairs, and into the room above the bar. This proved to be a sort of private lounge. It was rather shabby, but flames leapt upon the fireplace grate, warming the room. Seated in a red leather armchair before the blaze, his tattered shoes propped on a stool as if he were lord of the manor, was Billy Gully.

The cocky little fellow jumped up soon as we entered the room. "Wotcher, Wiggins!" Planting his hands on his hips, he eyed me suspiciously. "Is 'e in on this?"

"Mr. Munns works with me, same as you do," Wiggins reproved. He looked from one to the other of us. "You haven't been officially introduced, I believe. Billy Gully, this is Mr. Herbert Munns. Herbert, this is Billy, my chief man in the Baker Street irregulars. Very helpful these boys are, too!"

Wiggins gestured toward the other lads in the room, a dozen or so, all scruffy as Billy and all now standing, caps in hands, staring expectantly at us out of large, bright eyes. I recognized several of them as boys I had seen scampering up to Wiggins' rooms at Baker Street.

"Pleased to meet you, Billy," I said. Wiggins waggled his eyebrows encouragingly, and I held out my hand.

Billy stared at it as if it were a lobster claw, then shook it gingerly; afterward, he wiped his hand on his baggy pants. He sniffed in a businesslike way. "Well?" he asked Wiggins smartly.

"The photographs, Herbert!"

I took the packet from my inside coat pocket and passed it to him. He opened it and handed 'round the images, now nearly dry, of Samuel Jarrett. Silently the boys examined the dead man's features.

"Know him, lads?"

Some of them looked up, but none nodded yes.

"It's your job to identify him, then trace him. Divide up into your areas and begin at once. His name is Samuel Jarrett. No toff he; that's why I've come to you lads. Perhaps he was an actor. He was found in the Diogenes Club yesterday, stabbed by Baron Czinner, whom some of you know by other names—Brown, Seecombe, Dr. Scheele, Gundersen. Do any of you who lurked Czinner's hangouts recall a chap who looked like Jarrett?"

A shaking of heads.

"I might 'ave, Wiggins," Billy offered, sounding miffed. "But there was so many coves sneakin' in and out o' Seecombe Exportin' . . . I wish I'd knowed you wanted this Jarrett spotted. I could 'ave followed 'im easy and 'ad 'im pat!"

"I'm certain you could have," Wiggins said. "I only hope it's not too late. It's urgent, boys; I want your best. If anyone can find him out, you can. Billy and Spiker, stay behind. The rest of you, be off! Follow the usual procedures. And good luck!"

"Right, sir!" The boys pushed the photographs into their shirts and jammed their caps onto their heads. "We'll do it, sir!" Then through a side door they slipped from the room. I imagined them stealing out by a back way, separating, melting into London's narrowest lanes.

Turning his cap nervously in his hands, the boy whom Wiggins had called Spiker stood near Billy. I examined him

—skinny as a slat, his frame giving his trousers and coat few angles to cling to. He appeared painfully shy. His long, tangled, mouse-brown hair curled about a face blushing scarlet under its sooty smudges. His awkwardly grinning mouth showed more black gaps than teeth.

Proudly, Wiggins introduced us. "Spiker is London's flashiest snakeman," he explained. "Her finest housebreaker, I mean."

I stared skeptically at the lad.

"Oh, he's reformed, Herbert—except when he works for me. Now—Billy, Spiker, I have a special job for you. A spot of midnight larceny, don't you know."

Billy's eyes lit, and he threw out his chest. "We can crack any crib!"

Spiker's head wobbled eagerly in agreement.

Wiggins grinned. "Splendid! Here's to a right smart pull, then! And let's hope the peelers don't nab us!"

### 3

Wiggins went to the curtained window and peered out. "We must wait until dark, gentlemen. In the meanwhile—"

He had cold meats and cheese sent up and four great glasses of porter. We joined Billy and Spiker by the fire. As we nibbled and drank I learned that the Ramsgate was one of various places where Wiggins assembled his boys when he had work for them. How had he met them? I asked.

Billy spoke up: "I were the first," he said, gnawing like a pirate at a chicken wing. "It were three year ago we met, weren't it, Wiggins? I were workin' the scaldrum dodge on Fleet Street—pretendin' to be a lame lad, doncher know. I were somethin' pitiful! Well, Wiggins caught me out, stripped off me gammy bandages, and 'auled me to 'is rooms. What were to come I didn't know, but I were scared right enow. 'I'll say you're good at your work,' Wiggins sez. 'First rate acting! I'm an actor too. How'd you like a steady job with me?' 'E told me wot 'e 'ad in mind. It sounded better than the chancy dodges I were starvin' on one day at a time, so I took 'im up on it. I brung t'other boys along, and we been with 'im ever since."

Billy sounded proud, his admiration—and affection—for

Wiggins plain on his crooked features. There were more reminiscences, and I listened, fascinated. Spiker said nothing, all the while gulping beer and stuffing down meat and cheese and growing no fatter.

At seven Wiggins rose. "Let's be off on our pull!" It was to be Seecombe Exporting, the establishment which Baron Czinner had set up on the Jamaica Road, he explained. By now it was all too clear what he intended: to crack the place—that was why he needed Spiker's talents—and I was chary of what might come. My daydreams at Cox's Bank had never included breaking the law. Nonetheless, I allowed myself to be led down some creaking back stairs, out, and along Wapping High Street toward St. Katherine's Docks. I felt a high excitement; I would not have backed down for anything.

Black clouds scudded across the moon, and a bitter wind blew up from the Thames. We crossed Tower Bridge and were soon on the Jamaica Road. A constable in his tall hat stared suspiciously as we passed, and I felt sure my expression gave everything away. But Wiggins flashed a cheery smile and touched his cap. The boys scampered ahead. The policeman scowled, but he did not stop us.

Ten minutes later we were opposite number 187, a dilapidated two-storied frame building, dark, with "Seecombe Exporting" printed on a board in front. The stairs leading up to the offices were brightly lit by a streetlamp, and I wondered how young Spiker would contrive to get us in without being seen. The rain, which had threatened, began to scatter down, and we ducked into a doorway. To my surprise there was someone waiting—a sharp-eyed, tow-headed tyke, who greeted us in a confident little voice: "Wotcher, me cock sparrows?" The boy could not have been more than ten. Billy referred to him as the "crow," and it was clear he had been stationed specially to keep an eye on Czinner's place.

" 'Lo, Freddie," Billy said. "Anythin' seen?"

"Not a soul," the lad piped up. "Dark these two days past."

"Mmm. I expected it," Wiggins said, "Too much to hope that Czinner would return. But he won't have been able to clear anything out either, so we may find some clues. Let's get on with it! Freddie, you know the signal for crushers?"

The tyke bobbed his head. "Righto, Mr. Wiggins!"

Wiggins touched his shoulder. "Stay here, then, and keep your eyes peeled; whistle if there's trouble." He glanced at Spiker. "The side wall, don't you think?"

Spiker nodded.

Wiggins poked his head out to peer up and down the road. I looked too. There were just a few distant coattails flying for cover by the light of the lamps stretching away in the gloom. Rain hissed on the cobbles. Number 187 Jamaica was at the corner of Pike's Mews, across the way. We hitched up our collars and at Wiggins' signal dashed for it, ending under the dripping eaves of the gloomy cul-de-sac just off the thoroughfare. I hoped we had not been seen.

Wiggins turned to Spiker. "Up to you, lad. Can you crack it?"

Shaking his damp hair from his face and looking all at once changed from the painfully shy boy I had met at the Ramsgate, Spiker sized up the job, his gaze roving over the side wall of the building and taking in every detail. When my eyes grew accustomed to the dark I was able to follow his glances. The wooden wall stretched some thirty feet high and was slick with wet, with not a handhold until the three windows set at intervals under the eaves. It seemed one of them was how we must enter if we were to manage the thing, but I thought the task looked impossible.

Fearing for Spiker if he tried it, I said so.

"'E can do it, all right!" Billy sniffed.

The game lad meant to have a go, at any rate. "That'll be the way," Spiker muttered almost inaudibly above the sound of the storm. He was peering up the brick wall of the foundry building next to Seecombe Exporting. He turned his large eyes to Wiggins. "No more'n ten minutes, sir. Satisfact'ry?"

Looking unconcerned, Wiggins waved a hand. "Oh, take your time, lad!"

I knew I couldn't stop them; the thing had been decided. Billy had been carrying a bundle under his coat; now he took it out—a black physician's bag. Hauling it to the driest spot under the eaves, he opened it. I stared; no surgeon I cared to visit would have used the implements which tumbled forth: hacksaws, picklocks, jemmies. It was a kit of cracksman's tools.

Billy sniffed as Spiker pawed through the implements. "Special made in Birmin'am," he said for my benefit. "We can do *anythin'* with these!"

I could only nod. Stripping off his coat, shirt, and boots, Spiker was left only in ragged trousers. I glanced at the sheer wall. What did he intend? Thin and white in the gloom, he did not seem to notice the cold. From the kit he took only a short metal rod and a length of rope before Billy gathered up the tools. Spiker tied the rope loosely 'round his neck and returned to where the foundry and the wood building met. There a little vertical ridge of bricks protruded, and I suddenly knew by Spiker's rubbing of hands and his single-minded look upward that he meant to scale the wall by means of the precarious purchase which these bricks afforded. I wanted to stop him; he would surely fall! But Wiggins made no protest, only watched the preparations with a confident smile. Wiping the rain spots from my glasses and gulping down my misgivings, I watched, too, chilled at what the brave boy was about to attempt. Spiker gripped the metal rod in his teeth and started up.

He was astonishing. He used his fingers and toes, slipping them into worn spaces where I thought not a knife could be slid. He climbed slowly but steadily, his hands and feet like four little animals cannily sniffing over the bricks, testing, finding holds, pulling up, then darting to look for higher purchases. Sooner than I could have believed he was a third of the way up, then half. If he fell now, he might break his neck. There were no eaves on the foundry, so the rain spilled over its roof at the corner and splashed down, threatening to wash the lad off. Wind whipped his trousers about his legs. But doggedly he went on.

I glanced at Billy—his sturdy arms were crossed; he looked grim—then at Wiggins. My friend's smile was gone, but he made no move to stop Spiker.

The lad was twenty feet up, then twenty-five, nearly at the top. At this point the sharp needles of rain must have stung his bare back. The water pouring from the foundry roof fell straight into his face and looked to be drowning him. Nothing stopped him however. He inched his way on. I held my breath. He slipped a bit; one hand scrambled for a hold. I squeezed my eyes tight. When I opened them, Spiker was swinging safely from the foundry roof. He turned his head and flashed a plucky smile.

Spiker then grabbed the zinc gutter of Czinner's building, pulled himself out of the torrent of water, and like a monkey, dangling, he made hand over hand for the nearest window. I gave a cry of admiration. Glancing at me, Billy looked triumphant.

Spiker reached the window. It was barred like the other two; Czinner kept a tight crib. I could not guess how the boy meant to get in. Wriggling and grabbing, his dangling toes stretched, touched the sill, and took hold, like fingers. Reaching down with one hand, he got a grip on a bar. Only then did he let go the gutter. He bent and crouched on the sill two dozen feet above our heads.

Footsteps pattered by on the Jamaica Road, and I was reminded that there were still passers-by, constables likely among them. I was glad for the gloom of the mews, which blanketed us. I hoped we would not hear the "crow's" warning whistle while Spiker hung on high.

The lad wasted no time. He pulled the rope from his neck and worked it in a double loop 'round two of the window bars. Then, taking the short metal rod from his teeth, he fit it between the rope strands and began turning. This produced its effect, simple and ingenious: as the rope tightened due to Spiker's leverage, the bars were slowly forced together. It must have been tricky to turn the rain-slick rod with one hand while the cold wind buffeted him about, but Spiker worked steadily, and before long one of the bars slipped from its mortar. He waited for a particularly noisy gust of wind to muffle the sound, then smashed in the window. He picked aside the shards of glass and let his skinny frame into the dark opening.

Success!

We lost no time in jubilation. Wiggins craned to see that the way was clear. It was. Thunder rumbled as we slipped 'round the corner and up the stairs of Seecombe Exporting.

As we reached the door, it opened; Spiker already had loosed the bolt. He let us in and closed the door after.

4

Inside it was dark. While Billy and Spiker made sure the shades were drawn, Wiggins groped for a light. Finding an oil lamp, he lit it, and shadows jumped up 'round us from its dim yellow glow.

"Smart work, Spiker!" Wiggins said, patting the lad's shoulder.

Spiker showed a shy, gap-toothed smile.

I had kept Spiker's clothes under my coat and now handed them to him, also giving him my scarf to dry his soaking hair. The boy was covered with gooseflesh and his teeth chattered, but he didn't complain. When he was dressed I gave him my coat to keep him warm. Only then did I look closely at Seecombe Exporting. A long counter with a hinged half-door crossed the room six feet inside the entrance. On the other side of the counter could be seen a rolltop desk, open and showing empty pigeonholes, four tall desks with spindly-legged stools, a couple of cabinets, a bookcase, and a metal floor safe. The room could have been any sort of office; with a couple of clerks shuffling official-looking invoices and an authoritative gentleman smoking a cigar at the rolltop, anyone might have been fooled.

"To work, gentlemen!" Wiggins urged, and we went at the place, turning out drawers, opening cupboards, even peering under the grimy carpets. We found more than enough dust but little else—just some bills of lading and ledgers, which Wiggins guessed were meant for show. At the end of twenty minutes we ended with very little.

Wiggins looked thoughtful but not discouraged. "Seecombe Exporting is in the Commercial Register," he said, leaning against the counter. "And here is its office. To someone who hadn't seen that its files were empty and its ledgers full of sham it would appear a perfectly legitimate business. My guess is that Czinner set it up so that he and his agents could go 'round nosing into British manufacture without ever being suspected of anything more than mercantile interest." He placed some papers, which he had pulled from a dustbin, on the counter before us. "These prove my point—letters from Woolwich, Yarmouth, Sheffield, Newcastle, Liverpool, Bristol, Plymouth, Portsmouth, Dover—all dockyard towns—inviting the exporter to examine various products in which the innocent manufacturers hoped to interest him. Clever! Of course, Czinner/Seecombe didn't go himself; he was too busy in his numerous other roles. But he sent agents—the various men you saw tramping up and down his stairs, Billy—with letters of introduction. See the official Seecombe letterhead? Very convincing! Unsuspected, Czinner's men went to our important ports, watched what came in and out of England, marked her industrial strengths and weaknesses . . ."

"Bloody spies!" Billy spat, peering under a shade into the storm.

"Indeed," Wiggins said, beginning to gather up the letters. He cocked an eye at the squat floor safe. "Bullock Bros. Ltd., London. Guaranteed Burglarproof," was painted on the black surface in gold script. "Can you crack it, Spiker?"

The lad never blinked. "I'll 'ave a go, Mr. Wiggins."

Looking worried, Billy turned from the window. " 'E'll 'ave to drill it. Do we 'ave time?"

Resolutely, Wiggins pushed the last of the letters into his pocket. "All night, if need be; it's the one spot left unexamined." Perching on a stool, he gestured at the metal box which stood on casters against the far wall. "Have at it, Spiker!"

At once Billy brought forth the cracksman's kit, and both boys knelt before the safe. From the bag Spiker took a sort of drill.

"A petter-cutter, Herbert," Wiggins explained coolly, crossing his legs, "one of the indispensable implements of the trade." He smiled thinly. "Bullock Brothers are rather too optimistic, I'm afraid. Spiker will clamp the tool to the keyhole to get leverage, then drill a small opening over the lock. Through this opening he will then work the wards. Isn't the mind of man ingenious? The drilling will take a while, however; make yourself comfortable, old chap."

There was nothing for it but to obey. Thinking of the constables on Jamaica Road, I lit a Rajah to occupy myself. Wiggins frowned at my clouds of smoke but made no protest. Soon Spiker had the drill attached and was turning steadily as when he had bent the window bars. We were silent for some moments. The rain drummed down. Occasionally a flash of lightning lit the shades and thunder rumbled after. The wind howled under the eaves.

Seeming to forget we were present, Spiker began to sing as he worked: "You are the 'oney, 'oneysuckle, I am the bee; I'd like ter sip the 'oney from those red lips, you see . . ."

The boy had a pretty voice. After a time Wiggins joined in, softly; then Billy. Even I tried a chorus, my throat croaking hoarsely, but I stuck to it. It seemed strange to be warbling away in that shabby office while outside it poured rain and we cracked a safe.

The singing died. My thoughts wandered, disconcertingly, to Madame Sophie Bernard's green eyes as the painter Sargent had depicted them. I found it hard as my uncle had to believe that she could be part of some plot against His Majesty. The truth was, I did not want to believe it. What could be her motive?

I heard some clicks. When I looked up, the safe door stood open. Wiggins was by Spiker's side in an instant, clapping him on the back and congratulating him. The lad's face flamed with pleased embarrassment.

We all crowded 'round the safe. Wiggins held the lamp to the opening and peered in. "Hello!" he exclaimed, eyes bright. A treasure trove, it seemed; the opening was crammed with papers. He pulled them out and carried them to the counter, where, as we watched, he began rapidly to sort through them. Except for a few letters and a small book in a green leather binding, they were all placards: "Fight the Social Oppressor!" "Organize!" "Strike!"

"Aha, these were to have been used by Gundersen, the socialist!" Wiggins held one up. "Czinner wasn't only a spy; he was an agitator too."

After glancing through the letters, he whistled softly. "As for the Dr. Scheele alias, read this." He handed me one of the letters. In no uncertain terms it offered arms to the Sinn Fein rebels.

"Czinner was an Irish sympathizer!" I said.

"Certainly not, Herbert."

"He was willing to use their cause, I mean."

"To further his own, yes. The devil! A genius in a way. I very much want to lay my hands on him." He was thumbing through the small green book. Suddenly his eyes grew bright, and he thrust it into my hands. "We've stumbled onto something, Herbert! Have a look."

The book seemed a ledger of names, places, and dates. Some names had parentheses after them, enclosing one or more other names. "A list of his agents?" I asked, glancing up.

Wiggins nodded. "I believe so, old friend." He beamed. "A profitable day's—and night's—work, what? Your uncle should be very interested in all we've done." He turned to our two young accomplices. "A smart pull, lads! You'll be rewarded. Now—" he stuffed the book into his coat pocket with the letters, "let's be off!"

He extinguished the light, and, after first examining the road, we scurried down the stairs into the storm. Billy gave a brisk salute before vanishing with Spiker along the rain-spattered cobbles.

Wiggins and I dashed in the opposite direction to hail a cab at Dock Head.

## 🦚 *Jack Merridew's Narrative* 🦚

I did not see Mr. Bliss again on the day he left us at Curzon Street. I returned to the Diogenes Club and performed my duties. In the evening Mr. Wetheridge gave me a message from Mr. Bliss that he would spend the night at Curzon Street and that I was to be there at ten sharp the next morning. About eight a great storm came up and rattled and crashed outside the smoking room, where club members huddled in gloomy little groups. It kept up for hours. Going to bed accompanied by white flashes of lightning, I huddled under my eiderdown and wondered how I, too, might help King Edward.

The next day was gray, but the rain had stopped, leaving

the roads shiny with puddles. I was at Curzon Street promptly at ten. Mr. Munns was there before me, sitting with Mr. Bliss by the fire, a pot of coffee and some cakes on a tray near at hand. Mr. Wigmore was absent.

"Ah, Jack! Come sit by me. Nephew here was about to tell me what's become of our remarkable new actor friend."

I took my place.

"That's just it—I don't know what's become of him. Nothing, I hope," Mr. Munns said, his back straight. "He simply popped off early this morning, and that's all I know." Chewing his moustache ends, he looked disapproving. "Wiggins is like that, I'm afraid—not a word, except to his man, Salt, who told me to come ahead. 'Wiggins'll be there,' he promised."

Mr. Bliss frowned, but his look brightened when Mr. Munns began to tell how he and Mr. Wigmore had broken into Seecombe Exporting. I was fascinated, too, especially liking to hear about the "irregulars," as Mr. Munns called them; I hoped one day to meet Billy Gully and Spiker.

Mr. Munns finished his story. "You have been busy!" Mr. Bliss exclaimed, leaning back, clapping his hands on his knees. "Excellent work! What would they say to all this at Cox's Bank, eh?" He twinkled.

"They would heartily disapprove, Uncle!" Mr. Munns replied.

"*I* approve, however. Why . . . what's that—?"

There was a pounding on the front door, a commotion in the hall; then Mr. Wigmore burst into the room. We all stared. Looking apologetic, Nancy shut the door after him.

"Wiggins?" Mr. Munns murmured, half rising.

"Yes, yes, Herbert . . ." The young actor stood swaying. He was dressed elegantly as I had seen him before, in a fawn-colored morning suit and silk topper, but whereas he had always seemed lighthearted in spite of the serious problem these gentlemen faced, he now seemed distracted. He rubbed his jaw; he gazed about the room as if to make certain it was real. "Dreadful experience . . . dead man . . . hysterical woman . . ." he muttered. Mr. Munns held out an arm, but his friend waved him off. "No, no, old chap . . . I shall recover. It's just that . . . I say, Mr. Bliss, have you any brandy?"

"Certainly. In the tantalus."

Still muttering and shaking his head, Mr. Wigmore dropped his hat, stick, and gloves on a chair and rushed to the cabinet. He poured a glass and took a large swallow. He seemed to calm. "Just the thing, don't you know! This affair gets deeper!" He blinked. "Has Herbert told you about last night?"

"Yes," Mr. Bliss replied.

"A splendid adventure—with its reward!" He fished in his coat. "Here." He held out a small volume, bound in green leather.

The old man examined it. "This was in the safe?"

A nod. "Along with inflammatory placards." Mr. Wigmore took another drink. "Czinner was an agent provocateur. The book proves he was a spy—if we needed more proof. I've examined it closely; it's unmistakably a list of agents, with spy posts, aliases, even an elaborate code."

Mr. Bliss was peering at him sharply. "*Was* a spy, you say?"

Mr. Wigmore looked glum. He sucked his cheeks, and his eyes seemed to be seeing some terrible scene. "Yes—was. The man is . . . dead." He dropped into a chair and took another large swallow of brandy.

"Damn!" Mr. Bliss slapped the book on his chair arm. "I had hoped we might bring him to ground, get information from him! Now—"

"Someone else has brought him to ground," Mr. Wigmore said.

"Who? How do you know he's dead?" Mr. Munns asked.

Mr. Wigmore turned bleak eyes on him. "I saw him, Herbert—what's left of him, that is."

The fire crackled.

"Tell us what you mean, Mr. Wigmore," Mr. Bliss said evenly.

Staring into the flames, the actor turned his brandy glass slowly in his hands. "I received a telephone call early this morning. From Pickering."

"Your friend in the Scotland Yard morgue?" Mr. Munns asked, on the edge of his seat.

"The same. He's in the habit of letting me in on anything unusual. 'There's a body here you might like to see,' he said.

114

He gave the details; I knew I must go at once. On the way I picked up Rose Mappin at Chelsea Gardens—you recall, the poor girl whose face Czinner, as 'Brown,' had marked up? I hadn't seen her since Nance Castle asked me to find Brown. Her cuts have healed, but the scars are not a pretty sight; there's not a customer would want her. Naturally she's very bitter." He took a breath. "Pickering let us into the morgue." He shuddered. "He showed us a body." He drained his glass. "It was Czinner. Quite dead. He'd been found floating in the Thames."

There was a silence.

"Why did you need Rose Mappin?" Mr. Bliss asked.

"To identify Czinner."

Mr. Munns frowned. "But you knew his face . . ."

The actor was quite pale as he looked 'round at us. "That's just it: there was no face," he opened his hands helplessly, "no head at all. Nor arms." I could barely hear the last words, whispered: "Just a torso and legs."

"Good God!" Mr. Munns breathed.

"The act of desperate, determined men!" said Mr. Bliss.

Feeling chilled and very frightened, I watched Mr. Wigmore, who was staring again into the fire. I could not imagine Baron Czinner as he described him; yet I knew it must be true. What would happen to the king?

"You see," Mr. Wigmore went on, "I had given Pickering a description of Czinner, including a birthmark on the left thigh which Rose had told me about. You recall how we wondered if, hunted by the police, Czinner would be allowed to live? I was covering all chances. It was by the birthmark that Pickering guessed the remains were those of the man I was seeking. I had to have Rose along to make sure—poor girl! It was him, all right; she knew at a glance. She wailed and flung herself about, and do you know why? Because, in spite of the horrible way he had died, he was beyond her tormenting; she still wanted to make him suffer for what he'd done! She tore at her scarred face. In the end a doctor had to be called to sedate her."

Mr. Munns stirred. "Dreadful! More brandy, Wiggins? You've had a morning!"

"No, no. I'm myself now, I think." As if to prove it, he took one of the little cakes and poured coffee.

Mr. Munns rubbed furiously at his eyeglass lenses. "I'm more than ever glad they don't know we're onto them! Imagine, hacking off a man's head and arms to keep him from being identified!"

"We must play a very close hand, Herbert!" Mr. Bliss warned.

"I have more to tell," Mr. Wigmore said.

"You have the floor."

Mr. Wigmore ate a second cake. He leaned back and crossed his legs. He seemed to have recovered completely, even looking smug about what he had to reveal. "It's about Madame Bernard—and Teddy." He went so far as to wink. "When Billy told me yesterday morning that the Frenchwoman had snuck out at midnight to meet Czinner, I took it upon myself to send Salt 'round to her house in Norfolk Street. Keeping a sharp lookout, he lounged about and followed her head butler, Mr. Giddings, to the Running Footman off Charles Street, a public house frequented by servingmen. Salt is a fellow of many talents—he's been to sea; fought in the Afghani War; served as footman to Lord and Lady Glendinning of Grosvenor Street, so he well knows the servingman's fondness for gossip about the master and mistress. There's a great deal of that in the Running Footman. (Dressed as a butler or driver, I myself have pinched some nice bits of information there.) At any rate, Salt sidled up to Mr. Giddings—white-haired, red-nosed, a fellow full of airs, who likes his pint pot and, fortunate for us as you'll see, is willing to crow to anyone who'll buy it for him. Giddings is not top hole; all the Norfolk Street help are on temporary hire from an agency—and good luck with that! At any rate, plying Giddings with drink, Salt got out of him that he'd often seen His Majesty himself at Norfolk Street when the master was away. You can imagine the winks and leers; Salt played up to them. Giddings may be an old toper, but he prided himself on dates, said he remembered exactly when Teddy was last there. 'No!' said Salt. 'Bloody yes!' said Giddings. 'Bloody October eighteenth!' And he banged his pot on the bar."

"But that couldn't be, Mr. Wigmore," I exclaimed, feeling my face flame red as everyone looked at me. "I mean . . . Mr.

Bliss, sir, you read it to me from the Court Circular. His Majesty was at Londesborough then."

"You're perfectly correct, Jack. He is still there. Which means—"

"—that the man must have been Samuel Jarrett in disguise!" Mr. Munns exclaimed.

"Right you are, Herbert!" Mr. Wigmore beamed. "It was the last time the disguised Jarrett visited Madame Bernard too."

"Because he was murdered next day," I got out.

"In the Diogenes Club library!" Mr. Bliss put in, slapping the green-leather spy book again.

"And now Baron Czinner is dead too," Mr. Munns said gravely.

"So Madame Bernard is part of it, sir?" I asked Mr. Bliss.

"I'm sorry to say she must be. Do you imply, Mr. Wigmore, that, disguised as Bertie, Jarrett had visited the Frenchwoman on other occasions?"

Stretching and crossing his legs, Mr. Wigmore folded his hands placidly on his stomach. "Undoubtedly. Of course, the real king visited her, too, but so did Jarrett; they may have looked alike, but they showed different personalities. Here are some facts, odd on the surface, that Salt wormed out of Giddings. The servants were ordered to stay below-stairs during certain of His Majesty's visits. But during certain others they worked under no such prohibition and often observed the king striding into the house and vanishing into the drawing room with Madame Bernard—almost as if he were meant to be seen by them. He *was* meant to be, I believe! Furthermore, on these more public occasions, Madame Bernard and the king always had great rows during which she would sob and beg to be free of him while he abused and threatened her. 'I thought the old fellow'd *kill* her!' Giddings said about their last fight. In fact, he saw the king strike her to the ground before he trundled off in a fury."

Mr. Bliss sat with a pinched expression. "That was Jarrett, of course. Hired to give Bertie a bad name in front of a pack of servants? Damn it all, what for?"

"Oh, I have some ideas about that." Mr. Wigmore sipped coffee. "There's more, however." He leaned forward. "The last visit was different from the others. In town just for the day, Madame Bernard did not expect the king; Giddings was certain of that. He himself let him in. 'Drunk, he was,' Giddings told Salt. 'Imagine, the king tight as a tic! He went at milady something awful!' It was Jarrett, as we know, and this time it wasn't the usual roaring that she must continue to let him have his way with her, but something about refusing to do what she wanted him to—something about a letter he had got possession of and about 'telling all'—just what Jack heard in the library. Naturally, Giddings didn't know what to make of it. Madame Bernard obviously was agitated, but she managed to calm the fellow. She got him into her drawing room. She made a single telephone call. You might expect it to have been to Czinner, but it wasn't. Twenty minutes later Giddings admitted a second man, who joined Madame Bernard and her supposedly royal guest behind those closed drawing-room doors. Can you guess who he was, this second visitor?" Mr. Wigmore smiled. "I find this quite the most interesting fact of all. It was—"

"Allow me, Mr. Wigmore," Mr. Bliss interrupted, raising a hand. "Herr Wilhelm Luscher, Bertie's latest companion?"

"How the devil—?" Mr. Wigmore stared.

"Right, am I? Willy to his friends—and, not coincidentally, an attaché with the German embassy. Does that suggest things to you, Mr. Wigmore? He and Madame Bernard managed to shut up Mr. Jarrett for a time, but twenty-four hours later it proved necessary to kill him. Czinner did the deed for them, but in doing so crippled his own usefulness; then the police were after him. So he, too, had to die."

"Did one of them . . . ?" Mr. Munns looked horrified.

"No, Herbert. They merely would have given the orders."

"How did you know?" Mr. Wigmore asked.

Mr. Bliss described his talks with Lord Rothschild and the Duchess of Devonshire.

"We both have been at work then! We've solved our mystery!"

"Thank heaven," Mr. Munns said, again rubbing his glasses. "Now we may give the infernal matter into the hands of the police."

Neither Mr. Bliss nor Mr. Wigmore spoke.

Replacing his glasses, Mr. Munns peered in dismay from

one to the other of them. "A German plot against His Majesty, the Frenchwoman somehow mixed in—surely we can't remain silent!"

Briefly eyeing Mr. Wigmore, who was all at once studying his boot toes, Mr. Bliss then lit his pipe. "Silent? Perhaps we must be, Herbert—for the time being at any rate. We believe we've uncovered some plot, but what real proof have we? Anything substantial? Oh, we can offer vague rumours from Paris; we can call upon the word of a drunken butler; we can subpoena a number of disreputable little street scamps; we can show some letters and bills from Seecombe Exporting—which, I must remind you, we stole—and there is a letter from Bertie to Lord Hardinge and two blue-glass eye lenses. It all adds up in our view: an elaborate and bizarre conspiracy. Don't mistake me, I think we're right. But we must carefully consider how our little theory may be taken by others. Shall we speak out against Madame Bernard and Herr Luscher? First ask yourself if we can prove that Seecombe Exporting was a mask for Baron Czinner's spy activities. Can we prove a connection between Czinner and Willy Luscher? Between Luscher and Madame Bernard? A German, an Austrian, and a twenty-year-old Frenchwoman conspiring against the king of England—who would believe it? Are you willing to confess to gimlet-eyed Nelson Faraday that you broke into a Jamaica Road office last night? You may be brave enough to face his strict sense of justice, Herbert, but for my part I'm reluctant to admit to him that I've withheld evidence which I took from a corpse. Willy Luscher is Bertie's great new companion, Madame Bernard the royal mistress. They have the king's ear, his confidence, and much more. Dare we accuse them? Of what? Of hiring Samuel Jarrett to impersonate His Majesty, when we don't yet know the why of it? It sounds a fantastical story, and we—an eccentric old man, a boy, a former bank clerk, an actor—would very likely be crucified for fools if we opened our mouths. The upshot would be that the German and Madame Bernard would be left free to carry out their plot—or to invent some new deviltry. No, gentlemen."

Mr. Bliss rose and put his back to the fire. "For the time being Bertie's police guard will discreetly keep watch on our suspects; Esher will see to it. For our part we must see this thing much farther before we speak our reasons into official ears."

"Put that way . . ." Mr. Munns conceded, though he did not look happy.

"And there's the book," Mr. Wigmore added.

Mr. Bliss was still holding it. "Quite. Caution must be our watchword. If we act precipitously we may put the wind up the agents listed here, inadvertently set up a general alarm, and destroy the value of this little volume. You've performed a great service to England in obtaining it, Mr. Wigmore. With your permission I should like to see that it falls into the proper hands in Whitehall—I have friends there who won't ask questions about how I came to have it, and with it they may play havoc with German spying activities."

"By all means," Mr. Wigmore said. "Good grief, I still don't understand how the Frenchwoman got dragged into this!"

Mr. Bliss tut-tutted. "Luscher is said to be powerfully attractive to women; he's glib, worldly—utterly ruthless, I imagine. Dedicated to his cause, devoted to the upstart emperor of the Germans, who would like nothing better than for the world to scrape to his nation. No doubt Luscher is ambitious too; he would use anyone, in any way, to gain his ends."

"He is . . . using Madame Bernard, then, sir?" I asked.

"I believe so, Jack. Tragic for the foolish young woman; she's bound to be hurt by it. Hmm. I wonder if there's any way to see the thing through without destroying her."

"And her husband?" Leaning forward to take another cake, Mr. Wigmore cocked a bright blue eye at Mr. Bliss.

"He's a mystery. Part of the plot? I should like to think not. Still . . ." The old man scratched his jaw with his pipe stem.

"Two murders already," Mr. Munns reminded softly.

Rain began to patter against the Curzon Street windows.

Mr. Bliss thumped his stick. "We must see there are no more—Bertie's, nor ours!"

Mr. Wigmore merely leaned back, hands behind his blond head. He smiled broadly. "I love a little danger!"

Pensively Mr. Bliss sent clouds of smoke toward the ceiling. "I'm convinced that Sandringham, November ninth, is where and when the end of all this is to come. Madame Bernard and Herr Wilhelm Luscher will be there; Czinner, but for his death, would have been too." He fixed his wrinkled yellowish eyes on each of us in turn. "We must be there as well! I intend to see to it!"

"Hurrah!" cried Mr. Wigmore.

Mr. Munns chewed his moustache ends.

"I, too, sir?" I asked.

"You have my word on it, lad!"

I was thrilled and wondered if it might be there that I should have some part in saving His Majesty.

II

*Enemies*

*Observed*

# Simon Bliss's Narrative

Three weeks remained until November the ninth and Bertie's grand birthday party at his country estate in Norfolk. The thing would last the weekend, stretching to four or five days for some, and sixty or seventy guests were likely to be present: royals, nobility, equerries, financiers, a rajah or two, a rich American, an actress—Bertie loved the theatre and had gone a long way toward making the profession respectable. Three weeks. My instincts—and our evidence—told me the king was safe for the time being, but we could take no chances; so the very afternoon following our second meeting at Curzon Street I telephoned Lord Esher for a third time in as many days. I came to the point at once: "Add Herr Wilhelm Luscher to your watch list, Reggie," I said.

Reginald Brett, Lord Esher, was a shrewd man. Presently a royal equerry, he had been offered important public political positions but preferred to act behind the scenes. He was very close to Bertie; he had a fine sense of the way the wind blew in the corridors of power, and he could be trusted. But I was stretching his goodwill.

"Blast, Simon, it will spread Superintendent Quinn's men very thin. Watch Luscher too? Affable Willy? Whyever for?"

"Just do it," I urged. "I'll explain soon as I can."

He consented. "Very well, but I do want explanations.

It's difficult, you know, keeping all this behind-the-scenes manoeuvring from His Majesty; he has a nose for foolery."

"It's not foolery. And he isn't to know a thing, not even to suspect. Above all, neither are Luscher and Madame Bernard."

"Mmm." There was a silence, during which I imagined his sharp mind sorting through meanings. "I'll see to it, of course; I've learned to trust you, Simon—don't let me down. As a matter of fact, it will be easier soon; the Londesborough party is dispersing, most coming to London for some days before the big bash at Sandringham. His Majesty and Willy and Sophie will be going their separate ways for a time."

"Good," I said, somewhat relieved.

After a few more words we rang off.

There was one more call to make: "Hello, Lottie?" I reached the Duchess of Devonshire at her London house.

"Shame on you, Simon!" her rasping voice reproved. "You've interrupted me at bridge. You want something, of course."

"Something important, Lottie," I confessed.

"Well, well, out with it! I'm missing the greatest excitement!"

I had to laugh. "A thrilling rubber?"

"Certainly not! Gossip! We are doing for Lady Primrose, and I want to be in on the kill!" I heard the pearls rattle at her throat as she chortled.

I explained that I wanted an invitation to Bertie's birthday party. Could she get me one?

"Quite impossible!"

"Lottie! Queen of society? You can manage anything."

She sniffed. "Shameless flattery, Simon. But I won't do it."

"Can't, you mean?"

"Oh, you're very clever. Really, I must get back to my game."

"I'm playing no game; this is no whim. It's dreadfully important. Please? For an old friend? Only you can do it."

She hesitated. "Oh, very well, I shall see. Perhaps I can manage it through Alice Keppel; she owes me several favors. I hope you appreciate that I'm spending them on you; they're precious coin! Mmm, yes, Alice will be the one—she still has a great deal of influence with Bertie." Another chortling laugh. "No one is so close a friend of his as a former mistress."

"He must have a great many close friends, then."

"Ha, none so close as Alice Keppel! She may win him back." Slyly, "However, he continues to make a fool of himself over the Bernard woman, you know."

"Does he?"

"Yes. Have you pondered that bit of gossip I told you about her and her ... *friend* in Paris?"

"I've thought about it. I appreciate all you've done and shall do for me, Lottie."

"Oh, you're a wriggling fish. But I have you in my net. Have tea with me Wednesday—you owe me that."

"Surely," I agreed.

We rang off—she to return to trading in reputations, I to hoping her efforts on my behalf would prove fruitful.

That Wednesday, over tea, Lottie gave me her answer, making me squirm for it, smiling her thin, mandarin smile through which hints of her former beauty still showed. "Success, Simon. You shall be at Sandringham," she announced. "The king even looks forward to seeing you. Aren't you proud of me? Aren't you pleased with yourself?"

I was more pleased—and relieved—than I could tell her.

Stays creaking, eyes wickedly bright, she leaned forward to tap my arm. "Won't it be amusing, all of us there together—you, me, Willy, Sophie, and His Majesty? No pity that oily Baron Czinner will be absent, however! Wasn't it ghastly news about his death?"

"Ghastly," I repeated. The press had been full of the story, dwelling on grisly details—Rose Mappin had identified the body; the head and arms had not been found. Of course, there was nothing about Frederick Wigmore having brought her to the morgue; Rose had agreed to remain silent about that. Nothing about Czinner's numerous aliases apart from "Brown" either.

"Who killed him, Simon?" Lottie asked, watching me sharply.

"I can't say."

Leaving her house some time later, wrapped in greatcoat and scarf, I walked under ice-gray skies part way to my club, the poor Diogenes, which had been further shaken by Czinner's awful murder. Tapping along the pavement, I tried to ignore the sharp cold that once would have invigorated me. I felt grimly satisfied. My invitation to Sandringham was assured; Jack would come along as my valet. But now I must see to Frederick Wigmore and my nephew. I thought I knew how to manage that and, hailing a cab, thanked the stars for old friendships. Frederick Ponsonby, another royal equerry, was next on my list.

Ponsonby—Fritz—was Bertie's assistant secretary, second only to the redoubtable Sir Francis Knollys. I knew Fritz would be in town to prepare for the king's sojourn before he went to Sandringham, so I telephoned direct to Buckingham Palace.

"Simon!" he said when I had finally, with much difficulty, convinced intermediaries to give me a line through to him. "I've been directed to add your name to the guest list. Are you storming the citadel of royal favor at last?" His voice was breezy; he sounded pleased to hear from me.

"Briefly. For one weekend at least. Are there to be theatricals, Fritz?"

He chuckled. "Afraid the guests won't be enough to amuse you?"

"I'm speaking of the official entertainment."

"Oh, there's always plenty of that. You know His Majesty is bored if there's the least lull in the proceedings. Yes, a play is to be performed."

"Ah, I had hoped so. Will you lunch with me tomorrow? I want to discuss certain matters. Kettner's? At one?"

At the popular rendezvous on Greek Street, Ponsonby frowned, fidgeted, and hedged while he consumed *faisan rôti* and a light savory—I had a little consommé and ignored my filet of sole—but at last he agreed to the alteration in the play which I urged upon him, though obviously it puzzled him. He leaned back, smoked a cigarette, and regarded me. "I don't quite understand, Simon. However, the substitution isn't difficult, and I'll arrange it as you ask; a word with His Majesty should do it. Mr. Frederick Wigmore is to have the part of Hardcastle, correct? Hmm. The young actor's made a bit of a name for himself in comic roles—I've seen him once or twice; very amusing. The king should be pleased. And you—you've become a patron of the arts, have you? And Wigmore's your protégé?"

I gestured dismissingly. "As you wish."

He sighed, eyes twinkling. "No, as usual, as *you* wish, Simon."

Our conversation turned to political matters. "How are the king and his nephew getting along?" I asked cautiously.

"The German Kaiser? You very well know His Majesty's opinion of him; that hasn't changed. Wilhelm continues to grate on every occasion—he's the rusty hinge of Europe! I share His Majesty's view; between you and me, Simon, he's a fanatic, growing more dangerous by the day. That's off the record, of course. Neither the king nor anyone near him would publicly say so; we want to preserve some chance for peace."

"Serious you think things are?"

"They may be. The military build-up ... " Reflecting on the visits he had made with Bertie to Berlin, Ponsonby lost all his good humour. "The atmosphere there is oppressive—all spiked helmets, heel clicking, and truculent stupidity. No finesse. The Germans are best at iron-glove diplomacy—and iron-glove wit; that's for sure. Wilhelm is surrounded by England-haters—the Generals von Scholl and von Kessel. Von Bülow's no better. But Count Eulenberg, the closest friend, marshal of the emperor's household, is the worst—a fat, effeminate, leering fellow. I can tell you, Simon, it was all I could do to keep from running whenever he came near."

Fritz's sunny disposition and sense of proportion never deserted him for long, and I left him cheerful enough, he assuring me again that he would do as I asked. But I felt gloomy and spent the rest of the afternoon in my room at the Diogenes Club communing with Apollo. Things were arranged for Sandringham, and the king's private police guard were on the watch, Esher alerted; we had done what we could. But I was uneasy. Puffing my pipe, in the curling smoke I pictured Bertie, the stout, white-bearded, snappish old monarch who had developed perhaps too great a fondness for personal pleasure from being for years kept, by his stubborn mama, Victoria, from his ambition of serving his country. This prohibition was his tragedy, yet, since becoming king, he had done well, proving England's finest diplomat. He had single-handedly won France to our side in 1903—the Kaiser would never forgive him that—and just this year another alliance had been confirmed by the signing of the Anglo-Russian treaty. Bertie had had a hand in that too; the Kaiser must be seething!

The question in my mind was: did Wilhelm II, emperor of Germany, have a hand in the plot to discredit his uncle?

No sure answer to that. I had met the emperor once, in the days when I had been, however peripherally, a part of Bertie's circle. I had found Wilhelm intelligent—and boorish. Even then I had feared what his dreams of military glory might lead to. He had a sleek, handsome face; high cheekbones; eyes that glittered, demanding admiration and laughter at his jokes. They were insecure eyes, and I had pitied him; but I could not pity him now. He had black hair and a black moustache waxed up at the ends into arrogant spikes—an absurd thing. He was not to be laughed at, however. He admired his uncle, envied him, hated him. Whether or not he were privy to the plot, he most certainly would enjoy seeing Uncle Bertie—and England—humiliated.

Days passed. The autumn weather was unexpectedly mild, with crisp, clear skies. Delighted at my news of his role at Sandringham, Frederick Wigmore began to work up his part. The play was *She Stoops to Conquer*, and it was to be performed, as theatricals were at the Norfolk estate, on an improvised stage in the ballroom. It would be done the night before Bertie's birthday.

Mr. Wigmore invited my nephew and me to his rooms one afternoon to see his make-up; it was an astonishing job. The actor could not be more than twenty-eight, slender and handsome, but he emerged from his bedroom the very image of fat, balding, plethoric old Squire Hardcastle. He acted the part convincingly, too, for ten minutes, obviously enjoying every bit of it, thwacking chair legs with his stick as he clumped about railing against city ways.

"Amazing!" I had to say.

Pleased, the young actor beamed through his make-up. "You think it will answer?"

"Perfectly." I had news to give him; we had received an unexpected bonus from Ponsonby's efforts: Bertie remembered meeting Frederick Wigmore, had often chortled at his antics on stage since then, and, knowing he would be at Sandringham for the play, had invited him as a guest.

"Splendid!" Mr. Wigmore exclaimed.

We decided then and there that Herbert was to go as his manservant.

One problem remained. We believed something disastrous was planned for the party—but what? And how were we to prevent it?

# ❦Frederick Wigmore's Narrative❦

## I

"Hurry, Herbert!" I pounded on Herbert Munns's door. "You will miss your chance!"

It was Sunday, the twenty-fourth of October. In two weeks King Edward would celebrate his sixty-fifth birthday, and we must see he did it safely.

"Herbert!"

In his dressing gown my friend opened the door, his moustache prickly in disarray and his thinning brown hair seeming to fly about his ears. "I can sleep through church bells but not through your infernal pounding, Wiggins." He frowned and rubbed his gray-brown eyes, whose pouches were emphasized by sleep. "What time is it?"

"Eleven. Time to see Madame Sophie Bernard."

He blinked. "What . . . how . . . ?"

He was ordinarily slow, and far too meticulous for my taste, but this morning, when I told him Salt was waiting near Rotten Row with a victoria, he dressed in ten minutes. Shortly we were strolling along Baker Street beneath a pale blue sky, birds twittering in the trees at Portman Square.

As we went I explained, "I want to get a look at our enemy; I want to take her measure. She's riding this morning in Hyde Park."

"And how do you know that?"

"Salt. He's been watching her house. As you know, she and Monsieur Bernard arrived in town yesterday. Salt saw her groom readying her equipage, sauntered over, and chatted the fellow up. 'A black-eyed, tight-lipped bloke!' he described him, but he managed to worm out of him that his mistress would be in Rotten Row at noon. I thought you'd want to join me."

"Oh, I do."

We hurried along. It was splendid weather, crisp and invigorating. I was pleased to be going up to Sandringham as a guest of His Majesty: we would do for Luscher, Madame Bernard, and their plot! In the meantime, I was working up Hardcastle; I wanted my performance perfect for the king.

We turned right at Oxford Street and were soon at Marble Arch. We leapt across the thoroughfare, among jingling carriages and tooting motorcars. There, waiting on the corner, was a trim victoria, its calash top folded back. On the driver's seat: dependable Salt, wearing handsome dark-blue livery—somewhat baggy on his wiry frame—and a gleaming top hat, with red and green feathers in its band, that sat wobbling on his ears. A chestnut mare stood in the traces.

Salt touched his folded whip to his hat. "Mornin', guv'nors. Is their lordships ready for a ride in the park?" His face split in a grin. " 'Andsome rig, ain't it? Sorry about the liv'ry, Wiggins—best I could do on short notice."

"It will do splendidly!" I climbed up, Herbert following. "Wherever did you get it?"

"Oh, Lord Glendinning's driver lent it to me. The master don't know a thing! It must be back by four."

"Plenty of time. Good work! Now let's be off."

Salt flicked his whip, and we moved along tree-lined Park Lane, the imposing townhouses of this fashionable street gliding by to our left, the grassy swards of Hyde Park to our right. Near twelve we were at Hyde Park Corner and, when the noontime euphony of churchbells began to peal across the city, were rolling under the bright autumn leaves overhanging Rotten Row.

I leaned forward. "Madame Bernard's carriage?"

"A black brougham," Salt informed. "Never fear, I'll call out when I sees it."

I settled back. Sunlight flickered through russet leaves. Rails separated the road from the footpath, from which strollers gazed at me and Herbert, no doubt mistaking us for titled gentlemen leisurely enjoying the Sunday. I smiled kindly upon these mortals and thoroughly enjoyed my role of Lord Wigmore.

"You look a bit jumpy, Herbert," I commented. He was fumbling to light a Rajah.

"I am. After all, to see Madame Bernard, a murderess . . ."

"A beautiful young woman, that's all we really may be certain of. Your uncle speculated that Luscher is using her; I'm inclined to agree. Czinner's murder? The German will have given the order; Madame Bernard may have known nothing about it until after the fact."

Puffing his cigar, Herbert looked skeptical. "It's what I would like to believe, too, Wiggins, but . . . well . . . what about her husband? If only we knew his part in it."

"Mmm, yes—no part at all or a significant one? Ah well, we'll resolve it somehow. What ho, Salt, is that it?"

"Righto, Wiggins!" He gestured with his whip.

I peered ahead, along the wide, tanbarked way. In the season it would have been difficult to pick one conveyance out of the throng, but now, with so few vehicles on the path, I spotted the black brougham at once. Why had Madame Bernard chosen to ride in a closed carriage on this beautiful day? For privacy? So as not to advertise her beauty?

Herbert fidgeted, adjusting his topper and poking at his glasses. I was excited too—thrilled—but tried not to show it, leaning back and draping an arm nonchalantly over the seat back. We could not see the Frenchwoman, of course; we must glimpse her as we passed. We readied ourselves—even Salt, who pulled himself up in his outsized livery. The brougham drew near, its two horses smartly handled by a rather fierce-looking fellow, the driver Salt had spoken to in Norfolk Street. Salt kept his head down, his hat brim low. Then the brougham was next to us on my side, passing. Herbert craned his neck, leaning hard against me and staring roundly. I muttered in disgust as I glanced into Sophie Bernard's carriage window. I felt great disappointment. The brougham was gone in an instant, I with the merest impression of lavender tulle, a pale face, auburn hair; I had hardly seen her at all!

"Damn and blast!"

"I didn't see a thing!" Herbert exclaimed.

"Not for want of trying. If you'd pushed me any harder, I'd have landed in her lap. I'm determined not to waste the day! Salt, turn around."

"Right you are!" He wheeled the victoria about. Within moments we were just behind the brougham.

"Ease alongside her now."

Salt did so and held us not five feet from her carriage. But it was no good. The woman was sitting back in the shadowed interior, and I could not have glimpsed her unless Salt had pulled forward and I had turned 'round to stare, a much too obvious move.

I decided on drastic means; I leaned forward and whispered the order.

It was loud enough for Herbert to hear. "Wiggins, are you mad?"

Salt was well-enough pleased to do it. "If you'll pay for any damages to milord's carriage," he said. "Don't want to get my driver chum in hot water."

"I'll pay, of course."

Salt's lips curled. "'Appy to oblige, then!" And, flicking our mare's flank with his whip, jerking the reins to the left, he jolted our victoria into Sophie Bernard's brougham.

I had not meant for him to strike her so hard. There was a crash and an awful scraping sound as metal-rimmed wheels met. Herbert bit on his cigar, his hat flew off, and his hands leapt to his nose to save his glasses. For my part I lurched into Salt, nearly knocking him from his perch. I fell back, out of breath.

What had we done?

Madame Bernard's driver cursed, and I glimpsed a tight, black, thundercloud look as he pulled on his reins. Red-faced, he drew to a halt by the rail so other carriages could pass. Salt manoeuvred our victoria to the side of the path just ahead.

There were no pedestrians about; no one had noticed our

collision. I was perfectly happy not to have drawn a crowd. Herbert had retrieved his topper from the carriage floor and was dusting it with sharp little flicking motions. "Extremely foolish, Wiggins! Extremely!"

"Bloody fool!" Madame Bernard's driver exclaimed. Glancing back, I saw him leap from his perch and stride toward us.

I got down quickly. "Stay where you are, Salt, old fellow. We don't want him to get too close a look at you." Turning to face the burly driver, I raised my voice—and an admonitory finger, which I shook under his nose. "You, my good man, are the fool! Can't you see where you're going? You'd best not have scratched my carriage!" I bent to examine the black paint; fortunately, only our wheel rims had clashed and, aside from a few scratches, which, likely, Lord Glendinning would never notice, there wasn't a mark. I stared again at the driver; he was enormous—broad-shouldered with great working hands. "Lucky for you, my man; I'd have had you dismissed if there were any damage!" I sniffed his breath. "Have you been drinking?"

His jaw dropped.

"You *have* been drinking! I shall speak to your mistress!"

And, sidestepping before he could get those great hands on me, which the look in his snapping eyes plainly told me he was about to do, I was in an instant at Madame Sophie Bernard's brougham door. Footfalls crunched ominously behind me in the tan, but I hardly heard them. I was staring into the carriage at a remarkable face framed by a plush red-leather seat. John Singer Sargent had tried, but he had not done her justice. She leaned toward me. One small, white hand rested on the door, and the scent of Chypre struck me like a warm breath. All at once I was dizzy with perfume and beauty.

2

Sophie Bernard wore an embroidered mauve blouse, green jacket, and green velvet skirt. Over her shoulders was a Limerick lace scarf; at her neck a white-lace collarette, below which, under still more lace at the top of her blouse, were delicate collarbones and the deep hollow of her throat. Her auburn hair was upswept as it had been in Sargent's portrait, but showed, even in the dimness of the carriage, subtle lights which the artist had failed to capture. Perched on her hair was a little curve-brimmed hat decorated with osprey plumes. What I saw of her figure was fine and rounded. Her face was enchanting—perfectly oval, fine-boned, with a soft blush on the cheeks; her complexion, onyx-white; her nose, small but remarkably strong; her mouth, small also but with a delightfully plump lower lip that trembled as she gazed—with distinct displeasure—out of faintly exotic sea-green eyes.

Clumsily I doffed my hat, and I smiled, foolishly I'm sure. My mouth moved, unable to utter what I wished—that she was a vision and that I waited on her command.

"*Fou!*" she exclaimed.

It somewhat broke the spell. I was indeed beginning to think myself a fool.

Madame Bernard's driver was still pawing the earth behind me.

She seemed to look through me. "Well, Monsieur Rance?"

"Yes, ma'am!" He leapt for the door handle and bowed, flushing, as she stepped down, pert as a pigeon—a pigeon with ruffled feathers. Mr. Rance looked half-smitten with her; me he shot a black look.

Carrying a green parasol, Madame Bernard planted its tip firmly in the tan as she thoroughly examined the brougham. I thanked my luck it was unmarked.

"And now, Monsieur," she pulled her diminutive self up and fixed those disconcerting green eyes upon mine, "why did you deliberately run into me?"

Her voice was soft, piquant with a French accent. I wished her words to be sweet rather than angry.

"But I didn't, ma'am," I protested, gesturing helplessly. "An unfortunate accident—"

She struck the earth with her parasol. "*Ne mentez pas!* Your driver lashed his beast, flicked the reins. Why?"

"He never would deliberately do such a thing."

Her eyes narrowed; she raised her parasol, and it began to hum in furious circles over her shoulder. "You followed me, Monsieur!"

"But—"

The eyes flashed. "You will dare to say I am mistaken?"

136

"No, Madame Bernard, but—"

"Aha!" She looked triumphant. "How do you know my name?" She thrust out her chin. "Who are you?"

I had trapped myself nicely. Glancing back, I saw Salt and Herbert watching from the brougham with very little pity. Obviously Madame Bernard had seen us pass the first time and knew we had turned 'round. I took a deep breath; there was nothing for it but to brazen it out. In spite of her anger, I found I liked this young woman—for more than her beauty. She was sharp-eyed, and she had spirit. I did not like to think her Luscher's pawn. I bowed my head in defeat, as I did so noting that a small, closed carriage had drawn up behind the brougham.

"As you wish, Madame. My name is Frederick Wigmore, and I would be an ignorant and unfortunate man if I didn't know your name or your reputation as one of the most beautiful women in France. I've seen your photograph often in the illustrated papers. I made a special pilgrimage to view your portrait at Carlyle's. Allow me to say," I flashed my most charming smile, "that Mr. Sargent did not do you justice."

She softened only momentarily. She was used to admiration, flattery—from the king of England himself. I seemed only to have fed her anger.

"A pilgrimage? Does a pilgrim rudely strike his idol? Does he then lie to her?"

I was in a dreadful state. My face felt hot as a stove. I stammered, "I . . . I . . . ." My hands clutched my hat brim as if it were the only fixed object in a storm. (I ended by ruining a perfectly fine topper.) Either Madame Bernard was a passionate woman easily set off, or something more than my carriage's running into hers had put her into her state. Which? Childishly, she stamped her pretty foot, and I saw how young she was, barely half a dozen years older than Jack Merridew. She was His Majesty's mistress; she was likely, too, a pawn in a German plot. Was it all proving too much for her?

Disconcerted as I was, I pitied her; I wanted to comfort her. "Madame Bernard," I began, stretching out my arm, with no idea what I meant to say or do.

I was saved from deciding, from making an even greater

fool of myself perhaps—Sophie Bernard *was* dangerous; she stole a man's judgement—by a rough hand on my shoulder spinning me about. I found myself staring into a pale, livid face that seemed touched with madness.

"What, Monsieur, have you done to my wife?"

A fist was raised to strike me.

### 3

It was Monsieur Armand Bernard—tall, dignified, and in a fighting pose; I recognized him at once. I concluded it must have been his carriage which had drawn up behind the brougham.

"Monsieur," I breathed, aghast.

Fist still raised, he stared, seeming hardly to recognize me. He knew me, though, and I him.

Monsieur Armand Bernard's money came from winemaking; he owned great vineyards, inherited from his father and grandfather, in Burgundy. He was a sensitive man, a connoisseur. So far as I knew, he loved and admired England. He especially liked our theatre and, seeing me on the stage, had made my acquaintance; we had more than once discussed plays and acting over sherry at the Siddons Club. I liked him, though he seemed almost in his way a child, inexperienced in the world, too trusting. He was forty-five, his wife the first feminine passion of his life; I had not seen him since he brought her to London. Ordinarily he spent only a few weeks at a time, among friends, at galleries, taking in the latest plays; he had been here six months this visit. Why? For the social round? Because Sophie glittered here? Because, noblesse oblige, Teddy couldn't do without his mistress? Knowing his gentle nature, I was astonished to see him in this belligerent stance. I was embarrassed too; I believe I would have let him strike me if he liked.

He faltered, blinked. "Monsieur Wigmore? Is it you? Oh, but I am very sorry. *Je regrette* ..." His usual precise, almost sweet tone was cracked, like fine porcelain shattered by a blow.

"Quite all right," I managed, flustered too.

Only then did he lower his fist. "You must forgive me. I cannot imagine *you* ..." His expression was chagrined—but touched with suspicion, an emotion I had never expected to see on his trusting face. He was much changed, still with finely bred features—strong bones, the jaw a trifle long, fine mouth, a trim moustache, dark hair touched with distinguished gray, perhaps a bit more gray than I remembered —but something inside him had gone awry, making him look haggard and pale, causing his slender fingers, used to caressing objets d'art, to twitch at his sides. His gray eyes were set in gaunt, sleepless hollows. Even his skin seemed gray.

"Well, Frederick, what has happened?" There was a nervous edge to his voice.

I did not know how to answer. Had the Frenchman been pursuing his wife? Had he seen our victoria wheel about? Had he seen Salt's manoeuvre?

Madame Bernard saved me. Still twirling her parasol, she came between us. "So you know Monsieur Wigmore, Armand? That is enough for me." Her head barely reached her husband's shoulder; he regarded her sombrely. "*Un accident*," she said. "*Cela n'a aucune espèce d'importance*—our carriages collided, nothing more. Monsieur Wigmore has apologized; it is enough. I am not hurt. Let him alone." She half smiled at me, showing a hint of pink tongue between her white teeth. That smile alone might be worth the world! Monsieur Bernard did not fare so well. "You were following me again!" she accused, her parasol beginning to hum. "Weren't you following me, Armand?"

The Frenchman merely smiled sadly, as if a regrettable scene with which he was all too familiar must be played again. "A husband must look after his wife, *chère* Sophie." He attempted to take her arm, but she pulled away.

"Not by following her! I will go about on my own, Armand; I will not be pursued. This foolish jealousy must stop!"

"Ah!" It was the plaintive cry of a wounded man. "Foolish . . . ?"

It was Madame Bernard's turn to blush. "We will not discuss this in front of Monsieur Wigmore. I wish to go." She glanced ahead, along the wide expanse of Rotten Row, at the silhouette of a rider, far distant, half hidden by a chestnut tree, beneath which his horse nibbled grass. The rider sat tall and straight and seemed to be looking our way.

Her husband followed her gaze. I saw him shudder. "Sophie . . . ?"

"No, Armand! I shall go now. Good day, Monsieur Wigmore." The smile again—heart-stopping; a little frightened too? "Perhaps we may meet again under pleasanter circumstances. For now, *adieu.*"

Scraping, Rance hastened to open her door. Briskly she vanished into her carriage.

"I shall follow you to Norfolk Street?" Monsieur Bernard called.

"*Comme tu le veux,*" came her indifferent voice as her carriage moved off.

Gazing after his wife, Monsieur Bernard seemed to be watching some tormenting scene.

I felt very sorry for him. "Pity I met Madame in such an unfortunate way," I said awkwardly. "She's . . . very beautiful."

"Ha!" He turned a ghastly smile upon me, and ironic little barks of laughter tumbled from his lips. His eyes were wild. "Ha, I am a lucky man, *n'est-ce pas?* Ha ha!" Tipping his hat, without another word he wheeled and stalked to his carriage.

Pondering briefly, feeling shaken, I watched him climb in. Then, before his carriage could pull away, I dashed for the victoria. "Salt! Quickly! Fall in behind the Frenchwoman's brougham!"

Herbert groaned.

"You barely got out o' that with yer skin!" Salt commented as he pulled away smartly. He caught up with the brougham.

"We've done what we intended. More," Herbert said, tight-lipped, gripping his hat brim. "Let's return to Baker Street."

"Not yet." I was peering ahead. "Who *is* that fellow on the horse?"

The man who had grazed his mount by the chestnut tree was still far distant but had pulled his mare from the shadows and was trotting toward us, riding easily—fine form!— tall and slim in his saddle. As he got nearer I made out a trim, dark riding coat, Wellington boots, and a short, natty topper.

Herbert was nervously chewing his moustache ends. "I noticed him too. He was watching everything."

" 'E was indeed!" Salt said over his shoulder.

"And Madame Bernard was watching him," I added. "I think we may guess . . . Now, Salt, old fellow! Pull to the right as far as you can!"

"No more accidents!" Herbert cried.

Salt did as ordered, expertly. Glancing back, I noted Monsieur Bernard's carriage behind us. I gripped Herbert's arm and leaned close. "Never fear, I've learned my lesson. I only want a better view, of both the approaching gentleman and Madame Bernard. Ah, as I expected, she is at the right-hand side of her coach, the side the fellow will pass on. See, you can just catch a glimpse of auburn where she leans toward the window. Magnificent hair, isn't it? No, no, don't crane your neck so obviously! And . . . there . . . the horseman is near . . . he's passed her. Did you see his smug look? The white flash of her hand as she signalled?"

"Then he is—" Herbert croaked.

"Indeed. Herr Wilhelm Luscher, the partner in crime! Herbert, you simply must seem not to notice him as he passes!"

Putting on a bored expression, I followed my own advice, pretending to be oblivious of the young German prancing by our victoria. In truth, through narrowed lids, I took in every detail: handsome face, I had to confess it; blue eyes—did they briefly stray to me?—full, blond moustache; red lips; and a strong, squarish jaw, too blasted pugnacious for my taste. He wore a superbly tailored riding outfit and had a masterly way with his mount. Poor Sophie Bernard! I took an intense dislike to Willy Luscher's thin, supercilious smile.

When Luscher had passed, I risked another glance backward. Monsieur Bernard's drawn features were just visible in the right-hand window of his carriage, darting a glare of seething hatred toward the German.

Unconscious of the look, or ignoring it, Willy Luscher spurred his horse toward the Serpentine.

"Did you see that, Wiggins?" Herbert had glanced back also.

"I did indeed. The German is playing a dangerous game—dangerous for himself as for anyone. Well, well, he and Madame Bernard had an assignation here today; that's clear. Moreover, unless he's a very good actor, the poor doubly cuckolded husband is no part of their plot. I pity him, Herbert!"

"He looked like murder."

"Really, old fellow, your choice of language!"

" 'Ome, Wiggins?"

"Oh, you may take your time, Salt." I leaned back. "I want to think about this . . ."

# ❧Herbert Munns's Narrative❧

### I

I was up early on the Monday after Wiggins took such chances in Rotten Row—this time not because I could not sleep, but because I had work to do: I was to follow the German, Herr Luscher, while he was in London. Uncle and Wiggins had concurred at a council of war in Curzon Street Sunday evening. "You're the man for it, Herbert!" Wiggins had insisted. "Quite," Uncle had agreed, thumping his stick, his yellowish old eyes showing new pride in me.

I had merely bowed my head. "Any way I may help . . ."

I was content to do the job—rather pleased to be chosen, in fact. I had traced "Brown" to his aliases of "Seecombe," etc., to the truth of his being Baron Sigmund Czinner. I had done well in that and similar work. Wiggins had been right: my nondescript appearance was an advantage. I rarely was noticed and, if I were, was discounted. I could see it in people's eyes—this fellow is harmless; he doesn't exist. It was what had made me feel wretched, useless, a mere integer, at Cox's Bank. Now I had found my niche, however, and, though on the surface I may have appeared a mere lump of coal, inside I smouldered, I glowed. No one knew except

Wiggins, Uncle, Jack, Mr. Salt—no matter. I knew too: I was helping to save the king.

I dressed in my brown tweed suit, cream-colored waist-coat, tan four-in-hand—ordinary city clothes. We guessed Herr Luscher would remain in London until the party at Sandringham. The king was here, and so was Madame Bernard; too, Luscher had work at the German embassy. He was staying at the York Hotel in Oxford Street; from now on that would be my "lurk." (Associating with Wiggins was making me quite adept at criminal argot.) My face behind a newspaper, I would lounge in the York's lobby, one eye on the lift and the other on the stairs; I would note where Herr Wilhelm Luscher went. His Majesty's personal police guard could keep an eye on the German only when he was at the same country house as the king; therefore I alone had the present responsibility of watching Luscher, and I thought it just that he, who consorted with spies, should be spied on himself.

It was barely 6:00 A.M. I was about to ring Mrs. Cannon for a bit of breakfast when a familiar peremptory knock sounded. I guessed who it must be and beat Salt to the front door.

"Good morning, Billy," I said, as Billy Gully, scruffy and odd-looking as ever, sauntered in with his cocksparrow walk.

"Ungh." He glared at me suspiciously as ever. "Mornin', Mr. Munns." Without another word he stomped up the stairs.

Having some moments before I must leave, I followed the lad. When Wiggins himself opened, it was both Billy and I whom he greeted.

"Gentlemen!" The actor was in his caftan, his blond hair tousled. Though he obviously had just got up, his blue eyes were bright. "Come in, do!"

We entered. Scraping his feet and twitching his shoulders, clearly disliking to speak in front of me, Billy nonetheless got to the point soon enough: "We've traced the Jarrett bloke, Wiggins."

"Splendid news!" Wiggins dropped into his armchair by the fireplace and crossed his legs. "Tell us all about it."

It was very like what we had expected. Samuel Jarrett had

been an actor, of a cheap, tawdry sort—yet with a talent for mimicry. He had played the provinces mostly—travelling repertory groups, music halls, even carnivals; that was why Wiggins, who well knew London's theatrical scene, had not heard of him. " 'Is specialty were an act in which 'e did the king," Billy told us, "if that 'elps any."

Wiggins and I exchanged a glance. Billy and his boys had never been told about the blue-glass eye lenses.

"It may be significant; we shall see," was all Wiggins said. "You've done well, Billy. Your reward—" From his caftan pocket he pulled a roll of one-pound notes. Billy watched sharply as he counted exactly eighty into the smudged palm. "Ten each to you and Spiker; five apiece for the rest of the boys. Tell them I'm pleased, Billy, and to stand by. Be off now."

Stuffing the money into his shirt, Billy saluted smartly. "Right, Wiggins!" he said and scampered out the door.

"Very generous," I said skeptically when he was gone, "but how long will five pounds last those poor, dirty boys?"

Wiggins looked dismayed. "I hope you think better of me than that, Herbert! I see they have a roof over their heads, warm beds, plenty of food. You should watch them eat! Did any look starved to you? I insist they learn to read and to cipher, too, though they'd much rather do detective work. I take good care of them in a sort of dormitory house kept for me by a kindly old couple. Not all my fees go to fancy clothes and a motorcar! You would approve, I think; you must come by some day and have supper with us 'round the big trestle table, all the boys there and Mr. and Mrs. Settles too. Plain, hearty English fare and the boys digging in—a fine sight! Now," he clapped his hands on his knees and leapt up, "I'll convey the latest to your uncle. Billy's news explains a great deal. Likely Czinner got the idea for the impersonation by chance, from seeing Jarrett mimic Teddy on the stage; that was how it all began. As for how it may end . . ." Briskly he rubbed his hands. "Well, I find I'm very anxious to finish Willy Luscher at Sandringham. Perhaps we may prepare a few surprises for him, eh? Ones he may not like?" Taking my elbow, he led me to the door. "Get along now, Herbert. The York Hotel's your lurk . . ."

144

It was, indeed, my lurk for the next dozen days. Wilhelm Luscher's habits proved precise. He was punctual as a metronome, coming down at ten to be off to his embassy in Northumberland Street, where he remained until one each day, after which he would take luncheon or tea at some Mayfair establishment—never Madame Bernard's, however; the conspirators must have decided, due to her husband's watchful, mad jealousy, that their meeting was unwise. Herr Luscher was a precise, genial-seeming young fellow. He walked briskly; he was always polite, ever smiling. His only vice seemed to be a bulldog pipe, which I often saw him smoking. Ladies' eyes followed his figure, in dark-blue frock coat; gentlemen nodded and seemed to like him. He was pleasant to the hotel staff. Could any man really be sunny as he always seemed? I took great care to keep my *Times* up when he passed in the plush lobby, before I followed at a discreet distance. I did not think he had paid the least notice to me in Rotten Row, but I wanted to take no chances; there was something about his pinpoint blue eyes, something clear and hobnail sharp, at odds with his constant, affable smile. His eyes were rarely at rest; they roved, they evaluated, they seemed at times, when he believed no one was watching, to sneer. They could seem lazy, at ease, like trout in a shoal; then, at sight of a fly—some word, some revealing gesture— they would dart . . .

Had I not known the man was a plotter, I might have been taken in; privy to the truth, I grew less and less to trust his bright surface, felt more and more alarmed. He was much too good at his game—Uncle had been right! We had nothing definite on Herr Luscher, and, should we accuse him, it undoubtedly would be we, rather than the German, who would be disgraced; the fellow would dance free with a smile and would then do as he pleased, for England's harm. He had taken in everyone—except us. I kept close watch.

Only once did anything untoward occur. Luscher had a manservant, a great hulking fellow with a low-slung jaw, a squarish block of a head sunk in broad shoulders, and the arms and hands of an ape—a giant of a man who seemed more a pet than a servant; like a dog, he showed a fierce, dumb loyalty to his master. Herr Bünz he was called—no first name that I could discover. People might smile at Willy; they looked at Bünz in horror. He slept in the room next to the German's in the York Hotel; he came downstairs with Luscher, went in hansoms with him, and waited outside like a black shadow while his master lunched with Lady This or Lord That. And when Willy went about in the city, strolling with an ivory stick, Herr Bünz was always there, looking too big for his gray suit, his enormous head jammed in a billy-cock hat which he wore straight as a board across his brow. His piggy eyes were mean as a boar's. He never walked with Willy, but several paces ahead of him, or several behind, sometimes as much as a block—a scout breaking trail, a mutt following a spoor. Herr Bünz did not make my task easy. I did not credit him with much intelligence, but he had an instinct, and more than once I had to jump to keep those slit-eyes from catching sight of me. Would he report to his master that a suspicious stranger was following? Or—I shuddered to think it—would he take matters into his own huge hands? I guessed it had been Bünz who had separated Baron Czinner from his head.

One day less than a week before we were to travel to San-dringham—a chill, gray day with bleak November fogs then seeping in—I was careless. It was past four in the afternoon, and Herr Luscher was strolling 'round the great wheel of Piccadilly, heading for tea with Count Hatzfeldt at the Cafe Royale. Bünz was nowhere in sight. The skies were lowering, the light very dim. Every vehicle wore lit lamps, yellow cat's eyes. One could hear the clip-clop and jingle of horses, the putt-putt of motors, but one could barely make out the vehicles. Pedestrians loomed, then were gone, like spirits; London might have been Limbo. I had been trailing Willy Luscher for half an hour; I was chilled to the bone; I cared nothing for whether Bünz were about or no—I only wanted my quarry, whom I must follow very closely due to the fog, to turn into some warm place so I could melt the chill from my limbs.

Near the intersection of Jermyn Street a hand shot from a gray drift of fog. Then narrowed eyes, which seemed to my startled soul like those of Satan himself, were inches from my nose. A quite unsatanic breath, stinking of garlic sausage

146

and beer, hotly struck my face. "*Ihr Name?* Who are you?" came a guttural growl. It was Bünz, staring truculently from under his billycock hat.

I could not utter a word. My heart was pounding. My arm ached from his grip. My first thought: that if I could get free I might vanish into the mist; my second: that no man could loose Bünz's iron hand unles Bünz himself willed it.

"My good fellow!" I managed at last, struggling, hearing my own fitful squawk.

"*Name!*" Angrily he began to draw me toward a dark, rectangular shape—an alleyway.

Panicked, I fought. My feet stumbled. At that moment I longed for my cashier's cage at Cox's Bank. "I say! Help!"

He clamped a meaty hand over my mouth and nose, muffling my cries. I could not breathe.

The alleyway loomed.

I could think only of poor Baron Czinner.

A bobby—lovely sight!—rose up in the gloom, stern-faced. "What's up, gentlemen? Bit of a disagreement, hey? Hands off now, sir, or I'll be forced to—" He brandished his club.

Releasing me, Bünz struck the bobby down—a single blow to the neck, the policeman groaned, crumpled; simple as that. I made quite sure that when the manservant turned to grope for me, I was gone.

Thoroughly shaken, I gave up my job for that day. I slunk away in the fog. Back at Baker Street, Wiggins soothed my ruffled feathers with brandy before his fire.

"How dreadful for you, old fellow! I'm glad the hulking brute didn't get you in that alley. Whisk," he made a cutting motion across his throat, "and no Herbert Munns! Mmm, we shall have to take account of Bünz in our plans. Will he be at Sandringham, do you think? At any rate, you aren't to follow Luscher any more; I'll have Billy send one of his little soldiers into the fray—and make sure the lad takes no chances."

At Curzon Street that evening, after telling Uncle about Samuel Jarrett, we debated the wisdom of my going up to Sandringham.

"I'd still like Herbert along," Wiggins said.

"I'm inclined to allow it," Uncle said, puffing judiciously

on his long-stemmed pipe. "We don't want you left out, nephew; we may need your talents. What may we make of Bünz's stopping you? You're certain neither he nor his master noticed you before the incident, is that right? Then it was only a sudden suspicion on Bünz's part that made him do it. A stupid man, loyal as a dog—just the thing for Willy; the manservant would probably hang for him. As we've speculated, the bright young German will use people how he may. Good God, what if you'd been innocent? What if he'd got you in that alley? Yes, yes, I too think it likely Bünz was the one that did in Czinner. We must be careful of him; we must hope he does not come up to Sandringham. If he does, Herbert, watch out! Now, have I told you what Jack has agreed to do?"

Wiggins and I glanced at the small, brown-haired boy seated by the old man's chair. "No."

Uncle stirred, the glow from the grate making the wisps of white hair about his ears seem to flicker like St. Elmo's fire. He touched a gnarled hand to Jack's shoulder; Jack gazed at him trustingly.

Uncle looked grim as I had ever seen him, proud of his boy too; and I guessed it had not been easy for him to ask what he had of the lad. "Damn! We must discover what is to happen at Sandringham! To that end, Jack is to be our spy in the Bernard household."

# 🐝 Jack Merridew's Narrative 🐝

## I

At last I was to do something to help Mr. Bliss, Mr. Wigmore, and Mr. Munns! Frightened, but excited, too, determined to do the best I could for King Edward, in the chill dawn of November the first, I knocked and waited outside the servants' entrance of number 24 Norfolk Street, the big Mayfair house which Monsieur and Madame Bernard had taken for their London stay. My knees knocked in the cold. Tightly I clutched to my chest the little valise that contained only a change of clothing, my washing things, and a few books.

"I don't like to ask you, lad," Mr. Bliss had said, his kindly yellow-gray eyes meeting mine, a hand on my shoulder. "I would much rather Mr. Wigmore set one of his boys to the task. But they haven't the necessary skills—domestic skills. You know how a house is run. More important, you speak French, which you learned at Lady Blassingame's as a tot; some German, too, *nicht wahr?*"

"*Ja, mein Herr.*"

He had smiled, a trifle sadly I thought. "*Sehr gut*, Jack." Sternly, he searched my face as we stood in his room, Apollo looking down. "You've served me well. Always ready, always eager. I appreciate it. You're a brave lad, like a son to me." His hand tightened on my shoulder. "And you're willing to do this?"

"Oh, yes, sir."

"Mmm. It's not only for me, you know. It's for Bertie— His Majesty—for England."

"Yes, sir."

"Otherwise—" He scowled. "Things are not otherwise, however, and there's no sense pretending they might be! Now listen carefully." He explained that he would get me a place as footboy—boy-of-all-work it would be, the lowliest job ("The Diogenes is plush compared to it, lad ... ")— through Bedford's Domestic Agency, Regent Street. "It's highly prestigious; no one will suspect you aren't what you seem. There shouldn't be any danger. Just keep your eyes skinned, your ears open. Pay particular attention to Madame Bernard, where she goes, who she sees, how she seems. You may learn nothing—there's so little time until Sandringham—but you may pick up something we may use, some scrap ... " I was to report each day.

So I waited in curling morning mists. I had left behind my identity of Jack Merridew, Diogenes Club page. I was now Jack Merridew, footboy, sent 'round by Bedford's to fill in at the Bernards'. Shaking from more than the cold, I stood what seemed a very long time, uncertain if I had been heard, not knowing whether to knock again. The big, three-storied Tudor house leaned over me.

The door banged open. I blinked in sudden light. The silhouette of a man loomed, tall and thin as a sliver. His dark shape bent; a face peered into mine.

"Merridew?" came a sharp, high-pitched voice like a whine. "*Jack* Merridew?" His breath was like old cheese.

"Y-yes, sir."

The silhouette shot upright, put hands on its hips. "Um. Not much of you, is there? Are you a strong boy? There's plenty to do! Well, well?" He gestured impatiently. "In with you, you little perisher! Don't let in the bleedin' fog!"

He nudged my shoulder roughly and nearly slammed the door on my leg as I stumbled forward. I began to see that the task Mr. Bliss had set for me might be hard.

We were in an entrance hall. To the right, through double-glass doors, were the lights of a kitchen. I dared to glance up at the man who had let me in and found watery gray eyes, with drooping lids, meanly fixed on me. He sniffed in a superior way. "The name's Raddles—*Mr.* Raddles to you, Merridew, and don't you forget it!" He was the underbutler, he explained. He wore tight black livery. I guessed he might be twenty-five. He had very little chin, but a great, pale beak of a nose. He seemed very proud of it, waving it about as he spoke and sniffing with it importantly after every few words. "In you go (sniff)!"

He pushed me into the kitchen—was everything here done by shoves?—a big, warm room hung with copper pots and full of the smell of breakfast being prepared. Down the center ran a counter on which two trays were being readied by a scullery girl in a dingy, grease-spotted apron and tattered rag of a maid's cap. She seemed in a mad, dithering rush, whimpering, brushing at stringy wisps of dark hair, tossing china, silver, and napkins onto the trays in no sensible order.

"That's Jessie." Mr. Raddles nodded at the scurrying girl. "And that—" he flung a hand at a squat, beefy woman with huge arms and amazing orange hair which must have been dyed, "is (sniff) cook, Mrs. Wumble. Say 'ello to Jack Merridew, Gert."

The squat woman turned from the stove and, hands on her hips, a spatula sticking out of one hand, squinted at me like a pirate.

"Pleased to meet you, ma'am," I managed.

150

"Merridew, is it? The one Giddings said to expect?" She tossed her head. "Giddings, Mr. 'igh and mighty!—Mr. *Drunk*!" Half-turning, she beat at some sausages sizzling in a pan as if they might get away from her. "That'll do for you!" she said. She shook a finger at me. "Now, listen sharp, Merridew. You may 'ave been 'ired by them Frenchies," she rolled her eyes with no goodwill toward the upper floors, "but you're to serve us first, understand?"

"Yes, ma'am," I had to say, Mr. Raddles giving me another sharp shove, though I wasn't sure what she meant.

She made it clear: "There's a 'ierarchy 'ere, a 'ierarchy, mind you. Giddings on top—bloody Giddings!—and the rest of us some'eres between. You're on the bottom, understand? But you'll get your share if you just keeps mum, 'ave you got that?"

I thought I did, very clear. "Oh, yes, ma'am," I said. The servants were eating like royals, cheating on the bills, skimming all they could. It was a habit in more than one great house, Mr. Bliss had told me; it even happened in the Diogenes Club.

I caught Mr. Raddles' drooping-eyed wink. "Oh, Jack's a smart lad (sniff). 'E'll do fine!" He started. "Lordy, 'ere comes the devil 'imself!" Adjusting his livery he leapt to help Jessie with the trays. "Look sharp, now!"

There had sounded a sort of confused rumbling at the head of the servants' stairs. Feet appeared, slow, clumsy, nearly missing a step; legs; then the whole stout gentleman, white-haired and red-faced. He had the look of a drunken lord. It must be Mr. Giddings.

"What's up? What's up?" The man's expression was like thunder. He stumbled and, only by a lunge at the newel post, saved himself from sprawling on the kitchen floor. He recovered quickly and, growling like a bear, shot a look 'round the room. "Well?" he boomed. Smiling in a treacly sort of way, Mrs. Wumble stirred her sausages. Mr. Raddles snapped to attention. Whimpering, Jessie dropped a fork. Mr. Giddings' pale blue eyes met mine. I clutched my valise even tighter. I saw why, though he might be tipsy, the servants had leapt to their jobs: he looked fierce, as if he might tear me limb from limb.

He stomped forward. "Damn you all for lazy devils! Why

aren't the master's and mistress's breakfasts up yet? We have a sweet thing here; you want to spoil it? Jessie, straighten those trays; they're disgraceful! Mrs. Wumble, get those sausages and eggs on plates! And you, Raddles, you young fool, is this the new footboy? Get him upstairs and into his livery at once. There's work to be done!"

"Yes, sir!" Mr. Raddles choked and began to poke me toward the stairs.

Mr. Giddings glowered at me as I passed. "I *beat* boys who don't do their work," he snarled and looked very pleased to have let me know it.

"Yes, s-sir." Docilely I let Mr. Raddles shove me upstairs. As we climbed I glanced back. Mrs. Wumble still smiled. Attempting to fit a rosebud in a vase on Madame Bernard's tray, Jessie pricked herself and knocked the vase to the floor. She burst into tears. Mr. Giddings roared as the belowstairs door shut.

Mr. Raddles led the way with a queer sort of loping walk, his head held very high, his great beak swaying. I was glad to follow; he could not shove me when I was behind him. This was the Bernard house, and as Mr. Bliss had instructed, I looked carefully about me. The place was let furnished; therefore the tables and chairs could tell me nothing. Everything seemed very fine. All I could think of was that Madame Bernard had passed up and down these stairs. Had she left any trace? The wooden treads rang hollowly with our footfalls. Somewhere a clock ticked.

On the second floor Mr. Raddles crept by the third door from the landing. "Madame's room," he sniffed. "You'll stay clear of 'er if you know what's good for you!"

From behind the door came a trill of laughter and ladies' voices speaking French. To think that she was just beyond that door!

"Always jabberin' with 'er maid," Mr. Raddles muttered. He resumed his grand parade when we were past. "Them Frenchies!"

At the end of the corridor he nudged me up a narrow flight of stairs to a tiny, chill room under the eaves. My heart fell; this was where I was to sleep. But it was no worse than Hanwell School. I shivered myself into ill-fitting livery while Mr. Raddles lazed on the iron bedstead and smoked a cigarette. Then he jabbed me downstairs, and the day's work began.

I spent an hour in the boot room off the kitchen cleaning and polishing the Bernards' footgear. Mr. Raddles did not help, only leaned against the jam watching out for Mr. Giddings. "See you take extra care with the mistress's boots, 'ear! Madame Sophie prides 'erself on 'er pretty ankles, so I don't want news of a bad job of blacking from 'er or almighty Giddings. If I do, you'll answer to me!"

Next, Mr. Raddles and I saw to it that the brass scuttles in every room were filled with coal. Mr. Raddles led the way and turned the knobs; I carried the coal bucket and dirtied my hands at the hearths. Shortly before noon we came to Madame Bernard's bedchamber.

"She's out, thank God," Mr. Raddles said. "I saw 'er go off." He opened the door as if it were his own private room and strode in. I followed.

The first thing I noticed was the scent, a woman's, of perfume; it made me almost dizzy. There were a high, silken bed and a forest of toilet articles—gleaming, glass-stoppered bottles—on the elegant dressing table; a big cheval glass, too, by a tall, mahogany wardrobe. I tried to imagine Madame Bernard reflected in the glass but couldn't; I had seen her only in a newspaper photograph.

I must have been gaping. One of Mr. Raddles' sharp jabs brought me to myself. "Look sharp at the scuttle, Merridew (sniff)!" While I worked, sneezing from coal dust, he preened before the glass. He spat on his fingers to paste back his limp, black hair.

At luncheon the servants gathered 'round the big oak table belowstairs. The food was lordly; I wondered if the master and mistress ate so fine. Seated at table's head, Mr. Giddings started the platters, which made their way to me, the lowly footboy, picked nearly clean. I didn't mind; I was too excited to eat. Slanting through the area windows, the midday light was bleak, but the conversation was lively enough.

I only listened. Three souls completed the staff: Mary and Frances, giggling housemaids who seemed to enjoy teasing Mr. Raddles; and Mr. Rance, the tall, sour-looking coachman. There were two more servants, I learned from the conversation: Monsieur Dasté, Monsieur Bernard's personal valet, and Mademoiselle Cosette, Madame Bernard's maid. These two kept to themselves. They had rooms near their master's and mistress's and had their meals sent up. The belowstairs servants envied this. "Their airs is outrageous!" Mrs. Wumble declared at mention of them, sawing her roast beef as unmercifully as she had beat her sausages. "They don't deserve such treatment. Hit's not right, hit's demoralizin'!"

"'Ear, 'ear!" Mr. Raddles agreed, banging down a salt cellar.

"I *like* M'amselle Cosette," Jessie put in meekly.

Mrs. Wumble glared while the housemaids giggled.

There was talk of Madame Bernard's relationship with the king. It seemed the servants' favorite subject. They had all at one time or another heard terrible rows, in which the man they thought to be His Majesty threatened Madame Bernard and she begged to be free of him. They sniggered over Monsieur Bernard's position in the matter.

Only Jessie seemed to feel sorry for him. "How the poor master has changed," she said.

"Oh, indeed!" Mrs. Wumble croaked. "'E was 'appy, all right," she leered and winked, "'afore 'Is Majesty give 'im the 'orns!" She cackled loudly.

Fists bunched on the table, white-haired Mr. Giddings boomed like a magistrate, "It's just as well that the master is preoccupied!" Then he, too, winked as he poured his third great glass of wine. "A preoccupied man does not watch his affairs too closely, eh?"

Everyone laughed heartily.

After lunch Mr. Raddles set me to hearthstoning the front steps. "See you do a proper job!" he said before he vanished into the areaway.

Glad to be free of his mean eyes, his nose, his jabs, I began to scrub. The fog had lifted to a gray mist. The red brick townhouses of Norfolk Street looked glum. I was wondering if I might really do anything here to help Mr. Bliss, when a dignified gentleman in a dark suit and black topper got down from a carriage and slowly, gloomily it seemed to me, climbed the three steps of number 24. I thought he didn't notice me kneeling at my work, but as he was about to open the door he turned.

"You are the new boy?" He had a French accent. His voice was sombre as a parson's. It must be Monsieur Bernard.

"Yes, sir," I said, jumping up. "Jack Merridew, sir."

"Ah!" His tone was kind, but he gazed at me as if I were not there. Sunken hollows lay beneath his cheeks; his eyes were sunken too. He seemed a ghost of a man; he did something very strange, which gave me a chill. Placing a bony hand on my shoulder, he gave me a gentle but firm rocking back and forth. His mouth opened, another black hollow in his face, but nothing came out—whatever he had meant to say was too painful it seemed. "A mere boy," he managed finally, "you have much to learn!" He glanced up at his wife's bedroom window. His expression turned gloomier still. He turned and entered the house.

I was shaken by this. Poor Monsieur Bernard!

Though I was worked harder in this household than ever at the Diogenes Club, I found a moment before supper to carry up paraffin for the lamp in my attic room. I had slipped *Michael Strogoff* into my valise and hoped to read more of Mr. Verne's novel before going to sleep. Madame Bernard's door was ajar, and I heard her angry voice as I tiptoed past. I hurried to the narrow staircase leading to my room. Hidden by the rise of the stairs, I looked back to see Mr. Giddings trundle out her door making quick, apologetic little bobbings of his head. He stammered and wore a sickly smile. Madame Bernard continued to rail at him, half in English, half in French, about the wretched staff. She did not show herself. Then the door was slammed in Mr. Giddings' face, and he stalked off muttering and mopping his brow.

When at last I was allowed to go up to my room at eleven after scrubbing pots for two hours, all was silent. Had Madame Bernard gone out? Her perfume seemed to fill the corridor. In bed, neither my shivering nor *Michael Strogoff* nor my thoughts about the day could keep me awake. The book slipped to the bare wooden floor, where I found it in the morning when I rose at six to Mr. Raddles' sharp poking of my ribs. "Up, Merridew! More boots!"

It was November the second; in seven days His Majesty would be sixty-five years old. That same morning I met Madame Bernard.

Feet up, Mr. Raddles lounged in the warm kitchen while I labored in the boot room. "Lord lumme!" I heard him mutter at the falling of a bell shutter. His feet clattered on the floor. "It's Madame's room! What the devil can she want?"

Mrs. Wumble stopped rattling her pots and pans. "Giddings is out," she warned. "You'll 'ave to go up."

There was a silence, in which I imagined Mr. Raddles' pale nose growing even paler. "Damned if I'll face 'er!" he exclaimed. "Merridew can do it!" His beak loomed in the boot-room door, and he poked my ribs with a toe. "Up, boy! See what Madame wants. And mind your manners! I don't want no trouble."

Wanting to go, afraid to go, I went up to the mistress's bedroom. I knocked at her door. It flew open and she was there.

Madame was barely taller than I and wore a pale blue dressing gown. Her red-brown hair was like a cloud about her shoulders. "Cosette?" Her small, beautiful face frowned. "You are not Cosette!" Brushing past me she glanced quickly up and down the corridor. "*Où est cette bonne?*" Her green eyes flashed as she looked at me suspiciously. "Who are you, child?"

I hated for her to call me a child. "The n-new footboy, Madame," I stammered.

"And what do you want?"

"I was sent to answer your bell."

"A mere footboy? *Hélas!* I shall speak to Monsieur Giddings about this! *Alors*, since you are here, help me." She whirled; a fog of perfume seemed to surround me.

Somehow, I followed her into her room.

"There!" She gestured toward a heavy morocco-covered armchair.

I did not understand. "Y-yes, Madame?"

"*Là-bas, là-bas!*" A small, white finger pointed.

Gulping, I spread my hands helplessly. I understood Monsieur Bernard's pain—I would do anything to change her fretful frown to a smile.

"My reel of thread. *Rouge*—red. It is there. Get it, you idiot boy!"

At last I understood. The embroidery frame by the bed . . . she had been working, and her thread had rolled under the heavy chair. She wanted me to retrieve it.

At once I fell upon my hands and knees, felt about under the chair, and pulled forth a reel of red cotton. Standing, I handed it to her, my reward a pretty smile that made me forget all her harshness.

She swayed in her rustling blue gown. "What is your name, *mon petit garçon?*"

My throat was so dry I could hardly answer. "Merridew, Madame. Jack . . . "

"*Ah, Jacques? Merci beaucoup, Jacques.* Now go, leave me alone! If you see my maid tell her I am very angry! And tell Monsieur Giddings that I wish to speak to him!"

As if I weren't there, she turned to the embroidery frame. I backed out and softly closed the door.

Going downstairs—floating, it seemed—I could still smell the room and her; I could still see her white skin, pink lips, green eyes. Beautiful. Yet I did not forget that Mr. Bliss had warned me to beware, and, thinking of the mysterious plot, of poor Monsieur Bernard, of Baron Czinner's cut-up body, I caught myself. I must be careful not to let Madame Bernard's beauty blind me to my task.

I was to report each day, both to give news and to reassure Mr. Bliss that I was well. I was not certain how that was to be managed. "We'll see to it somehow, lad," Mr. Bliss had told me. "I'm working it out with Mr. Wigmore. Just wait for our signal." Having been in the house for a day, I did not see how it was to be done; I was almost always watched.

When I returned to the kitchen, Mr. Raddles sent me to give the order to the coal man, whose cry had been heard through the area windows. "'Alf a ton'll do, 'ear? (sniff, sniff)."

Wrapping a scarf about my throat, I went out into the morning, yellow fog clinging to me and seeming to wrap the house. The coal wagon waited above, a skinny man and a boy perched on its seat.

" 'Ow much today?" the man asked as I came up.

"Half a ton, sir," I said and was startled to see him wink.

"Salt's the name, Jack," he hissed. "Mr. Wigmore's man."
Relief flooded me. He cocked a thumb. "This 'ere's Billy."
He jumped down. " 'Ave a nice chat, lads. I'll see to the
coal."

While Mr. Salt busied himself fixing the chute to the cellar opening, the boy jumped down, too, and thrust out a
smudged hand. "Billy Gully. Jack Merridew? Pleased to
meet yer. Give it to me quick, now; Salt's swift at 'is work."

"How . . . how did you manage?"

He frowned. "No matter. It were this way or some other.
This 'un worked. Out with it now. Wot news?"

I told him everything I had seen and heard, all the while
watching this boy who helped break houses for Mr. Wigmore. He wasn't handsome, with his pushed-in nose and
dirt, but he had a cocksure air. He wore a battered cap at an
angle across his brow and sucked his teeth as I spoke. I
wanted him to like me.

"It ain't much," he said skeptically when I was through.

He was right; I flushed.

"Now look 'ere, Jack." He poked my chest. "Wiggins an'
old Bliss 'ave told me all about this matter." He peered up at
the Bernard house, wreathed in fog. "And yer brave to go in
there, I'll say. I'm yer man in case o' danger, don't you ferget
it. I'll be lurkin' about if you needs me. Just you step out that
door—" he cocked a thumb at the servants' entrance, "and
me or one o' me boys'll see. Make a sign like this," he pretended to cough, "and I'm at yer side 'afore you knows it."
He pulled a cosh from his back pocket and smacked it in a
palm. "I'm the equal o' any two men, I can tell yer!" He
looked so wicked, I believed him. Then he grinned as Mr.
Salt sauntered up. "Coal's done, must be off now. Good
work!"

The two jumped on the wagon, and Salt flicked the reins.
They vanished in fog. His boys? Shivering, I peered into the
gloom but could see no one watching. I hoped they were
there nonetheless.

That evening Madame Bernard went to see Camille Clif-
ford in *The Gibson Girl* at the Vaudeville Theatre. From
belowstairs I heard her greet a party of friends before they
all swept off in their carriages. Later I was sent to the library
with a decanter of port. I found Monsieur Bernard in a

leather armchair staring into the fire, a book open, face down, in his lap. He looked bad as I had seen him the day before—sad, but angry too. He drummed nervously on the chair arm. From the servants' talk I knew that he was here almost every night brooding and drinking.

"Your port, sir," I said, setting down the tray.

He did not speak; the firelight danced in his glistening eyes.

Silently I crept from the room.

## 3

Wednesday Mr. Raddles jabbed me awake as usual. On Friday the Bernards were to leave for Sandringham, so I had only two days more to discover something which might help Mr. Bliss.

I carried out my morning tasks while Mr. Raddles watched and prodded and complained I did them ill. I had by this time glimpsed both the maid Cosette and Monsieur Bernard's man Dasté a number of times. Cosette was small and dark, with black hair; Dasté a tight-lipped man with skin pale as a toadstool and a pencil-line moustache. Both carried their noses high. Late in the morning I climbed the stairs with the coal bucket. Mr. Raddles had decided I knew the job well enough to manage it by myself, while he remained, feet up, in the warm kitchen. When I reached the second-floor landing, I heard angry voices coming from Madame Bernard's bedroom. I hesitated but thought I must go ahead with my work; too, I wished to hear any conversation. "When people are angry, Jack, they often say the most revealing things," Mr. Bliss had said. The corridor was deserted, so I crept to the bedroom door. It was ajar. I paused, straining to make something of the torrent of words.

I started as Cosette suddenly burst out, shaking her head and clicking her tongue. Ignoring me as if I weren't there, she rushed by. Monsieur Dasté poked his sleek head from his room just down the corridor. The maid joined him, murmured a few words, and, arms folded, they stared with disapproving looks at the mistress's room. She and her husband were having a row.

Cosette had left the door half open. Slowly it swung back. I was hypnotized and stood rooted as the bedchamber came into view—the wardrobe, the glass, and the high, silken bed with the embroidery frame beside it. Monsieur and Madame Bernard were facing one another half a dozen feet apart. They did not notice that the door had opened. I held my breath, feeling ashamed, as if I ought to creep away. Yet my feet would not move. Tall and thin as a ghost, Monsieur Bernard seemed to be struggling to control some deep emotion. He wore a dark suit. Madame Bernard was about to go out, it appeared, for she wore a lavender flared skirt and coat and a small hat covered in ribbons. They hissed at one another, speaking mostly French with occasional English words and phrases. My French was not good; I could not make out everything. Sandringham was repeated several times.

"*Tu es pénible, vieux fou!*" the mistress cried, her small chin thrust forward. "*Laisse - moi faire ce que je veux!*"

"*Ce que tu veux?*" Monsieur Bernard took a step nearer. "As in Paris?"

Her green eyes flashed. "Do you accuse me?"

Fists clenched, he drew himself up. "You know of whom I speak," each word falling like a stone from his lips.

Another torrent of French burst from Madame Bernard. Twice I heard the name Herr Luscher. I would remember that for Mr. Bliss.

I watched the husband's complexion turn purple with fury; his look frightened me. Suddenly one of his thin arms snaked out, gripped his wife's shoulder, and jerked her to him. Turning white, she appeared terrified. The Frenchman's features worked; he seemed mad. He shouted into her upturned face terrible insults. Again I heard Herr Luscher's name, and that of the king. Madame Bernard twisted helplessly in his grip.

Looking aghast at what he had done, Monsieur Bernard let go his wife as suddenly as he had grabbed her, then thrust her away. He passed a fluttering, long-fingered hand over a perspiring brow. He seemed to sob, but there were no tears: "*Je t'en supplie . . . pardonne- moi . . . chère Sophie . . .*"

She laughed nervously. She tried to pull on fawn-colored gloves, but her hands shook too. "*Arrêtons cette dispute! Je vais m'en aller.*"

A searching look. Monsieur was suspicious again. "*Qui vas-tu voir?*"

Madame Bernard gave a small start as she noticed me. She seemed relieved and said, as if nothing were wrong, "Ah, Jacques. Here with the coal? Come in, come in." She managed to get on her gloves. "I am merely calling on Lady Glendinning, that is all, Armand. Don't be harsh with your Sophie." She made to touch his cheek, but, rigid, he turned away.

"I *shall* be at Sandringham," he said through clenched teeth.

Was she about to fly into another rage? Glancing at me darkly, all she said was, "As you wish," before she hurried out. "Cosette, Cosette!" I heard her call. The maid followed her to the stairs.

Brushing past me, Monsieur Bernard stalked to his room. I busied myself at the hearth.

I must report to Mr. Bliss. Soon as I could, I slipped free of Mr. Raddles' eye and out the servants' door into the area. It was another gray day, but the fog had lifted. People strolled by on the pavement above; no sight of Billy Gully. I pretended to cough. Billy did not appear. Worried that I should be missed indoors, I was about to pantomime coughing again when a dirty bundle dropped out of the sky to land with a thud beside me. It was my saviour, all right, smudged and cocky as ever.

He uncoiled himself. "This way, Jack." He drew me behind a large dustbin, where we could not be seen. "Wot's up? Trouble?" His cosh was in his hand.

"No." I told him about the Bernards' argument.

He clapped my shoulder. "Righto. I'll tell old Bliss and Wiggins. Cheerio!" He was up the stairs like a snake.

Marvelling at him, wishing I knew his tricks and very glad he was near, I went back into the sad, awful Bernard house.

That evening I helped Mr. Giddings and one of the maids to serve supper, it being Mr. Raddles' night off. The master and mistress sat opposite one another at the long table in the upstairs dining room, Monsieur dressed in black as usual. Madame Bernard wore a gay pink dress. Candles flickered; the white damask and the silver service gleamed. Miles seemed to yawn between husband and wife, yet they seemed close, too, as if a spark would ignite their friction like powder. Monsieur Bernard said nothing, ate little, only brooded. Madame chattered in English about her afternoon with Lady Glendinning, exclaiming over Catherine and Heather, the dear children, and saying how she should like to have babies of her own some day. I was charmed by her musical voice; it was easy to forget how sulky she could be. Monsieur Bernard winced at the mention of children.

Later, when Madame had again breezed off with friends, Monsieur retired to the library and his decanter of port.

4

Thursday morning it rained. The two housemaids had the day off. The next day everyone would be 'round to help prepare for the journey to Sandringham. In the steward's room Mr. Giddings was entertaining Mr. Vamberry, the wine merchant. Mrs. Wumble crashed about among her pots and pans. Jessie was peeling potatoes, Mr. Raddles watching her and jeering. I went up to dust the woodwork on the ground floor. Monsieur Bernard went out early. I saw him, accompanied by dapper Dasté, pass through the entrance hall in his tall, black hat, trailing gloom. Bundled against the weather, Cosette left shortly afterward. This was unusual, the French maid being used to keeping her mistress company until Madame herself went out, and I wondered what Cosette's errand might be. The upstairs floors were empty for the time being, except for Madame Bernard—and me.

At 10:00 A.M. I finished polishing the bannisters of the entrance hall staircase and went into the library opposite the front door to dust the long rows of books, as Mr. Giddings had ordered. I left the door slightly ajar. The electric lights were lit. Rain sheeted the windowpanes. Thunder rumbled.

I was feeling disappointed to have learned so little in the Bernard household, when I heard the front door open. There had been no knock. Wondering if Monsieur Bernard had returned unexpectedly, I went to the library door to peep out. Just as I reached the door it began slowly to open. In stepping aside on the soft carpet to avoid it hitting me, I ended out of sight against the wall. A black-haired head appeared and looked 'round the room. It was Cosette, face still damp from the rain, wearing an odd cold expression. She glanced in only briefly and did not see me in the angle between the door and the wall. Silently, she closed the door.

Alerted, I pressed my ear to the oak. The wood carried sound well, and I heard the click and creak of the front door again. Then came whispers—someone had entered with Cosette. Two pairs of footfalls ascended the staircase; one, I thought, sounded heavier than the other. A booted gentleman's?

I cracked the library door and peered out. I glanced at the stairs, but whoever had gone up was already out of sight. The entrance hall was empty. Carrying my cloth and tin of polish so I would appear only to be about my work if anyone asked what I was doing, I went to the foot of the stairs. From below came a faint echo of Mrs. Wumble's din; from above, nothing.

Careful to make no sound, I began to climb the stairs. Cosette's behavior had interested me; I hoped to find out something for Mr. Bliss at last. At the drawing-room landing I glanced down the corridor. No one in sight, no sound; they had not stopped here, it seemed. I continued up. Had the man who had entered with Cosette been brought to see Madame Bernard?

I stopped just below the second-floor landing and, through a bannister opening, peeped cautiously up over the edge of the stairs. I was just in time to see Cosette go alone into her room. The corridor was empty. The man must have gone into Madame Bernard's bedchamber. I was tingling; surely this was something significant!

But I hesitated, afraid. Recalling what Baron Czinner had done to Samuel Jarrett, and what had been done to the baron in turn, I shuddered; my mouth was dry. But I must see the thing through!

I climbed the remaining steps, crept to Madame Bernard's room, and, trembling, put my ear to her door.

At first I could make out nothing for the pounding of my heart—what if the door should suddenly open? Clamping my jaw tight, I pressed my ear closer. Sound carried well, and—yes—I had been right: there was a man's voice as well as Madame Bernard's. The pair spoke mostly English; they seemed most at ease in it, and I guessed neither knew the other's language well. Occasionally Madame Bernard spoke French. The man had a German accent, used German words and phrases. I knew at once that he must be Herr Wilhelm Luscher!

I gasped, realizing what danger I was in—also that I must stay to listen. I kept my ear to the door.

"Willy ... !" The Frenchwoman's voice was as I had never heard it, sighing, longing. I heard a rustling sound— her dress as the German embraced her?

Her words continued a moment later. "I had to see you Willy, *cher* Willy—please forgive me for sending Cosette. I know we agreed that it was dangerous to meet until ... until this thing is done, but ... I have been so many days without you, and ... I have not been able to put Armand off. He insists on accompanying me to Sandringham. He has got very bad, Willy. I'm frightened! Yesterday morning I thought he would strike me ... "

Herr Luscher sounded playful. "Nearly struck my Sophie? How dare he!" He laughed. "After all, you are only his wife."

"Don't make fun of me, Willy."

"There, there, no need to worry, *mein Schatz*. When it is over I will whisk you away from the stupid Bernard. We will celebrate in Berlin!"

"Berlin?" She sounded hopeful. "Do not call him stupid, Willy. He suspects, *knows*!" Her tone changed, almost to pity. "How he suffers!"

Herr Luscher's warning tone chilled me. "No change of heart, Sophie ... ?"

"No, no!" she replied quickly. "My husband is impossible! I love only you! It is just that Armand suspects me, questions me. He tolerates the king's attentions—what else can he do?—but you, he hates you, Willy. And he broods and plans. I don't know what he may do."

The German sniffed. "He will do, he can do, nothing. Let him come to Sandringham! After all, the invitation is for two. It will make no difference."

"It will be harder to find moments alone with you."

"Ha! Charmingly romantic, Sophie! And impractical. It is just like you French. No, we must forget romance until ... Have you the pistol?"

I started at these words.

"Of course. Hidden in my wardrobe since you gave it to me. I will put it in my handbag for safekeeping tomorrow before I go. Oh, how I hate the thing and what I must do with it! The king is a fool, a bore—disgusting!—with the stink of cigar smoke and his latest meal always on his breath. You do hate it that he touches me, don't you, *chéri?* And yet to . . . to *shoot* him—he *is* evil as you have told me, isn't he, Willy? It must be done?"

Coldly, firmly: "As I have said."

I was terrified.

"Murder! To think of it!" I imagined Madame Bernard wringing her hands; I wanted to wring my own. "Jarrett, Baron Czinner—dreadful! You said the baron would simply disappear. Oh, Willy, I did not know you meant to have him killed."

"I intended no such thing; I've told you so! I told Bünz he was to vanish, meaning only that he must be persuaded to leave the country." Herr Luscher sounded amused. "Bünz simply interpreted my orders in his own efficient way; he's a funny fellow! Mmm. It is unfortunate that the young prostitute identified Czinner's body, but that will not matter either. The stupid English police are baffled, and we are free to do as we have planned. I think it is for the best that Jarrett and Czinner are dead."

"And we must go on without them?"

The German had been pacing; his footfalls stopped. "Faint heart, Sophie? Gird yourself for your task; you are to have a place in history! Of course we shall go on. On his visits to you in royal disguise, Jarrett made you the abused, wronged mistress. When the English king is dead, your servants will testify to the terrible rows you had, to how he struck you. Your liaison with the pompous fool is well known, and when, out of pretended fear for your life, you shoot him on his birthday, the world will sympathize with your outraged young womanhood; it will vindicate you. The French will be up in arms that their countrywoman, wife of so respected a pillar of society as Armand Bernard, was treated so callously—you will give full details both on the witness stand and to the press—and the Entente Cordiale will crumble. These English, who think to dominate Europe

165

for their own ends, must be stopped! You, Sophie, are the instrument!"

He practically crowed this. I cowered outside the door. It was the whole plot: England would be disgraced because of scandalous lies about the king. The Norfolk Street staff had been duped to make those lies seem true. With the burden of this secret, and the knowledge that His Majesty was to be shot on his birthday, I felt suddenly very alone and helpless in the long upstairs corridor. If Herr Luscher knew I had heard, I would die as Baron Czinner had, and likely this time Bünz would see to it the body was never found.

The Bernard house seemed a terrible trap. I wanted to dash down the stairs, out the front way, and escape to Mr. Bliss along the rain-darkened streets.

I lingered, hoping to learn something more.

"A faint heart?" Madame Bernard was saying. "Everything I have done has been to prove my heart to you!"

"Then do not suggest stopping now, *Geliebte*. Only this last task stands between us. When it is done, you shall have me completely."

"Oh, Willy . . . " Another embrace?

"And now I must go. It would spoil everything if your husband should find me here. Courage, Sophie! In three days the deceptions will be over." Herr Luscher's footsteps approached the door.

Panicked, I knew I had stayed too long. I heard his hand on the knob. What to do?

Just to my right, in a brass urn, stood a leafy aspidistra on a bamboo stand. I fell on my knees and began to dust the stand just as the door swung open. Gleamingly polished black boots appeared. I rubbed at the bamboo furiously, wondering if it and the boots were the last things I was to see in my life. I glanced up; I did not have to pretend to be surprised to see a man standing there.

Then I was strangling, jerked from the floor by a firm hand grasping my shirt at the throat. Feet dangling, I hung in the air. Herr Wilhelm Luscher—blond hair, lean features, ice-blue eyes—stared into my face. Things turned red; I could not breathe.

Behind the German I glimpsed Madame Bernard, looking

166

distressed. "What are you doing, Willy?" she cried. "It is only the footboy. Stop!"

He held me a moment longer; I thought I would faint. Then he dropped me, and my legs collapsed as I hit the floor. I had been clutching my tin of polish but lost it now, spilling its oily contents on the carpet.

"Augh! See what you have made him do!" Madame Bernard cried. "Get up, boy, get up!"

I struggled to my feet.

She was glaring at me. "How you startled Herr—" she caught herself, "Herr . . . Werner!" She wrinkled her nose at the wet spill of polish. At that instant I could not help thinking of Samuel Jarrett's blood spilled on the Diogenes Club library floor. "Herr Werner is my . . . jeweller," she went on. "He has come to deliver a . . . a gift which I secretly asked him to make for His Majesty's birthday. You know Monsieur and I are to go up to Sandringham tomorrow. The gift is a surprise; no one is to know about it. You will tell no one that Herr Werner was here?"

"N-no, Madame."

She gestured, with a little, nervous laugh. "It is only that, jealous of his artistic secrets, Herr Werner—"

"Enough!" the German snapped. Looking enormously tall in his dark suit, he bent toward me and showed white, even teeth. "The boy understands to keep his mouth shut." He fingered my Eton collar. "Don't you, boy?"

"Oh, y-yes, sir!"

Thunder rumbled. Glimpsing behind Madame Bernard the rain-smeared window that let on Norfolk Street, I was dizzy for a breath of freedom.

With another warning look at me, Herr Luscher straightened and pulled on his tall hat. "Keep the boy indoors, Madame. It is shocking weather; you would not want him to catch his death. And now I must go. No, no—no need to call your maid." He touched my shoulder. "The boy will see me down."

Madame Bernard frowned, glancing from me to Herr Luscher. "But—"

"Lead the way, boy," he muttered, bowing to her. "Good day, Madame. The . . . *gift* which you are to carry up to Sandringham? I trust it will do the job."

Madame Bernard murmured something. I led the way along the hall, my neck hairs prickling. On the way down Herr Luscher walked beside me, his long legs stepping, stepping. I dared not look up at him, but in a sort of numb fear I watched the bannister sliding by. When we reached the front door would he grab me and force me out into his carriage? Would I never see Mr. Bliss or the friendly Diogenes Club again?

At the lowest landing he stopped me. I chanced a glance at him. He was peering down at the empty entrance hall, listening. His features were sharp and handsome. He released me; we descended and crossed the carpet. Herr Luscher opened the door a crack, then glanced out. Seemingly satisfied, he pulled back the oak.

Norfolk Street was awash with rain. Lamps lit, carriages and motorcars splashed by. On the stoop loomed a muffled figure—a huge man. He had been peering up and down the roadway but now turned, his face flat and ugly, with dull pig's eyes. It must be Herr Bünz, who had attacked Mr. Munns in Piccadilly—the man who had murdered Baron Czinner! My heart sank.

Herr Luscher glanced a question.

*"Die Luft ist rein,"* the man replied in a thick voice.

I could not help staring at the coarse, stubby-fingered hands hanging at his sides; they had done such an awful deed! Then I saw he was staring at me. I gazed back, gulping. His eyes had a way of holding me; I couldn't breathe, couldn't move.

"Ungh!" came a sound from his throat, meaning what, I did not know.

Suddenly Herr Luscher's fingers were on my collar, tight. "Remember, boy, no word of this!" Then, miraculously, he and his man were gone, and I was left safe, with the hiss of rain, the echo of Mrs. Wumble's clanging belowstairs, and my own thudding heartbeats mingling in my ears.

I staggered with relief and must have sat for a quarter of an hour on a step, staring at an old armorial portrait on the wall. I did not think, or care, about the shoves I would get if Mr. Raddles found me doing nothing.

Afterward, soon as possible, I snuck out the servants' entrance. Rain streaming in my face, I peered about, pantomiming coughing. As before, Billy tumbled into the area-way. He drew me under the eaves, and I poured out my adventure.

"Brave work!" He thumped me on the back. "Bloody German! I wish you was one o' me boys—per'aps we may work together some day. Meantime, not to worry. Old Bliss'll 'ave the tale in twenty minutes. And I'll stick tighter'n glue. If the smarmy Luscher bloke comes back, I'll cosh 'im right enough! Cheerio!" He scrambled up the steps.

At four Monsieur Bernard returned. He and his wife ate supper in silence; then Madame retired to her room to begin packing for Sandringham. I saw her go up. She looked sad. What a burden she carried—to have to shoot a man, the king! But was her sadness for that, or because she mistrusted Herr Luscher's love? I felt sorry for her. I felt sorry, too, for gaunt, brooding Monsieur Bernard, to whom I again carried port in the library.

That night I hardly slept for the drumming of the rain on the slates, for remembering Bünz's heavy hands and piggy eyes, and for wondering if we would still go up to San-dringham or if, the plot being known, all our plans would be dropped.

I had done my job in the Bernard house! What was to come of it all?

# Simon Bliss's Narrative

## I

At 6:00 P.M. on the evening before I was to go up to Sandringham, my cab splashed to a halt before the doors of Brooks's Club on St. James Street. A steady rain hissed on the hansom's leather top. Through the wet darkness, the club's windows shone with an inviting yellow brilliance. Umbrella raised, blackthorn stick tapping on the slick pavement, I clambered down and hurried through the downpour to the tall double doors for my rendezvous with Willy Luscher. The young German did not expect me, but we would meet nonetheless. One of Mr. Wigmore's boys, replacing Herbert, efficiently dogging the German's steps, had traced our quarry here.

That same boy had earlier reported Luscher's visit to the Norfolk Street house. Luscher had been fetched from the York Hotel by a black-haired woman, Madame Bernard's maid. I had hung fire; then Jack's report had arrived from Billy Gully: my lad was safe; he had discovered the plot entire!

I had been relieved at last to know it all, but far from certain what steps to take. Sitting before my fire in the Diogenes Club, I had worried over the problem all afternoon, while thunder crashed above London's rooftops. About five, when daylight began to fade, I got word that Luscher had gone to dine at Brooks's Club. It was a piece of good luck. I had been contemplating going there anyway to consult with Lord Esher and had set out at once.

A cheery coal fire burned opposite the club's front doors. I gave my name to the head hall porter, and, after checking his book, he had me shown to the thickly carpeted smoking room. Red damask draperies descended from valances above the tall, water-sheeted windows fronting St. James Street. Portraits of distinguished members past and present—noble front benchers, bewigged magistrates, soldiers clutching cockaded hats to their breasts—lined the walls. Above the black marble mantlepiece hung a huge, ornate mirror, the glass etched at the top with an elaborate *V.R.* Leather sofas and armchairs were scattered about, ashtrays on brass stands sprouting like mushrooms beside them; the low, round tables were piled with London's dailies. Sunk in well-padded leather, some club members dozed or read, while others stood about chatting and gesturing with cigars and pipes. All wore evening clothes. Soon the dinner gong would sound. There was something reassuringly alike about all London clubs.

Reginald Brett, Lord Esher, sat in a group of four men near the fire. He nodded as the page boy left me at the door. I nodded back but was in no hurry to speak to Reggie, especially in other company. First: Herr Luscher; it was past time we met.

Some young men stood nearby. I heard a German accent, turned, and there he was—no need for someone to point him out. Leisurely filling and lighting my pipe, I strolled closer and studied him from under my brows. He was about six feet tall, slim, athletic, and looked at first glance affable enough and harmless, wearing his impeccably tailored dark suit with the nonchalant ease of one born to its cut. His blond hair was combed back. He had a curling blond moustache, beneath which a sensuous, almost petulant, lower lip protruded. Only his nose, long and aquiline, suggested any haughtiness. His blue eyes were heavy-lidded, with thick, nearly white, lashes.

I listened to the young men's talk as I puffed. Debutantes, horse racing, and motorcars made up its substance. If these fellows were the statesmen of tomorrow, I hoped their minds were less frivolous than their conversation! Effortlessly, young Willy contributed his part, while his gaze wandered seemingly at random about the room. He wore a bright, vague expression—the affectation of boredom of every rich, callow young man. Only I seemed to know the expression was a mask; he was contemptuous of us English. His gaze drifted to the bent old man smoking a pipe nearby and moved on; he appeared uninterested in me.

Dangerous pup! Stepping forward, I jabbed his arm with my pipe stem. What would he do if he realized I knew his secret plan and was determined he should never carry it out?

He had just finished an anecdote about an experience at Ascot. He had told it well, with just the right touch of self-deprecation, and his circle burst into laughter. He was expert at small talk, all right—just the thing Bertie doted on—and I saw how he had enchanted the king. A foot taller than I, he turned slowly and glanced down. "I beg your pardon?" The locution sounded odd in his German accent. I had struck his arm rather hard and fancied I saw a flicker of hostility in his pale blue eyes.

"Herr Luscher?" I inquired, chewing my pipe stem.

A nod. Cautious? I could not tell, the mask was so firmly in place. "I am he." A definite hint of pride.

"Simon!" It was young Frank Cardew. I knew him, a fledgling M.P. Bright-eyed, he shook my hand and introduced me 'round. "Willy, have you met Simon Bliss?"

"I have not had the pleasure."

"Oh, you must meet Simon!" He introduced us.

The German placed his heels together, made a little bow, heartily shook my hand. "I am very pleased . . ."

"Thank you, Herr Luscher." Under other circumstances I might have found his formality charming; now I was very glad to let go his hand. "You're the Herr Luscher I've been hearing so much about, Bertie's new friend?"

"Bertie?"

Frank Cardew laughed. "Simon's rather informal, Willy."

The German echoed the laugh. "Your king, you mean? A jolly fellow! Yes, yes, I'm pleased to say he lets me be his friend. I am more than that, however."

"He is!" Frank said, a chorus agreeing. "Splendid chap!"

I did not comment that I, too, knew he was more.

Frank glanced at me slyly. "Collecting, are you, Simon?" He winked at Willy Luscher. "People, to be exact. Watch out; he'll scoop you up in his net, then he'll have all your secrets. He's said to know everything about everybody."

"Oh?" Mere polite interest. He was damnably cool!

"Indeed. Rumour has it that all society's secrets are in a locked box—in Simon Bliss's head."

"How interesting." The German's heels were together again, his hands behind his back. "And do you wish to have a secret from me?"

I puffed smoke. "If you have one."

"Ah, no! Except that I am so pleased to be in England."

"That won't do!" one of the young men protested, watching us with an expectant smile.

"Yes, you must do better than that," another urged.

"For example," I said, taking my pipe from my mouth, cocking an eye, "what do you make of the murder in the Diogenes Club?" I hadn't been able to resist; immediately I regretted my rashness.

There was an uneasy silence as everyone—except Luscher and I—shifted his feet.

"Murder . . . ? Diogenes Club . . . ?" He sounded bewildered.

Frank seemed delighted at the subject. "Simon has a morbid bent; criminals and coppers are his best friends! Yes, the murder. You must know the story; it's been in all the papers. A . . . Baron Czinner, I think his name was, stabbed a man in Simon's club, then was himself found a few days later—quite without his head."

There was jittery laughter.

Herr Luscher frowned. "I have heard of it, of course, but—"

"Czinner was a countryman of yours," I prompted.

At once: "Ah, no, he was Austrian!"

"So you do know something about him?"

"That he was Austrian."

"You never met him?" It was foolish, but I wanted to crack that mask!

"No."

"Why, then, did you recommend him to Natty Rothschild?"

"See, Willy?" Frank Cardew crowed. "I told you he knows everything!"

For the first time Herr Wilhelm Luscher looked displeased. Enough! I told myself; I did not want his displeasure to turn to suspicion. "It is still true that I never met him," he said, recovering easily. "He had some dealings with my father—business dealings. I merely remembered that papa had spoken well of him. Yes, yes, now I recall saying something to Lord Rothschild. It's amazing you should know about it."

"It's nothing," I muttered. "Natty's an old friend. He merely mentioned it in passing."

"Yet you remembered it . . ." Suspicion now?

"Mere showing off, Herr Luscher. That locked box Frank mentioned? It's full of more trivia than scandal." Shamelessly, I trembled on my stick to show my frailty—harmless old Simon Bliss.

"Remarkable nonetheless." He seemed soothed, but I could not be certain. "Please do call me Willy." He shook my hand again.

"And you must call me Simon." It stuck in my throat to say it.

"Old friends already?" Frank Cardew asked, a little bored. "Glad to be the instrument." He made a face at his empty glass. "I'm for another drink. Will you chaps join me?"

Herr Luscher and I declined. The rest strolled off to the bar. Willy had not been drinking at all. To stay alert? To take our measure?

I continued to take his. "Shall we?" I gestured at a black leather sofa nearby. "These old bones . . ."

"Certainly."

We sat, the German looking a picture of ease, with crossed legs, one arm draped over the sofa back. Above us hung an ill-painted equestrian portrait of some forgotten hero of the Indian campaign.

"So. You are with the embassy?" I asked.

"Yes."

"And what does a young diplomat do?"

"Oh, nothing important. I shake hands at receptions and help to prepare the state visits of our dignitaries; occasionally I accompany the diplomatic pouches to Berlin. That is all—*eine Kleinigkeit.*" He glanced at me, and I saw him make a decision. "I wish I could do more to help your country and mine to grow closer, however," he said earnestly. "Whenever I return to Berlin I praise your English ways and your cheerful, brave people at every opportunity."

I swallowed hard. "I'm very glad to hear it. Do you know the Kaiser?"

His eyes gleamed. "Not as a friend. But I have met him."

"Splendid fellow!" I said, not meaning it for a moment. I watched Luscher take out a pipe, a handsome bent bulldog with a flat saddle mouthpiece. "Your emperor has the right idea—he gives the orders; he is a *real* king . . ."

For a moment I thought he would laugh. "You are a monarchist, Mr. Bliss?"

"Simon. Please."

"Indeed. Simon." His voice grew soft. Thoughtfully, he lit his pipe and for the first and only time looked sly. "Yes, he *is* an emperor . . ."

"Mmm. I should think," I said carefully, "knowing the affection our king has for you—your unique position, as it were, for doing good—your embassy would use you . . . that is . . ."

Showing white, even teeth around his pipe stem, he chuckled, a light rippling sound. "Do I use my influence with His Majesty to promote goodwill, do you mean? Naturally." He was airy about it.

"Good." Glancing across the room, I saw Reggie Brett eyeing us. "Much as you love England," I said, "you must look forward to your sojourns in Germany—visits with family and friends. Have you a sweetheart there?"

"Ah!" Puffing smoke, he rolled his blue eyes roguishly. "But there are so many women ..." He chuckled again. "Why choose one?"

"Quite. You are young yet." I was thinking of Sophie Bernard. Would Willy merely discard her when he had finished with her? I disliked him intensely then.

He rose; his bright, callow look was set firmly in place. He clicked his heels. "So very pleasant, Simon, but I see friends whom I must greet. Alas, a diplomat may not remain long in good company but must spread himself thin."

"Oh, do spread yourself," I said crisply, pulling myself up with the aid of my stick. "Will you be at Sandringham?" I asked before he could escape.

His wheat-colored lashes blinked. "Yes."

"So shall I. We will have more opportunity to talk then."

Another bright smile, more heel clicking, a curt shake of my hand. "I shall be delighted." And, blond head held high, glancing about and nodding to this man and that, he was gone, trailing pipe smoke.

I could not help feeling relieved—and greatly disturbed. I was glad to go to Lord Esher.

2

As I approached the four men by the fire, the dinner gong sounded, and the knots of conversing men began to fall apart in a general movement toward the dining room. Dozing old club members, who would not have been roused by an explosion, snorted, climbed upright, and trundled off to the primordial call.

Lean, distinguishedly gray-haired Reginald Brett, Lord Esher, rose to greet me. His handsome moustache did not hide his mobile mouth and quick half-smile. "I thought you had forgot we were to dine together, Simon."

I shook the hand of the man known to his political enemies as the grand vizier of England. "I was preoccupied, milord."

"So I saw, with young Willy Luscher. What do you make of him?"

I gave him a sharp look, and his humorous eyes crinkled, yet with a touch of concern. I had known Reggie's father, Viscount Esher, a Master of the Rolls, and had followed closely this eldest son's unusual career. Since Eton, Reginald had been intimate with Lord Rosebery and as a very young man had caught Queen Victoria's eye. He had worked for her; now he was her son's most trusted advisor—the power behind the throne, the jealous called him. He was said to be an intriguer, a usurper, dangerously ambitious—all false. In his subtle way he worked for England's best interests. He had trusted me in the matter of police protection for Bertie. Now that I knew the German plot I must trust him for good advice.

"Willy?" I said blithely for the benefit of the three other men. "Quite charming."

"I don't much like him, myself!" rapped a swarthy, bouncy little man, jumping up to shake my hand. "Hello, Simon." He was the raffish Marquis de Soveral, Portuguese ambassador to England. His swarthy skin and simian features had earned him the nickname, the "Blue Monkey," and his amusing ways had made him one of Bertie's closest friends, part of the inner circle; he was one of Her Majesty's favorites too. He made no secret of his hatred of Germany.

"Hello, Luis," I said. "What's wrong with Luscher?"

Soveral screwed up his face. "His spiked helmet and jackboots, that's what—they always make a man unattractive!"

"Tut-tut, Soveral." White-haired Sir Francis Knollys liked to pour oil on troubled waters. He had been Bertie's private secretary since 1870. "Willy is one of His Majesty's favourite friends," he chided as he shook my hand. "Simon."

"Um. I'm inclined to agree with Luis," grumbled a broad-shouldered, stormy-looking man—Admiral Sir John Fisher, a legend, England's greatest sailor since Nelson. Fisher took my hand in a stonelike grip. He towered over us. If ever England and Germany met in battle on the high seas, Fisher's present effort to modernize our navy would make the difference between victory and defeat.

"Let's not argue. You'll eat at our table, Simon?" Francis Knollys asked.

"Yes, thank you. I want to have a word with Reggie first."

"Oho! Intrigue!" Soveral rolled his eyes. "Old Simon Bliss has some plot hatched! Well, we'll never get it out of him. I should prefer not to waste my time. Let's intrigue with some roast beef instead. Gentlemen?"

He led the way with his prancing walk. Fisher and Knollys followed.

Reggie and I were left alone in the big club room, which lay silent except for the rain spitting at the windows, the soughing of wind, the hiss of the fire. From panelled walls portraits of the formerly great stared into an idealized future. I sank into a chair near Reggie. If only those gallant soldiers on dramatically rearing horses and those wise-eyed statesmen could be resurrected to England's aid now! It was a dark hour. It was not just Willy Luscher's plot that I fretted over, but the course of nations at odds, rushing toward some terrible confrontation.

I gazed into Lord Esher's intelligent gray eyes.

"Is it time, Simon?"

"For relevations? Indeed." I thumped my stick. "Though I'm damned if I know what to do with them!"

# Jack Merridew's Narrative

Friday morning the entranceway of number 24 Norfolk Street was crowded with tall, studded wardrobe trunks, hatboxes, rugs, and travelling cushions. It was cold and bright after the rain. I had slept very little and had been awakened early as usual by Mr. Raddles' sharp jabs. "Let's see them Frenchies off!"

The staff was happy to see Monsieur and Madame go; they could then live like royalty without having to hide anything. Like a slave I had carried down most of the master's things with very little aid. I ached from the work as, at ten, having helped load a special luggage van—it had just pulled off to St. Pancras Station—I stood on the pavement and watched stout, white-haired Mr. Giddings puff and blow as he saw the Bernards off. Monsieur Bernard stalked down the steps, seeming to see nothing out of his bleak eyes. He got into the brougham driven by Mr. Rance. Madame Bernard followed a moment later, her cheeks flushed. She was very pretty in a feathered hat and lavender travelling coat, but she did not look happy as she might. She clutched a beaded bag, which, if she had done as she had promised Herr Luscher, contained the pistol with which she meant to murder the king. She climbed into the brougham, and Mr. Rance drove off. From twenty paces away I heard Mr. Giddings' sigh of relief as he turned to go in.

Shortly afterward I took my chance and slipped out into the areaway. Collecting my valise, which I had hid behind the dustbin the day before, I escaped through the mews in back, but it was only when Mr. Salt met me with a hansom to rush me to Curzon Street that I breathed easy. The Bernards would hear no story of a runaway footboy until they got back from Sandringham. By then it would not matter what the servants told them.

I was let off at Mr. Bliss's door. Mr. Wigmore and Mr. Munns waited before the fire in the drawing room. They greeted me warmly and congratulated me on the success of my venture. "Sherlock Holmes himself would be proud of you," Mr. Wigmore said, and I flushed with pleasure.

"Where is Mr. Bliss, sir?" I asked.

The actor reached for a fruit tart. "Blasted if I know, Jack. The old fellow's usually punctual, and us with so much undecided . . ." He frowned but seemed nonetheless to enjoy the pastry.

"Patience, Wiggins. Uncle will be here," Mr. Munns said, soberly rubbing his bushy moustache.

Just then there was the sound of carriage wheels at the curb. A moment later Mr. Bliss ushered in a tall, distinguished-looking gentleman. They gave their hats and coats to Nancy, who withdrew. We stood as Mr. Bliss led the stranger to the fire.

"Lord Esher, this is Mr. Frederick Wigmore, Mr. Herbert

Munns, and Jack Merridew," Mr. Bliss said. To me he added, "Glad to see you safe, Jack. Brave work!" And he squeezed my shoulder.

Lord Esher shook everyone's hand, even mine. "So you're the lad discovered Wilhelm Luscher's plot? I'm very happy to know you!"

"Thank you, sir," I said. I liked Lord Esher. He had gray hair and sharp but kind gray eyes. I knew he was a man whom Mr. Bliss had confidence in.

"Sit down, Reggie, sit." Mr. Bliss himself sank into his chair. We all took our places.

"I'm glad to meet you, too, Mr. Wigmore," Lord Esher said. "I've seen you on stage; I must say your real appearance quite startles me. I understand you are to perform for His Majesty, for all of us, tomorrow night."

"If we decide to go through with this thing, I shall," said Mr. Wigmore, smiling. "And you, milord, you've been seeing to it nothing happens to Teddy?" He stretched out his long legs.

"Teddy? Mmm, yes," Lord Esher looked amused. "I've been doing that indeed. Now I know the reason, I'm very glad for it. Well," he placed his hands on his knees, "the problem now is to decide what to do next."

"Quite," Mr. Bliss murmured. He looked tired, and the lines around his eyes were deeper than ever. I hoped he was not doing too much.

"Simon and I have discussed the matter at great length," Lord Esher went on.

"Late into the night, I might add," Mr. Bliss put in.

"And we are inclined to think that His Majesty ought not to be informed."

Mr. Munns blinked. "Whyever not? Isn't that dangerous? Uncle . . . ?"

Mr. Bliss passed a hand before his eyes. "Let Reggie tell you our thinking, Herbert."

"Certainly, but—" Agitatedly, Mr. Munns began to polish his glasses.

"There are many considerations," Lord Esher said, "but first allow me to say that I'm quite aware of the seriousness of the threat. More than a man's life is at stake. His Majesty is central in European politics; he isn't called the 'Uncle of

Europe' for nothing. And it's more than that he's related to nearly every royal house from Greece to Norway. He's the most respected of all monarchs. If he should ignominiously fall, as Willy Luscher plans for him to do, using that poor Bernard woman, it will rock the already unstable balance of powers. No nation will be unaffected. I don't want to see Europe's huge standing armies, which are larger than at any time in history, on the move. At the very least, good relations between England and France will end, anti-English sentiment will flare up everywhere, and Germany, heading the Triple Alliance with Austria-Hungary and Italy, will be left to call the shots in Europe. England will be at Germany's mercy."

"Then the plot must be made known!" Mr. Munns's moustache was bristling.

Lord Esher pursed his lips. "May I?" He poured himself coffee, leaned back, and crossed his legs. "Made known to whom, Mr. Munns? To the police? Let us say we tell the police, and an investigation is launched. Do you think the English press, not to mention the French and German newspapers, indeed those of the world, would not hear of it? They would, surely; the lurid light of scandal would flood every corner of the affair, and I'm rather afraid it would be you and I—His Majesty too—who would be made to look the fools, not wily Herr Wilhelm Luscher and Madame Bernard. Whose word do we have? Jack's?" He nodded to me. "Don't mistake me, *I* believe you—but to accuse a respected German who is an embassy official, and a beautiful Frenchwoman, on the evidence of a page boy and some . . . ah . . . highly irregular investigations on the part of a stage actor? Well, gentlemen, it may not be done!"

Mr. Munns fidgeted. Eyes bright, Mr. Wigmore listened while he popped several more tarts into his mouth. Mr. Bliss nodded glumly at every word.

"And then, His Majesty's delicate relations with Madame Bernard," Lord Esher continued. "We cannot take the chance of those becoming general knowledge." He lowered his lashes over his cup. "What is understood among gentlemen and ladies might not be understood by the public."

"It is not always understood even by gentlemen and

ladies," Mr. Bliss commented. "Monsieur Bernard, you know."

Lord Esher nodded. "Indeed. Too, what sort of light would these accusations cast on His Majesty's judgement in his choice of friends? A very bad one, I think. Do you see, Mr. Munns," he spoke kindly but firmly, "why we must consider very carefully what's to be done?"

Mr. Munns sucked his cheeks. "Mmm. Well, yes. Now you put it that way. The public must not know, but," his pouchy eyes stared, "surely His Majesty ..."

Lord Esher gazed at the ceiling. "His Majesty? Yes, we might tell His Majesty." He looked sharply at Mr. Munns. "The old fellow loves Madame Bernard, you know."

"But—"

"And he's enchanted by Willy. Youth. They flatter him. He's completely taken in, as was I. He *believes,* don't you see. It will be a great blow. Need we tell him?" He spoke intently.

Mr. Bliss gently thumped his blackthorn. "*Must* we tell him—that's the question."

"Is there perhaps another way?" Lord Esher asked.

"Would Teddy believe us even if we did tell him?" Mr. Wigmore put in.

Lord Esher nodded. "Our evidence is slim. And the king is not in the best of health—smokes too much, curses his broken wind. He's crotchety, is what I mean. He'd be liable to fly into a rage, stalk off, and grumble to Willy, 'Do you know what damn fool nonsense Esher's been pouring in my ear about you?' "

"It would be a disaster!" Mr. Bliss said.

"We must avoid it," Lord Esher agreed.

"So His Majesty's our enemy too? But where does that leave us?" Mr. Munns asked.

Mr. Bliss didn't look happy. "With our Sandringham plan."

"Plan?" Mr. Wigmore guffawed. "What plan?"

Frowning, Lord Esher leaned forward and struck a fist into a palm. "What's needed, gentlemen, is a method of prising Luscher and the Bernard woman free of the king— they're like barnacles!—without hurting him, without spoiling the old fellow's birthday. See here, we have him watched by the police, and his enemies are being watched too; Madame Bernard will get no chance to shoot him. That much is taken care of. But we can't watch them forever. Having Willy recalled to Germany and getting Sophie to give up Edward in favor of her husband—that's what's wanted."

"It's Luscher she ought to give up!" Mr. Bliss muttered. "He's the one making her do this."

"To act by indirection ..." Mr. Wigmore chewed these words.

We were silent for a time, the clock on the mantlepiece ticking softly, its hands moving toward the hour when the royal train would leave St. Pancras Station for Sandringham.

I wanted to help. "Sir," I said. "Herr Luscher meant to trap His Majesty by some scandal. What if there were some scandal about him instead? Something that would disgrace him, drive him off. Then Madame Bernard would leave the king."

Mr. Bliss looked at me, and for the first time his eyes brightened. "It's an idea, Jack! Nothing so horrifies society as scandal. And what a joke! To turn the tables on the bloody German!"

"But how?" Lord Esher began.

Suddenly Mr. Wigmore jumped up and began to pace, his face aglow. "How, indeed ... how ... how ... ?" He ran a hand several times through his shock of blond hair. "Gaming, that's it! A scandal involving gaming would do the trick. Remember the outrage over Tranby Croft at which a man's reputation was ruined? That's surely it! We know Luscher loves to gamble ..."

"I can testify to that," Lord Esher said. "He likes any sort of wager—it seems his weakness. I must warn you, however, that he likes to win—and usually does."

Mr. Wigmore stopped pacing and faced us. "Not this time." He beamed. "We shall, as it were, stack the cards against him! Luscher smokes a pipe, doesn't he? Herbert, you saw him smoke it often."

"Yes, he was never without it."

"A bent bulldog with a flat saddle mouthpiece, to be

exact," Mr. Bliss grumbled. "The fellow's an addict. But I don't see—"

Mr. Wigmore plucked at Mr. Munns's sleeve. "Hurry, then, Herbert! Up! We must be off to your workshop, where we shall prepare a device to do in Willy!"

Mr. Munns rose ponderously. "Wiggins?"

Mr. Bliss was on his feet too. "We shall hear your plan first, Mr. Wigmore, if you please!"

The actor glanced at the clock. "There is very little time. Oh, very well." He outlined his idea.

"I don't like it! Too many risks!" Lord Esher said when Mr. Wigmore was through. "Too many unknown factors."

"I'm sure I can bring it off, milord," said Mr. Wigmore. "Just give me the chance."

Mr. Bliss was smiling, nodding, looking thoroughly pleased—no longer tired. "You know, Reggie, I'm inclined to think he can do it?"

"Hurrah!" Mr. Wigmore crowed. He rushed to the door, Mr. Munns trundling after.

Just before he vanished Mr. Wigmore turned and winked. "Until Sandringham!" Then he was gone.

III

Sandringham

# ❦Simon Bliss's Narrative❧

Shortly before 2:00 P.M. Jack and I were on the platform beside the King Edward Special, which would carry us and numerous marquises, dowagers, and rich Americans with daughters eager to marry a title to Wolferton Station and Sandringham. The scene was bustling—steam hissing, people boarding, an army of valets and maids supervising the stowing of a mountain of coronet-emblazoned leather trunks. Overhead sprang the arch of the station; ahead, a maze of railway lines sped into the distance. It was cold, and my legs ached. Yet I felt very little discomfort: our decision was made; we had a plan. If only Frederick Wigmore could see it through!

"Board with me, lad," I said to Jack. I had decided to take him, to keep him near. He deserved his trip to Sandringham. The Bernards, Willy Luscher, and a number of others had gone up by an earlier train; there was little chance Jack would be spotted once we got to the Norfolk estate, and I wanted his company—wanted, too, to have him about in case quick work needed doing.

"Yes, sir," he piped up, his large brown eyes taking in everything. I smiled. He helped me to board, my last momentary anxiety relieved as I glimpsed Mr. Wigmore and Herbert hurrying through the wicket. They had made it, then; they had manufactured the device, a mere bit of cork, glass, and glue, with which Herr Wilhelm Luscher was to be discredited tomorrow evening.

It was only then, seeing Mr. Wigmore's confident mien, that I wondered what Luscher would do afterward. He would know he had been duped; he would be furious. Was he vengeful? Would he turn his malevolence against the young actor? We would have to face that when the time came.

The saloon car was elegantly appointed in royal purple, scarlet, and gold. A liveried servant showed me to a seat. "The boy may go to the servants' carriage now, sir, if you please."

"No, no, I shall keep him with me for a time."

"As you wish."

"Sit here, Jack." I patted the plush seat beside me. Jack took the place, gazing about at the well-dressed ladies and gentlemen who were filling the car. I watched, too, noting Lord Esher nearby and seeing Frederick Wigmore enter like royalty at the far end. He sat with Lady McKellar and immediately fell into animated conversation with her pretty nieces Charlene and Jane.

Then we were off. The Royal Special slid smoothly from under St. Pancras' roof and began to click ever more rapidly over the points. Somerstown, Camden Town, Islington, Stoke Newington, and Tottenham crawled by. Then we were past the tumbled cottages and broken chimney pots of the outskirts of London and rushing north.

The train rocked gently on the rails. There were thirty or so in our carriage, clustered in animated little groups, the women wearing hats soaked in feathers, the men in dark travelling suits, many sporting curling moustaches, the latest in lipwear. I gazed at the passengers over the top of my stick. Each was appealing to Bertie in his or her way, because of beauty, a talent for small talk, a talent with money. The ladies chattered about tea gowns, the gentlemen about the turf. Here and there above the shimmering surface broke an occasional piece of political acumen, a wise observation on the human condition, a flash of wit.

"Unknown to them, they are the extras in a great drama," I mused to Jack.

"Monsieur Bernard, sir, will he play a part in it?" the lad asked.

"I sincerely hope not! Except afterward, to forgive and forget and take back his wife, a wiser woman."

"I hope so, too, sir."

Masculine guffaws rumbled down the carriage.

"Sir, shall I . . . shall I get to see His Majesty?"

I looked into those serious brown eyes. "Perhaps you may even get to meet him, lad." He brightened. I patted his shoulder. "Off with you, now. Keep Mr. Munns company in the servants' carriage. Give him some hints on the proper way to serve a gentleman! As for me," I groaned up, "I'll talk to Reggie Brett."

Jack departed. I joined Esher's coterie, as at Brooks's made up of himself, Soveral, Knollys, and Admiral Fisher. As I sat, Reggie let me know by a brief, reassuring nod that he had done as we planned, telephoned to Superintendent Patrick Quinn at Sandringham. Quinn's men were to keep a sharp watch on Luscher and Madame Bernard. There was the pistol to be dealt with. "The Frenchwoman won't carry it around," Reggie had pointed out. "She'll secret it in her room until Sunday, when she's supposed to shoot His Majesty. I'll give the word to Quinn. He can search for it when she's out and substitute blank cartridges. That way she won't suspect a thing—nor, more importantly, will the German."

"Good," I had agreed. Knowing the pistol was harmless considerably relieved me. Now all that remained was the discrediting of Luscher—I hoped.

Frederick Wigmore apparently had charmed the handsome Lady McKellar. She was taking him 'round, introducing him.

"Have you gentlemen met Mr. Wigmore? An actor. So amusing!" Her laughter tinkled.

We said hello. Reggie and I had decided it was best not to acknowledge any friendship, so greeted the actor as if he were a stranger.

Soveral invited him to join us. "I have seen you, Mr. Wigmore. You are very funny indeed!"

"Thank you."

"You're performing for us tomorrow evening? I wish you well," I said.

Frederick Wigmore merely smiled. If he were on edge about what he must do, he did not show it. That was for the best, but did he have hidden doubts? I began to have them myself. So much was at stake!

One hour later we were at Wolferton Station, and Sandringham was but a fifteen-minute motor ride away.

# ❧ *Frederick Wigmore's Narrative* ❧

## I

The air at Wolferton Station was brisk. It matched my mood of high excitement. Oh, there was danger, risk. But what could go wrong? I had Willy Luscher's measure—a pompous, conceited cad! I would pull his strings like a marionette's; I would get him where I wanted him, then . . . snap! . . . the trap would shut and there would be nothing he could do.

Hands behind my back, head high, sniffing the air, I strolled the Wolferton platform while the line of black Daimlers which was to take us to Sandringham pulled up. A northeast wind was blowing, fluttering dresses; I had to hold my topper tight. I kept an eye out for Herbert and spotted him among the milling servants seeing to our luggage. He managed to get it loaded onto one of the first vans to pull off; then he himself departed in a huge carriage crowded with ladies' maids. Lucky Herbert! The last I saw, he was briskly polishing his lenses.

I found myself standing near old Bliss. Sotto voce, he was giving his boy orders. I eavesdropped: "You must go ahead, Jack. You'll be taken in by a back way. Ponsonby's seen to it that my room is close to the Bernards'. Look sharp so they don't see you! Cosette or Dasté might be about, too, so keep an eye skinned for them. Once you get to my room you'll be safe. Wait for me; don't go exploring. Understand?"

"Yes, sir."

Jack scurried to find the old man's luggage. Chatting, Bliss and I strolled toward the Daimlers, each with a liveried driver. Lady McKellar and her nieces captured me for their companion. "You can't escape us, Mr. Wigmore!" Charlene cooed. I acquiesced. Simon Bliss joined Lord Esher and, making jokes, the Marquis de Soveral pranced alongside them. When we were in our seats, we pulled away from Wolferton Station and started uphill, the funereal color of the caravan belying our high spirits.

The nieces kept up a magpie chattering. Lady McKellar sat tall and dignified. I watched the Norfolk landscape unroll, rather a bleak setting—bare commons and occasional clumps of pine trees. The sky was a depthless, blue-gray dome in which jackdaws wheeled. The hazy dot of the sun was halfway down in the west.

Then we were past the lodge, through the massive gate of ornate ironwork, and amid a glade of rhododendrons. This was Sandringham.

Charlene and Jane exclaimed over everything. I observed in silence. First came the park, with beds of flowers and groves of trees spreading pale shadows across the lawns. Here and there rustic-looking pavilions sprang up like mushrooms. In the distance, on a rectangular mound, rose the house itself, imposing but rather less elegant than I had expected, vast and rambling in a style I could not quite identify—Victorian? Tudor? Jacobean?—built of bright red bricks with a liberal application of brownstone. All those windows, hundreds of them! Gables, two huge cupolas! Pinnacles, balustrades, and weather vanes smothering the roofs! On the whole, it looked more like a grandiose railway station than a palace, but it must suit His Majesty's needs. It was not artistic—Teddy hated anything artistic—but it accommodated his guests; that was what counted. There were twenty thousand acres besides, containing a manmade lake and river, a croquet lawn, tennis courts, a nine-hole golf course. The stables were admired by connoisseurs; the piggery bred prize-winning Norfolks. Woods and game reserves provided unmatched shooting. Three hundred servants, including gamekeepers, gardeners, foresters, and stable-hands, saw to it that everything ran smoothly. Lucky

Teddy! His birthday would celebrate this opulence as much as anything—if Sophie Bernard did not put a bullet in his heart.

We approached down a long drive. When our motorcar had taken its turn before the entrance to Sandringham House, I followed Lady McKellar and her nieces up the wide, shallow steps and through a tall door. Lady McKellar swept into the Great Hall, was announced, curtseyed, and then warmly embraced Her Majesty, Queen Alexandra. Beside Her Majesty stood Edward, the king.

Nearby, a stuffed baboon extended a tray for calling cards. Behind this incongruous creature was the Great Hall, two stories high, panelled in light polished oak. I glimpsed hanging banners, suits of armor, the heads of tigers and antelopes staring down. Towing her nieces, Lady McKellar swept on; then I heard my own name announced and found Their Majesties' eyes on me.

Never had an entrance meant so much. Taking a breath, I stepped forward. Queen Alix, of legendary—and rather frigid—beauty, smiled. I bowed, "Your Majesty . . ." and kissed her white-gloved hand.

"Mr. Wigmore . . ." A pleasing sound, with a touch of Danish accent.

Briefly I met her eyes, deep set, violet, a trifle unfocused. "Very clever I *don't* think she is!" Queen Victoria was rumoured to have remarked of her. Alexandra was past sixty but still slender, her skin rosy, her piled-high hair, lying in tight curls on her forehead, an only slightly tarnished gold. Her lips were red. There was something girlish about her. She wore a mauve tea gown with orchids pinned to the bosom and a collarette of lace and pearls to hide the tracheotomy scar from her youth. Her vague, charming smile was said to be a fixture of her face. I quite liked her.

"Mr. Wigmor-r-re is a clever-r-r fellow," King Edward said, rolling his Coburg *r*'s and pumping my hand informally. "Splendid to see you again, sir!"

"Thank you, Your Majesty."

"What, what, Bertie?" It was Her Majesty; she was very deaf.

"Clever-r-r. Clever-r-r, I say!" the old fellow grunted. He

was chewing a cigar and pulled it from his mouth to speak in her ear.

"You needn't shout, Bertie!"

King Edward scowled and momentarily puffed smoke like an engine. He was portly, dressed in an impeccable short black jacket and black tie. His face was full, his complexion high, his receding hair combed smoothly back. His nose was long and sharp; a salt-and-pepper beard covered his Hanoverian chin. He was no more than five-and-a-half feet tall, but his swelling girth in the admirably cut clothes was majestic. He had the manner of a king. His congested blue eyes could develop a terrible fixity when he was angered, I had been warned.

Those eyes became merry again. The king seemed to be enjoying himself. "Mr. Wigmor-r-re's an actor-r-r, my dear. Ponsonby's ar-r-ranged for him to perfor-r-rm for us tomorrow night, you know."

"That will be very nice," Queen Alix said, blinking.

"Yes, yes." Teddy's rumble again. He nudged my arm. "We met at the Gaiety Theatre, wasn't it, Mr. Wigmor-r-re?" His look dared me to contradict him. Then, smiling, he gestured 'round at the Great Hall like a hotel manager showing off his lobby. "Welcome to Sandr-r-ringham!"

2

A tall, silver-haired equerry named Mr. Laney took me in hand, leading me through the Hall and along a wide corridor, past ornate mirrors, armorial insignia, and portrait after portrait of nobles and royals. As we proceeded, he explained, "His Majesty hates for anyone to be late. As you may know, sir, the clocks here are all turned ahead one half hour so there may be enough shooting on these dark, winter days; please set your timepiece accordingly. Dinner is served promptly at eight-thirty. Your man may wish to begin laying out your evening wear at once, formal dress of course. His Majesty has been known to cause a scene if a collar stud is found improperly fastened, so . . ." He allowed me to draw my own conclusion. "Guests may foregather in the drawing room any time after six," he added.

We climbed a sweeping flight of stairs, from the top of

which a dour bust of Queen Victoria oversaw our progress. We turned right. "This is the west wing, sir. Your room is just along here."

I took in everything, especially the brass holders on the doors, each containing the elegantly hand-lettered name of the room's weekend occupant. With special interest I noted the card on the door third before my own: "Herr Wilhelm Luscher."

"Ah, here we are," said Mr. Laney.

He opened and stood aside for me to precede him. I strolled in; it was a pleasant room—spacious, well appointed, with a canopied bed, a bay window overlooking the park, a fireplace in which flames leapt brightly. Through a door to the left was the loo.

Across the room Herbert glanced up from removing my coats and trousers from my trunk to the mahogany wardrobe. "Welcome, sir," he said with a perfect deferential nod. One would have thought him bred to service.

"Thank you, Munns."

"If I may help in any way, sir," Mr. Laney offered.

"Certainly, certainly. Thank you."

He withdrew.

Herbert and I beamed at one another. "Well, Wiggins?" he said.

"I just met the king! Splendid chap! Splendid room!"

"Mine's not so bad either." He explained that it was in the servants' quarters, not far away.

"Tut-tut, old fellow, you make a fine valet, but I'd be happy to finish putting away those things."

"No, no, I'll do it. Don't want to forget my place." He came as close as I had ever seen to twinkling.

I stood in the bay and surveyed the landscaped grounds while I described meeting Their Majesties. "No Bünz, eh?" I asked in a soberer mood.

His back twitched as he hung up a handsome black jacket which I had had specially tailored for the weekend. "No. I saw a number of gentlemen's gentlemen, but no sight of that hulk."

"He hardly seems the sort Luscher would bring along here, does he? Hmm." Staring out at the fields, copses, and coverts where, tomorrow, if the weather held good, one of

King Edward's great shoots would be held—I got an idea. I wanted to show up the bloody German in every way. He liked to wager? Why shouldn't I, too, take up a shotgun and demonstrate some real shooting? Could I manage it?

I described my plan to Herbert. He didn't look pleased. "Take care, Wiggins." Through with my things, he shut the trunk, and we rang to have it picked up. "There's something I want to show you," he said.

"Yes?" I turned from warming my hands by the fire.

Coming near, he pulled back the left side of his dark valet's jacket. He was clever with a needle and thread as with any of his gadgets and had sewn a hidden pocket into the jacket lining just under the arm. Just visible, a deadly chick in its nest, was his short-barrelled Webley's .38.

I whistled softly. "Very nice, Herbert! Do Bliss or Esher know about it?"

"No," he replied, letting the coat fall back. "They needn't." So nice was the positioning of the pocket and fit of the gun that no telltale bulge showed. His moustache quivered. His pouchy eyes stared. "I hope I shan't need the pistol, but I shall carry it just the same. I want to be prepared for anything."

## ❧Simon Bliss's Narrative☙

### I

Simon Bliss!" It was Bertie's deep, guttural voice.

I had just kissed Alix's hand. "Your Majesty," I said to him, bowing my head. I had no idea how the king of England would greet me. Angrily, because I had dropped out of his circle? With pleasure because I was back? We had had some entertaining times.

Cigar clamped in his teeth, the king peered at me from eyes blue, now not quite so sharply clear as they once had been—for that matter, neither were mine. He squeezed my hand warmly. "You devil! Alice Keppel said I must invite you, that you wanted to come. Why?" Slyly, "Have you br-r-rought me a pr-r-resent?" He chuckled, seeming to think it a great joke, then scowled. "You had better-r-r be amusing as you once were!" He laughed again. "Ha, ha, happy to see you again, old chap! We shall have long talks, shan't we?"

"I hope so, Your Majesty."

"Good, good." He clapped my back. "See you at dinner."

I passed on into Sandringham House.

Though I had known Bertie for over a quarter of a century, this was my first time here; so as I was led to my room I kept a sharp eye on everything, on the overblown furnishings and clutter of royal possessions as well as the layout of the sprawling house, in which it appeared one might easily become hopelessly lost. My room turned out to be on the second floor, east wing. By the hand-lettered card on the door diagonally opposite mine—"Madame Armand Bernard"—I saw that Ponsonby had done his work. Monsieur Bernard's door was next to his wife's.

Jack was waiting when the equerry showed me into my room. By a slight nod the lad let me know at once that he had not been spotted by either the Bernards or their servants. I was relieved.

"Dinner at eight-thirty. White waistcoat if you please, sir," the dignified Mr. James, who had showed me here, murmured as he started to bow out the door.

I stopped him. "One moment. Mr. Frederick Wigmore's room—where is it?"

He consulted his list. "In the west wing, third floor, sir."

"May I?" I held out my hand.

"Certainly, sir." He handed me the list. There was, in addition, a printed diagram of the house on which the guests' names were neatly lettered beside their rooms—an unexpected bonus. Of course, the allocation and disposition of rooms would have been thought out carefully as a battle plan by Bertie and his equerries. One's social status was reflected in his placement within the house. Putting on my reading glasses and squinting as if I had a hard time making out the diagram, I kept it for some time while I memorized the locations of as many bedchambers as I could.

"I met Mr. Wigmore on the train—charming fellow—and

may wish to send my boy to him with some messages," I explained to Mr. James. "Would you show the lad?"

"Happy to, sir." Mr. James took the diagram and traced for Jack the route he should follow to reach the actor's room. I watched over Jack's shoulder.

"Thank you, Mr. James," I said.

"At your call, sir." He withdrew.

"Am I to take a message to Mr. Wigmore, Mr. Bliss?"

I knew Jack was eager to see more of Sandringham, but I had to disappoint him. "No. You're to stick to this room. I shall have a daybed brought up; you'll sleep here too. I won't use you unless absolutely necessary. Sorry, lad; you understand."

"Oh yes, sir."

"Perhaps after Saturday night, when this thing has blown over, you may see a bit more of the place, eh?"

"I should like to, sir."

I smiled at him. "I'll see you do! I'll see you meet the king, by damn!"

He grinned.

"And now," I sighed, "I must get ready to go down. It's an endless social round here—out of one set of clothes, into another."

The lad began to unpack my trunk. Outside the bay window, the sky was shading to purplish dusk. I went into the bathroom and began to run water.

When I returned, Jack said, "There seemed an awful lot of servants, many more than guests. I nearly got lost among them."

"All to the good. Less chance of Cosette or Dasté spotting you—or Luscher's man, Bünz, if he's here. Help me out of this jacket. Yes, yes, that's it. Indeed, some guests bring as many as ten servants."

"Really, sir?"

"Oh, quite. The boots, too, Jack; there's a good lad. Yes, but Sandringham's got three hundred rooms, give or take twenty; it can accommodate an army. That will do; I can manage the shirt and trousers, I believe. You finish unpacking, hear? And lay out my evening wear. It's spotless, I hope—don't want to give Bertie apoplexy!"

197

I sank into the white-enamel, claw-footed tub and let the warm water wash over my shoulders, the heat helping to dissolve my aches and anxieties. "You've brought something to read, I hope?" I called through the open door.

"Oh, yes, sir. *A Man of Property.*"

I was amused. "Mr. Galsworthy's novel will tell you a great deal about England's middle class but very little about Bertie's friends. Still, it will entertain you until I return."

As I soaked, steam rising about me, I hoped Superintendent Quinn already had found Madame Bernard's pistol and substituted blank cartridges. I hoped, too, that he would continue to be guided by Reggie and not blurt out anything to His Majesty. I thoroughly agreed that the less hurt to come to the old monarch the better. Madame Sophie Bernard? A foolish young woman, self-centered, too beautiful for her own good. Twenty years old! Her face materialized out of the steam—oval perfection, auburn hair, those green, gently mocking eyes. She knew her power. I had met her at Lord and Lady Robbin's when she had been in England but a few weeks; already London had been conquered—not since Lillie Langtry was it so taken with a woman's beauty. She and I had spoken. She had liked me, I fancied; I was old and safe—she could flirt with me freely and never think of consequences. My heart had beat a trifle faster; I was susceptible too. The young woman was vain, capricious, shallow—not without cleverness, however. I hated to think what Willy Luscher had done to her—rather, what she had allowed to be done. Was it because he was the first man she had met who loved himself more than he did her? Was it the fascination of the unattainable? Thinking of her beauty, I understood that fascination. If I were younger . . . Ah, Simon, Simon!

Feeling even older than my years, a hundred rather than a mere seventy-two, I rose from the steam like a brontosaurus from a swamp and, wrapping a towel about myself, prepared to trundle downstairs.

## 2

The pace of activity in the great house quickened in the hours before dinner. In every guest room maids and mistresses must be fussing over the choice of gowns, jewels, and coiffures, while valets were brushing and adjusting their masters' coats and trousers, seeing that every seam was straight and that nothing had escaped the attention of the cleaners. Curling irons would be glowing warm for ladies and gentlemen alike. Bertie was punctilious about clothes. "The advantage of being rich is that one can be dressed correctly for every occasion!" was one of his maxims, and too short a coat, the wrong color gloves, or a decoration worn a trifle too high could turn him livid. Bertie doted on form.

Jack helped me with the ritual of dressing. At last I was ready. In the cheval glass I examined my attire—black tailcoat, white waistcoat, white shirt with high, starched collar—and was unimpressed. Blast, these elegant clothes were made for more dashing figures! But I did strike one splendid note, a concession to Bertie's refined sartorial taste: an ebon stick with a silver crook handle. My humble blackthorn was left behind.

"Mr. Munns will bring you supper, Jack. I shall most probably be quite a while—no one's allowed to bed before Bertie, and he's a notorious night owl. Read your book." I touched his elbow before slipping out. "I shall tell you all about it when I return."

Jack shut the door and locked it—I heard the click—as we had agreed. I proceeded along the corridor, deserted for the moment. From behind Madame Bernard's door came a musical peal of laughter. Monsieur Bernard's door gave off sombre silence. Eyes discreetly averted, a tall footman in deep blue jacket and black trousers hurried past to pop down the narrow servants' stairs like a mole into its burrow.

Discretion was a cardinal rule here. The brass nameplates and the expressionless footman reflected it. Love affairs were a late-night amusement of Bertie's set, but the lower orders must never know of them. So a great game was set in motion. When the master of a country house planned a weekend, he never located guests having an affair in double bedrooms or even rooms with a connecting door. Nevertheless, the consenting parties were always close enough so they would not have far to walk. The nameplates prevented any embarrassing muddle. After dinner was served, beds turned down, and sandwiches and Malvern water put out, the servants would retire. The proprieties had been observed and the game could begin in earnest. Upstairs, doors would quietly open, then close, and footsteps would patter along the darkened corridors. Belowstairs the servants would drop their pasted-on masks and chortle over who was sleeping with whom.

We were fairly certain Bertie would not attempt to slip into Madame Bernard's room in the night, but we were prepared to raise a diversion in case he should; we wanted to take no chance of leaving him alone with her.

I descended the staircase, nodding to people I knew. All were drifting toward the drawing room, but I detoured, exploring the ground floor, passing card rooms, a billiard room, the library, smoking rooms, small salons where ladies could gather to gossip, a conservatory, even a bowling alley. There were Louis XV mouldings and window curtains draped like dresses from Worth; palm trees; stuffed Bengal tigers; portrait paintings in gilt armorial frames. Bronze animals guarded huge fireplaces, and everywhere were little tables littered with mementoes—inlaid boxes, jade, semiprecious stones, and above all else photographs of great and famous relations, from the tsar of Russia to the queen of Spain.

Turning toward the drawing room at last, I heard a snarl. Bertie's long-haired, white fox terrier Caesar was crouched beside a fat-bellied Georgian chest, the remains of an embroidered seat cushion in his teeth. He snarled again, as if I meant to rob him of his prize, but I had no such intention. Caesar had the reputation of being able to do no wrong in his master's eyes, and far be it from me to interfere with the dog's destructive pleasure. I skirted the creature and tapped ahead on my ebon stick.

I walked into the drawing room. It was a brilliant setting, light scattering from the chandeliers. Somewhere out of sight, Gottlieb's band played the easy airs which were all that Bertie would tolerate—Offenbach and Strauss. It was nearly seven o'clock. Perhaps two dozen guests had come down and stood in small groups—the men in crisp, dark formal wear, medals clinking on their breasts; the women in long chiffon gowns of rose and pale blue with tiaras glittering in their nests of curls. Servants in scarlet tailcoats and black, gold-embroidered waistcoats carried trays of bubbling champagne.

I took a glass and pretended to drink while I looked for Lord Esher. I discovered him near the black marble fireplace talking with Harry Chaplin, an old friend of Bertie's, and Sir Ernest Cassel, the shrewd financial advisor. I was about to see if I could disengage him for some private words, when the Duchess of Devonshire appeared at my side. She was more jewel-encrusted than ever—fairly shimmering—and rather too décolleté for her age and proportions. She smiled slyly while her rouge threatened to crack. Her nose loomed longer and sharper than ever, and her eyes were wickedly merry; she was in her element.

"I shan't snub you, Simon." She carried a black fan, which she waved to emphatic effect.

"Oh, good."

"In fact, I shall stick like glue."

"Not necessary, Lottie!"

She looked displeased. "I want to know why you were so anxious to be here! Won't you tell me?"

"Perhaps."

She brightened.

"Some day."

"Phaugh! You're impossible!" She tapped my arm with her fan. "I got you here, didn't I? Do you know how I convinced Alice Keppel? By hinting that you would dump Sophie Bernard from Bertie's bed."

"Lottie!" I was genuinely alarmed.

"Oh, you needn't worry; I did no such thing. I wanted to see you jump, that's all. Poor Alice!"

"Alice Keppel can take care of herself," I said. "This little fling of His Majesty's with the Bernard woman—it will be over soon, I predict."

She examined me. "That is something, at least." Another tap with the fan. "You are a mandarin, Simon! But I like you nonetheless. Let's talk tomorrow morning, while the fools are out shooting."

I bowed. "It would be my pleasure."

At this moment Lottie's husband, "Harty-tarty," wandered into the room, looking startled to find himself there.

As always, his clothes were somewhat dishevelled. Only he, of all Bertie's cronies, could get away with dressing improperly. I greeted him; he repeated that he'd thought I was dead. Wrinkling her nose, Lottie led him off.

More guests arrived, Willy Luscher among them. Heading toward the fireplace, I paused to observe him. Intensely handsome in his black tailcoat, he flashed his ingenuous look about the room, his blue eyes, behind their apparent nonchalance, taking in everything. I felt a frosty chill when they discovered me, but nodded, as did he with a bland smile, and raised my glass. He took champagne, joined a laughing crowd, and contributed jokes. He toyed with his bulldog pipe.

Turning, I shook Reggie Brett's hand.

"Hello, Simon. You know Harry Chaplin and Ernest Cassel."

I nodded. "Good evening, gentlemen."

"Evening, Bliss." Chaplin, a friend of Bertie's from youthful Oxford days, was decrepit and gouty but still showed a twinkle in his rheumy eyes.

"Mr. Bliss." The gruff, heavily bearded, sharp-eyed Cassel ranked with Esher in royal influence; he invested Bertie's money with a Midas touch.

"Care for some exercise, Simon?" asked Lord Esher. "Excuse us, gentlemen."

He and I walked apart.

"Quinn's done the job," he said when we were out of earshot.

"The pistol's full of blanks?"

"Right where Madame Bernard hid it, in a petticoat pocket in her wardrobe."

"And Quinn's men are alerted?"

"Yes. The only problem is lack of them. Having to watch three people instead of one has spread his forces thin. But he's managing, he tells me."

I felt uneasy and must have shown it.

"Having second thoughts about young Wigmore's plan, are you? I'm more comfortable with it than I was. Whatever happens, the king will be safe; we've seen to that."

"Have we?"

He didn't answer but, as did I, glanced toward Willy Luscher.

"It isn't any lack of confidence in Frederick Wigmore," I mused, "but the way that clever villain may leap when he sees his game is up."

More guests drifted in, the air becoming animated with the clink of glasses, laughter, talk. Lottie Cavendish came up to us and, diamonds rattling, drew Esher away for one of her "talks." Momentarily alone, I lit my pipe and gazed 'round the room, filled with a glittering and varied array of personalities. Besides those I had spoken to or noted, there were Admiral Fisher, looking like a stormy petrel; Sir Francis Knollys; Ponsonby; Soveral; War Secretary Haldane; the French ambassador, Paul Cambon; the Austrian ambassador, Count Mensdorff; Bertie's oldest friend, Charles, Lord Carrington, president of the Board of Agriculture. From the world of commerce had come the breezy grocery magnate, Sir Thomas Lipton; the furniture millionaire, Sir Blundell Maple; and Lord Iveagh, the brewer. Slender, balding Baron Charles Hardinge, whose stolen letter I had found on Samuel Jarrett's body, strolled in. Lady McKellar conversed with Lord Glendinning while Lady Glendinning spoke to Willy Luscher. Swanlike Lady de Grey, Alix's great friend, paddled among us. Golden-haired Daisy, Princess of Pless, wore her famous seven-yard-long rope of Pless pearls. There were equerries too—Sir Arthur Bigge, Arthur Paget, and Sir Dighton Probyn with his white beard down to his chest. And, of course, the family—Arthur, Duke of Connaught, Bertie's brother; and the children: Prince George and his wife, May; Louise and her husband, the Duke of Fife; Maud and her husband, Prince Charles of Denmark; and the unmarried daughter, Victoria, whom Alix called Toria. There were numerous others, too, of like credentials.

And there was Alice Keppel, wife of the Honorable George Keppel, who acquiesced with exemplary graciousness to her relationship with the king. She had been perhaps the favorite of all Bertie's many mistresses and like Queen Alexandra kept Bertie's favor by not expecting him to be too faithful. She genuinely cared for him; she knew how to amuse him. I wondered how she took to Sophie Bernard's eclipsing her. I did not know her but, as she had engineered my invitation, we must meet.

Crossing the room, I introduced myself. In violet gown

and pearl collar, Alice Keppel turned from a group of friends, her turquoise eyes regarding me with lively interest. Her hair was a shining chestnut brown, her skin alabaster. She wore her mature beauty without vanity, as unconcernedly as she might wear an old macintosh.

"I'm pleased to meet you at last, Mr. Bliss."

"Pleased to meet you, ma'am."

"And are you happy with your invitation to His Majesty's birthday?" she asked in her throaty voice.

It was a delicate subject. I wanted to thank her but did not want the nearby ladies and gentlemen to overhear a discussion of how I happened to be here. "I am grateful, ma'am," was all I said, bowing, hoping she would not pursue the matter. She did not, and we conversed harmlessly enough about mutual friends until the pull of the crowd drew us apart. As we separated, Alice Keppel gave me a look of frank curiosity, and I knew that only her remarkable sense of tact had kept her from asking why it was vital for me to be at Sandringham this weekend.

Seeing me near, Willy Luscher approached, wearing his best golden mien. I braced myself for the encounter.

At that instant there was a break in the crowd behind him, and Monsieur Armand Bernard suddenly was visible as if through a divided sea, his face sheet-white but with spots of hectic color on the cheeks, his eyes burning in dark hollows, his nostrils flaring, his thin lips curling. He sent a look of killing hatred at the German's back. Then the crowd surged again and, like an apparition, he was gone.

I was shaken. I shuddered at what I had seen. Suddenly I realized that Luscher had stopped before me, was clicking his heels a second time, and had spoken:"*Bitte*, you do not remember me, Mr. Bliss?"

The ticking precision of his speech brought me to myself. "Indeed, indeed." I focused on the lean, inquiring face— sensuous lower lip, curling moustache, bland blue eyes in which a hint of affront lurked. "Certainly I remember you, Herr Luscher."

"Willy. Please." He glanced over his shoulder to where I had stared. "I thought for a moment that you did not wish to speak to me."

"Nonsense." I managed a smile. "Merely thinking an old man's thoughts."

"I see."

We conversed about nothing of any importance. I was happy not to have my ingenuity taxed; Monsieur Bernard's expression had filled me with dread. "Too many unknown factors!" Reggie had complained; I was seeing he might be right.

Frederick Wigmore arrived. He was handsome as a raven in his black jacket, and I saw several ladies glance his way— Luscher, too, with the barest hint of a frown. Jealousy? It was remarkable how alike they looked—both young, blond, handsome. Did Luscher sense a rival in the actor? Just so long as he didn't guess our game.

As if by chance, Wigmore strolled our way, not appearing to notice us. He had one hand in a trousers pocket and was gazing about in a half-bored fashion as if he were among royalty every day. He nearly bumped into me.

"Good evening, Mr. Wigmore."

"Ah, Mr. Bliss, is it?" He blinked and offered a limp hand, which I shook. "And who's this?" He peered at Willy Luscher.

The German clicked his heels. "Herr Wilhelm Luscher, sir."

"Yes," I said, stepping aside. "Herr Luscher is attached to the German embassy in London. Willy, this is Mr. Frederick Wigmore, an actor I had the pleasure of meeting on the train up. He's made quite a success in the West End and will be in the play here tomorrow night."

"Ah! I look forward to it. Happy to know you." Luscher stuck out his hand.

There was a perceptible hesitation, almost disgust, in Wigmore's taking it. "Um," was all he said, appearing distressed, and he escaped from the grip fast as he could. He made a face at the fingers which had touched Luscher's.

Something dangerous briefly swam in the German's blue eyes.

Uncertain what the actor intended, I was about to say something to fill an awkward silence, when Wigmore commented blandly, "So these are the nobs?"

"I beg your pardon? Nobs?" Luscher apparently had decided to ignore the odd behavior. He cocked his head and smiled politely. He continued to toy with his pipe. The muscles along his lean jaw tensed.

Wigmore stared at him. "Manner of speaking, don't you know. Nobs. Nobility." He sniffed. "Though most of them are no nobler than I under the skin; I fancy my character's good as any man's here." He looked Luscher up and down. "At any rate, I had the chance to come see them up close, so I did. They're not my sort—I prefer a bohemian crowd— but one or two must be pleasant chaps, and some of the women are quite pretty, though a trifle thin-blooded, if you know what I mean. Herr Luscher, eh? You run with their set, do you? I know you do; I've seen your photograph in the papers. Mmm. German, and a great friend of Teddy's—I'd like to know how you managed it! No, no, I can't say I like His Majesty spending so much time with a German, but then he's always done as he pleased, whether it was good for him or no." He gazed appraisingly into Luscher's face.

Willy's smile had frozen.

I wanted to draw Frederick Wigmore away; he was going too far.

"And what is wrong with your king's friendship with a German?" Luscher asked between his teeth.

"Germans simply cannot be trusted."

The skin on Luscher's face tightened. "I remind you that your king is of Coberg stock."

"That makes no matter. He was born in England; he is English to his soul! You are a German, fresh from Berlin. Don't mistake me, Herr Luscher; we may get on well enough if you prove to be a decent chap. But I won't pretend to like your race, and you must know it. That's how I am— honest. No dissembling from me." And he looked glowingly smug.

Luscher fumed.

"Mr. Wigmore," I said, alarmed, "perhaps—" We were fairly certain Willy would not recognize him as the man who had bumped into Sophie Bernard's brougham in Rotten Row. Luscher had been far away, and the actor had averted his face when the German trotted by, but I did not want any memories jogged, any suspicions encouraged.

206

Willy did not look suspicious. He controlled his anger. "If that is how it is," he said, drawing himself up proudly, "then I shall—"

"That is how it is, I say," Wigmore pressed.

I tugged his sleeve in warning.

"So!" Willy nodded blackly, his *s* becoming a *z*.

"*Zo?*" Frederick Wigmore had the audacity to mock him. I despaired.

I didn't think young Willy could draw himself up further, but he did. "I am proud of being German, Mr. Wigmore!"

"Tut-tut. A German is never the equal of an Englishman."

"*Gott im Himmel!*"

Several people turned to look.

"Indeed, your people are decidedly inferior in every way," Wigmore went on imperturbably. "For example, as sportsmen. Do you shoot, Herr Luscher?"

"I am an excellent shot."

"And I am a superb one. I should be happy to demonstrate, but . . ."

Luscher sneered. "Do you back down from your boast in the same breath with which you make it?"

"Not at all. But, not being so good a friend of Teddy's as you, I find that my name is not on the shooting list."

"What?" I thought Luscher would laugh. "You propose to prove that you are a better shot than I *tomorrow?*"

"I should like to very much. Can you arrange it?" He looked innocent.

"A contest, do you mean?" Luscher asked.

"Oh, an Englishman against a German? Hardly a contest."

Luscher smiled thinly beneath his curling moustache. "Perhaps more of a contest than you imagine. Would you place money on it?"

"Gentlemen . . ." I said.

Frederick Wigmore's hand was in his trousers pocket once more. Again he looked bored. "A thousand pounds?" he suggested, as if it were tuppence.

"A thousand?"

"Quite. Too rich for your blood, Herr Luscher? You said you were a good shot."

"The question is," Luscher retorted, "do you have that much money?"

"I have it, though I shan't need it. As I see it, the question is, will you pay up after I best you?"

For an instant I thought the German would strike him. I was prepared to step between them, to use my stick if need be to keep them apart.

Willy chose to laugh. "You are very amusing, Mr. Wigmore. Oh, yes, I can get your name on the list, I have no doubt of it; His Majesty listens to me. I shall tell him what a good shot you claim to be; he always likes new blood, and one more name won't matter. If you prove to be less than you boast, that will amuse him too. Our wager must be strictly between us, however, *ein Geheimnis*. Will you be a party, Mr. Bliss? Will you hold the stakes?"

I hesitated. This was not part of our plan; I did not like it. Yet Frederick Wigmore seemed to know what he was doing; he had handled Luscher well. If he could get him to gamble at shooting, he could surely manipulate him into the decisive card game.

"I'll hold your money," I said.

"You will have your cheque in Mr. Bliss's hand before we set out in the morning?" Frederick Wigmore asked.

"Sooner."

"I'll do the same. It *will* be amusing, Herr Luscher."

The German clicked his heels. "I will bring down more birds than you. I will do it for Germany!"

It was the actor's turn to laugh. "And I—I shall act for myself." Hands behind his back, he strolled off.

"He is very rude, your friend," Luscher ventured to comment coolly.

"Only an acquaintance. I apologize for him."

"You needn't. Too confident, he needs a lesson. I shall teach him one in the butts tomorrow. You mustn't fear his behaviour has made me think any less of Englishmen; they are splendid fellows!" He caressed his bent bulldog.

"I'm glad to hear you say it," I said, eyeing his apparent blitheness. I hoped Frederick Wigmore was not putting himself in unnecessary danger.

I called the preliminary skirmish a draw.

## 3

The band stopped playing. Conversation ceased. We turned, and there in the doorway, resplendent in the scarlet uniform of colonel-in-chief of the Guards, the blue ribbon of the Garter across his chest, stood Edward VII, king of Great Britain and Ireland and of the British dominions beyond the seas, emperor of India. Beside him in a white Doucet gown stood Alexandra—small, slender, her beauty slightly frigid, smiling her familiar vague smile.

An incident marred the grand entrance: Bertie's face grew red, and he sputtered with a fit of bronchial coughing. Alexandra grippped his arm uncertainly. We watched, appalled. A footman in scarlet livery and powdered wig came to the rescue, ignominiously slapping the king's back. When he had recovered, Bertie shook the man off like a dog shaking off water. "Damn!" I heard him mutter. The footman slunk back to his place.

"Gottlieb!" Bertie growled to his bandleader as he adjusted his coat. "Offenbach!"

Airs from *Tales of Hoffmann* filled the room. Bertie fixed a fierce smile on his face and strode forward. Limping slightly from the rheumatic fever she had developed after the birth of her third child, Alix moved at his side. Men bowed their heads; women curtseyed.

The portly, magnificent old gentleman passed easily among the crowd, dropping a word here, admiring a gown there, making jokes in his guttural voice. He waved his fat cigar like the royal sceptre. I watched his progress. He grew more jovial and animated, more purely, deeply pleased, with everyone he spoke to. If he were the "Uncle of Europe," these were his nieces and nephews. He bestowed his gruff grace on them. He was in his element, certain that no one would introduce a serious note or insist on an introspective moment to spoil the mood. Like a fat brigantine on shining waters, Bertie glided on a sea of small talk.

The royal ship spied and hailed me. "We shall have our talk now, Simon," he said, trundling over. Luscher had moved off. "There's much to catch up on, eh?"

"Yes, Your Majesty."

"Paugh! All this for-r-rmality. Well, well, it must be." I

knew he doted on it. "Now," he gripped my elbow and led me aside while he sucked on his Havana, "tell me why I've seen so little of you."

We conversed briefly about past times. I remembered why I liked the old monarch: he was sincere, with a brusque honesty. He understood why power had had to pass into the hands of Parliament; yet he would not accept a back seat and acted in every way he might to preserve not only England, but the world, from war—not naively, through pacifism, but by arguing that we must be prepared.

"I'm very glad you support the army and navy reforms, sir," I told him.

"Damned necessary! Long over-r-rdue! Ah, what's the wor-r-rld coming to Simon? Between you and me, my jacka-napes nephew on the Ger-r-rman throne is the wor-r-rst danger of all; I'm ashamed to be related to him! Preaching against democracy! Preaching peace and gear-r-ring for war-r-r! He's mad!"

"We shall stop him, sir."

"We?" He rumbled a laugh. "You and I, do you mean? Old men? Um. Well. Yes." He chomped on his cigar. "I shall do all I can."

"So shall I."

"Indeed?" He glanced at my stick, my bent back. "Good, Simon, good. See you do. Now, what do you think of Sandringham?"

"Very fine."

He smiled. "I believe that it is. Oh, not everything is fir-r-rst r-r-rate. Those paintings, for example." He gestured to-ward some overwrought allegorical designs hung on one panelled wall. "I'm told by experts they're no good, but I like them. They're well placed, don't you think?" He chuckled. "I may not know much about ar-r-rt, but I do know about ar-r-rangement. Ah, Jackie!" He beckoned to tall, weatherbeaten-looking Admiral Fisher. "I want to speak to you about submar-r-rines. Excuse me, Simon. We shall chat later."

I bowed my head, and the king drew the First Sea Lord aside.

I heard a tinkle of laughter, a musical French accent. I turned, and ten paces away on her husband's arm was Madame Sophie Bernard, wearing a floating lavender gown that made her eyes seem even more deeply green then I remembered them. Obviously she had just come into the room, and I was startled to see the change in her husband. No longer gloomy, he gazed down at his wife's fresh beauty with a look that suggested the beatitude of a saint. It was as if he had been transfigured, made ecstatically happy to have her nestled near. She ignored him, neither looking at nor speaking to him. That did not seem to matter; having her close was enough.

She was for the moment the centerpiece in an arrangement of admirers—mostly men, but some few women, too, commenting on her gown, her jewels. The women might be secretly jealous of her beauty, but they knew she was mistress to the king and thus must be granted every favour of kindness and attention. Was the young woman nervous to be in the same room with the queen, with Alice Keppel, with her true love, Willy Luscher, and with King Edward of England, whom she planned to murder? She was animated, certainly; her laughter was quick— perhaps too brittle? But if this were due to agitation I could not tell; after all, this was a grand occasion for everyone.

I looked around. Willy Luscher was far away. Avoiding the Bernards? The crowd had grown noisy again; Gottlieb's banal music cantered on. I watched Queen Alix. Smiling and blinking as if she heard every word that was said to her, she made her way among her guests. She loved parties, games. She was notoriously unpunctual, and I wondered how Bertie had got her to the drawing room on time. A little frightened of his good, pure wife, so different from and so wronged by him, Bertie usually glumly tolerated her lateness. In return for his indulgence she let him have his way with women.

Her Majesty warmly greeted Mrs. Keppel, who spoke carefully so the queen could hear. Alix's friendship with her husband's former mistress was a tribute to Alice Keppel's graciousness and tact, which had made a friend of her royal lover's wife. They conversed intimately. Both avoided Sophie Bernard.

Bertie did not. He was the king; he did as he pleased. A smile gleaming through his trim, salt-and-pepper beard, he talked for several moments to Monsieur and Madame Bernard, nodding his head drolly, chuckling, occasionally venturing to touch the young Frenchwoman's arm with his white-gloved hand. Monsieur Bernard maintained his dignity. He did not glare as he had at Willy Luscher, but stood in apparent calm, wearing an expression of polite interest. The wealthy wine merchant had been Bertie's friend long before the king had taken his wife as mistress. To all appearances they still kept up that friendship.

As for Madame Bernard, she laughed at Bertie's every joke. Her eyes, which her husband, standing slightly behind her, could not see, promised the monarch love, adoration, pleasure, and he fairly glowed at their sly, lidded gaze. Madame Bernard showed a pink tongue between rose-pink lips. May Bertie never know her true feelings! I prayed.

Across the room, wearing his brightest, callowest look, Willy Luscher watched her performance. I fretted.

The house clocks simultaneously struck 8:30. Led by Bertie, who offered Madame Bernard his arm, we marched off to dinner.

## 4

It was a stately procession of bejewelled women in long gowns and gentlemen in black tailcoats that made its way into the dining room. There the enormous table was exquisitely set for fifty, gleaming with silver, Meissen ware, crystal glasses, gold vases filled with sweet peas, carnations, and roses from the hothouses, epergnes of fruit and sweetmeats. We took our places.

Great crystal chandeliers shone above, and on the walls hung Goya tapestries, Sandringham's one outstanding art treasure, a gift of Alphonso XII of Spain. Just to the right of each setting were name cards, assurances that there would be no awkward jockeying for position at the last moment. Bertie was as finical about seating as about the pinning of orders on his chest, and the place allocations were meticulously made according to close considerations of politics and rank. Bertie and Alix were at the centre of the long table. Dukes, earls, and high-ranking politicians occupied the rarefied air nearest them. Lesser mortals such as Frederick Wigmore and I were allocated baser territory, barely inside the gates of Olympus.

As I sat down next to Lady McKellar, I noted the interesting placement of Madame Sophie Bernard beside Frederick Wigmore diagonally to my left. They were near enough so I would be able to hear their conversation. For the moment Madame Bernard hardly looked at the young actor, apparently not recognizing him as the man who had discommoded her in Rotten Row. Her attentions were for His Majesty, down the table. From under lowered lashes she sent him discreet glances. The portly old fellow's medal-encrusted chest swelled near to bursting.

Next to him, Alexandra smiled as her guests seated themselves. There was a lull while we turned our eyes to the hand-written menus in silver holders. Bertie was a gourmet as well as a gourmand; the menu demonstrated that. It was long—ten courses, eight wines—and had been prepared by the legendary Monsieur Ménager; it was no less than a culinary battle plan. I read with dismay: *Consommé Printanier à l'Impériale* (Coronation Sherry, 1837), *Filets de Truites à la Russe* (Madeira, 1853), *Poulardes à la Norvégienne* (Rudesheim, 1893), and *Selles Présalé à la Niçoise* (Moet Dry Imperial, 1892). There was more, including Monsieur Ménager's most famous creation: an ortolan within a quail, a truffle within the ortolan, *pâté de foie gras* within the truffle. We would end with *Petits Soufflés Glacés Princesse* and an 1800 brandy. I glanced around. As most of the guests were used to these endless meals, every eye sparkled in anticipation. How did their constitutions and figures bear it?

The upperservants, in dark blue tailcoats with gilt buttons embossed with the royal cipher, bore down on us carrying gleaming tureens of soup. They splashed our glasses full of sherry. I ate little and observed the proceedings.

Bertie's guttural voice led the soaring conversation, his complexion flaming redder as dish succeeded fabulous dish. Service was *à la Russe*—His Majesty first; then the white-gloved butlers made their way to us with groaning platters, tureens, and wine bottles. At the end of each course Bertie rang a bell for the dishes to be cleared away in preparation for the next onslaught of food.

To my right, handsome Lady Glendinning chatted with Sir Julius Zarchin. To my left was Lady McKellar. Across the table one of the McKellar nieces chattered to Frederick Wigmore. He smiled politely. Sophie Bernard spoke to Lord Glendinning.

The courses flowed by. In the midst of the *Céleri Froid à la Vinaigrette*, the Frenchwoman's green eyes glanced for the first time at Frederick Wigmore and widened. Leaning forward to take up my glass of wine, I looked down the table. Willy Luscher sat six places from me. I saw that though he was conversing with Francis Knollys he kept an eye on Sophie Bernard. He saw her surprised expression. He glanced at Wigmore, and a cold look flitted across his face.

Some instinct made him glance my way. I smiled and raised my glass. The German's white teeth flashed beneath his moustache as, silently, he returned my toast.

I sat back and poked at my celery, continuing to observe Sophie Bernard—milk-white shoulders bare above lavender lace; upswept auburn hair, a tiny tiara of diamonds sparkling among the curls. She was still, discreetly, examining Frederick Wigmore, and I sensed he knew she had noticed him. She touched the actor's hand.

Wigmore turned and smiled pleasantly. "Good evening, Madame Bernard."

"*Bon soir, Monsieur Wigmore,*" her voice purred.

He seemed to brighten. "You remember me, then! *Parlons français?*"

Sticking out her plump lower lip, she shook her head. "*Pas ici.* I would rather speak English." She fluttered her lashes. "You are a friend of the king?"

"Hardly his friend. I met him only once, three years ago. I'm an actor, you know; I'm to entertain him—you as well, I hope—in a play tomorrow night. The king kindly remembered me and invited me to join his guests. He's a great theatregoer."

"Ah, yes? You will entertain us? You were not entertaining the last time we met!"

"I hoped you had forgotten. Since not, allow me to apologize again for the unfortunate incident."

The tip of her gloved finger grazed his hand once more. "*Non.* I am the one to apologize. *J'en faisais trop.* I behaved

214

dreadfully over what was, after all, only an accident." She widened her green, almond-shaped eyes. "It was an accident, *oui?*"

"A regrettable one. It put you in danger."

She smiled.

"Although," Frederick Wigmore went on, "I almost wish that I had ordered my driver to strike your brougham."

"*Comment?*"

"Oh, I do, quite!" Now he smiled. "It would be proof of how much I wanted to meet you."

She did not look displeased but, "You must not flirt, Monsieur Wigmore!" she said firmly. "Let us talk of something else."

"The theatre, perhaps?"

"*Si vous voulez.*"

"May I join in?" I asked.

"Mr. Bliss, of course. Do you know Simon Bliss, Madame Bernard?"

Blinking charmingly, she shook her head.

I reminded her of our meeting at Lord and Lady Robbin's.

"*Ah, oui!* Monsieur Bliss." Her voice was light and gay. "But that was six months ago. So much has happened since then!"

"Indeed," was all I commented, gazing at her smooth, white brow.

The stony-faced valets presented us with a *Macédoine aux Fruits.*

"I met Mr. Bliss on the train," Frederick Wigmore rattled on. "We talked about plays, actors, actresses. Mr. Bliss doesn't like the music halls, but I dote on them!" He popped a piece of pomegranate into his mouth. "What do you think of them, Madame?"

She ignored the question. "Have you known King Edward long?" she asked me.

"Nearly thirty years."

"Oh, yes?" They were mere sounds. Delicately she chewed a strawberry. Thirty years—ten years longer than she had lived. I stirred, feeling a twinge in one leg. She was too young for time to mean much. Six months were crowded with events; thirty years—incomprehensible. Her gaze wandered along the table, paused briefly at Mrs. Keppel,

Alexandra, Bertie, drifted to her husband seated next to
Lottie Cavendish, then lingered on Willy Luscher. She did
not know I was watching. Her lips compressed, and a tiny
frown marred the perfect clarity of her brow. Pain, was she
feeling that? She, too, was bound to be hurt.

Frederick Wigmore made small talk about the theatre. Recovering, Madame Bernard laughed at his anecdotes—a
child's carefree sound. I kept watch. Willy Luscher remained in conversation with Knollys, Count Mensdorff, and
others; yet I knew he was keeping half his attention on us, on
Frederick Wigmore particularly, who was charming Madame Bernard—one more reason for the German to wish the
young actor ill; I did not like it that they were shooting together the next day.

Monsieur Bernard? Lottie Cavendish looked distressed at
being unable to divert him. He continually sent seething
looks at Luscher, which very few at the table could have
missed. They appalled me.

I was very happy when the ordeal of dinner was through.

5

After dessert the ladies withdrew to the drawing room
while the gentlemen lingered over brandy and tobacco. Bertie smoked a fat Havana. I puffed my pipe. Willy Luscher
took out his bent bulldog.

Blowing smoke from one of his Egyptian cigarettes, with
his legs crossed, an arm flung over the chair which Madame
Bernard had just vacated, and a smile playing on his lips,
Frederick Wigmore watched the German light his pipe.

Bertie never liked to stay too long away from the ladies, so
it was less than half an hour before he rose and sailed out of
the dining room to join them. His departure left us free to do
anything we pleased—except to go to bed. A few men
stayed to smoke and talk. I followed the rest to the drawing
room, where the ladies and gentlemen planned the frivolities
of the evening. Some men went to play billiards. Several
tables of bridge were formed, Bertie going to one of these
with Alice Keppel, Lady Glendinning, and Francis Knollys.
Alexandra was in high spirits and wanted to dance, so led a
large party into the ballroom. Caring for neither billiards nor
cards, I followed this party. As we went, Soveral hopped

alongside Alix. She giggled girlishly at his antics. This was mild behaviour compared to former days, when Bertie and Alexandra were younger. They both were fond of practical jokes, and rumors had circulated even into the eighties of visiting the Prince and Princess of Wales and finding a live lobster in your bed, of Alix shrieking with laughter as she slid down the grand staircase using a silver tray as a toboggan, of Bertie pouring a bottle of cognac down someone's— anyone's—shirt, at which protocol required the dampened party to rise, bow, and murmur, "As Your Highness pleases."

The Edis ballroom was high-ceilinged, seventy feet long, thirty feet wide, and glittering with lights. The floors were polished oak parquet, the walls embellished with Indian shields, tiger skins, elephant cloths, and the like. At Alexandra's order, Gottlieb's band struck up the customary opening quadrille, and she and Soveral led out. Her Majesty's slight limp never spoiled her love of dancing. I was not especially pleased to see that Frederick Wigmore had captured Sophie Bernard for his partner. Standing in an alcove, unaware I was observing him, Willy Luscher scowled as the actor led his mistress 'round the floor.

I stayed for a short while, but, restless, unable to stay put, I left and wandered about. I watched Esher, Ponsonby, and others in the billiard room for a time. Chalking his cue, the cheery Ponsonby drew me aside. "His Majesty likes your friend, Mr. Wigmore, Simon; he told me so. 'Ver-r-ry amusing!' he said. Will you ever tell me why you wanted him in this play?"

"For God's sake, Fritz, don't mention to anyone that Wigmore's my friend. Nor that I engineered his being here. I'll tell you everything I can, if I can, I promise."

"Very well, Simon."

Leaving the billiard room, I wandered past potted palms, hunting trophies, and numerous portrait paintings of royal kin and English heroes. One picture in particular struck me, a huge oil in a massive armorial frame, and I stopped before it. There, in an affected Louis XIV pose, wearing a fierce warlord mien, loomed Wilhelm II, emperor of Germany, a field marshal's baton in one outstretched hand, his moustache ends waxed up nearly to his eyes. I grimaced at the

militaristic folly represented by the pose. The man was ridiculous, but powerful—and, I agreed with Bertie, a little
mad. Caesar snarled from beside a stuffed boar. I thumped
my ebon stick and, nails clicking on waxed parquet, the terrier scampered off.

I entered the library, a peaceful haven I hoped. The
sounds of music and laughter were dim behind me. I closed
the oak door. Masses of richly bound presentation books
climbed to the ceiling. I thought I was alone; then I heard
the crackle of a fire and discovered Monsieur Armand Bernard sitting by the hearth, a bottle of brandy and a half-
empty glass at his side.

"Armand?"

"Mr. . . . Bliss? Simon?" He hardly seemed to recognize
me. Absently, he rose and shook my hand; then, after gesturing vaguely at a nearby sofa, he slumped back into his
chair. I was shocked at the change in him from former days.
He had shown a dignified self-possession; now he acted
strangely, as if occupying another world. He blinked and for
a time talked with almost childlike pleasure about his wines,
Paris, mutual friends; but he never mentioned his wife.
After some moments of this, he abruptly sank back, as if
collapsing, snatched up his glass, and tossed down the
brandy. His eyes became hooded and suspicious, and he
took to answering any question in monosyllables.

Only one thing roused him. "King Edward is an old
friend of yours, isn't he?" I commented. "Mine too. Pleasant
to see him enjoying his birthday . . ."

The Frenchman sat upright, gripped my sleeve. "He is a
fine man, a great man! I would do anything for him, make
any sacrifice . . ." He sank back. Pouring more brandy, he
fixed his brooding eyes on the fire.

Greatly disturbed, I left him to his ruminations.

It grew near to midnight. The click of cues and balls continued in the billiard room, the riffling of cards in the card
room. In the ballroom the livelier guests sang songs and
played charades. I glanced in to watch Daisy of Pless perform a Spanish dance to much applause. Then Alexandra
insisted everyone take off their shoes to see what difference
it made in their heights. She climbed into each pair and

wobbled about, her daughter Princess Victoria watching with obvious chagrin.

Feeling tired, I wandered onto the terrace and smoked in the crisp autumn air. The sky was black and clear, sparkling with stars. I longed for the next evening to be done, to know the climax of the drama. I hoped it would be as decent an ending as we could manage—hoped, too, that we had done the right thing. Our precautions seemed thorough. If Frederick Wigmore failed in his plan, all was not lost.

Long, rectangular bars of light fell across the terrace flags from the ballroom windows. Suddenly these lights winked out. I realized that I had been standing in the night air longer than I had intended and that Gottlieb's music and the guests' pealing laughter had ceased.

I went in to find everyone drifting off to their bedrooms. Only the card room was still active, one table playing on: a foursome of gentlemen under yellow lamplight—Lord Glendinning, Harry Chaplin, Frederick Wigmore, and Willy Luscher. Just as I entered, their rubber ended.

Looking pleased, the rubicund, muttonchopped Lord Glendinning pushed his chair back. "I say, Wigmore, we've properly trounced them!" He stroked his moustache roguishly. "Luck was with us!"

"Luck?" Wigmore finished figuring the score, then pushed the paper to the center of the table to show the result. "Not luck, milord. Superior playing!" And he glanced significantly at Willy Luscher.

The young German smiled thinly. Leaning back, he rested his fingertips carefully on the table edge. "An extraordinary margin of victory, Mr. Wigmore. *Ganz fantastisch!* I have never witnessed such success at bridge. You must admit you had the cards."

Wigmore shrugged superiorly. "A hundred honors in the last hand? If that's 'having the cards,' as you put it, you're right. But you and Mr. Chaplin had several matching suits and couldn't make your contracts. Admit that it was fine playing defeated you—ours against your blunders." Coolly, he gathered up the cards.

I saw Luscher's fingertips tense; otherwise he appeared at ease.

"No postmortems for me," Harry Chaplin grumbled. "I'm going to bed." He wandered off.

Excusing himself—"I say, Wigmore, I'll play with you any time!"—Lord Glendinning followed.

From a decanter on a nearby table I quietly poured a glass of port. Yawning servants waited patiently by the doors until we all should go up to bed so they might straighten the card room and turn out the lights.

Neither Wigmore nor Luscher appeared sleepy. Stretching his long legs, the German began to smoke his pipe. As if mocking Luscher's pose, Wigmore, too, leaned back, extended his legs, and lit a cigarette. He smiled at the German. Luscher's gleaming teeth returned the smile. The two looks met like knife points in the smoky air between them.

I sat in a dim corner, unaware if either man had noticed me.

"I do not mean to suggest you are not skillful," Luscher said after a moment.

Waving his cigarette, Wigmore was blithe. "You couldn't reasonably suggest that."

"But skillful at what, is another matter."

"Oh?" The actor sat up a little.

"Yes. I found it odd how often, whenever Mr. Chaplin and I got the bid, trumps were unevenly balanced against us in your and Lord Glendinning's hands. Do you recall, you once held six of our spades while Glendinning had none? I kept careful track, Mr. Wigmore: five times a similar uneven distribution occurred—unlikely in a mere two hours of play, wouldn't you say?"

"One cannot control chance."

"No? It is naive of you to say so."

Frederick Wigmore's eyes were hard. It was very clear that Luscher was accusing him of cheating, clear to me that he was correct. "And what do *you* say, Herr Luscher?" the actor asked.

"That there was more than luck and less than honest, forthright playing behind your win tonight."

"Forthright!" Wigmore sputtered laughter. "You speak to me of forthrightness! And you, a German, an embassy man, whose emperor is the least forthright of men? Let me tell you, Herr Luscher, we English invented forthrightness, and you had best take lessons from us."

"Lessons!" Luscher stared at the effrontery.

"Quite. Do you accuse me of cheating? Out with it, then, instead of shilly-shallying; let's hear your forthrightness. Ha!" He tossed the cards on the table. "I told you what I thought of German sportsmen. And now here is an example of your sportsmanship—you are trounced and all you can think of is to accuse me of foul play." He sneered. "How predictably you bear out my theories."

Luscher was livid. He leapt to his feet. "I will not listen to insults to me, my emperor, my country!"

"You earn them, Herr Luscher."

I was at the table, moving faster than I had in years. I gripped Luscher's arm, at the end of which a trembling fist already was half raised.

"This is unbecoming, gentlemen! Please calm your-selves!"

"Evening, Bliss," piped Frederick Wigmore, smiling brightly as if we had met on a sunny country lane.

"It's His Majesty's birthday. Nothing must spoil it," I went on, frowning at him. "Think of your positions here. You must stop this before it goes further."

"I shall have satisfaction!" Willy Luscher growled. But he lowered his fist.

The servants were alert now; they would have tales to tell belowstairs.

"Satisfaction?" Frederick Wigmore looked interested. "Oh, I should be delighted to give you satisfaction, though you won't like it." He rose. "As a matter of fact, I want some satisfaction of my own. Mmm. You have it in mind for us to stick one another with swords or to fire pistols at one an-other's heads, do you? That won't answer. Use some imagi-nation, Herr Luscher. It's cards that are the issue; we'll simply play again. Tomorrow night, say? After my perfor-mance? Yes, let's do—a different game, one at which it is not so easy to cheat." He seemed to consider. "Baccarat, I think. Yes!" he said brightly, as if he had just thought of it. "Bacca-rat's perfect. What do you say?"

Both Wigmore and I had been watching Luscher closely; this was the crucial moment.

"I am thoroughly tired of games, Mr. Wigmore!" The German rapped. "I would much rather shoot you."

"Ha!" Wigmore came 'round the table to stand facing him. "I might have guessed it! Earlier you suggested that, after boasting of our English prowess at shooting, I wished to back down from testing my skill against yours. I did not back down. Do you do so now? Are you afraid I shall beat you again and that your ridiculous accusations will be proved false?" He sniffed. "As I said, you well bear out my theories about Germans." He made as if to go.

A strangled sound rose in Herr Luscher's throat, but with obvious, red-faced effort he turned it into an ugly barking laugh. "Very well," he breathed, "very well. . ." Inwardly, I groaned with relief. "But—I want witnesses to your defeat!"

Frederick Wigmore turned back.

"What do you say to . . . your king himself?" Luscher sneered, no doubt believing he had struck a great blow. In truth he had played into our hands.

"His Majesty?" Frederick Wigmore gave a good imitation of momentary confusion. "To play with us also? Why . . . certainly!" He showed bravado: "Let's have other gentlemen too. Mr. Bliss, will you be there?"

"I shall. It's a civilized way of settling this. Shall I ask Lord Esher? I think he'll come. And Ponsonby—him, too, if you like. We must keep quiet about this, however. Gaming. . ." I rubbed my jaw. "Bridge is one thing, but baccarat, you know . . . the scandal of Tranby Croft . . . it touched many men."

Luscher clicked his heels. "We can be discreet. *Danke schön*, Mr. Bliss. I am very sorry you have been drawn into this disagreement between Mr. Wigmore and me."

"Think nothing of it. Happy to help."

"I shall tell the king about the game," Luscher offered. "Not that it is to settle a dispute, however—just baccarat among several gentlemen. He likes baccarat."

"There's a card room in your wing," I suggested, remembering the house plan which I had examined, "small and isolated. What do you say to that as the location?"

"Splendid," Frederick Wigmore said. "Of course, we'll need a shoe and some counters."

"Shouldn't be hard to come by. I'll see to them," I said.

"Then it's set."

"Yes," Luscher agreed stiffly. "I am very sorry for you, Mr. Wigmore." He went to the door. "Go to bed. You need rest for the shoot tomorrow."

Afterward, in the corridor, the servants out of earshot, the young actor nearly leapt with pleasure. "We've got him where we want him!"

We were walking toward the stairs. I was angry. "You took foolish chances, Mr. Wigmore! Don't push the German too far; he's dangerous."

"He'll have my head lopped off, will he? Like Czinner's?"

"A stray shot tomorrow . . .?"

"No, no, he won't do that. He needed goading; you have to agree."

"Yes . . ."

"I counted on your stepping in at just the right moment, and you did. You kept the pot from boiling over—that's for tomorrow night."

I stared at him hard. "See you don't make a stew of things."

He merely laughed.

## 6

I had to admit that, much as his improvisational methods fretted me, Frederick Wigmore had skillfully manoeuvred Herr Wilhelm Luscher into position. With any luck we would set him on his ear.

Back in my room I found Jack asleep in an armchair by the cold grate, *A Man of Property* on the carpet beside him. Ponsonby had had a daybed sent up as I had asked. I gently woke the lad. As he undressed, he mumbled a few questions about the progress of the evening, but he was barely able to stay awake for my answers. He had risen at six and travelled a long distance from Norfolk Street. Climbing into bed, he promptly fell asleep. I touched his tousled brown hair.

I was tired, too, but I did not retire at once. Instead, in my nightshirt and dressing gown, leaning on my blackthorn as on the arm of a friend, I stood for a time in the bay window gazing out across Sandringham's darkened fields. I pondered great questions as the huge manse sighed around me, its sounds seeming to be made up as much of memories of intrigues long past as adventures still afoot.

At last I went to bed.

# ❧Jack Merridew's Narrative❧

I woke to find Mr. Bliss pulling on his boots by the fire. I sat straight up and rubbed my eyes. The fancy gold clock on the mantlepiece said nine. Embarrassed to have slept so late, I jumped from bed.

"Let me help you, sir."

"Awake, Jack? Thank you, lad. Ah, that's better. Damn, once I could touch my palms to the floor; now I struggle to pull on a boot! Time is the enemy." His boots were on. "My tan waistcoat for breakfast, I think."

I fetched it from the wardrobe. Pale sunlight slanted through the bay window. A tea tray sat on the low table near us. I helped Mr. Bliss into his waistcoat. While he buttoned the buttons, I slipped into my shirt and trousers. Beckoning me to sit opposite him, he took out his pipe. I felt very much at home, as if we were in the Diogenes. Mr. Bliss lit up, and, as we sipped tea, he filled in the evening. He told how His Majesty had looked, what he had said. I wished I could have been there, just to watch and listen. He was worried about Monsieur Bernard. He described how Mr. Wigmore had managed Herr Luscher. Things were set up for tonight, but he was not pleased.

"Why, sir?"

He scowled, his features seeming to bunch up. "Don't know for certain, lad. I've seen schemes far better put together than ours come tumbling. It may turn out well, but I'm uneasy. Promise you'll stick close to this room!"

"I shan't leave it, sir."

"Good. I know it must be tedious. I'll send a message for Mr. Munns to join you for breakfast. He's lying low too; you can share one another's company."

I helped Mr. Bliss into his brown morning coat. Leaving the ebon stick behind in favor of his blackthorn, he went downstairs.

I settled myself into the windowseat with my book, but I couldn't read. I kept glancing into the courtyard below, where the gentlemen on the shooting list soon would assemble with their breech-loaders. My part in the saving of the king seemed to be over, but I might catch a glimpse of him when he started out for the coverts.

# Herbert Munns's Narrative

WIGGINS told me next morning how he had boxed in Luscher. He seemed quite bright and gay, confident of himself. "Old Bliss objected to my methods, but they did the job," he said, expertly knotting his tie.

"You'd best listen to Uncle," I advised.

He surveyed himself in the mirror. "Quite fine, I should say. I'll wager the bloody German hasn't a morning coat nicely cut as this one." He turned. "What? Listen to your uncle? Certainly I shall; I admire the old fellow. But I must handle this my own way. Herbert, don't look so sour! Tomorrow it will be over and you can get back to your workshop. I say," he patted my shoulder as he headed for the door, "you did a splendid job on that little device you rigged up; it will be featured in our private baccarat game tonight—your moment to 'shine,' after a manner of speaking." He laughed at his joke. "Hmm." He paused, hand on the knob. "Do you know, Madame Sophie Bernard has charm. I danced with her several times. Pity she's been hooked into this dreadful affair. Well, well, as I say, it's over soon. For now—" he opened the door, "I must go down to play my part. Have I told you that you make a splendid valet? You do, decidedly you do. Still got your pistol? Tsk tsk, Herbert, you shan't need it." And he was gone.

Patting the bulge under my left shoulder, I was happy for the comfort of the firearm. I frowned at the closed door. I liked Wiggins, but his charm went a long way, and I didn't trust the seeming offhandedness of his attitude—hard to tell how much of it was assumed and how much actual. My young friend's play-acting spilled far too far into real life.

I rubbed at my moustache. Intending to obey Uncle's request to keep Jack company, I went into the corridor. It was deserted. I started toward the east wing. I looked forward to talking with Jack; he, too, loved London, enjoyed observing, acting quietly. I kept my eyes peeled as I knew I must. I had not seen Bünz, but there were hundreds of servants and I easily could have missed him among them. Too, I so far had kept to my cramped quarters except for my moments with Wiggins. Recalling the burly man's stubby fingers clamped over my mouth, his other hand on my arm dragging me toward that alleyway in the fog, I fervently hoped my precautions were for nothing; I wanted him not to be here.

But he was.

Some ladies' maids scurried toward me, chattering officiously. They paid me no heed—the servants' hierarchy was strict as that of the guests, and I was merely an actor's valet. The maids' chatter ceased behind me. There was something abrupt about its ending, and I glanced back. Bünz stood outside Herr Luscher's door.

Loomed, I should say; he seemed a giant. Inwardly I gasped. He no longer wore his billycock hat, and his head appeared like a cannon projectile. He looked queer, awkward, frightening in his manservant's clothes, like a dressed-up ape. No wonder the maids had stopped chattering. They crept by, Bünz watching them suspiciously as he had watched everyone who came near his master in London. He must have just left Luscher's room; he had not been in the corridor when I passed. The maids vanished. Bünz's awful eyes began to swivel toward me.

I jerked my head 'round and kept walking, placing one foot before the other—slow, slow—feeling hot, hearing a ringing in my ears. Let him not charge after me! Had he glimpsed my face? I thought not. We valets all looked alike from behind, didn't we?

Reaching the servants' stairs, I turned into them at what I hoped was normal speed, then scrambled down. No thundering footsteps followed.

I was relieved but jittery all the way to Uncle's room. There seemed miles of corridor. I knocked.

"Who is it, please?" came Jack Merridew's voice.

"Herbert Munns."

He opened. He looked pleased to see me but grew alarmed when I told him about my encounter. "You must tell Mr. Bliss and Mr. Wigmore soon as possible, sir," he urged.

"I shall indeed. Let me catch my breath."

Plopping down, I mopped my brow. Cox's Bank and death of old age seemed less dull prospects now.

## Simon Bliss's Narrative

### I

In the dining room I found that the long, mahogany dinner table had been spirited away, after the manner of the stage management of things in great houses, to be replaced by several small, round tables set for breakfast. It was nine-thirty. Perhaps a dozen guests had come down, among them Lord Esher. The indefatigable Daisy of Pless giggled with the McKellar nieces at one table; Armand Bernard sat alone by the tall windows facing the park. Gazing into the wan morning light, the Frenchman looked more drawn than ever, as if he had not had a wink of sleep. His hands twitched nervously; he did not eat.

Esher was at the sideboard filling a plate.

"Can you find enough to eat, Reggie?" I asked, joining him.

He laughed. "I think so."

Before us was an army of food—eggs fried, scrambled, boiled; toast, muffins, crumpets, scones; bacon and sausages; steaks and chops; chicken and woodcock; boater and haddock; deviled kidneys frizzling on a hot-water dish. There were yards of edibles.

Putting a bit of toast and kipper on a plate, I followed Esher to a corner table where we could survey the room.

In handsome morning coat and gleaming shirtfront, waving his cigar and jovially greeting everyone with a roll of his Coberg *r*'s, Bertie trundled in.

"He looks well," I commented, leaning my stick against a nearby chair.

Esher glanced up from under his brows. He nodded but frowned. "It's Madame Bernard who's keeping his complexion up. Damn, Alice Keppel was better for him! Not that he shouldn't have his pleasure, but . . . well . . . he's always gone too far in everything—cigars, brandy, women; there's no changing him now. It's the smoking that's catching up with him. Did you hear him coughing yesterday?"

"Just so long as it's not Willy Luscher who catches him," I said.

"Mmm. Or the Frenchwoman?"

"Quite. Superintendent Quinn reports nothing?"

"All safe and secure. No patter of feet in the night—not royal feet at any rate."

"It does me good to hear it."

While we ate we watched the guests wander in: ladies in pretty morning gowns—there must be at least twenty changes of dress for each woman here; not one would be caught dead wearing the same frock twice—gentlemen in short coats and dark trousers. Queen Alexandra arrived early for once, sailing in with smiles for everyone and nodding, "Yes, yes," to anything anyone said. Mounds of food were scooped onto plates, a third of it eaten, the rest left to whatever fate befell leftovers—His Majesty's guests could not be concerned about waste. The blue-liveried servants hovered at the edges of the room, appearing from their neutral expressions to be deaf and blind to everything. As always, small talk was in order, and most of the guests practised it expertly.

Frederick Wigmore sat with Lord Glendinning. Sophie Bernard, her skin freshly glowing against pale green chiffon, joined Lottie Cavendish, who dripped with diamonds. Willy Luscher came in flashing his teeth beneath his curling moustache. Sophie Bernard glanced at him, and I caught the troubled look in her eyes. From his windowseat, apart, Monsieur Bernard glared at the German.

Luscher sat with the king and Ernest Cassel, their table near ours so I could hear every word of their conversation.

Bertie related his favorite story, how Persimmon had won the Derby in 1898. Cassel yawned. Luscher, who must have heard the anecdote countless times, beamed with interest, as if every detail were new. Bertie laughed his bronchial laugh, slapped his young friend on the back, called him "Good fellow!"

The shooting list had been posted. Luscher indeed had made good his promise to see that Frederick Wigmore was added to it. Shortly after ten Bertie rose and, his gruff voice daring any man to be late, announced that the gentlemen on the day's list would foregather in the courtyard promptly at ten-thirty. Then he strode off to dress for the coverts. Frederick Wigmore and Willy Luscher left too.

At eleven the distant thudding of the guns began to sound from the fields.

### 2

The two great shooting parties of the year at Sandringham were this, for Bertie's birthday, and the one in December coinciding with Alix's birthday. Both would stretch out for two weeks, though not everyone stayed—or was invited—for the whole time. Most of the ladies found them tedious as I did; they were locked up in the great house—whichever one it might be, Sandringham or some other away from city diversions—while their husbands pounded away at the birds. Gentlemen who didn't shoot always were invited to keep these ladies company, and affairs inevitably began or were resumed. Many husbands didn't mind; they were happy to have their wives occupied.

We who remained behind that morning sought amusement. Ladies were to be seen in the library with books or glimpsed tête-à-tête in alcoves behind potted palms. Soveral, a nonshooting favorite, flitted from group to group, and wherever he lighted laughter was to be heard. Other gentlemen played billiards, bowled, sat in the smoking rooms and talked.

Lottie Cavendish and I had our stroll about the grounds, chatting about old friends, intrigues long past, affairs long ended. The country air seemed to have mellowed her; she did not pry into my reasons for being here.

Later I found Queen Alexandra in the ballroom overseeing its transformation into a theatre for the play. Workmen labored to erect risers and wings. Alix appeared to want to supervise—the setting up of the stage must have seemed to her like the erecting of a giant doll's house—but she succeeded only in getting in the way of the work, and Ponsonby, the equerry in charge, flashed me a grateful look when I diverted her. The queen chattered about her children and pet dogs, but little else seemed to interest her. I grew exhausted from yelling politely so she could hear and soon retreated from her bright, blank smile. To Ponsonby's despair she went back to annoying the workmen.

I came across Madame Sophie Bernard, alone, writing letters in the Great Hall, looking lost among the jumble of furnishings. I wanted to talk to her but hesitated—tired of being in everyone's eye, she must have chosen this vast, empty room in order to be by herself. I approached, the carpet deadening my sound; she did not notice me. Near, I glimpsed the greeting on her letter—*Chère Maman*—and was reminded that until eight months ago she had been Mademoiselle Sophie Thierry, sleeping under the roof of her mother's house at 23 Rue du Clos, Paris. Her father was dead. Her mother was the respectable Madame Blanche Thierry. She had a brother, Jacques Thierry, a young lieutenant in *La Garde Républicaine*. I had learned a great deal about young Madame Bernard over the last two weeks. I knew the stories of the wild life she had begun to lead at eighteen, to the despair of her mother, the chagrin of her brother, and the delight of the Parisian demimonde, which had toasted her beauty. I knew that shortly after that time she had met wealthy, eligible Monsieur Armand Bernard and consented to marry him. And I knew that there had been a shadowy love affair with Willy Luscher during the summer before her marriage. Madame Bernard was a troubled young woman who could glitter and dance merrily one night and weep over a letter to her mother next morning, a young woman of feelings so powerful and ill-directed that she would murder to please her lover. Seated at an elegant Louis XVI secretaire, she wept as she wrote.

"Madame?" I began. I felt sorry for her. The curve of her neck . . . her child's small hand moving the pen—I wanted to help.

She started, glanced up; she could not control her tears. "You. What are you doing here? Leave me alone!" And snatching up her letter, she fled from the room.

Gloomily I sank into the chair she had vacated, her delicate, tragic scent lingering about me.

Shortly I went up to dress for luncheon. Damn the social round! The thunder of guns still echoed from the grounds. How was Frederick Wigmore faring against Willy Luscher?

# ❧Frederick Wigmore's Narrative❧

### I

I bounded upstairs after breakfast; the shoot was about to begin. Herbert was not in my room—had he stayed with Jack Merridew? No matter, my clothes were laid out, a handsome outfit which Sewall of Savile Row had made up: blue-serge Norfolk jacket and vest, gray whipcord breeches, knitted golf hose, tan blucher shoes, a checkered woolen cap.

It was quarter past ten. Dressed and ready to go down, I heard a knock. A servant waited at the door with a folded note on a tray. It was from Herbert:

Wiggins:

Bünz *is* here. I saw him outside Luscher's door just near your room. I don't believe he saw me, but I think it best I remain with Jack for now, in case he's lurking about.

Take care!

Herbert

I didn't like it. But there was nothing I could do. Hoping my friend was right, that Bünz hadn't seen him, and hoping, too, that this new development would not change our plans for that night, I hurried downstairs. The shoot must occupy my attention.

A dozen or so gentlemen waited in the courtyard, Willy Luscher among them. I did not like to admit how well he looked in his tweeds. He flashed his toothy smile everywhere, even at me, but I knew what the look hid—determination to get back at me. He looked confident. I was not entirely sure of myself—oh, yes, I confess it!—but I would not let him see. Smiling back, I turned and chatted with Harry Chaplin.

Precisely on time His Majesty strode out among us, his belly girded in a magnificent jacket, a Norfolk hat rakishly tilted across his royal brow, a fat cigar poking from between his fingers. "R-r-ready, gentlemen?"

We heartily answered yes.

Growling with satisfaction, he led the way to the three open, motorized brakes which would drive us to the coverts. We climbed aboard and were soon beyond the park, out upon the gently undulating Norfolk plain, with its quiet brown-and-mauve background of distant hills. Along one side of the road meandered a hedgerow of hawthorn and wild rose; on the other was a low stone fence. Here and there the red roofs of the king's tenant farmers appeared and disappeared, smoke trailing up from their chimneys. The sky was vast and clear, but gray. It was crisply cold, our breaths white clouds. Pungent country smells of earth and grass blew against our faces, reddened by the biting air.

Luscher shared the king's brake at the head of the procession. I was in the brake just behind, nervous with excitement, for I was embarked at last on one of the famous shoots I had read about in the illustrated papers. Practically the whole twenty thousand acres of Sandringham were given over to the propagation of game. Teddy had raised the bag of birds enormously from the annual two or three thousand when he first purchased the estate. Dozens of cottages had been erected for gamekeepers, and over thirty thousand pheasants were hatched each year, fed on grain, and then let out when they were full grown. The tenant farmers were expected to subordinate their interests to the preservation of these birds, and their crops suffered in consequence; one paid for working the king's land.

The men who were to act as beaters carried blue-and-red flags and wore smocks and scarlet headbands so they could be spotted easily. Early on the morning of the shoot, the keepers in green-and-gold livery would have led them to their places. Then the head keeper would have ridden about on a sturdy cob to check the disposition of the forces. Game carts would have been rolled out to the positions where the firing was expected to be hottest. Now, near eleven, the preparations were complete. When we arrived—we were to shoot partridges at Flitcham Farm—the loaders waited patiently with guns, cartridges, and dogs.

We got down from the brakes under thick oak branches, the equerry-in-waiting going 'round to inform the gentlemen where His Majesty had placed them. I had drawn a number between Luscher and the king. I glanced at the German. Looking smug, he touched his cap. Had he arranged this positioning? It was not good. A thousand pounds of my money was riding on the number of partridges I should bag, but I knew that at the end of the day the equerry would record in the game book only those birds picked up for each man. Teddy had the notorious habit of claiming all those on the ground near him as his own, even if the man next to him had shot them. I was that man. Luscher would be far enough away to escape the depredations and might even encroach on my territory. I was caught between the two of them.

Silently I cursed the German but forced another smile as we marched to our places in the butts.

Huffing and puffing, King Edward stomped through the weeds ahead of me. "Willy pr-r-raises your shooting, Mr. Wigmor-r-re," he barked over his shoulder. "I am anxious to see you handle a gun."

"I only hope to do as well as Your Majesty," I called.

Out of breath, he waggled an arm to indicate that he had heard.

We took our places. We were strung out in a line, each man several yards from the next. Not far away were some woods from which the beaters would drive the partridges. They would fly over; we would bring them down—it was called a *battue*.

We waited, a breeze cutting through the grass. His Majesty kindly had provided shotguns and chosen two loaders for me from among the neighbouring farmers. I had learned to handle a gun from a former client who had paid me by teaching me to shoot on his Sussex estate, but I was used to walking up my game with a dog and picking it off with a muzzle-loader. I had trained a fine eye and steady hand that way—I was a splendid shot—but here the game would be flushed for me; I had only to stand and wait for it. That should be simple. I had two dogs. My two loaders stood nearby, each holding a fine breech-loader, which he would pass to me as I needed it. I should surely make a large bag. But Teddy himself was to my right. Would I end by counting as many birds as Willy Luscher?

I began to think I may have been foolish in my challenge, but I had little time to reflect on it. Among the trees came glimpses of the red-and-blue flags of the beaters, then shouts; birds began to rocket against the wide, gray sky, and the booming of shotguns filled the air.

The word *battue* was appropriate: the indiscriminate slaughter of unresisting numbers, in this case partridges raised for the express and only purpose of flying for an instant in front of gunsights, then being exploded in a sad puff of feathers for the satisfaction of the finest gentlemen of the land. I felt the sadness but little of the satisfaction as I hammered away with the rest. A smudgy screen of smoke began to drift down the line where the guns swung and fired, swung and fired. *Crack ... crack ... crack!* The birds wheeled, jerked, and fell, each one seeming to leave a dirty pockmark in the sky where it was hit, a brownish streak of doom as it plummeted. To have good loaders was half the battle. Mine were excellent fellows, though perhaps not quite so good as Willy Luscher's, whose men reloaded his hot guns with machinelike rapidity. He rarely missed a shot. But neither did I. I caught a gun from my right, swung it up in one motion, pinpointed my bird, dispatched it, gave up my gun, and caught another from my left. Catch, swing, fire; catch, swing, fire. The curtain of smoke rose higher, burning my nostrils like the stink of hell. The yipping dogs rushed ahead, ran back, dropped a limp bird, then crashed into the undergrowth once more. The beaters' flags continued to wave, their voices raising a fountain of birds against the sky. The fountain rained down under our relentless fire.

I glanced at the king. His face was an extraordinary red,

almost flaming, his eyes beady slits, his brow soaking wet with perspiration, as he ponderously blasted away, raising his gun with a grunt, firing it, and thrusting it angrily into the hands of his loaders, poor men whom he cursed fulsomely, whether he missed a shot or no, blaming them for everything—for his wind, which had been broken by years of dissipation, for his gouty legs, for his bronchial cough. He hit a remarkable number of birds, however, and kept his eye on mine as well. He seemed to share an uncanny intelligence with his two hounds. If he missed a shot he would glance slyly at one of these eager dogs, and it would bound off to rob one of mine of its mouthful. My dogs always deferred without protest to his, which showed no more sense of noblesse oblige than he.

The slaughter went on. My shoulder ached from raising the guns and from the constant rhythmic pounding of the recoil. My eyes smarted with smoke.

And then it was silent, the first drive over.

At my feet was a pile of dead birds. Tongues hanging out, my dogs lolled, panted, and gazed up at me with soulful, pleading eyes. I patted the dogs. My loaders complimented me; I thanked them. I looked down the line to where Willy Luscher stood. He appeared fresh and unwearied—rather exhilarated, in fact—and waved to me.

I raised an aching arm but had to blink because of the sweat running into my eyes. I discovered that I had a splitting headache from the roar of the guns.

In the distance, behind us, workmen like tiny elves raised a brightly colored marquee that billowed silently and gently in the wind. There we would have lunch.

But not yet. We walked to new positions. The shouting began again. The blue-and-red flags flashed once more. The birds whirred up in a mad, frantic cloud, and a hot breech-loader was thrust into my hands.

The thunder of gunfire resumed.

2

There were three drives that morning. At the end of the third booming round, Edward stomped through the crackling grass to congratulate me. I could barely hear him for the great dull wind that seemed to be blowing through my cranium.

"Fine shooting, Mr. Wigmor-r-re!" He looked at my birds, then glanced back at his own place, where his men were laying out braces of partridges. "Hmm. You seem to have a larger bag than I ..." A scowl started on his brow, but he would not let my besting him spoil his day of avicide in the bracing air. The angry lines melted. He beamed. "You ar-r-re enjoying yourself. Excellent!" He clapped me on the back; my head throbbed. "I like to see my guests have fun. Come! We'll walk to lunch." Heartily he waved to Willy Luscher. "Join us, Willy!"

Men were relinquishing their guns to their loaders and beginning to cross the field toward the marquee billowing a hundred yards behind us. The bleak curtain of smoke drifted upward, and with it the souls of the dead. Eager dogs fetched in the last-killed partridges.

Looking fresh as when he had fired his first blast, Luscher strolled up. I glanced at his bag of birds; it was unmistakably larger than mine.

"Don't count them yet," he murmured. "There are five drives after lunch."

Teddy wheezed as we walked. "What's that, Willy?" He paused to light a fat cigar.

"I was just telling Mr. Wigmore that he does not look well," Luscher said as we started off again. "Is it hard work for you, the shooting?" he asked innocently.

I forced myself to match his brisk stride. "I shall finish the afternoon," I replied with a blitheness I did not feel. *And you*, I added to myself.

We approached the marquee. Horse-drawn carriages were pulling up beside it, the ladies and gentlemen who had remained at Sandringham House disembarking. The women had changed from morning gowns into sturdy tweed suits; the gentlemen also were dressed in the height of rugged out-of-doors fashion. Looking invigorated by the crisp air, Alexandra arrived in a dashing little trap drawn by two ponies. Inside the marquee the servants had laid down a handsome feast of hot dishes which had been transported in heated metal boxes. We found whatever places we liked at the long

trestle tables—this was an informal meal, with no prearranged seating. The ladies asked about the shoot. The gentlemen boasted of vast numbers of birds raining down.
"Jolly good morning!" they complimented the king, and he
roared with laughter to hear that his shoot was a success.

Wanting only to nurse my aching head, I participated
very little, only watched through pain-dimmed eyes. Seated
nearby, Madame Bernard was subdued. No wonder; she believed she would commit murder tomorrow. Where had she
chosen to do it? At what time of day? Was it to be a public
or private execution? Poor, foolish young woman! Her gaunt
husband sat across from her. It gave me chills to see him
looking destroyed. He gazed lovingly at her, like a saint contemplating a relic. His eyes glittered strangely. His beautiful
wife's self-possession had seemed unflappable, but she could
not meet his stare. Gnomelike, silent as I, Simon Bliss sat at
the end of the table and watched them both.

Then I caught my first glimpse of Bünz. Old Bliss must
have seen him at the same moment as I because I saw him
start. A hulk of a man appeared at the marquee entrance,
then glanced about. His eyes were mean as Herbert had described; his hands, hanging at his sides, as terrifyingly ham-
like. It must be the fellow.

An equerry murmured to him, no doubt asking what he
wanted. Bünz thrust the man aside and approached Willy
Luscher, who did not look pleased to see him. Bünz's ugli-
ness startled some of the guests, and King Edward frowned
at the interruption. Bending, behind a hand, Bünz whispered in Luscher's ear.

"It's nothing, my man," I heard the German say loudly,
waving Bünz off. "Trivial. You should not have disturbed
me!" He smiled 'round an apology.

It was I whom Luscher's eyes sought and found as his
servant moved away. What was I to make of the suspicion
that flickered on his face? Simon Bliss must have seen it, too,
for he glanced at me grimly. He must by now have heard
about Herbert's glimpse of Bünz. I knew I must speak to the
old man soon as I could.

It did not prove possible after luncheon, however. Queen
Alexandra insisted all the nonshooting members of the party

follow her on a tour of the stables and model farm. My headache little better for having eaten, I trudged back toward the coverts. I heard footsteps behind me. It was damned Luscher.

He caught up with me. Hands in his jacket pocket, head held high, he gazed at the landscape as if he were window-shopping in Bond Street. "Why are you squinting, Mr. Wigmore? Five more drives to go. Are you sure you are up to them?"

"Naturally."

He rubbed his hands briskly. "I, too, look forward to them. By the way, have you a manservant?"

"Every gentleman has a manservant."

"Quite so. But yours—does he have a bushy moustache and wear glasses? Is he a middle-aged fellow?"

"Yes. Mr. Munns. He's been with me many years. Thoroughly dependable. Why do you ask?"

"Oh, my own man is dependable, too, if a trifle officious. He came to tell me about some problem with a gift for King Edward which was supposed to have arrived by messenger. It hasn't arrived—damned inconvenient!—but the news could have waited. In passing, he said he'd seen a man come out your room whom he thought he had glimpsed once or twice in London."

In passing? "Your man has a good memory to remember that," I said, alarmed though I didn't show it.

"Oh, he has very sharp eyes." Luscher looked at me. "Of course, the man he saw in town may not have been yours."

We had reached the new position. I faced him. "Likely not. Herbert does not go about much."

"Mmm." Luscher already looked bored with the subject.

I did not think he was bored; I was convinced Bünz had come to tell him not about a gift, but to say that he thought it had been my manservant who had followed them in London.

Luscher lit his bent bulldog. I watched him closely. In my wardrobe was a pipe so like his that only the most expert eye could tell them apart—purchased at Dunhill's just the day before, while Herbert labored over his device. Luscher's pipe would be his undoing—if we were not undone first.

"When did your man think he saw mine?" I asked.

"About a week ago, I believe."

I managed an offhand laugh; considering my splitting head, it was a fine performance. "It couldn't have been Herbert, then. He's been in Kent the whole of the past fortnight, with his dying mother. Only returned to town yesterday, in time to come up with me."

"Ah!" Luscher's response expressed nothing I could interpret.

My loaders and dogs returned; so did every man's. Luscher waved to King Edward, who had taken his place and already was growling at his poor loaders. Luscher clucked his tongue. "I believe you have fewer birds than I. You boasted perhaps too much yesterday, yes?"

Teeth gleaming beneath his curling moustache, the German turned and strode to his place. I stared after him glumly.

Shortly the flags were waving again, the guns booming, the birds rocketing up and plummeting out of the sky. My ears rang and my shoulder ached from the recoil of the shotguns. Several times in the course of the five remaining drives Luscher seemed to shoot wild, and pellets whizzed audibly near my head. Once my left loader cursed, and both men fell back. When I glanced at Luscher he seemed not to notice me but grinned fiercely as he unerringly picked off birds. Angrily I held my ground and called to my loaders to stand with me. They did, but reluctantly, and their rhythm was shaken. For my part I was disconcerted by Luscher's shooting near and by the news about Herbert; I was too blinded by my throbbing head to do well. When blessed silence fell at last and the equerry came 'round to write our scores in the game book, Luscher recorded 146 birds, I less than a hundred. My only consolation was King Edward's pleasure in besting me by more than twenty birds. He jarred my head with a hearty clap on my back. "You're a fine fellow, a spor-r-rtsman!"

With a gloating glance Luscher strode off with the King. I dragged after to the waiting brakes. The day had not begun well—I had traded £1000 for a splitting headache and ignominious defeat. The day was not over, however!

The brakes rolled back toward Sandringham House across fields ochre under the afternoon sky. From the motor ahead, His Majesty's chortling laugh rattled down the line.

3

Our hunting tweeds went to the brushing room to be restored. I wanted only to nurse my head but knew I could not get out of making an appearance at tea, a full-dress occasion. Herbert was waiting in my room when I came up. He had drawn a bath and laid out my black jacket and black tie.

"Thank you, old chap." I sank into the warm water. "Ring for some brandy, will you?"

"Certainly." He pulled the cord for a servant, then stood in the bathroom door. "How was the shoot?"

I told him.

"Sorry to hear it. You got my message about Bünz? What shall we do?"

"You spoke to your uncle?"

"Yes. Lord Esher too. We met in Uncle's room, with Jack. I was afraid to leave it."

"And what do they think?"

He hesitated, rubbing his moustache. "That we should go ahead with our plan." He stared solemnly. "Wiggins, I don't like it."

"Nor do I." The warm water was having an effect; my aches began to diminish. "But I'm determined to finish Luscher as we've agreed. It's just."

"And dangerous. Wiggins, Bünz saw me; he'll make his master suspicious."

I waved a hand. "Not enough so he'll withdraw from the baccarat game. I know Luscher's sort—he had some of me this afternoon, and he'll want the rest tonight. He won't be content until he squashes me, whereas I—" I found my spirits rising, "shall squash *him*."

Herbert still fretted. "But Bünz will have an eye out for me. It's a wonder he didn't follow me this morning."

I glanced at him sharply. "You're sure he didn't?"

"Yes."

"It probably takes a while for things to penetrate his brain. You're right, Herbert, he's beastly looking! You simply must be extremely cautious for the next several hours;

240

that's all it will take. Stay here until I've made up for *She Stoops to Conquer* and keep the door locked; then go up to Jack. I'll scout the way for you. You two can hold down the fort in Bliss's room until the thing is over. You'll be safe."

"I only hope you're right."

Downstairs at tea, servants pushed wooden trollies of meat pies, fruits, and other delectables from table to table. Feeling somewhat restored, I spoke to Simon Bliss. Glancing about with his shrewd, yellow-gray eyes, he looked like Voltaire.

"Take no chances, Mr. Wigmore," he advised. He sucked on his pipe grimly. "Thank God this thing soon will be finished!"

Willy Luscher came into the room. Noticing Bliss and me together, he came over. The old man nodded hello.

Luscher placed his heels together. "Has Mr. Wigmore told you the result of our wager?"

"He has. Congratulations, Willy. I have here—" Bliss pulled an envelope from his jacket, "your cheques. These must go to you." He handed them over. I forced myself not to look disappointed; I should very much have liked to put that money toward a new motorcar.

Luscher knocked his heels together again—tiresome habit! *"Danke."*

Simon Bliss excused himself to join the Duchess of Devonshire and her husband.

Luscher looked infernally smug. "And what do you think of German prowess now?"

"Everyone has a lucky day."

"Oho!" He laughed gaily. "What was that you were saying to me about sportsmanship last night, Mr. Wigmore?"

I was silent.

"You will be happy to know that King Edward is pleased to join us at baccarat."

I was, but did not say so.

"He will witness another defeat, *ja?*" Smiling, Luscher thrust a hand in a pocket. "You and Mr. Simon Bliss were in such serious conversation when I arrived. You looked quite . . . how do you say . . . quite gloomy."

"We were discussing the theatre. Tragedy," I added.

"I see. And you first met on the royal train—you did not know one another before?" His blue eyes followed the old man. "An interesting character. Collects secrets, I have been told. Does he really sometimes help the police, as I've heard?"

"I wouldn't know."

"Of course not, of course not." He slipped the envelope into his jacket. "Thank you for the cheque, Mr. Wigmore. I shall be pleased to take more of your money later tonight." Another blasted click of the heels before he wandered off. "Ha, ha! I have no reason to think your baccarat will be better than your shooting."

*It will be surprisingly better, Herr Luscher!* I said to myself.

Just then Lord Glendinning accosted me and gave me a quarter of an hour's dissertation on his stables and aspirations for the Derby. At five everyone went to find before-dinner entertainments. I spent the time in the billiard room but, still recovering, played ill.

Since I had to prepare for the play, I was excused from formal dinner. First I examined the ballroom. The makeshift stage was admirable; some of the cast already were in costume and were giving their parts a last-minute rehearsal to get the feel of the stage. I went up to my room at about seven to apply my make-up and found Herbert waiting.

"Still alive I see, old chap," I greeted him when he unlocked the door.

He did not look as if he found my remark funny. He fetched my make-up case. I placed a low table in front of the cheval glass and turned a lampshade so the light would fall on my face. I opened the case. The smell of grease paint and spirit gum cheered me.

Herbert stood behind me, his dour expression reflected in the mirror.

"Don't worry; Luscher won't escape," I urged.

"He's wily."

"We are wilier; he's in our trap." With a grease pencil I began to apply ageing lines about my eyes, to draw furrows in my brow, to carve two great channels from my nose to the corners of my mouth. "Hand me my skullcap and side whiskers, please."

Herbert passed me the implements which would help turn me into the blustering old country squire.

"Is the shiner at hand?" I asked as, tucking in my hair, I pulled on the skullcap.

"Right here." I began to fix the salt-and-pepper side whiskers to my jaw with spirit gum as Herbert pulled from a pocket the device with which smug Herr Wilhelm Luscher would be brought low.

The gadget lay in his palm, tiny and flashing. It was simple: a thin circle of mirror with a cork backing, known in cardsharper parlance as a "shiner." It fit into the bowl of a pipe and enabled the man who held the pipe just so to see every card dealt at a table, even in baccarat. In my wardrobe was a bent bulldog pipe, a twin of Willy Luscher's. I would fit the shiner into this pipe and carry it to our game. I would see to it that the German won heavily, an easy task since the baccarat shoe and cards which Simon Bliss would supply had been modified by Herbert. Then, at just the right moment, when Teddy looked most displeased at losing—he hated to be beaten at anything—I would nudge Luscher's arm; he would drop his pipe. I knew sleight-of-hand, and the pipe he picked up, thinking it his, would be the one which I had prepared to finish him. "Herr Luscher's cheating!" I would exclaim—to outrage on his part and grave looks from the other gentlemen. "A ser-r-rious accusation, Mr. Wigmore," Teddy himself would rumble. "Where is your pr-r-roof?" I would grasp the German's wrist, shake the pipe from his hand, and reveal the shiner. Dismay!

A gentleman did not cheat. A man who cheated was no gentleman. Such persons were ostracized by society; they lost reputations and position, and doors closed against them. Tranby Croft, the card-playing scandal which had rocked Teddy when he was Prince of Wales, was proof; it had ruined Colonel Gordon Cumming, nearly ruined Teddy, and His Majesty could take no chance of such a scandal touching him again—he would have to dismiss Willy Luscher from his society.

Simon Bliss and Lord Esher would see to it the tale did not stop there; they would take Willy's ruin the rest of the way. He would be finished in the European capitals by Christmas.

I looked forward to seeing the look on Luscher's face when he knew I had bested him. He might accuse me of an elaborate trick, but who would believe it? What was my motive? Bliss and Esher would defend me.

I finished applying my make-up, rose, and slipped into my costume. I looked in the glass. Old Squire Hardcastle stared back fiercely.

"I am an instrument of justice, Herbert!" I exclaimed.

# 🐚Herbert Munns's Narrative🐚

### I

It took Wiggins an hour to apply the finishing touches to his make-up and costume—everything must be perfect!—but when he was through I was amazed; I hardly knew him. It was nearly nine. Below, dinner must be in progress; the play would begin soon. I had fixed the shiner into the bulldog pipe hidden in the wardrobe, ready for my young friend when he came up for the baccarat game. Peeping through a crack in the door, I watched him scout the corridor for me. He winked at a lady's maid, who stared as he passed. Then, glancing down the servants' stairs, he beckoned. "Hsst! All clear, Herbert. Hurry!"

The corridor was momentarily empty. I popped out of his room. A hand on my shoulder, he saw me off down the stairs. "No Bünz in sight, thank heaven. I'm inclined to think the fellow is all memory and no brains; knew a chap like that once in music hall days—remarkable! Go straight to Bliss's room. He and I will come there after the game. We'll celebrate! Off you go, now."

"Good luck, Wiggins."

A beaming smile. "Thank you, old man."

We parted, he to go to the ballroom and I to keep Jack Merridew company until the adventure was through. I was beginning to feel hopeful: there were indeed only a few more hours of it. Wiggins could bring it off; he shone under stress. Simon Bliss and Lord Esher would be there to help him. And Superintendent Quinn's men were keeping watch, dressed as servants, hovering near Luscher's and Madame Bernard's rooms. All was well.

I made my way through the house to the east wing, darting a glance 'round each corner as I went. No Bünz. If I had seen him I should have made tracks. I calmed my shivers by telling myself this was no foggy London street but a great house packed with four hundred people, police among them. If Bünz got his hands on me, help was near. Probably he wasn't watching for me. What could he have against me other than vague suspicion? Too, his master would want no commotion caused on the day before his plan was hatched. As ever, our great advantage was that Herr Luscher did not know we were onto him. And, if worse came to worst, I had my pistol.

I reached Uncle's room without mishap; across from it was Madame Bernard's door, next to that her husband's. By now both must be below in the drawing room, as Luscher must be, so the detectives keeping an eye on them would be below, too, among the liveried servants. I knocked on Uncle's door. After asking who it was, Jack opened.

"Come in, Mr. Munns, sir."

I did, briskly, feeling relieved. "Can't tell you how happy I am to arrive, Jack."

We locked the heavy oak door. A fire burned in the grate. Outside it was black, a mist having risen so that not even the lights of Wolferton down the hill were visible.

Jack had been reading a book.

"What've you got there, lad?"

He showed it to me. "A copy of the play Mr. Wigmore's in tonight. Mr. Bliss brought it up. I was trying to picture Mr. Wigmore as Squire Hardcastle but couldn't. How does he do it?"

"He's very clever."

His small boy's face grew serious. "I . . . I hope things turn out well tonight, sir."

I sat in an armchair. "It's out of our hands. We simply must wait for news."

"Yes . . ." He sat too.

"Well, what shall we talk about? Tell me about the play. I don't know the plot."

"Yes, sir. It's very funny." His brown eyes brightened. "It's about a narrow-minded country squire and a stuttering young man and a clever girl who—" There came a knock at the door. "I expect that's supper; Mr. Bliss said he'd have a tray sent up." He raised his voice. "Who's there, please?"

"Supper," came the muffled word.

"I'm not especially hungry," I said, as the boy went to the door, "but—"

Jack Merridew flew back into the room. The door, which he had just unbolted, crashed open.

Bünz loomed in its rectangle.

I jumped up, heart pounding; had everything gone awry? The huge man lunged in, seeming to fill the room. He kicked the door shut. His slit-eyes found Jack, who was staggering back.

Recognition gave those eyes a mean, fizzling glow: *"Du bist's!* You are the boy in the Bernard house!" His voice was a grunt.

"The . . . the Bernard house? No, sir, I—"

Bünz took a threatening step forward.

"See here, my good man," I said, drawing myself up. "You've made a great mistake. This is Mr. Simon Bliss's boy, and this is Simon Bliss's room. How dare you burst in this way? You'll have to leave."

"Ungh. You . . . !" he said, ignoring my words, the awful eyes now fixed on me. With a sinking feeling, I stared back. His slack jaw worked. He recognized me, that was certain; Jack too. Wiggins and my precautions had been for nothing. With his animal instincts and tracking skill the brute had followed me.

I felt a great fool. Terrified, too, for all our plans.

The big man took another step. I began to raise my right hand toward my jacket. Good lord, would I have to shoot him?

Jack stood between us. Seeing my move, Bünz struck the boy a swift, backhanded blow. I heard its thud on his shoulder and saw Jack tumble. Then, before I could act, a pistol was in Bünz's fist; he was standing not three feet from me, staring down, and the cold barrel was pressed against the centre of my brow. He prodded, hard. *"Nein!"* A slow smile spread his lips but did not light his eyes.

Defeated, I lowered my hand.

Looking dizzy, Jack climbed to his feet.

"All right, lad?" I asked.

"Y-yes, sir." He massaged his shoulder.

Trying to ignore the pistol above my eyes, its steady pressure, the distinct possibility of a bullet at any instant shattering my brain, I said, "Awfully sorry. Awfully. What are we to do?"

## 🪷*Simon Bliss's Narrative*🪷

### I

The predinner gathering in the drawing room was much like the day before: the women smiling and drifting in their gowns; the gentlemen standing with one hand behind their backs in the fashionable bluff attitude, smoking cigars, keeping up the flow of small talk. For the time being, no untoward event ruffled the decorum. I stood apart and watched. Drama bubbled below the bright surface, the featured players being His Majesty, Madame Bernard, Herr Wilhelm Luscher, and Frederick Wigmore. And I—would I be called upon for more than a supernumerary role? I hoped not; let the thing play itself out without me. But I would be ready.

In full regalia, beard and moustache in place to a hair, decorations fighting for space on his chest, Bertie shone, every inch a monarch, his great belly again cleaving the sea of adoring guests like the prow of a triumphant ship. His complexion glowed; his small, white teeth gleamed from between his moist lips; his puckered eyes, intensely blue, stared with utter confidence into every face. In an expansive mood, he waved his cigar, dispensing largesse.

Smiling, her bright veneer like the patina on a fine old commode, Alexandra arrived late.

I listened to the king speak with Willy Luscher. The German played his part of admiring young man well, and it was sad to see with what fatherly affection Bertie regarded him. Our trick would prove a blow to the monarch—better that, however, than for him to discover Luscher's desire to humiliate and murder him.

Sophie Bernard arrived, this evening in pale blue. At once I saw that she was agitated. Her green eyes seemed to burn, she twisted her hands, she hardly spoke to the gentlemen and ladies who greeted her. She went to the centre of the room.

The king approached her, looking solicitous. A tender gaze filled his congested old eyes. He was infatuated with her; what did it matter that wisdom and experience should have taught him better? My concern aroused, I watched them, and so did many others; they became the focus of the room's discreet attention.

Bertie said something to the young woman—I could not hear what. He attempted to touch her slim, white arm, but she jerked it away and stared at him angrily, with a look of tragedy too. Appearing puzzled, hurt, he again stretched out his gloved hand. Amazingly, she struck it aside.

There was a catch in the general babble of conversation, quickly covered over by rapid talking—no one must embarrass the king; no one must appear to notice! I caught Lord Esher's eye; he looked shocked. Near him, Ponsonby was aghast. It was an extraordinary thing to strike a monarch—a favored mistress might do so in private; the royal personage might tolerate it there—but it was never done publicly; it was the greatest faux pas.

I was not completely surprised, however. If Madame Bernard was to shoot King Edward and be believed in her claim that she had done it because he made lecherous demands and threatened her when she would not submit, she must have witnesses to his habit of abuse. She already had her servants, gulled by Samuel Jarrett's impersonation. Now she was creating a final dramatic touch for Bertie's friends. They would make quite an impression sweeping into the witness box to do what, under oath, they must: describe the scene they had witnessed at Sandringham. They might be forced to add what a temper Bertie was known to have and how he had always been a rake. It would be damning!

I glanced toward Willy Luscher. A dozen paces away, he watched the exchange with a pleased, veiled look while he stroked the stem of his pipe. No doubt he had put Madame Sophie Bernard up to this.

Bertie froze. His lips hung open on the endearment he no doubt had been about to utter. His eyes were a turmoil of shock, disbelief, and anger. His face grew red. Sophie Bernard stepped back and stared defiantly, her slender arms held out from her sides as if ready to fly up in defense should he attempt to strike her. It was a masterly performance. Tears sprang up in her sea-green eyes. Her exquisitely thin shoulders trembled. Next to her, the portly, dissipated Edward appeared, for all his grandeur, pathetically gross, the beast to her beauty. What had he done? No one could tell, but one must sympathize with the wronged young woman. She acted her part magnificently.

*"Ne me touche pas! J'en ai assez d'être dérangée! Laisse-moi seule!"* she said, not loudly but clearly, with an artful catch in her throat. Bertie must stop abusing her!

The king spoke French fluently. Clearly he understood her words, though his stare of disbelief showed he had no idea why she said them. How many others had heard her? I glanced 'round—enough for her purpose. And they would give the words the worse meaning, just as she and Willy Luscher wished them to do.

For a moment, facing one another, Bertie and Madame Bernard seemed frozen, balanced on the edge of a disastrous scene. Conversation began to die around them, to dwindle to nervous confusion. The room seemed explosive, they its flash point.

Abruptly the young Frenchwoman whirled and walked to her husband. Relief was palpable. Not far off, Monsieur Bernard had watched the exchange with a queer, detached expression, as if he were merely observing butterflies dart in the summer air. His reedlike figure swayed as he accepted his wife's arm. Abstractedly he patted her small, white hand and smiled sadly down at her. His eyes swam with his inner torment. Standing near him, I heard his hoarse whisper: *"Ne souffre pas, Sophie. Ce sera bientôt fini.*" Do not suffer, Sophie. Soon it will be over.

I shivered at the calm, sepulchral confidence of the utterance. What did he mean?

Madame Bernard shivered also; gooseflesh sprang out on her bare shoulders, and fear started up in her eyes.

Across the room, Bertie's expression stayed black as thunder.

## 2

Dinner was hardly a jolly affair. The long table glittered under the crystal chandeliers, and course succeeded rich course, each a masterpiece to eye and palate. But the gleam of gold and silver, the bejewelled bosoms and crisp white shirtfronts, and the extravagant dishes seemed tokens of a doomed civilization which Bertie, rumbling like a volcano at the head of the table, was about to bury under an explosion of wrath. We were brighter and noisier than ever, but our talk had a frantic edge, as if a moment's silence might allow the disaster to fall upon us.

When happy, Bertie had a gruff, avuncular charm; when displeased, he made things intolerable. He glowered, fidgeted, fumed, and drummed impatiently on the tabletop. Every five minutes we were treated to an awful scene in which he reduced some butler to ashen-faced, snivelling helplessness. At these moments we chattered loudly, but never loudly enough to drown out his snarls. Even Alexandra heard him, her smile gradually altering to a miserable wreck of itself. Only Mrs. Keppel, who once had been able to control the king's tempers, sat silent while we suffered. Sophie Bernard talked in a subdued voice to white-bearded Sir Dighton Probyn seated beside her. She looked more miserable than Alexandra; thus she, and not the queen, had the old man's sympathy.

Monsieur Armand Bernard sat across from me. Grown strangely gay, he talked about French politics of two decades ago as if they were present history. On my right and left, Lady Glendinning and Lottie Cavendish looked at him oddly, but none of us contradicted him. After a time he became confused in his words and faltered, but continued to smile brightly, looking about eagerly and occasionally saying, "Yes, yes?" as if seeking approbation for some unspoken idea. He drank glass after glass of wine; his speech became thick; his eyes grew glazed in their gaunt, dark hollows.

At last dinner was over, and with relief we escaped from our chairs, where we had seemed to be held prisoner, to go to the ballroom where *She Stoops to Conquer* would be performed. Pointedly, Bertie chose to escort Alice Keppel. The handsome, turquoise-eyed woman accepted his arm with restrained grace. As Bertie walked with her toward the dining room doors, I saw him fix his piercing blue eyes on Sophie Bernard. His anger appeared gone. His look at the beautiful young Frenchwoman was filled with bewilderment. What have I done? it asked.

I knew the answer: he had fallen in love with the woman who intended to put a bullet in his heart.

We went into the ballroom. Spirits rose. The threatened storm had not broken, and Bertie, now in Mrs. Keppel's hands, might be placated. We were about to be entertained. The raised platform was finished in spite of Alexandra's interference. On either side of the room, wings jutted out to form a proscenium. Temporary stage lights hung from the ceiling. Gottlieb's band was in the gallery, ready to provide music.

Chairs had been arranged in semicircular rows facing the stage. Bertie sat front row, right, with Mrs. Keppel by his side. Willy Luscher took the end seat next to Mrs. Keppel and managed to goad the king into a brief, harumphing laugh. I deliberately sat behind the trio and eavesdropped on their conversation. Lowering his voice, Luscher reminded Bertie of the baccarat game to be held after the play.

At last everyone was seated, Gottlieb's band sounded introductory airs, and the huge electrified chandeliers fell dark, leaving only the stage lights glowing. Sophie Bernard sat a few seats to my left. In the dimness I saw Bertie glance back at her once more. His expression was stern but yielding; he would forgive her, it said. But the Frenchwoman would not look at him. Bertie jerked his head back toward the stage. Willy Luscher smiled thinly in the dim light. The play began.

# ☙Jack Merridew's Narrative☙

What are we to do?" Mr. Munns asked.
I did not know. I was frightened. My shoulder
ached from Bünz's blow. Managing to find my feet,
I could not take my eyes from the pistol which the huge
manservant was pressing against Mr. Munns's brow.

"You are the man in London!"

Mr. Munns blinked behind his glasses. "I am Mr. Frederick Wigmore's man. He lives in London; naturally I reside there too. You have the advantage of me, sir. Your pistol, by the way, is unnecessary. Please put it away." His moustache ends were quivering. I thought him very brave to stand up like that.

The German's eyes were cold little marbles. "*Erzählen Sie mir doch keine Märchen!* You followed my master in London! I saw you!"

"Your master?"

"*Herr Wilhelm Luscher, wie Sie ja Wissen!*"

"Herr Luscher? The German attaché? Ah! Well." Mr. Munns managed a shaky smile. "My master, Mr. Wigmore, knows Herr Luscher, I believe. There's some misunderstanding. Let's call them both; they can settle it—"

"*Nein!*" Bünz bumped Mr. Munns's forehead with the gun barrel. "We will call no one for now."

Mr. Munns paled, blinked, swallowed. "As you say." It was a hoarse whisper.

"Leave him alone!" I cried, stepping forward.

A mean smile spread the German's lips. With a huge arm he pushed Mr. Munns into a chair. Then he turned his pistol on me. I found myself staring into the black hole of the barrel.

Bünz kept his eye on Mr. Munns. "You are the man in London?"

"No, I—"

Suddenly the German's free arm snaked out, had me by the throat, and bent me back. His pistol bored into my temple. I gasped for breath; my ears rang, but I could hear well enough: "I will hurt the boy. The truth now! You followed my master in London, *ja?*"

"Yes, yes!" came Mr. Munns's defeated cry. "Let him go!"

The awful pressure left my throat. Bünz dropped me like a sack.

"Boy!" the German barked.

I looked up dizzily. Again Bünz had the pistol pressed to Mr. Munns's brow.

"You worked in the Bernard house, boy?"

"Yes."

"I saw you when my master left?"

"Y-yes."

"You are Mr. Simon Bliss's page, but you were there. Why?"

I was standing shakily. "I had a job for a time; that's all, sir . . ."

"Bah!" But he took his pistol from Mr. Munns's brow. "You are lying. Both of you are lying! I do not know why you are here together, but my master will have the reason. Stand up!" he barked at Mr. Munns. "When I came in, you started to reach into your coat. Why?"

"For . . . for my other glasses. These are for reading, but when you burst in—"

"Um." He was suspicious. "Let us see those other glasses. Move your hand carefully."

Cautiously Mr. Munns reached into his coat. My heart thudded, hoping he would not try to pull out the hidden pistol which he had showed me at breakfast that morning. He would never get to use it; he would surely die.

I was very relieved to see that Mr. Munns did indeed have a second pair of spectacles in his breast pocket. He showed them.

Bünz smiled meanly. Taking them, he crushed them beneath his boot. Then laughing, "Ha ha!" he snatched Mr. Munns's other glasses from his nose and with a splintering sound crushed those too. More laughter, rumbling choking, while Mr. Munns squinted, looking helpless. I hated the German then.

"*Schnell!*" Bünz rapped. "We will go to my master's room. You, Munns, you walk first. Then this boy. I will come after him. I will keep my pistol in my coat pocket, so, just behind his head. Do not try to run or make an alarm. I will shoot him if you do." He smiled. "Then I will shoot you."

A heavy hand on my shoulder, Bünz pushed me toward the door, which Mr. Munns opened. *"Gehen Sie nur!"* Feeling the gun barrel in his pocket nudge the back of my head, I did as I was told.

We went along the corridors, up and down stairs, to reach the west wing. In celebration of His Majesty's birthday, his guests' servants and many of the Sandringham staff had been invited to stand in the back of the ballroom to see the play, so the big house seemed nearly deserted. We passed a footman or two, but these men ignored us. I felt very low, less bad for myself now that my first panic was through than for Mr. Wigmore's plan, which might go awry. Too, Mr. Wigmore might be placed in danger and not know it, whereas we, Mr. Munns and I, knew very well what we faced.

Was there anything we could do? I asked myself as we went, Bünz's breath grunting behind me. Could the German be distracted so Mr. Munns might somehow get out his pistol and fire? But would that do any good? Mr. Munns hadn't his glasses; how well could he see without them? We were in a very tight spot.

We reached Herr Luscher's door and went in. The room was much as Mr. Bliss's, with a bay overlooking the grounds. Without taking his slit-eyes from us, Bünz closed and locked the door, then gestured for us to stand in the alcove. We did. Outside it was darker than ever, as if a great blanket smothered the moon and stars. Bünz seemed to be thinking—difficult work it appeared; his wide brow creased with effort. At last, going to the bureau, he picked up a pen and, switching the pistol to his left hand, keeping watch on us, he scratched a message. He slipped it into an envelope and rang the bell.

We waited—too long for the German, it seemed. Muttering, he rang again, nearly pulling the cord from the wall. I glanced at Mr. Munns, who met my gaze with worried, pouchy eyes. "Courage, Jack," he murmured.

"Do not speak!"

We were silent. Bünz scowled as minutes ticked away. At last a knock sounded on the door.

"*Schweigen Sie!* Quiet!" he warned us again. He opened the door part way.

"Yes?" I heard a footman's polite inquiry from the corridor.

Bünz showed the envelope. "For Herr Luscher."

A hesitation. "Your master is at the play, is he not?"

"*Ja.*"

"I'm very sorry, then, but I mayn't interrupt a royal entertainment with a message."

Bünz's pistol was out of sight of the footman. He kept half an eye on us. I watched his rocklike knuckles whiten on the butt. "It is an emergency!" he snapped, looking terrible. "Herr Luscher must read this!"

There was silence. The footman yielded. "If it is an emergency, then . . ."

"*Ja, ja*—an emergency. I cannot go myself." He thrust the envelope through the opening. "You must deliver it now!"

The footman left. Bünz closed and locked the door. Under his glowering gaze we waited helplessly for the result.

# Frederick Wigmore's Narrative

I wore dark green breeches, white cotton stockings, and rustic shoes with brass buckles. A padded harness gave me a stout belly. Over this was a plain white waistcoat and simple green country frock coat. A brown tricorn hat completed the costume. I was the copy of a Gainsborough portrait of an old gentleman farmer. I had just played my first scene as Hardcastle. Much laughter. Jolly applause at my exit.

I felt exhilarated. I was doing splendidly, my anticipation

of the baccarat game giving my acting an extra spark—that and the fact that it was lords, ladies, and royalty I played for.

Off-stage, listening for my next cue, I peeped at the audience through a crack between the flats. Willy Luscher was in the end seat, front row, near old Teddy, Mrs. Alice Keppel between them. How I looked forward to disgracing the smug German! The king looked gloomy and fidgeted. Why? Not my acting, I hoped! And why was Mrs. Keppel beside him rather than the favourite, Sophie Bernard, who sat apart wearing a downcast expression?

On stage again! In the midst of performing I had no chance to watch the audience, but when I returned to my spyhole some moments later I looked for Monsieur Bernard. I caught sight of him in the third row, just behind his wife. Frightful! His face was like a skull, he sat stiff and straight as a statue, great tears rolling down his cheeks. I felt sad to see them, no result of my acting. Bloody Luscher had caused them! Soon Monsieur would have his Sophie back!

Young Kate Hardcastle was speaking under bright lights: "In this hypocritical age there are few who do not condemn in public what they practice in private and think they pay every debt to virtue when they do so."

Her shy lover, Charles Marlow, replied, "True, Madame. Those who have most virtue in their mouths have least of it in their bosoms."

I did not listen to Kate's response. In his row-end seat, Willy Luscher was a dozen paces from the side entrance to the ballroom. A footman had come through this door and was approaching discreetly; he held out his silver tray. With a small look of surprise Luscher took the envelope. The footman retreated under Teddy's disapproving frown. Glancing an apology, Luscher opened the envelope and examined a single piece of paper. I squinted to read his expression but could make out no more than a slight tightening of his damned habitual smile. The king looked a pointed question. Slipping the message into an inside coat pocket, Luscher leaned past Mrs. Keppel and spoke behind his hand—some excuse was made, I presumed. Then he slipped quietly out. His Majesty returned his scowling attention to the stage.

This exchange had taken little more than a minute. Few

persons seemed to have noticed Luscher's departure, but Sophie Bernard had not missed it. Her alarmed eyes stared at his empty chair. Simon Bliss, too, had seen; seated behind King Edward, he frowned with concern.

I looked about the room for Superintendent Quinn. Lord Esher had pointed him out earlier, and I spotted the man in the back row, but I was not reassured. His eyes were fixed on the comic antics on stage. Obviously he had not seen Luscher leave. I hoped his men were more alert than he.

Then I was on the boards once more, soliloquizing about young Charles Marlow's impudence.

## ❧Simon Bliss's Narrative❧

I was greatly disturbed by Willy Luscher's departure from the play. What had been in the note that drew him off? Who had written it? I hoped it had been some consular communication and feared it was not. I consoled myself with the thought that the king sat before me; with Bertie safely here nothing disastrous could happen, could it? I did not like what appeared to be Superintendent Quinn's careless work: none of his disguised policemen had left to follow Luscher. Had the man assigned to the German been so distracted by the play that he had failed to see him go? Damned incompetence!

*She Stoops to Conquer* ended shortly before eleven-thirty. I twitched throughout and was not relieved when the chandeliers flared on. Luscher had been gone for half an hour and had not returned.

Gottlieb struck up a stirring air, and the cast came on stage to take their bows. Frederick Wigmore received a loud, well-deserved ovation and grinned through his Hardcastle make-up. I wished I felt as cheerful as he looked. We rose. The actors and actresses came down from the stage. The audience went forward to congratulate them.

And then I saw Cosette, her black eyes darting. I well

knew the maid from several glimpses of her in the corridors. She hesitated at the side entrance, looking agitated. Spying her mistress, she brushed past me and touched her arm. Madame Bernard started. Cosette whispered something in her ear. The Frenchwoman searched her face and asked a question. Cosette nodded sharply. Madame Bernard rushed from the room, the maid at her heels. Had she been summoned by Willy Luscher?

I glanced 'round. Damn, were Quinn's men counting their toes? They were nowhere in sight. The crowd of ladies and gentlemen formed a close-packed throng. Had anyone besides me seen Madame Bernard escape? I did not know but could not take the chance that no one would follow; I must pursue her myself.

I began to make my way toward the side door, but it was difficult to get through the crush. Seconds counted if I were not to lose the trail in the great house, and, cursing my old legs and arms that were not strong enough to assert themselves better, I was sorely tempted to crack some noble heads with my stick to make a path.

I reached the door. As I opened it I glanced back, hoping to catch Frederick Wigmore's eye, or Lord Esher's, Quinn's at the very least. I could see none of them. I saw Bertie, however. And he saw me. He glowered through a brief parting in the crowd. Perhaps he had seen his Sophie go; now I was scuttling out too—rude of me, but there was nothing for it. I made no apology, not even a glance of one. Monsieur Armand Bernard stood near Bertie, his dead-white face wearing the expression of an avenging angel. I shuddered, then I was gone, the door firmly shut behind me.

Blessed silence after the chatter of the throng; I was in the carpeted corridor that paralleled the ballroom. I glanced to the right and left—no one in sight. Desperately I listened for footsteps, but not even the rustle of a gown indicated which direction the women had taken. I made a hasty decision. In one direction the corridor led to the drawing room, dining room, and library; in the other to the grand staircase. I guessed that Madame Bernard and Cosette had gone up the stairs and hurried toward them.

As I went, speculations tumbled through my mind. Had Willy Luscher sent for Madame Bernard in order to explain some change of plans? If so, what change? I could not get Armand Bernard's startling hate-filled look out of my thoughts.

Straining on my stick, forcing my old legs to extra effort, I climbed the broad stairs. In half an hour the game of baccarat was supposed to begin in the west-wing card room. With every step up I grew surer that that game would never take place. Something had gone wrong. Somehow Luscher had found out about our plan. What would the wily German's instincts lead him to do? Was Jack safe? Was Herbert?

The stairs forked at the first landing. The footman who usually stood there had gone to see the play, so I had no one to ask whether Madame Bernard and her maid had passed that way and, if so, which direction they had taken. I decided to try Madame Bernard's room first and ascended toward the east wing. With all the guests and servants below, the upper house was silent. Hurrying along the deserted corridors, with their varnished portraits and staring stuffed animals, I felt alone in the mansion. The thud of my stick sounded loud on the parquet.

I came to the Frenchwoman's door. To my left was her husband's room, behind me my own. I listened but heard nothing. I pressed my ear to the oak; still not a sound. I tried knocking. No response. Madame Bernard had not come this way. Had she gone to Luscher's room? Perhaps not. Perhaps my fears were for nothing.

I wanted to assure myself that Jack was safe and to alert him that I might need him. I took out my key to unlock my door but was chilled to find that the latch turned easily in my hand. It was not like Jack to ignore or disobey an order! I thrust the door open. My heart sank. The coals of a dying fire glowed upon the grate. My playscript of *She Stoops to Conquer* lay on the carpet by the armchair where Jack sat to read. But the lad was gone. Where? And where was my nephew, who was to have kept him company? Then, stepping into the room, I discovered on the floor, beside one of the chairs that flanked the fire, two pairs of wire-rimmed spectacles. Unmistakably Herbert's, they had been violently crushed. I was sure then that Luscher's abrupt departure from the play was a prelude to disaster, and that these crushed glasses were its first effect.

I felt more alone than before and knew that I must have help—Quinn's, Esher's, Frederick Wigmore's. I must have strength with me. In a confrontation with the Germans my stick would not prove an adequate weapon.

Hurrying out of my room I started back down the corridor but stopped ten paces along it. Monsieur Bernard's door was open. I glanced inside but saw no one. Cautiously I walked in. The room was high-ceilinged, with bed, wardrobe, and fireplace. Monsieur Bernard was there. He had been standing by the bureau, out of sight of the corridor. He was removing something from a drawer. He turned with the thing in his hand—a pistol. Wild-eyed, he pointed it at my breast.

"Where is my wife, Mr. Bliss?" he demanded, trembling with hysteria, his finger tightening on the trigger.

# Jack Merridew's Narrative

I watched the clock on the mantlepiece after Bünz sent his message. There was nothing else to do, unless it was to look into his eyes, which were dull and stupid and mean and made me shiver, or to stare at his pistol, which never stopped pointing straight at us. It was quarter to eleven. The play must be progressing, Mr. Wigmore acting Squire Hardcastle. How I wished to be there rather then here!

Near eleven there was a sound in the corridor. Bünz lurched to one side of the room so he could see both us and the door. The door opened.

Key in hand, Herr Wilhelm Luscher strode in. He saw me at once. "*Um Gottes Willen!* The boy from the Bernard house! Bünz, what does this mean?"

"*Ich weiss nicht, mein Herr.*" Bünz explained in German how he had found Herbert and me in Mr. Bliss's room. I understood most of what he said.

Eyes narrowing, Herr Luscher's gaze found my face. He

wore black evening clothes and seemed slimmer and taller than ever, handsomer too—and more dangerous. All I could think of was how he had jerked me off my feet outside Madame Bernard's bedchamber.

"So . . ." he said, rubbing his jaw. *"Hat dieser Kerl mich die ganze Zeit in London?"* he asked of Bünz, shifting his gaze to Mr. Munns.

*"Ja."* The manservant nodded.

Herr Luscher was a foot from Mr. Munns in an instant. "My man says you followed me. Don't deny it if you know what's good for you—and what's good for the boy."

"I don't deny it, sir," Mr. Munns said, sounding very humble. "I should never have denied it. There's a good explanation. My master made me do it. Mr. Frederick Wigmore, you know. He hates Germans. I have nothing against them, you understand. I *like* them. But my master . . . he has something against them, don't ask me why. He knew you would be at Sandringham—he reads the papers very close—and when he found out he was to come up, too, why, he set me to following you. He wanted to find out your habits, seemed fascinated by them. I was his man; I had to do what he said. I figured, no harm in it. Then I saw what he meant. He meant to show you up somehow. Obsessed with the idea, he was. I told him I'd sometimes seen you at cards, that you seemed to like playing, so he planned to lure you into a game and beat you by cheating. That was his idea of fixing you—not mine, mind you; I don't believe in cheating. But what could I do? As I said, I was his man. Ha, ha! He was in a foul temper when you set him back that thousand guineas at the shoot, where he thought to beat you too. Thinks a lot of his shooting, he does! But he didn't beat you, did he? Between you and me, sir, I'm very glad; my master needs taking down a peg or two. Well, now you know the truth, we may go, mayn't we? It was all a misunderstanding."

I thought Mr. Munns very clever to have made this up, but I saw from Herr Luscher's eyes that it would not wash. He only seemed to grow angrier.

"Lies!" he spat. "Why were you found with this boy, who only two days ago was footboy in the Bernard house? I caught him outside Madame Bernard's door—listening to our private conversation, I'm certain. I should have obeyed my instincts and got rid of the *Landplage* then, but I was too distracted by Sophie's complaints and demands." His features twisted. "The beautiful Frenchwoman—a fool! There is a race to hate—the French! They have no more right to affront Germany than England does. Both your nations will fall together!" He smiled thinly. "You see how honest I am about my intentions, Mr. Munns. May I hope for the same from you? Quickly! I have not much time!"

"Our masters will soon be up from the play," was all Mr. Munns said, quietly. "The boy and I must get back to them."

The German sneered. "Masters? Yours is Mr. Frederick Wigmore, you say. And yours—" he looked coldly down at me, "is Mr. Simon Bliss?"

"Y-yes, sir."

"The man who sometimes works for the police? What were you doing in the Bernard house?"

"It was only temporary, sir. Mr. Bliss did not need me for some days, and—"

"*Maul halten!* More lies. Mmm. I have a number of times observed your two 'masters' in close conversation. They met on the train, they said. Another lie. There is some conspiracy afoot, among all of you. What is it?"

"I don't know what you mean, sir," Mr. Munns said. "I've explained. Now, if we may go—" He made a move.

Herr Luscher struck him hard in the chest; he fell back. "You have explained nothing, you stubborn Englishman! Well, it will do you no good. Stubborn but stupid. It's cleverness that will win this game."

Seeing how he made Mr. Munns stumble, I wanted to shout to the German that if he had been clever things would not have come to this pass for him. But I bit my tongue; Bünz's pistol never left us, and I was sure he would shoot me at a word.

Herr Luscher grasped my collar; his hot breath hit my face. "What did you hear outside Madame Bernard's door, you blasted boy?"

"N-nothing . . ." I choked.

"Did you report it all to Simon Bliss?"

"No . . ."

"You devil!" I heard Mr. Munns say. I felt him tensing

near me; he might have attacked Herr Luscher, got himself shot or beaten, but the German already had let me go and with a disgusted cry had turned away. He began to pace, glancing from us to the clock, then at the deep blackness outside, which matched the blackness of his expression.

On being released, I had stumbled a pace behind Mr. Munns; my right arm was partially concealed from both Herr Luscher and his man by Mr. Munns's coat. It was hard to know that the Webley pistol was just inches from me and that there was no way to get it.

Was there no way? I was frightened to think there might be. All I needed to do was to raise my concealed hand, slip it up the back of Mr. Munns's coat . . .

Could I shoot a man? I had never fired a gun in my life. The idea caused me to burn. While I trembled and flushed and tried to work up my courage, Herr Luscher came to a decision.

"Bünz," he ordered, stopping his pacing, "find the Frenchwoman's maid. Send her to the ballroom to tell her mistress to come here. No one else is to hear the message, understand?"

"*Ja.*"

"*Gib mir dein Gewehr.*"

Bünz handed him his pistol.

"Go now. *Es ist wichtig.*"

The manservant left.

Herr Luscher sat in an armchair facing us. He leaned back and crossed his legs. He held the pistol offhandedly, as if it were a toy, but I knew he would be deadly with it. He was watchful but very cool, in a bragging mood.

"So you, Mr. Munns, are Mr. Wigmore's man? Or claim to be? Well, I can tell you, all your master's efforts will come to no good. I have a new plan! After Frederick Wigmore challenged me I made inquiries about him. 'A charming fellow, an actor, that's all I know,' everyone said. I did not find him charming—I have a finely developed instinct for deceit—so I persisted, until I found one old lord who knew more. He said Mr. Wigmore had helped a friend of his in a matter which ultimately needed the police. Wigmore did splendid work, the lord recalled: 'A fine detective!' I was immediately suspicious; I have been since yesterday."

Herr Luscher took out his pipe. "But I, too, can play-act; I showed nothing." He frowned as, with one hand, expertly, never taking the pistol from us, he packed the pipe. "Now that I'm certain Wigmore is not what he pretends to be, I shall see he does not stop me! In fact," he leered behind a cloud of smoke, "I shall stop *him*—dead, if need be. And you, boy—your master, Mr. Simon Bliss, who pretends to be so frail, leaning on his stick, he resides in the Diogenes Club, does he not? And was the man who reported Samuel Jarrett's death to the police?" He nodded. "I read so in the papers. That tells me enough! Did Bliss paw over the dead body? Did he find a certain letter which Jarrett stole from us, and which fool Sigmund Czinner failed to recover? Was it the first clue? Did that lead him to Sophie and me? Did he then set you to spying in the Bernard house?"

He did not seem to expect an answer; he did not need one. He guessed enough.

Would there be any chance to get Mr. Munns's pistol?

"It can't do any good to keep the boy and me," Mr. Munns began.

The German's eyes lit. "Oh, yes! You and he will be hostages; thus you will do a great deal of good—for me." He kept looking at the clock. "How much of my plan do you know, I wonder. That Madame Bernard was to shoot your king tomorrow? Aha, not even the blink of an eye? So you did know; you're cleverer than I thought—not typical Englishmen. Well, your cleverness will do no good. It's annoying, I admit, to have to give up some of the finer points of the thing. I've endured a great deal for it from the Frenchwoman—her sobs, her sighs, her clinging, her amorous demands—though not all of it has been unpleasant. I'm angered it was for so little. But not for nothing. Madame Bernard will get no chance at Edward tomorrow, I see; so I shall finish him myself tonight. He blocks the path of German triumph. One way or another he must die." He smiled as he balanced the gun in his hand. "I shall be very pleased to put a bullet in the fat fool."

"You'll never get away with it!"

"Oh, yes. When poor, beautiful, infatuated Sophie Bernard arrives, I shall inform her of the change in plans and say that I am forced to leave her." He clucked his tongue.

"She will take it hard, but there is nothing for it. She soon will find some other man to console her, perhaps her ineffectual husband! I shall send Bünz down to ready one of the king's motorcars for my escape. He is quite persuasive; he will manage it easily enough. You, Mr. Munns, will go with him. Jack will stay to be my shield. Your king will come up for the baccarat game. I shall simply wait in the corridor by the servants' stairs and shoot him. How it will please me to see the look in his eyes just before I fire! Shock and confusion will follow. There will be an alarm, of course, but I shall get down the back stairs to the waiting car safely enough. I may not have to use Jack—" His eyes hardened. "But I will if I must. The king's police guard will hop to work, but they will be cautious if there is danger of injuring a child. And I will kill Jack before I let them take me! Once in the car, I know Sandringham's environs like a native; I have made it my business to know them, and I have scouted an escape route for just such an emergency as this." He glanced at the smothering blackness pressing against the windowpanes and smiled. "Convenient of the fog to come up tonight! Bünz and I will not take the main way but will go by country roads where we will never be followed. I have friends sympathetic to Germany's cause near as King's Lynn. There are many such sympathizers in England, you know. They will hide me and see to my escape. You two will go with me. Of course, if there is no trouble, I will set you free in town. So, you see, my game is not quite up, as you had hoped. I shall live to see England fall!"

I knew, then, that I must do something. The German's plan might very well get as far as murdering His Majesty. He would shoot anyone who tried to stop him—Mr. Bliss, Mr. Wigmore. And I did not believe he would free Mr. Munns and me at King's Lynn; we would be left dead in the fog.

"Surely I shall be hostage enough," Mr. Munns was saying. "Let Jack go."

I forced myself to concentrate on my task. Mr. Munns wore a short coat, the pistol pocket just above his waist on his left side. I was not tall. So long as he did not move I could work my arm up the back of the coat, reach the Webley, and, if I were ever so careful, remove it unnoticed. I could raise it, prepare to shoot, and at the last moment move my arm from behind Mr. Munns and fire. I no longer asked myself if I could kill; I must!—and before Bünz returned.

It was past eleven. "No," I heard Herr Luscher's voice. "Two hostages are necessary, in case one is . . . used up. You both will come along."

Cautiously I began to lift my right hand. My shoulder was level with Mr. Munns's waist. I must slide my arm up the back of the coat without causing any revealing movement of the cloth. Careful, careful. As I raised my hand I kept my eyes on the German; I wanted to seem to be listening to him, whereas truly I could hear very little but the blood pounding in my ears. My trembling fingers reached the hem of Mr. Munns's coat and slipped under it. He did not know my plan. Another inch and he would feel my hand. What if he started at the touch? Another chance I must take.

Herr Luscher had been speaking to Mr. Munns, boasting. His glance brushed my face and, terrified, I froze. His sharp blue eyes seemed to read my thoughts; I was sure he guessed my plan. His pistol gleamed. My mouth was dry. I gulped for air.

The eyes went back to Mr. Munns; his pistol did not shoot me. "We have spies in every port and industrial town of your country. . ."

I nearly fainted with relief; he did not suspect. I pushed my hand upward, felt Mr. Munns's shirt. Then I touched his back.

"Give up killing the king," Mr. Munns had just urged.

"He must die!" Herr Luscher had snapped.

Mr. Munns jumped at my touch, but the German seemed to take it as a response to his anger. He laughed. Suddenly he stood, glanced at the door, then at the clock.

Again frozen, through icy fear I, too, saw that it was eleven-thirty.

Herr Luscher frowned. *"Verdammt nochmal! Wo ist Bünz?"*

Let him not begin to pace again! That would bring him in sight of my arm, now reaching up the back of the coat toward the pistol. Mr. Munns guessed what I intended; he shifted his left side nearer me, at the same time folding his left arm across his body to conceal my movements. I might succeed!

There was a knock; my heart thumped.

"Bünz?" Herr Luscher called, looking at the door.

It was now or never. Already I felt the hard bulge of the gun through the cloth pocket. I slid my hand up. My fingers touched metal.

At Bünz's muffled *"Ja,"* Herr Luscher unlocked the door. I pulled the gun from Herbert Munns's pocket.

Then Bünz was in the room, and the door was closed and locked once more. Herr Luscher was asking in German if his manservant had done as he was told.

A heavy nod. *"Ja, mein Herr."*

I stared down at the pistol in my right hand, concealed by Mr. Munns's legs. I was hardly able to believe I had got it. It felt awkward, heavy, a clumsy thing. I was terrified to use it. Must I now kill two men?

"Madame Bernard's maid has gone to fetch her; she will be here soon." The German was speaking to us. Bünz had his pistol again and was holding it on us as before. "You will not witness my farewell scene with her, Mr. Munns," Herr Luscher went on. "You are to accompany my man below, where he will see that one of His Majesty's handsome black Daimlers is waiting when I am through. *Bring den Wagen zum Seitenausgang,"* he ordered Bünz. He motioned toward the door. "Walk ahead of him, Mr. Munns."

Bünz waved his pistol. *"Schnell."*

What should I do? Fire now? Or try to conceal the pistol behind my back until Bünz had taken Mr. Munns away, then point it at Herr Luscher? Perhaps I should not have to shoot anyone then. I trembled with indecision. My right arm hung limp and heavy. The Webley weighed like lead and seemed to pull my shoulder, which Bünz had struck, with a dull pain. I could not drop the weapon; I could not raise it either. In a moment Mr. Munns would move, and I would be revealed. Bünz would put a bullet through my heart.

Mr. Munns did not move.

Herr Luscher's look was icy. "No show of stubbornness! We will harm the boy if you resist."

"Jack—" Mr. Munns said. He was waiting for me to act. I

must! Slowly, hand shaking, I forced my arm up, pulling the pistol as if out of a bog that sucked at it. Up, up, I dragged it, but my fingers felt so weak that I doubted I could pull the trigger. My ears rang. I thought I would faint at what must come next.

There was another knock at the door, and my hand fell to my side.

Herr Luscher glanced sharply at Bünz. The servant stepped aside so he could watch both us and the door. Herr Luscher called out. Madame Bernard's voice answered, "Willy?" and the German opened.

Wearing a blue ball gown, the Frenchwoman rushed into the room. Her perfume filled the air. Her beautiful face was pale, stricken. She swept into Herr Luscher's arms. He held her, but his expression was hard. He forced her away from him.

She searched his face. "*Cher* Willy, what is wrong?"

He jerked his head at us. "As you see."

Madame Bernard noticed Bünz's pistol as her eyes moved to us. She bit her lip and stared bewilderedly. ". . . *Jacques?*" Her gaze was fixed on me.

For a moment I forgot the pistol. She was so beautiful! I flushed red, feeling—knowing—I had betrayed her.

"But . . . but why is this boy here?" She looked at the German again.

"Foolish woman, because he is a spy! He is Simon Bliss's page boy. The man next to him is Frederick Wigmore's valet. He followed me in London." He smiled bitterly. "Surrounded by enemies. We are found out, Sophie. It is all over."

Madame Bernard stared; then she looked relieved. "I am not to kill the king?"

Herr Luscher shook his head. "It seems you never would have got the chance to aim your pistol."

She burst into laughter. Tears flooded her cheeks. "I am glad, Willy, glad! I did not want to kill him. I hate him! He is an evil man, a tyrant—you have told me so. But I did not want to kill him, though I would have done it for you. Anything for you, *mon amour*, you know that. Haven't I proved it a thousand times by what I have endured? But I am glad that we are found out. Someone else can kill him now. We still have each other. We can escape to the Continent, to Berlin, as you promised. I will pack some things. You will see how fast I can be ready, how willing I am to follow." She touched his cheek. "No, I will not pack! We will go as we are. We will be so happy!" Throwing her arms 'round him, she kissed him again and again.

Herr Luscher gripped her shoulders. He stared at her. "I said it is over, Sophie." His voice chilled me. *"Everything* is over . . ."

She trembled. "But . . . but . . ."

My heart broke for her. Herr Luscher kept staring coldly, yet with a little smile, as if he enjoyed her pain. I glanced at his manservant—and saw Bünz was staring at her, too, with dumb, calflike devotion. Through nothing else could have, she had distracted him. His pistol was lowered. I must shoot him now.

Knowing it was the moment, I felt as if I stood on the brink of a steep cliff and might be swept off at any moment. There was a great windy roaring in my ears. Moving as if my body weren't my own but some other lad's, which I watched in a dream, I raised the pistol. Madame Bernard and Herr Luscher stood a dozen feet away from me. Her hands gripped his evening jacket so tightly that the black cloth was crushed. Bünz still stared at Madame Bernard, but his slightest glance would show him my pistol. I slid to the left; he did not look. I steadied the Webley with both hands and squinted along the barrel. Bünz's breast was in the sight. He was a huge target; I could not miss. Now . . . now . . . This morning Mr. Munns had allowed me to hold the pistol. "You must squeeze slowly, Jack," he had said. "Do not jerk it as you fire." I squeezed. Slowly. There was no explosion. My hand shook with effort, and I felt I would burst from the strain, but it was no good. Then I remembered: I must loose the safety catch.

I had come to my limit; my arms fell to my sides.

Suddenly I was gazing down Bünz's gun barrel.

*"Schiess!"* I heard Herr Luscher shout. He and Madame Bernard were staring at me.

*"Schiess, Bünz!* Shoot, shoot!"

I was lost. Bünz was smiling meanly, crookedly; his awful eyes seemed to hypnotize me. Mr. Munns had showed me where the safety catch was, but I could remember nothing now, could only imagine black death blasting at me from Bünz's pistol.

However, there was no need for him to shoot and rouse the house; I was frozen; he saw that. He lumbered toward me.

Coming between us, Mr. Munns tried to stop him. "No!" I heard his cry, before, with a blow, Bünz had felled him. He tumbled to the right; I glimpsed blood on his brow where the pistol barrel had struck.

Then Bünz was at me. He lifted his gun hand once more and swung at my head. Thoughts tumbled through my brain: *King Edward must be saved! I must not disappoint Mr. Bliss! Mr. Wigmore's cleverness must not go for nothing!* Mr. Munns must not die! Squeezing my eyes tight shut, so I would not see the huge paw swooping down, and gripping the Webley, I turned my head and ducked. Almost too late.

Bünz's pistol clipped my skull, and my head exploded in a flash of pain. A surge of darkness changed to bruised purple; then there was a reddish wash of light by which I could make things out. I was on my back on the floor by the hearth. I moaned and shook my head. There was a brass Georgian ceiling lamp above me. I was aware of Mr. Munns groaning to his knees some feet away, of Herr Luscher and Madame Bernard watching. Something hard and cold was in my hand. What? A pistol, with which I was to do . . . what?

Bünz's thick face floated into view. He planted legs huge as tree trunks on either side of me. He had struck me, I remembered, and might have killed me if I had not ducked. He had not liked my escaping. Face like a storm cloud, he leaned and raised his arm again. This time he would finish me.

I remembered what I must do with my pistol.

"No, no, not the boy!" I heard Madame Bernard's cry.

My thumb found the safety catch. I flung up my arm and fired.

There was a deafening crack and a shock that numbed my arm. Bünz jerked. His hand, already in downward motion, missed my head but struck my pistol, knocking it from my grasp. I heard it thud away on the carpet. Arms hanging apelike, Bünz swayed. His nostrils quivered. His mouth dropped open. He looked bewildered. His puzzled eyes squinted. His pistol dangling from one finger, he opened the hand he had swung at me and stared into the palm as if to examine something. I saw the back of the hand—a black dot.The dot dripped blood upon my chest. I had hit him, but only his hand. Now he would murder me!

The blood spattered from my chest onto my face, warm droplets. I clenched my teeth and bunched my hands. Imprisoned between Bünz's legs, I wanted to cry out, but could only choke.

Queer—Bünz did not attack. His eyes were clouded, his face strange. I squinted up. Dark red worms crawled from his hair down his brow; they wriggled along the sides of his flat nose. Blood! They were blood! My bullet had pierced his hand and struck his head! His pistol clattered beside me, and he touched his brow. Then he heaved a sudden great sigh, crashed to one knee, and fell upon his pistol, capturing me with the weight of his legs. His dead eyes stared at me.

Sobbing, I turned my head away; only then did I smell the stench of cordite on the air.

"Are you all right, Jack?" It was Mr. Munns, struggling to his feet.

"I'm . . . I'm alive," I managed.

"Not for long. *Schweigen Sie!*" Herr Luscher snarled. Releasing Madame Bernard, he stooped and snatched up Mr. Munns's pistol, which Bünz's blow had knocked almost at his feet.

Pressing a fist against her lips, Madame Bernard stared at the dead manservant's body.

Livid, Herr Luscher gibbered, "You have spoiled everything, boy! Everything! I should have killed you at the Bernard house. I will make up now for not doing it!" He raised the Webley. The play was over, the guests coming upstairs. He knew the shot I fired would bring inquiries. He could not wait for His Majesty; he must flee—but first he would finish me. The pistol shook with his fury, but I knew he would not miss.

Knowing I had saved King Edward, I prepared to die.

Just then the door flew open, lock splintered, from a crashing blow. Herr Luscher whirled.

An old man was crouched in the opening, a man I had

never seen in my life—bald, with white muttonchop whiskers, stout, wearing old-fashioned clothes, as if he were dressed for a costume ball. His fiercely bristling brows were fixed in a scowl. Agile as a boy, he leapt at Herr Luscher.

Then I knew him—Squire Hardcastle, Frederick Wigmore! "Wiggins!" Mr. Munns cried.

Herr Luscher fired the pistol. I flinched. My heart sank to see Mr. Wigmore jerk as the bullet struck him. Bravely he came ahead, grasped the German's arm, and struggled with him. But he was hurt and weakened by the shot. Herr Luscher's face was inches from his. "Wigmore," I heard him hiss in triumph, "I've beaten you . . .!" Mr. Wigmore stumbled, his eyes glazed. Barely able to stand, he leaned on the German and aimed feeble blows. Herr Luscher struck them aside, freed his pistol, stepped back, and fired again. Madame Bernard screamed. I gasped, wanting to take the bullet myself. The actor clutched his chest, swayed, and crumpled to the floor, a dark stain spreading across his waistcoat.

Mr. Munns rushed to him. "Wiggins! Wiggins!" He loosened the tie and collar. Mr. Wigmore's fingers moved; he was alive.

Herr Luscher levelled the pistol at Mr. Munns. "And now you!"

Madame Bernard clutched at him. "No more!" she sobbed. The German tried to shake her off, but she clung to his arms, his neck. "Please stop! We must escape. You and I! While there is still time!"

Pulling free, Herr Luscher slapped her face. She staggered back, hand to her cheek.

"Escape with *you!*" the German sneered, his mouth twisted in contempt. "You were never meant to go with me. *Verdammte Hure!* I have enjoyed you as one enjoys a low woman, but I do not love you, Sophie. I intend to escape alone, and if you hinder me I shall shoot you as I mean to shoot the rest of these meddlers!"

She blinked. She stared. Her mouth moved. She shook her head, her beautiful red-brown hair, undone by his blow, beginning to fall free to her shoulders. *"Mais non, non . . ."* She held out her arms.

Herr Luscher struck Madame Bernard's arms aside, and she sank into a pitiful heap on the floor. He turned toward Mr. Munns again.

Out of the corner of my eye I saw a movement in the open doorway. Another man stood there; he was tall, thin, with a pale, ghostlike, terrifying face. Herr Luscher glimpsed him, too, and started. The apparition pointed a pistol at the German's breast.

Herr Luscher swung his own pistol 'round. There was a deafening exchange of shots and the sulphurous smell of cordite again. I cringed and put my hands to my ears. When the noise died away in a rattling echo, Monsieur Armand Bernard, his pistol smoking in his hand, strode into the room.

With a sickened, disbelieving look Herr Luscher stared at him. Then the German's firearm slipped from his hand onto the carpet. He pivoted slowly on ankles that wobbled; he doubled at the waist and began to fall. His face was waxen, his ice-blue eyes already dead and staring when he struck the floor.

I was confused. I understood nothing. I wanted Mr. Wigmore to be all right. I wanted to be safe in the Diogenes Club with Mr. Stalker, Mr. Wetheridge, the rest of the staff, the clubmen, my familiar daily tasks. I wished I had never found Mr. Samuel Jarrett's body on the club library floor. I wanted Mr. Bliss.

And then my master was there, and I knew I was safe at last. "Mr. Bliss, sir," I sobbed. He brushed past the tall Frenchman and glanced at Mr. Wigmore. "Good God, is he—"

"I'm doing all I can," Mr. Munns said, looking miserable.

"Yes, yes. Jack." He thumped to me on his stick, knelt, pushed the hair from my brow with a leathery hand, and stared at me with those yellowish old eyes, which I loved. "Thank heaven you're safe!" He stared at Bünz, still lying half across me. "Whatever happened?" He helped me to struggle free.

"B-Bünz followed ... Mr. Munns. He ... brought us here. Herr Luscher ..."

"Never mind, Jack. Later. You may tell me later. We must get a doctor for Mr. Wigmore." Hand 'round my shoulder, he started me toward the door.

Monsieur Bernard caught our eye. We paused. Wailing, Madame Bernard had thrown herself across Herr Luscher's body. She plucked at his blond hair, searched his sightless eyes. "Willy, Willy . . . !" Her husband knelt beside her, gently disengaged her, and lifted her to her feet. He held her close, stroked her hair, murmured while he rocked her. One of his arms dripped blood from the sleeve, and there were flecks of red on his lips. He was injured. How badly? He must have been in pain, though he did not show it. His expression was almost joyful. But the hollows of his cheeks were dark, his cheekbones were like knife edges, and the glitter of his eyes frightened me. Madame Bernard stared at him but did not seem to know him. He looked down at her as if she were a hurt child.

Then Monsieur Bernard shifted his position.

"No . . ." I heard my voice.

He still held his pistol. It was pressed against his wife's breast.

I felt Mr. Bliss stiffen. "Monsieur!" he cried.

The Frenchman shook his head slowly, as if to say it must be. "To end her pain," he said softly, "and mine." He fired.

I flinched. Madame Bernard struggled against her husband; then she sighed and slumped in his arms. Monsieur Bernard shuddered. They fell together.

I sobbed. Mr. Bliss held me.

On the mantelpiece, in the corridor, throughout the great house, clocks struck midnight. It was King Edward's birthday.

Through the blur of my grief I saw a portly figure outside the door. My vision cleared. It was the king himself. Mr. Quinn appeared and held His Majesty back from entering the room. The king did not yet know what horror was here.

"Baccar-r-rat, baccar-r-rat!" King Edward thundered, red-faced. "I come for bacar-r-rat! On my birthday am I not to play as I wish?"

IV

*Afterward*

# Jack Merridew's Narrative

At 2:00 P.M., Sunday, one week after the king's birthday, Mr. Bliss, Mr. Wigmore, Mr. Munns, and I sat before a cheery coal fire in Mr. Bliss's room at the Diogenes Club. We—even I—were dressed in Prince Albert frock coats with satin lapels and silk buttons, gray-and-black-striped trousers, and black patent-leather shoes with white spats. I had never worn clothes so fine. The gentlemen's tall silk toppers sat in a row on the chest of drawers, their pearl-gray gloves and sticks in a heap beside them. We had just come from Buckingham Palace, where His Majesty himself, Lord Esher looking on, had growled his thanks for our saving his life. I felt very proud.

"The king seemed rather sad this morning, sir," I said to Mr. Bliss.

The old man took his long-stemmed pipe from his mouth. "Little wonder, Jack—just a week since Sophie Bernard died? Bertie loved her as much as any woman in a career of women. She was a taste of youth, a last chance to imagine himself a gallant knight instead of an old Don Quixote. And the shock of discovering Willy Luscher's true colors—it was a great deal to sustain. No wonder Bertie went into seclusion. But he will survive! Already Mrs. Keppel consoles him."

"I wish I had a woman beautiful as Alice Keppel to console me," sniffed Mr. Wigmore. "After all, I'm injured too!"

That was true. He sat next to Mr. Munns, opposite Mr. Bliss and me, his chest swathed in white bandages, his left arm in a sling. His face was still pale from loss of blood, but he was recovering nicely due to the fast work of Sir Francis Laking, His Majesty's physician.

Mr. Munns grunted skeptically. "Um. That very pretty chorine from the Gaiety Theatre whom I saw leaving your rooms this morning?" he commented, staring over his spectacles. "She did not console you?"

Mr. Wigmore flamed red. "Ah . . . after a fashion, Herbert, yes," he murmured.

"I'm only happy you're among us to be consoled," Mr. Bliss put in. "Willy Luscher's first hasty shot hit your shoulder; it's fortunate his well-aimed second was stopped by that great padded belly you wore."

"Oh, quite!"

"Foolish of you to burst in like that, Wiggins," Mr. Munns reproved.

"Not at all. If I hadn't, Jack would be dead; so might you. Listening at the door after I rushed up from the play, I had to do something when I heard Jack's shot. Good job, lad, shooting Biinz like that! You're the real hero."

It was my turn to blush.

Mr. Wigmore made a tent of his hands, tapped the fingers together, and smiled into space. "We're all heroes, in fact! Yes, it's turned out rather well; indeed it has. Have I told you, Herbert, that I'm thinking of writing my memoirs?"

"Often."

"This story will be their showpiece!"

Frowning, Mr. Bliss stirred. "Don't publish it yet. Not that I don't think it rather a good idea for all of us to write down the parts we played, for future historians. Now, however, the truth must be suppressed."

Mr. Wigmore nodded. We all understood why.

On the Benares brass tray was a week-old Sunday *Times*. What the public knew of the tragedy was printed there. It was a scandal, but not disastrous for the king. Mr. Quinn had removed him quickly from the scene of the crime. Mr. Munns and I were spirited away too. Cosette and Dasté had been detained until Mr. Quinn discovered that, though they both knew that Herr Luscher had been Madame Bernard's

278

lover, neither knew about the plot against the king. The official story was that the thing was a crime of passion caused by the triangle among the Bernards and Herr Luscher. Bünz had been shot along with his master by the enraged Monsieur Bernard. Mr. Wigmore was an incidental victim wounded trying to placate the gentlemen. English society kept its mouth shut tight about His Majesty's true relations with Madame Bernard, so the antiroyal press had been unable to implicate him. The king's life and the monarchy had been saved, His Majesty's reputation hardly stained.

Mr. Wigmore rose. "We must be off. Have I told you, Mr. Bliss, Jack, that George Edwardes has offered me a part in his new musical comedy? He begs me to do it! Well, well, perhaps I shall; after all—" he glanced at his bandaged arm, "enough detective work for a while, eh?" He smiled. "Come, Herbert, old chap; you can test me on my lines." He turned at the door. "By the way, Bliss, what's the news about that spy book we found?"

A firm nod. "My friends at Whitehall are making good use of it."

"Splendid."

He and Mr. Munns left. Feeling sorry to see them go, knowing our great adventure was over at last, I collected the tea things and was about to carry them down when Mr. Stalker himself arrived to announce Inspector Nelson Faraday. Chewing on a cigar, scowling, the policeman trundled into the room, stared suspiciously into every corner, and toyed with his Albert chain.

"Must speak to you, Bliss!" he huffed.

I left quietly with my tray.

Some time later, shortly before supper, Mr. Bliss called me up again. Inspector Faraday had departed. A storm had broken over London, and rain lashed the windowpanes. I found the old man by the French doors, leaning on his stick and staring out at the blustery night. He turned, and I saw at once by the light in his eyes that something was afoot.

"I have news, Jack!" he exclaimed. "Nelson Faraday has a baffling new case which wants my help." He thumped his blackthorn. "By damn, I'm ready for a new adventure! What do you say, lad? Are you ready too?"

I didn't answer right away. Suddenly I seemed to smell

Madame Bernard's perfume, glimpse her green eyes. I recalled my terror, how I had ended by shooting a man. A great many ideas and feelings flooded me then. Was it just a month since I discovered Samuel Jarrett's body? I felt as if years had passed since; I felt older. Did I want a new adventure? Adventures could bring pain. And yet . . .

"I'm ready, sir!" I piped up.

"Good." He squeezed my shoulder, and I was pleased to see the sparkle in his eyes.

We sat close before the fire. The old gentleman told me about the new case. Outside, the storm howled. Below on Pall Mall gentlemen dashed from their carriages through the tall, mahogany doors for a quiet evening at the Diogenes Club.